TWO FAMIL
TORN BY BI

'If you love me, Juliette,' he said, 'then let me show you how to love a man.'

Her answer came in kisses, insistent nibblings at his neck and ear.

'You are beautiful, Juliette, really beautiful.'

Juliette's body was taken over by waves of pleasure. She did not hear Angus' voice, and unti. many weeks later she could not really remember what had happened, but she carried the feeling with her, for it was insanely powerful and continued, rocking her, longer than seemed at all possible. She who had been tossed and tormented by her awakening sexuality all the days of summer and all the nights of fall, was entirely ready for this feeling, and it invaded her entirely; she was racked with ecstasy unlike any she had imagined or might ever feel again . . .

Also by Cynthia Van Hazinga in Sphere Books:

THE GEORGIANS

The Georgians II

White Columns

CYNTHIA VAN HAZINGA

SPHERE BOOKS LIMITED
30-32 Gray's Inn Road, London WC1X 8JL

First published in Great Britain by Sphere Books Ltd 1982

TRADE MARK

Printed and bound in Great Britain by ©ollins, Glasgow

PROLOGUE

Savannah, Georgia
Spring, 1800

Toward dawn, the fog began to lift. It would burn off by ten. The sun slumbered wearily, hotly, just past the horizon, knowing its power, colossal, shining. Its first rays would scald the waiting city with clear, golden light. The fog kept the last secrets of night—the last sailor creeping home, the town crier making his last rounds—and blurred the first signs of morning life. Gulls mewed with mindless sadness and took wheeling wing over the docks and reed-choked riverbanks.

The first light of day crossed the tangled masts and riggings of the big sailing ships asleep at the docks and in the harbor. They had come from across the seas, from Havana and Portsmouth, from London and Liverpool, from Port au Prince and Le Havre. Every week the ships came now. They brought Savannah fame and fortune, exotic cargoes whose pungent spicy smells mixed with the salty, damp air, the wood smoke from the town, and the raw, clean smells of progress: of sawing and building and ginning.

In the hour between night and day, the waterfront seemed bigger than it was. Fog and shadows extended the bulk of the warehouses, magnified the width of the wooden docks. In the silver-gray light, the cotton gin alone at the end of the docks loomed big as a fortress. It was the biggest in Georgia; also the finest, the newest. In gold lettering on black, the sign outside read I. Barstow and Sons.

And then, at an hour too early to be abroad, came Ira Barstow. He crossed Bay Street on foot, alone, aloof, and elegant in an unwrinkled white linen suit. Ira Barstow, cotton merchant, citizen, patriarch—a man in his full maturity, complex and yet uncompleted, a man still extending his life, still seeking change, demanding increase and growth from the future.

He looked up at the gray canopy of the sky. It hushed the restless, unceasing whisper of the water beyond, a familiar sound that always hinted of wider horizons—shores far beyond, ships to come, new days, new opportunities. He scanned the street. It was empty and quiet. He was out early, he who was always early. Today he was early by a full hour.

He had taken his usual route from his home to his warehouse and his cotton gin. A dream had summoned him. Sleep had evaded him half the night; during the rest, helplessly, he had dreamed of lost love and old troubles—bygone troubles, for his life was easy and safe now. He had suffered and prevailed. Now he was free and had seen his own children born free. He had seen his business grow and prosper, seen the town where he was born grow from a swampy, feverish village to the most important cotton-shipping port in the South. He had seen Georgia change from colony to state, seen a nation born and fought for its rights. He had shed blood and thanked God for the republic. His long life had always been full of people: family and friends, business colleagues, and others who were less and more than that, but in this key hour he was alone. He recalled his dream. He had dreamed of fire—a subtle, snakelike fire creeping through his store of cotton, bursting into huge red flames, gobbling the air, lighting the sky, casting a pall of smoke over the Bay.

His heart beat faster. It was only a dream. The tree-shaded mall was empty. Here on the docks everything was calm and chill. Within the hour the first workers would come, the steam engines would hiss to life, the day's heart would begin to beat with its regular rhythm.

He paused in the middle of the sandy street and looked up at the big front doors of his brick warehouse. In an hour they would stand open and scores of stevedores would pass through them, moving sacks of raw cotton in and ginned bales out, shifting the wealth of the outlying counties into the holds of the square-rigged schooners.

He opened a small side door with his key. The air inside

the cavernous warehouse was dry and smelled sweet and dusty. It was silent and very dark. He called to the night watchman. Getting no answer, he called again. He paused for a minute on the threshold.

From the shadows outside the warehouse a man watched him; two men waited for him in the shadows inside. His watchman was sprawled behind a mountain of cotton bales with his throat slit, his head back, his eyes open in death.

Slowly, his Paris-made boots creaking softly, Ira Barstow entered the warehouse and walked the narrow path between cliffs of cotton. Above his head swallows soared from nests to rafters. A pale column of light followed him from the open doorway.

He was surprised but not alarmed by the watchman's absence. Likely he had fallen asleep. He would warn the man, then forgive him, as he had so many others less able and conscientious. As he crossed the warehouse he was surprised again.

From the far end of the building came the unmistakable sound of the cotton gin beginning to turn, the hiss and sputter of the first steam-powered gin in Georgia, the clanking of its sharp steel disks. His step quickened. It was so early; yet the first crew of men had already started up the gin. How had he lost a sense of the time?

Calling out, he hurried toward the gin room. The machine's clanking and scraping masked the footfall of the man waiting inside the gin room door. His blow caught Ira Barstow solidly. He fell forward.

"He's all yours," the man said.

Ira Barstow struggled to focus. He shook his head; the blow had stunned him. Kneeling, he looked up into the faces of the two men. They were wide, ignorant faces, but they were recognizable. The man with the ugly white-stubbled face had worked in the warehouse for a few months and been laid off. The bald man with the red beard had learned to run the gin, and then been fired for stealing.

"What do you want?" Ira Barstow asked. His voice was cool, his accent refined.

"Look at the boss man's Frenchie suit," the ugly one sneered.

"Hold off your gab," the bald man said in a raspy voice.

He fixed Ira Barstow's ankles together with a long twist of wire and prodded him to his feet. The muscles on his right arm rippled under a tattooed horse's head.

The gin coughed and rattled into full operation. Steam spit and whistled, and the big wheels turned faster and faster; lint and dust flew out of the empty rollers. In the dimness, the gin seemed huge. It took on life—that of a big-toothed iron monster. The whirring spinning of the oversize cylinders seemed dizzying and frightening.

"What do you want?" Ira Barstow asked. His voice revealed no fear. He could smell rum on the men.

"Be quick about it," the red-bearded man said. Broad and long-limbed, he towered over Ira, who had his father's stocky build and his father's bright blue eyes, though his skin was as dark as aged rum, as his mother's had been.

"Get him over here," the red-bearded man shouted. The din of the machine was deafening.

Ira struggled desperately. He was strong, but no match for the two younger men. One of them flipped him up into the feeder bin that held the cotton until it tumbled into the rollers.

The other man began to beat at his head with a hammer he seized from the anvil at the foot of the gin. Ira screamed.

Horrified, he reached out to push himself away from the rollers spinning beneath him but his fingers caught. He screamed again as he felt the sharp metal disks cut through them and pull his arms into their teeth.

One of the men retched at the sight of the blood. Blood splashed back at Ira's white suit. Pain glazed his eyes and they rolled back. He swallowed his last scream and slid between the rollers with a sickening crunch that stopped the gin.

Both men ran.

In less than an hour the first shift of workers would arrive at the warehouse.

CHAPTER ONE

A Surprise at the Exchange; Two Marked Men; A Family Reunion

Every seat in the Cotton Exchange was taken, and those who could not find seats crowded the steps outside. They were a good number, and owing to the heat of the afternoon and the length of time many of them had waited already, some of the spectators and hangers-on had forgotten the solemn purpose of the gathering and had begun to drink rum and take snuff, smoke home-grown tobacco and gossip.

The funeral for Ira Barstow was to be held in the Cotton Exchange and at twilight—two unconventional arrangements, but arrangements that solved certain problems. In many ways it was an unprecedented situation. Ira Barstow himself had been a member of the African Baptist Church, the first black church in the entire republic, but he had been, in a way, a Barstow, and the Barstows had always attended Savannah's first church, Christ Church. But four years ago, in the calamitous fire that had destroyed two thirds of the city, Christ Church had burned.

Meanwhile, the Cotton Exchange had been built, a handsome structure with a spire and an observatory from which vessels could be seen ten miles at sea. It was a place for the buying and selling of cotton, built while cotton prices soared and Georgians nursed visions of vast and sudden wealth.

The Exchange, presently the largest building in Georgia, had been designed by the cultivated and celebrated émigré architect Adrien Boucher, who had come to Savannah three years earlier and undertaken a wide variety of building projects. Most of the money for building the Exchange had been put up by Ira Barstow, the best-known, most community-minded, and richest cotton factor in Savannah. In many ways it had been Ira Barstow's Exchange. It was located right down Bay Street from his warehouse; he had proposed its construction and traded more cotton on its floor than anyone else.

And now he would be buried out of it. His body would be blessed and his soul consigned to eternal peace. It seemed fitting and right, and at the same time it bypassed the problem of whatever else to do with a rich and well-connected black freeman.

"Who done him in, d'you suppose?" one rosy-cheeked servant girl asked another, seated beside her on the sunny steps.

"No one knows," her friend answered. She grinned. "Course there were lots who would've liked to. 'Twasn't right, if you ask me, an African man bein' so rich as he was. Did you see the gown on his wife when she went in?"

"I did. Silver lace, and me in brown linsey and her as black as Satan's kitten. But she's a Barstow, and all the Barstows are different—they always have been."

"Or thought they were."

"It's the same thing."

It had been eight days since Ira Barstow was murdered, just enough time to get word to the family on Saint Simons Island and for family members to rally themselves and make the dangerous, difficult journey up from Brunswick along the coast. It was Mary Barstow, Ira's wife, who had insisted that they be informed of Ira's death, and who had waited for the messenger's return before she agreed to set the date for the funeral.

"They won't come all this way, Mama," Ira's oldest daughter, Alice Ann, had told her mother. "Not in the yellow fever season."

"They'll come," Mary Barstow had insisted. "The Barstows are a strong family—maybe too strong—they're a strict people. I can say so to you, daughter, 'cause you're only half Barstow. I know how Mr. Roland and Miss Jenny feel about your father, how they've always felt . . ."

The thought of it reminded Mary Barstow of her loss and she forgot the rest of her argument and succumbed to tears. She might have said that Ira had been Roland Barstow's cotton factor, had loaned him money and advanced him credit on every year's cotton crop, had set up Kate Barstow (poor widow that she was) with a clever Yankee overseer who had made Blackwoods profitable in ten years. Before that, Ira had fought beside Kate's husband Byron in the Revolution, saved his life on one occasion. He had sewed up Roland Barstow's head when a crazed Indian had taken off the top of his scalp, and he had saved Jenny, when she was a girl of sixteen, from being carried off to England by her Tory uncle James Dunlie.

Mary Barstow had married Ira late in life, but she was well versed in the legends of his family's history and awed by it. The Barstows were a proud family, a complicated family, one of the first families in Georgia. They were close-knit, and getting closer despite the spread of the generations, for Roland Barstow had married his first cousin Jenny Stone and Kate Barstow had never remarried.

A sob escaped Mary Barstow as she waited for the preacher to speak. She was nearly too tired to cry. She had cried for eight days, ever since the horrible shock of seeing Ira carried up the front walk on a stretcher—or what had been Ira, a ghastly, bloody wreck of what had been Ira. Mary felt nausea rise at the recollection of his mangled face. She gasped, and felt Kate Barstow's hand—cool and dry in lace gloves—grip her own.

"Oh, Mary," Kate whispered, "I know. Close your eyes and think of your children. Your own life must go on." Kate was the Barstow woman most respected for her composure and genteel tranquillity. In this respect, she had changed; as a young woman (after all, she had Indian blood) she had been passionate and quick-tempered and impatient, but life had smoothed her out as the waves of the ocean polish a stone—life and the ceaseless days of motherhood and quiet plantation life.

"Yes, ma'am, yes, Miss Kate, I know," Mary sighed, rocking back and forth in her pew. Her daughter Alice Ann leaned over to fan her with a lacy shield of woven palmetto. It was smotheringly hot in the Exchange although all the big windows were open and the back door stood ajar. It was time for the ceremony to begin, past time, and where was the preacher, Ira's younger brother Samuel?

Alice Ann gulped. Her eyes stung with tears. What would their life be like without him? It was unthinkable. She had been afraid ever since he was killed, afraid to sleep, afraid to go out in the streets, afraid to look into the eyes of the people she met. Why had they done it? Who could hate her father so? He had seemed untouchable—they had all felt untouchable, but with the full awareness that they lived upon sufferance that all Savannah's free blacks felt. Alice Ann winced. She did not understand it, but she knew that her life had changed completely and irrevocably on the day her father died.

Juliette Barstow, who sat in the pew behind Alice Ann and her family, did not understand it either. Juliette was sixteen, in the first flowering of mature emotions and desires, and she had never before felt such grief as she did now for her Uncle Ira. "My *fa*vorite uncle," she had called him since she was old enough to walk, running into his arms at the first sight of him when he came to visit at Sea Groves or, more rarely, when she and her father journeyed to Savannah to see him.

"My *fa*vorite niece," he had always answered her. It was a ritual, an unvarying litany, and when they had exchanged that delightful greeting, Juliette had always jumped into Uncle Ira's arms, always taking delight in the smell of starched white linen and the spicy scent of his skin, always rummaging through his pockets for the round white peppermints he hid there for her to find.

Uncle Ira was the first person to die whom Juliette had loved. She had been shocked and grief-stricken when the messenger reached the plantation. It had seemed incomprehensibly abrupt. Why, only two months ago he had visited them at Sea Groves. A letter had come from him last week, predicting a fair rise in cotton prices, inquiring after the spring plantings. Until she reached Savannah with her family, Juliette hadn't known that Uncle Ira was murdered; she hadn't believed it until she was allowed to view his body, and now she was shaken to the roots.

"How could God allow this?" Juliette had demanded, wide-eyed and pale, to her parents' alarm, when she began to understand that Uncle Ira had been maliciously killed. "How could God let this happen to him? He was a good man, all good. If God let this happen, I hate him. But

I don't believe he could. I believe Satan has gained control . . ."

"Juliette, you must stop. Many of God's gifts to us are beyond easy understanding. Remember, darkness shows us worlds of light we never saw by day. It is our duty and privilege to walk this earth by faith and not by sight. Not another word," Roland Barstow had told his daughter. Roland himself had lived through enough death and pain, enough random violence and senseless pathos, to see beyond Ira's death. Roland, the head of the family, was a calm, fair-minded man, even-tempered and generous. He could not cry openly for Ira Barstow, but he would miss him as much as anyone else. He knew his debts to Ira—they were more than anyone present could guess.

Juliette obeyed her father out of respect, but it was only in the numbness of exhausted grief that she could sit quietly in the Exchange and wait for the ceremony to begin.

Morgan Barstow, Juliette's brother, sat next to her. He was uncomfortable in a stiff suit and starched collar. Morgan, just eighteen but already a man in his family's eyes, hated being in Savannah as wholeheartedly as he mourned his uncle. To his dying day, Morgan would dislike cities and mistrust city people—dandies, he thought them. Depression gripped him as soon as he left the plantation. Savannah, actually a dusty town of about five thousand at the beginning of the new century, seemed to him a sinful place, and he was overwhelmed by its array of possibilities and dismayed by the confusion that his eyes and mind beheld.

Morgan's eyes wandered around the crowd seated in the Exchange. Who were they all, he wondered. Businessmen—pale and weak-looking, decked out in silk stockings and imported woolens. Old militiamen in uniform, honoring Uncle Ira's role in the fight for freedom. There was Adrien Boucher, the French architect. Morgan recognized a group of men from the Merchants and Planters Coffee House, where he had often gone with his father and Uncle Ira. Most of the others in the room were strangers to him—the influx of new people into Savannah was greater every year. They came from the North—mountain people, Yankee farmers and traders—and from the Old World—Scotch-Irish, refugees from the Revolution in France. Life in Savannah was sufficiently dull that most townspeople turned out for any good-sized event, and the circumstances of Ira Barstow's death made it the most spectacular crime anyone could remember.

Morgan scowled at them, scornfully, with the intolerance of youth. To him, they were all thrill-seekers, gossips, meddlers taking an inappropriate interest in a matter that was none of their concern. He would have restricted the funeral to family members, but his father, who made all the arrangements for Mary Barstow, had made everyone welcome. Morgan sensed that the community was titillated by the gruesome nature of his uncle's death; he was shocked and mortified by it. They had come to stare at and speculate about a grisly accident that he felt was a private family sorrow, and he hoped that they would all be disappointed—that they would be soothed into sorrowful respect by the simple solemnity of the occasion and go home soberly.

But it was Morgan who was to be disappointed, not the crowd. A hushed rustle at the back of the room caught his attention. He turned. The big, oil-soaked cypress torches just outside the front door of the Exchange had just been lighted. There was an acrid, smoky smell, and some wisps of gray smoke blew into the room. More people turned. There was a hush, then a ripple of chatter.

Morgan stared. Instead of the expected minister, a tall, white-haired man dressed in outrageous full-length pantaloons swept into the Exchange. Morgan had no idea who it was. The man wore a black feathered hat nearly as broad as a sugar barrel, a red coat, a striped satin waistcoat of an intense and gaudy turquoise brocade, deep gold lace in a waterfall down over a red satin cutaway, and matching gold gloves.

A total silence fell over the crowd. Morgan could not take his eyes off the stranger. His face was wrinkled, his deep-set hazel eyes swept the room with an expression—of what? Amused curiosity? So it seemed. And then he smiled, or tried to smile, and the gesture sent a chill through his frame, a shudder no less ominous than the first symptoms of fever.

Flanking the stranger, Morgan gradually noticed, were two younger persons, an extremely gaunt, broad-shouldered young man, blond and foppish but undeniably handsome, and a dark-haired girl with skin as clear and pale as a child's and large, long-lashed eyes as blue as the older man's waistcoat.

"Who is it?" Juliette whispered to her parents, and Morgan leaned toward them to hear the answer. "Who are they?"

Roland did not answer at once, but both children could see that he was disturbed. They heard their mother gasp. Aunt Kate, they could see, was crying softly into her handkerchief, but perhaps that was for Uncle Ira.

"Why has he come now?" Jenny Barstow asked her husband in a carrying voice. It trembled so that Morgan reached over and touched his mother's elbow.

"What's wrong, Mother?" he asked.

"Damn him, why has he come now?" Jenny demanded.

"Who is it? Who is it?" Juliette asked again, her voice rising. Morgan turned away from Jenny to hush her.

Roland Barstow rose slowly to his feet. His wife reached up, trying to stop him, her hands shaking wildly. Both Morgan and Juliette stared at their father as he faced the strange man.

"So you have come back, James," Roland Barstow said. He was a tall, solid, well-built man. He had been white-haired since his twenties, by a freak of nature, but the intervening years had aged him gently. His body showed hard work and exercise—it was lean and square, and he wore his only broadcloth suit. Roland's pale blue eyes fixed on his boyhood companion, his lifelong rival, whom he had not seen in eighteen years.

Everyone else present waited, silently, for Roland to finish speaking. "So you have come back to Georgia," he said in a cool voice that suggested neither welcome nor surprise.

"You always knew I would," James Dunlie said. He smiled again, and again Morgan felt an unhealthy chill.

"This is no time for our personal reunion," Roland said. "Later, James . . . we will have time for that."

James, Morgan thought wildly. . . . Our Uncle James, who was a Tory and who sailed off for England like a coward when the British gave up Savannah? His mind scrambled to remember what he had heard of Uncle James . . . very little. Both his mother and Aunt Kate hated to speak of him. He didn't think Uncle James had been in touch with any of them for years. It was strange, wasn't it, that he had appeared so suddenly.

"Those must be our cousins," Juliette whispered to Morgan. She had given James Dunlie only a cursory glance, but something about the look of the young man fascinated her.

Roland sat down, and James Dunlie and his family crossed the Exchange and made their way to the front pew, opposite the Barstows, and waited there until two young men got up to make room for them. As they took their places, the minister came in, the froth of whispers settled down, and Mary Barstow began to cry loudly.

For eight days the two men James Dunlie had hired to murder Ira Barstow had been on the run. At first they had tried to run south, for one of them—the red-bearded brute named Bob Jasper—had a wife in Liberty County, but the coastal roads were dangerously flooded, beginning just south of Cockspur Island, and when they began to realize how difficult it would be to spend the British gold in the poor ramshackle towns and taverns of south Georgia, they changed their minds and their route and headed north.

The days of hasty, misdirected travel had given the two men time to think—and quarrel. Two days after they had first left Savannah, they were abreast of the port city again, and the other man, the rough-looking tattooed ex-hostler named Jake Fox, was all for going back into the city and trying for more gold out of James Dunlie.

"Shut up, you ugly fool!" Jasper raged at the suggestion.

"He give us so much—means he'd give us more to hush us," Fox argued.

"We don't even know his name!" Jasper said.

"Can't be two like 'im in Savannah, now, can there?"

Jasper agreed to that, but he didn't like the idea all the same. The Englishman had paid them royally, overpaid them, to the extent that they roused suspicion every time they tried to spend one of the shiny disks of British gold, but he didn't feel good about seeing the Englishman again, ever.

"Who was he, d'you think?" Fox asked.

"Now, how would I know?"

"Lots of us hated that Barstow, but he paid in gold.

There would've been plenty willin' to knock 'im off for a pint of ale."

"Listen, Fox, I know that, you know that, but he didn't know that! See? Only what if he's found out? What then? Think he wouldn't invest another round on gettin' us beat up and robbed to git some of it back? How about that, eh?"

"Well . . . he might," Fox coughed. He had a low, racking cough that sometimes doubled him over and sometimes ended in blood.

"I ain't as stupid as you, Fox, and I ain't goin' back to Savannah while there's anyone alive who remembers Ira Barstow. This mess'll stink for years, as God's my witness."

"God! Your witness! Don't make me laugh!"

"Anyway, I wouldn't of done it, 'cept for the money."

"Course not."

"*You* would of, Fox, you just said you'd have bumped the old man for a glass of ale."

In reply Fox gave Jasper a punch that knocked him off balance and made him so angry that he cut at Fox's right arm with his bowie knife. Fox howled in pain and stumbled backward.

"Had enough?"

"Murder, bloody murder!" Fox howled, coughing so that he went first red, then white.

"Oh, sweet Jesus, how stupid you are! Now, hold it down, you fool, you'll rouse the dead."

Coughing and sputtering, Fox could not speak until Jasper had helped him straighten out and waited while he caught his breath. "I never said a glass," he sputtered finally, "I never said a glass, I said a pint!"

Jasper laughed at that and clung to his comrade's arm. "You are a simpleton, Fox. Lucky for you you've got me. Now, listen to me. We've got to stay out of Savannah, right? It's not safe. Let's jump a coach at the next decent tavern and go to Charleston, right?"

"Right."

"And watch your tongue; we're in this together. Don't tell anyone where we've been or where we're going to."

"Right."

Riding on in near-silence through the night, watching the moon, listening to the call of a whip-poor-will, the two men came upon a roadside tavern a few miles along the road. They gave their horses to the slave who met them at the front gate; then they went back to the well yard, where another slave poured water over their hands from a gourd he dipped into a big wooden trough.

Fox met Jasper's eyes and they both smiled. This, this then, was the style of life they needed and deserved, and thanks to the fancy Englishman they could afford it.

Inside the tavern they found six or seven men gathered around the fireplace, drinking and smoking huge dark cigars. The table was made of rough sawed boards resting on forked poles driven into the dirt floor. Rain had seeped in under the doors so that the floor was two inches deep in mud. Supper, when it came, was boiled fowl and rice in sufficient quantity to rule out complaints about quality, and a coach for Carolina and points north was due in the early morning.

"Lawd, this is the life," Fox exulted, leaning back in his chair and spitting into the fire.

"Where did ye say ye were goin'?" one of the men by the fire asked Jasper.

"I didn't," Jasper said, swallowing ale.

"Charleston," Fox said. Jasper gave him a murderous look.

"Guess you haven't heard," another man said, lowering the front legs of his chair until they just touched the muddy floor.

"Heard about what?" Fox asked.

"Fever. There's yellow fever in Charleston—a contagion of it. They're dyin' at the rate of fifty a day, so the coachman said yesterday."

Jasper frowned. It could well be true; it was the beginning of fever season, and swampy, seaside Charleston was subject to bad scourges. Damn! Squinting at the fire, he began to plan. Perhaps the thing to do was to get away from cities altogether, go upriver into the woods, into the new territory where a man's past was of no interest to his neighbors, where land was cheap, two shillings an acre, he'd heard, and aside from the Indians, life was peaceful.

As he drank, the idea sounded better and better to him. He'd—they'd—take a flatboat up the river to Augusta, buy supplies there, and move on west to the good fertile land.

He'd heard they were raising tobacco up there. Hell, in a few months he'd even be able to send for his wife.

"Guess I'll get to bed," Fox said, while Jasper was still planning the future.

"No," Jasper said.

"What?"

"Not yet," Jasper said in what he hoped was a low voice. "I want to talk to you—private. Just wait. Have another drink."

Fox obliged, and after a time the other drinkers left the fireside and went into the other room, which was lined with hard and narrow beds and from which the sounds of a variety of snores could already be heard. The tavernkeeper retired to his own quarters in the ell of the building, and it was so still that a baying hound made Fox jump.

"We ain't goin' to Charleston," Jasper announced.

"No? Just 'cause of what he said about fever?"

"Partly. I say we should strike out for the new land in west Georgia. That's where there's a good life to be made."

"A few hours ago you wanted to get out of Georgia."

"So what? Are you comin' or ain't you?"

"I . . . don't know, Jasper. I wanted to see Charleston and have a good time."

"Are you comin' or not?"

"Now?" Fox asked, seeing Jasper rising and pulling on his tattered linsey coat. "Right now?"

"Yep. I want to be out of sight of this place by the time my food settles. Something about this place I don't like. Are you coming?"

Fox needed a leader and he knew it. "Aye," he said sourly. He tossed a gold coin onto the rough table.

"I already paid," Jasper said, picking it up.

Moving quickly and quietly, they saddled their own horses and were on the road west to the ferry before the slave who kept the horses was back with the constable.

"They're gone," the tavernkeeper told the constable, standing in the doorway in his nightshirt and cap. "Jest proves I was right. There's no honest way two ruffians like them could come up with those gold coins. See? Look."

He held out a solid gold guinea, worth a year's lodging, and the constable looked at it in awe.

* * *

The coffin containing the earthly remains of Ira Barstow had been blessed, and wept over, and lowered into the earth, and now the members of the Barstow clan had assembled at the house on Abercorn Street for the customary collation. It was a family reunion of sorts and would have been even without the unsettling arrival of James O. Dunlie and his children.

Kate Barstow had not wanted to come at all and had made her sentiments known precisely and politely to both Roland and Jenny. Jenny had taken Kate's part. "I had hoped, dear cousin Roland, never to be under the same roof with that man ever again in my whole life," Kate had said, in her soft, firm, ladylike voice, but Roland had pleaded with her and won her cooperation by asking for her help and support.

"This is something we must deal with," Roland had said diplomatically to the two women, both of them shaking with nerves as they waited for their carriages outside the Exchange. "Years have passed since the end of the war; Georgia has pardoned her Tories; our personal difficulties with James Dunlie seem very long ago. Oh, perhaps you are right, Miss Kate, it may be too much to ask you to do. . . ."

"Yes, it is," Jenny had insisted, her lips white and pressed together in a hard, straight line. "As for myself, I cannot bear him; I never could; I can never forgive him, never!"

Roland looked at his wife very seriously. "My dear," he said, "I know you have been wronged by James Dunlie, perhaps we all have, but when I stop to think of God's goodness to us, to you and me, to all our family, I cannot find it in my heart to hate him any longer. Poor James!"

"You are a better Christian than I," Jenny said stubbornly.

"After all, he is my blood kin," Roland said. "We were raised together. That is the reality."

"Poor Lucifer!" Kate Barstow had mumbled, and then stopped, ashamed of her loss of control and astonished by the strength of the feelings that gripped her. Perversely, because she was so violently opposed to forgiving James Dunlie, or even to seeing him, she forced herself to go along with Roland and Jenny. After all these years, she marveled, after all this time, I feel such pure hatred for that man that it might have been yesterday. I have always believed he was responsible for Byron's death, and I believe it still!

Kate's thin shoulders shook with tears as she followed Jenny into the carriage that would take them to Abercorn Street from the burying ground.

"Think of poor Mary Barstow," Jenny reminded her. "I'm sure our presence will help her to bear this first night."

Kate nodded. It seemed disloyal to her dear, long-departed husband Byron to forgive James Dunlie. Seeing him would make old wounds bleed again. And yet, James Dunlie and her heroic husband had been brothers, twin brothers, though as different as day and night, and it was the will of the Lord that we forgive our enemies—that we forgive those who trespass against us. . . .

Hand in hand in the carriage, Jenny and Kate wept all the way, and Juliette, who sat up front, next to the driver, looked back at the two women and begged them to stop, and cried a little in sympathy, and wondered, and did not understand.

The Dunlies had arrived at the Cotton Exchange in their own carriage, a fresh-painted black calèche, and Roland agreed to ride with them.

"I suppose you remember the way," he said evenly to James Dunlie, when the two men were seated inside.

"Of course I do," James Dunlie said. "I have forgotten nothing."

"Quite so," Roland said. "It has been such a long time . . ."

"Eighteen years."

"We had heard nothing," Roland said. "They have been eventful years for us . . . for Georgia and the republic . . . for the family." Roland spoke slowly; he was ill at ease with this flamboyantly dressed man who was almost a stranger, seemed like a stranger. His accent had changed; he had aged immensely; but to all indications his general outlook, which had always been one of hasty intolerance, of superiority, of self-interested determination, had not changed. "Your wife? Rosalind?" Roland asked.

"Dead," Dunlie said. "I heard nothing from you, either." For the upstart republic, for the ex-colony of Georgia, he cared not a whit, but he was intensely interested in the family and its fortunes. He had anticipated this conversation for years. For years he had planned the details of his return to Georgia; so far it had gone superbly. He had been delighted with the impact of his sudden appearance at Black Ira's funeral and the results of the investigations he had conducted since his arrival in Savannah ten days ago.

Roland, he had learned, was the functioning head of the family. He occupied Sea Groves, the seaside plantation that his own father, Angus Dunlie, had established and built on land given to him by James Oglethorpe on Saint Simons Island. In the days of their youth rice had been the main crop at Sea Groves, but now, James had heard, Roland mainly planted the long-staple cotton they called sea-island cotton. Byron Barstow's widow had done the same at Blackwoods Plantation. Roland had struggled to make the new crop pay; he had worked closely with Ira Barstow to clean and package and sell and ship the cotton. Over the years prices had risen and the size of his harvests had increased, although now, because of the invention of an efficient winnowing machine by a Yankee named Eli Whitney, the easier-to-raise short-staple cotton was becoming more plentiful in inland Georgia.

Roland and the rest of the Barstows had prospered, according to what James Dunlie had learned in Savannah, but they had not become conspicuously rich or even free of care. Except for Ira Barstow. Outrageous as it was, annoying as he found it, Ira Barstow had combined a business genius with courage and a will to work very hard, and his fortunes had mounted to the point where, so it seemed, he was carrying the rest of the family.

Or at least those living on Saint Simons Island. Another branch of the family, among them his nephew Pittman Stone, had gone inland. So far, James Dunlie had not received any reliable reports of their fate, although he had launched an effort to reach them.

"How does Savannah look to you, James?" Roland asked, as the carriage passed the fine houses along Bull Street and turned into St. James Square.

"Rather small, I must admit," James Dunlie said. He smiled in that odd, slightly sour way his son had inherited. It looks poor and shabby, James thought. It all looks provincial and drab beyond belief. Why, even the slums of London have better buildings than these.

"I had thought it would be grander," Angus Dunlie added. Roland looked at the young man across the carriage from him, a young man who bore only the faintest resemblance to the youth of twelve whom he remembered; his years in England had made an Englishman out of him. As for the daughter, who had been born in England, she was pretty and graceful enough, though she had an intense stare and a slightly dissatisfied expression Roland found unattractive. Exposure to Juliette will do that one good, Roland thought generously. His own daughter Juliette was the delight of his life—so unspoiled, so sensitive of soul and delightful of disposition. Not that Morgan was any less satisfactory. Roland was well pleased with his family; he adored both his children and had never suspected that a love as strong and sustaining as that between himself and Jenny could endure without flagging over so many years.

"The fire in November four years past left Savannah desolate and distressed," Roland explained. "It was the most terrible fire ever experienced in America, they say."

"But spared the house on Abercorn Street?" James Dunlie asked.

"Aye, and Cousin Kate's house on St. James Square. You see it—there?"

"Yes, yes," James Dunlie said. During the ten days he had been in Savannah, staying at a shabby boardinghouse on President Street, he had walked every street in town and experienced a full range of shocks and pleasures in seeing what still stood and what did not. "How fortunate we are . . ."

We? Roland wondered. He reflected for a moment on Dunlie's use of the word and then plunged ahead. "Have you come to Georgia to stay, James? What is the condition of your fortunes? Will you be wanting to journey south to Sea Groves with us? Excuse me if my questions seem rude or improper. I hardly know how to express all the things I am thinking—or understand what you must be thinking. There's no use denying we know each other very well, that bad blood has existed between us, or that many years have passed . . ."

"Here we are," James Dunlie said in reply. "Here we

are at my father's house. When I left it the lilacs were not as tall as the windows, but now . . ."

I cannot press him, Roland thought. Who knows what he has endured? All this will sort itself out in good time. James's speaking of the lilacs had touched him; he was a good and sensitive man; he had never been able to hold a grudge against James, although even as a child he had been tricked by him and tried by him, again and again.

"Let me savor this moment, Roland," James Dunlie said. "I will answer all your questions and more over a glass of rum in my father's old study. How long I have waited for this moment!"

Roland smiled and felt almost embarrassed as he handed the reins to a slave and followed Dunlie up the front walk. Pushing ahead of the others, James Dunlie moved briskly toward the front door. It stood ajar. Taking a deep breath, as if he had longed to breathe this particular air and no other, he paused on the threshold and then plunged in without looking back at his children or at Roland, who followed rather hesitantly.

"It's not nearly as fine as our house in London," James Dunlie's daughter, whose name was Livia, said to her brother.

"Far from it," Angus said. "It never was and it hasn't improved."

"Do you remember it well?" Livia asked.

"Of course I do," Angus said.

"You don't remember me," Juliette Barstow said brightly, not wanting to eavesdrop. She stood just inside the white wooden fence, half-hidden in the shadows. "You couldn't. I wasn't born yet. I'm your cousin Juliette and I have a brother, Morgan." Juliette curtsied respectfully as she spoke. Her mother had sent her out to welcome her cousins; she had conquered her natural shyness and was rather pleased with herself.

"No one does that anymore," Livia said, staring at Juliette. "Except servants."

"How do you do?" Angus said, bowing slightly. "How charming to meet you."

Juliette blushed at the unkindness of Livia's remark, but decided to tackle it head-on. "I'm sure you will be able to teach us all many things that you have learned in London," she said.

What a sweet voice she has, thought Angus, but that accent! She is like a country lass. Well, I suppose she is a country lass. I shall leave her to Livia. "I should like to meet your brother," he said, drawling deliberately in a way Juliette had never heard before, "and to see your mother again. She was kind to me when I was a child."

"Do come along and see her," Juliette invited. "Mother is kind to everyone—you'll see."

"How boring," Livia said in a voice that Juliette could not quite hear. She decided that she must have misunderstood.

"What? What did you say, Livia?"

"Tell me," Livia Dunlie said, letting Angus go ahead and lacing her arm through Juliette's, "dear cousin, I have a question—is it customary to socialize with Africans here in Georgia? I hardly expected it, but there seemed to be a whole tribe of them at your Uncle Ira's funeral."

Juliette's jaw dropped. She struggled for words and tears stood in her eyes as she spoke. "Why, why, Cousin Livia, not usually, but you see . . . well, Uncle Ira was a Negro and he was part of our family, in a way. You see, he was a free Negro, not a slave. In fact, his father was white and he was Gibson and Andrew's grandfather, in a way . . ."

"How dull family histories are," Livia said. Her bright blue eyes widened as they approached the house. "Oh, at least there are enough candles in here, you can't imagine the dreadful place we've been staying."

"Oh, have you?" Juliette was shocked, but determined to mind her manners and keep her temper, if she could. "Well, Mother says you must stay with us now, and we shall all do our best to make you comfortable."

"Thank you," Livia said. She handed her shawl and reticule to a vastly plump, broadly-smiling black maid in the front hall and remembered her original question. "Is your family peculiar, then, Juliette, or is there miscegenation all over America?"

Juliette trembled. "I don't really know; perhaps Papa can tell you."

"I see. Well, I shall look forward to finding out. What caused the color of their skins, Juliette—do you know that?"

Juliette would have rather dropped through the floor straight to China than stand there discussing the color of

Negro skin right in front of Lizzy, the maid she had known all her life. It just wasn't done, it wasn't ever done; the Barstows owned slaves, took care of them from cradle to grave, fed them and taught them, but they never, ever, discussed them, not to each other and not in front of *them*. It was awful, but how could Livia be expected to know? She was just arrived from London, after all, where life was different—how different Juliette had never before this moment suspected.

"No . . . I don't," Juliette confessed in a shaking voice, "although perhaps it is a particularly virulent form of leprosy. I have heard that. Or perhaps it's because of the sun in Africa. It's terribly hot there, you know."

Livia sniffed, dissatisfied with both suggestions. "Of course it's hot in Africa," she said. "Well, we shall discuss this another time. Now I want to meet the others. Which one is your brother?"

CHAPTER TWO

The Invasion Begins; An Odd Pair; Jenny Admits Her Suspicions

An hour or so had passed since the members of the Barstow family had welcomed their cousins the Dunlies into the old house on Abercorn Street. According to custom, the family of the deceased had a solemn obligation to entertain those who had come to pay him last respects, that is, to supply them with food and drink and an opportunity to visit with friends and relatives, some of whom had gathered from considerable distances. In this case, it was Roland Barstow who had invited funeral guests to his home, and to ease the pain of the occasion and to bolster spirits, he had provided a brandy punch, five gallons of wine, a dozen kegs of ale, and quantities of cold roast meat, oranges, and plum cakes.

The house was filled almost to capacity; candles burned in every downstairs room; doors and windows stood ajar; and friends and relatives moved freely from one conversation to another, meeting and greeting each other, exchanging condolences and embraces. Very shortly, a somber gathering of those to whom this was truly a painful occasion had come together in the formal parlor. Mary Barstow and her children were there with the free black minister Samuel Barstow; Ira's other brother was there, standing silently behind Mary's chair, and so was Kate Barstow, who had chosen this company as much to be free of James Dunlie as for any other reason.

James Dunlie had gone directly into the study as soon as he entered the house and remained there, conversing with Roland and taking no interest in the purpose of the gathering.

"How affected I am to be in Father's study again," James Dunlie said, toying with the silver penknife and silver-rimmed magnifying glass which his parent, Angus Dunlie, had used in his old age and which Roland used now. How affected he was James Dunlie could not easily say. In fact, he was controlling, with effort, his feelings of bitter resentment and rage that all this was Roland's and had been for all the years he had suffered poverty and exile in England. "Father told me that James Oglethorpe often visited him here, but of course you know that, Roland. Do you recall that General Oglethorpe gave me a gift of six hundred acres on Saint Simons Island on the occasion of my christening?"

"Yes, of course I remember," Roland said, nonplussed by his old rival's air of fierce possessiveness, as well as the many other surprises of the evening, but still courteous to a fault. "This house is sixty years old—one of the oldest in Savannah. Many historic things have happened here."

"Quite so," James Dunlie said, opening the top desk drawer to examine its contents with a sweeping glance. He remembered, far more powerfully than the old family stories about Oglethrope, the day he had opened this same desk drawer and removed a chamois pouch holding fifty pounds in gold. He looked up into Roland's pale and guileless eyes and glanced at the jagged scar along his hairline. Roland had never known that it was he who had hired the Indian to scalp him, to seek him out in camp among the other aides to General Wayne. The skin had healed amazingly well.

"I hope you will begin to feel at home here," Roland said.

"You say this is not your primary residence," James Dunlie said.

"Ah, no. Thanks to the able and faithful offices of our cousin Ira Barstow, I have been able to avoid all the business of ginning and marketing cotton—business doesn't suit me, I'm afraid. Perhaps I am like your father in that respect."

"Very little," James Dunlie said. "But you prefer the country?"

"Immeasurably. This house is good enough for a place

in town, but I never linger here. The ladies like to come to town in season for a matter of weeks or months, but I . . ."

"So you will return to the island directly?"

"Tomorrow. And . . . if it suits you . . . I welcome you and your children to accompany us to Sea Groves."

James Dunlie stared. His deepset hazel eyes gave no hint of his bitter feelings. In planning his return to Georgia, he had underestimated the extent of Roland's charity and forgiveness, but he would change his plans to take them into account. Roland's good-natured hospitality cloyed; he did not believe in it, anyway, for during the years of his exile he had hardened his heart irrevocably against his Georgian kin. In the dark recesses of his mind, they were responsible for all of life's pains and injustices. Even as he faced Roland, he did not see him clearly; instead of a kindly gentleman farmer, he saw a deliberately insensitive dolt. No man could be as open as Roland appeared to be; therefore, he was not truly open, he was conniving and deceitful. Dunlie resolved to use all his wit to outguess him and to seize every advantage.

Accordingly, he frowned at Roland's invitation. "I believe I would be more comfortable here," he said bluntly. In truth, he longed to see Sea Groves again, but under other circumstances. In Savannah, poor city as it was, he would be better able to advance his fortunes and further his plans for taking over the entire family holdings, Roland's only part of them.

"My dear James, you do not realize! No one will remain long in Savannah. There is danger—yellow fever has already settled into Charleston, and a summer which begins cold and wet and then becomes hot and dry is likely to be the most fever-ridden!"

James stared suspiciously. Was he being tricked? "Do you see a correlation between temperature and fevers?"

"No one knows the origin of fever. Perhaps it is brought in from the Indies. I have heard a good case for last year's epidemic bursting to life in a bad crate of coffee left rotting too long on the wharves. But at any rate, it is furthered by rain and heat, and once it begins it rages until the first cold weather—that I know."

"So everyone leaves the city in summer?"

"Everyone who can possibly afford to do so. But in your

case, I should insist on it . . . we have so many things to talk over . . . so very many things, quite apart from my natural concern for your health."

And I for yours, James Dunlie thought. I should like to see you dead. An internal shudder expressing the violence of his thought ran swiftly along his back and spine and resulted in an odd and uncontrollable tremor of his neck. Roland stared awkwardly, not in the least comprehending what was wrong, and just at that moment his daughter Juliette appeared in the doorway of the office.

"Papa," she inquired, "am I disturbing you? Excuse me, Great Uncle James . . ."

How like Jenny she is, James Dunlie thought. He was not at all pleased at being called Great Uncle by this grown child, although her genealogy was accurate. He scowled at Juliette.

"What is it, daughter?" Roland asked.

"Mother asks if you would come now, to join us for refreshments," Juliette said. "As soon as you are able, of course."

In fact, in the next room, Jenny Stone Barstow's patience was being strained, nearly to its limit, by the outlandish presence of Angus and Livia Dunlie.

Seeing Angus again, a man grown from the troublesome child she had known so well in the last years of the war, had unsettled Jenny and shaken her composure.

"How like your father you have grown to look," she had said mildly when tall, lanky Angus had come to her and hugged her affectionately, exclaiming "Cousin Jenny! Or must I call you madam?"

It's not the poor boy's fault he reminds me so of his father, Jenny had told herself. Foremost among her feelings for James Dunlie was revulsion, but she was ashamed of the feeling and chastised herself for a sinful lack of Christian charity.

"You may call me cousin, as you used to," she said, "as may your sister. Welcome to our house, Cousin Livia."

Livia Dunlie put out her gloved hand stiffly. She stared at Jenny, her bright blue eyes frankly analytical, seeing a strikingly handsome woman, past her prime, of course, but composed and aristocratic of bearing. Jenny's dress, an oldfashioned green silk moiré, set off her green eyes, and her hair—still dark and lustrous, without a trace of gray—was piled high on her neck to show the fine lines of her bosom and shoulders.

"Thank you, ma'am," Livia said, "I never 'cousin,' 'aunt,' or 'uncle' anyone. It's presumptuous, don't you think? Perhaps it's only provincial. I expect we shall have to strive to avoid provincialism here. It *is* a small town, isn't it? I suppose you acknowledge that! But can you recommend a capable dressmaker to me? The best in town. It's terrible, I can't bear to think of it—half my dresses were ruined in the crossing. Some stupid tar stowed my chest in a part of the hold that was *submerged* by water! They are ruined, completely!"

"I do all my own sewing," Jenny said softly, "but I shall be happy to help you replenish your wardrobe, Livia."

"Mother makes all my clothes, too," Juliette said. She had followed Livia in stunned silence from the front hall. Juliette had never heard a woman speak as rapidly or as freely as Cousin Livia; she was dazzled, and in her mind she had likened Livia's arrival to the appearance of a comet, although comets were sometimes reckoned to be portents of disaster. Juliette resolved to rethink the comparison when she had time and opportunity to retire to her own room and the solace of her journal.

"I never had a mother. Mine died the day I was born," Livia said, pausing for dramatic effect between the twin announcements.

Poor child, sympathetic Jenny thought at once, she has missed a mother's love and instruction. I suppose that's why she seems so overbold, so abrupt and demanding. I was already a little girl when I lost my mother, and I missed her painfully, I recall. Jenny looked at Angus and was startled to see that he was watching his sister with an expression of amusement.

It was her first inkling that they were an odd pair, and she put the vague notion aside as she turned to Angus to answer his questions about the whereabouts of Gibson Barstow, and Andrew and Adam and the other cousins he remembered from his childhood in Georgia.

"Darling Livia, you were so amusing! I could barely keep from shaking with laughter!" Angus drawled to his sister Livia some hours later when they were alone in the tiny attic bedroom at the Widow Bullard's boardinghouse on President Street.

"Whatever are you talking about, Angus? There wasn't a light moment during the entire evening. Why, the company was dull, the conversation halting, there was no music at all, and our cousins seem so doltish I suspect their minds are defective, or at least dwarfed!"

Angus laughed at that, and drew on his pipe. Dressed in a dark red brocade smoking coat, he reclined on a low couch; it was his bedroom, but Livia had left hers, one flight below, and crept up the narrow stairs to join him.

"Laugh all you like! It's I who have nothing decent to wear and shall be trapped for hours tomorrow in the company of that dreadfully childish Juliette—'My mama makes all my clothes,' she said. Only think of it! She has no pretensions, that witless pieface!"

"She's quite pretty, actually," Angus said provocatively.

Livia rose to the bait. "Pretty? As a pink-cheeked piglet is pretty! And her brother—a more maniacally sober character I have never encountered. He reminds me of a big-eyed calf, to retain the notion of the barnyard. Faugh!"

Angus drew again on his pipe and watched his sister fume and prance around the attic room. Shadows danced and smoke from the two candles he had set beside his couch rose in columns to blacken the low, hand-cut rafters. In truth, he disliked his cousins as much as Livia, for the most part, but he was always less free with his opinions. Life had taught him many lessons, but the one he found most consistently sound was that of holding his tongue. He had no confidants save his sister, and her only to an extent.

"Do you think they are as close as we are, dear Livia?" he asked teasingly.

Livia turned from the small dim looking glass mounted over the chest of drawers. "You jest," she said, abandoning an examination of her chin.

"Not at all. I raise the question soberly."

"No one on earth loves her dear brother as I love you, Angus. I cannot fool with you about that. You raised me, Angus, you alone, and you taught me everything I know. I belong to you completely. There! Is that what you're asking? If any others are as we are? I think not."

"Is there nothing you wouldn't do to please me, then, Liv?"

"What pleases you pleases me. You know that."

Livia paused and looked at her brother when she had spoken. She was not as bold, or as confident, as she seemed to be. Her struggle to win and hold her older brother's attention had so far dominated her life, and he was cool enough, enough older, and cruel enough to tease her at his will, to play her like a hooked fish. Women, he thought, were pure creatures of emotion and passion—not that Livia had not a sharp enough mind, for one of her sex, but he knew well that her actions, her motivation, her spirits, were always at the call of her blood.

"Angus, why do you stare at me so? You are like one of those star-struck Barstows!"

He only smiled, and she went on as her confidence diminished.

"I suppose you think I am foolish, Angus. You have been cold to me ever since we arrived here." Livia turned to hide the insecurity that might show in her eyes. Constantly, ceaselessly, she was tormented by the fear that he would send her away, laughing, admitting that what they meant to each other was wrong. She knew he had the power to do so. In all her life they had been parted just once, when Angus had conspired with her father to send her to a small school in Lancashire. She had hated it and missed her brother passionately. After three months she had lost so much weight and was so obviously listless and unhappy that her father had taken her home again. Without Angus she had felt lost, completely rudderless. Without him, her life lost its purpose, as well as its focus, for he had shaped her so—as a small and pretty child, she had become her brother's pet and creature.

"Don't be naughty and cry, now, Livvy," Angus said. He was both tense and weary. It was late. His head was heavy from smoke and brandy, and the candles were burning low. Still, he was not averse to it, and Livia seemed desperate, as always. He looked at her crossly, in a way that had always been one of the signals that he wanted her, for the ritual of their congress followed certain very prescribed lines.

"I'm not naughty, Angus," she said, petulantly, posing for him at the side of his couch.

"Yes, you are. Very naughty." He frowned and she knelt quickly on the floor at his side with a gesture that was both graceful and unselfconscious.

"What will you do to punish me?" she asked.

"I think I will send you away."

"Please, Angus, don't! Please . . . keep me, I beg you. Keep me and teach me how to be good."

"I think you are beyond education."

Her voice rose into a wail. "Don't send me away! I can never be happy without you."

"How else can I punish you?"

"Any way that you like."

He reached down with his left hand and maliciously slapped at her breast. She groaned softly and shut her eyes.

"You must beg me," he said softly. "Implore me to instruct you."

"Yes . . . yes, please. Try to teach me."

He seized her nipple, sliding his hand into the neckline of her fitted, high-waisted gown. He twisted it so that she gasped with pain.

"Hush, Livia. Or I shall have to be cruel with you."

I know he loves me, Livia thought exultantly. I know he loves me when he gives me pain. This is what we two have that no one else can have. Tears filled her eyes and slid down her cheeks but when she opened her eyes, they were shining.

"What shall I do?" she whispered.

"Stand up. Take off your clothes and come back to me."

She did as he said and stood before him; her body was pale and smooth-skinned and glowed a faint ivory in the candlelight. She was exquisitely shaped, with small breasts standing out boldly and tipped with large, dark nipples, a long, slim waist, and strong, rounded legs and thighs. He stared at her, seeing the child she had been as well as the woman she was, seeing the likeness between her more diminutive but similarly long-limbed body and his own. There were strong family likenesses, from the squareness of their shoulders to the shape of their calves—he savored them, studied them, and sighed.

"How naughty you are," he said. "What is that bruise on your leg?"

"I don't know," she whispered. "I don't know, Angus."

"I shall spank you for that. Come here. Bend over."

She did, in a flash of bare limbs, pitching herself at him as he lay, reclining, diving at his body with a lust and hunger that suggested long privation. Angus lay motionless for a moment; her full weight was on him, and then he began to slap her bare buttocks with the flat of his hands, solidly, each blow firm. Her smooth skin reddened and grew hot. She trembled with pain, but did not pull back.

"Oh, please, Angus!"

"Hush!" Her voice annoyed him, interrupted his own pleasure, which he felt more immensely and pervasively with every blow, every blow which pressed her sleek body against his. Tears streaming out of her eyes, she nuzzled into his neck and clung to him tightly as he continued to hit her.

She rocked against him, then, giving into it, and their bodies meshed in a tangle of legs, breasts, bellies, thighs, a wholly natural and perverse coupling that exploded into sheer and inevitable pleasure-taking as they grew hotter and hotter and moved faster and faster until they both gasped and slid apart.

Open-mouthed, still naked, Angus slept alone, and when Livia was sure he was sleeping soundly, she dressed quietly and crept down the steps to her room below. As she passed her father's doorway, she heard the familiar sound of his snoring and remembered that the next day they were all to sail south to Saint Simons Island.

As was her custom, Jenny Barstow rose very early the next morning. Her husband had not slept well and she had been fully aware of it, as a good wife would be; nor was she baffled as to the source of his troubled restlessness. He was upset, all of the family was, at the sudden and total invasion of their long-gone cousins, the Dunlies.

Roland and Jenny had talked late into the night, sharing their feelings about the Dunlies. Roland insisted that it was their natural and Christian duty to forgive James Dunlie his past cruelties and to forget them. His children, Roland reminded Jenny, were blameless innocents, as far as they knew.

Jenny had wondered at that. She had sensed a peculiar

and desperate ruthlessness in their natures, but she did not mention it to Roland.

"It's because my own life has been so blessed," Roland had said. "I feel so fortunate in my own happy marriage, my own strong and healthy family, that it is easy for me to be generous to James. Think of it, Jenny! James and I were raised together, just like brothers. We're just two years apart in age, though God knows what sufferings have aged him so. His mother was never kind to him; she always favored me and James knew it, but childish resentments between men of our age are inappropriate, as are holding political grudges between relatives.

"James was a Tory and I was fervently committed to the cause of liberty, as were you, but you remember that my mother, and my grandmother, were Tory sympathizers. There were some good reasons for it, in those first confused years of the war, and anyway, Georgia has pardoned those old loyalists, long since."

"I shall never be able to forget the way he treated me while you were away with Elijah Clarke and General Wayne," Jenny had said. "I hate to think of it! I believe you and I loved each other already, though we had not admitted to it. He kept me prisoner in this house, Roland. He nailed my window fast. He stole your letters to me, and mine to you. He abused me physically, and had you and Ira and Gibson not intervened, he would have carried me off to England!"

"Oh, Jenny!" Roland had exclaimed, taking her into his arms and covering her soft neck and throat with gentle kisses. "Of course I cannot bear to think of it! You are right, dear, to resent such insane behavior, but perhaps it wasn't as clear at the time. You were so young; you may have misjudged his intentions. James may have thought that he was taking you to safety, as he did his own family. And think of the intervening years, dearest wife. Think of the happiness of our love and our life while he was so far away in England. That is what softens my heart, that and the pricking of my conscience—for James is the natural-born heir to this house, and to Sea Groves, and yet he has none of it."

"He seems to have plenty," Jenny had said. "Those clothes!"

"If our own tastes are simple, we can't blame him for

that. And it's clear to me that he has thought about this homecoming for a long time, perhaps ever since he left Savannah aboard the *Bethia.*"

"It's late," Jenny had said, her voice resigned if not her spirit. "Come to bed, dear husband, and take comfort in my love."

He is too good, she thought the next morning as she watched Roland, still sleeping. It is not in his nature to hold a grudge, nor do his principles allow it. She frowned, and even stifled a sob as she washed her face and dressed herself, for she loved Roland with her whole heart, just as she had at twenty-two; she would do anything to help him and shield him from harm.

But she could not so easily forgive James Dunlie, although not to do so was in violation of her husband's wish and her marriage vows. As the day's first sunshine filtered into the little morning room at the back of the house, shining through the willows that had been only saplings when she was a girl, she settled herself there, accepted a cup of tea from the housekeeper who had come with them to Savannah, and prepared herself to write a letter.

It was a letter she knew she must write, a difficult duty to discharge. Someone must tell Abby of Ira's death, she thought, and it must be done as soon as possible. Poor Abby; it would be a blow to her.

The Abby Jenny addressed was her old friend Abby deLyon, now Mrs. William Warrington of New York City, a woman who was not only rich and happily married but powerful and well connected, a woman whom no one but Jenny Barstow would have described as "poor." But Jenny was a romantic, and remembered the old days—days when Abby and Ira Barstow had been wonderfully in love and had both lost themselves in a romance that had crossed religious and racial lines and had deepened and flourished under the edge of the sword. Abby and Ira had met when she was a nurse and he an aide to Doctor Jack Barstow, Roland's father, and their passion, a phenomenon so stirring and true that it had completely won Jenny's sympathy, had been suddenly and painfully destroyed when, in the confused and desperate days right after the Revolution, Ira had disappeared from Savannah.

Jenny sighed and stared at the blank page, remembering those terrible days. Abby had been completely heartbroken, unable to speak or eat. Mourning had possessed her and she had lost interest in living. And Ira! It was awful to think what he had endured. Ira had been seized, they found out in the weeks that followed, falsely abducted and deported to Jamaica in the *Celia,* a British ship carrying loyalist property out of the country.

Desperately, hopelessly, Abby—all of them—had tried to trace Ira, but he was dead, according to the scanty reports that reached them from Kingston. Accepting the inevitable, Abby had left Savannah, gone north to New York where she had family, and had gone about making a new life for herself, as had Ira, when he miraculously escaped and returned to Georgia in 1790.

It was a romantic story, one of the most romantic Jenny knew, fully as romantic as her own history with Roland. Hardly anyone else remembered it, she felt sure, and no one else knew of its last chapter, the time when Ira and Abby had met in Virginia Springs and renewed their love, admitted eternal fidelity, and decided to part forever. Only Jenny knew that. She herself had not seen her old friend since the day she left Savannah for New York, but throughout the years they had been faithful correspondents. Jenny knew that Ira had always and would always live in Abby's heart, their separate lives and "second" marriages notwithstanding, and she knew that the news of his murder would cause Abby great pain.

With this all in the back of her mind, then, Jenny sat down to write Abby.

> My very dear Abby,
>
> It is with a sad and listless heart that I must write you with very painful news. There is no way to hide the truth. I pray you will accept this and be able to use the reality of this information to better understand the nature of eternity and the briefness of life.
>
> My dear friend, Ira Barstow is dead. It pains me to wound you with this announcement. You may be anxious to know of what he died, and that part of the reality is even more painful. He was murdered! By whom and for what reason we do not know; suffice to say that the intelligence has struck our family and the community like a thunderbolt. He was much loved

> and respected in life and is much mourned in his passing.
>
> Dear Abby, I can well imagine how you must be reeling at the force and suddenness of this news; believe that I am, also, as is my beloved family, especially my daughter Juliette, who loved her Uncle Ira so easily and with such great heart.

Jenny wiped her pen and stopped to think. It seemed cruel to voice her own resentments and suspicions, to stir up poor Abby's passions any more than was necessary, and yet . . . Abby would understand that she needed to air all her thoughts. Abby, above all others, would want to know. She added:

> Terrible as it is, I must confide in you about another sudden and shocking development. James Dunlie has returned to Georgia. He is here in Savannah. Unbeknownst to us, he had been staying in town and appeared at Ira's memorial service, decked out in red and gold like a finch, with his two children. I cannot forgive him, Abby, for his past, nor can I accept him with a welcoming and Christian heart, as Roland can. But worse, and may the Lord forgive me my wicked suspicions—if they are unfounded—I cannot help connecting, in my mind, his reappearance with Ira's death. He was murdered, after all, and I have always believed James capable of murder, always known his bitter resentment of Ira's goodness and success. It seems *too* coincidental, dear friend, that James should stage his return to Georgia on the very occasion of Ira's death by violent means.
>
> Abby, I cannot go on. We sail today for the Island, Dunlie and his children with us, to take refuge in our home. You can imagine that this leaves me with a heavy heart, a heart made even heavier than the terrible news which I am so sorry to send to you. May our Lord comfort you, and the love of your dear family, to whom we all send love, and the sincere sympathy of your
>
> Ever affectionate,
Jenny S. Barstow

"Good morning, mother," Juliette said, appearing in the doorway of the morning room just as Jenny had penned her signature. "Why, whatever is wrong? You look quite stricken!"

"Nothing, my dear, I was just finishing a letter to my dear friend Abby Warrington. Please join me." Jenny looked up, and there, right on cue, was Bella, the housekeeper, with a tray of teacups and hot cornbread.

"Are you sure, Mother? Are you feeling quite well?"

"Yes, dear. I am well. And I am glad that today we shall sail for Sea Groves, aren't you?"

"Yes, of course! Thank you, Bella." Juliette kissed her mother affectionately and sat down to take tea.

CHAPTER THREE

Everyone's Agent Agrees to Everything; A Sea Voyage; A Homecoming

The varied and beautiful land of Georgia could not be called tropical, for its winters bring killing frosts, especially in the inland Piedmont region, but also along the broad and fertile coastal plain. Nonetheless, the months of summer in Georgia are not merely long, providing her a growing season the envy of her northern neighbors, but they are relentlessly and roastingly hot. There are some who have said that Hades itself couldn't be hotter than a summer day in Georgia.

It was on such a sultry day that the Barstows and their relatives, the Dunlies, were to set out from Savannah for Saint Simons Island. The sky was clear that day, and the unclouded sun beat ceaselessly on the land, bleaching the blue from the sky, melting the clouds, and glinting intolerably off the shimmering surface of the river and the sea.

The hour appointed for the Barstows' departure was noon, the very latest possible for reaching the landing at Tybee Island in time to take ship for Saint Simons Island. The first leg of the journey would be in a longboat, covered with a sailcloth and rowed by a dozen burly slaves. Roland had set the hour himself; he had business to transact in Savannah before leaving, and yet he longed to be on his way home.

Accordingly, having risen and breakfasted in the coolest part of the day, he left the house on Abercorn Street and walked the few blocks to the riverfront through the city he knew so well, noting the new houses rising along Bull Street, noticing the sapling pride-of-China trees that were being planted along the streets and squares laid out by General Oglethorpe more than sixty years ago. Roland had been named executor of his good friend Ira Barstow's will, and he meant to comply with the duties of that office.

Roland felt sadness and regret as he approached the fine frame structure Ira Barstow had built and winced when he saw the sign, so optimistically proclaiming I. Barstow and Sons. The sons, he knew, were merely children. According to the terms of Ira's will, control of the business would be held by Ira's white partner, a mere figurehead in Ira's lifetime, until the boys were grown.

The partner, a tall, lanky man with red whiskers named Carlton Raye, was waiting for Roland in Ira's old office.

"Good morning, sir, good morning, Mr. Barstow," Raye said, smiling through yellow teeth when Roland paused at the door. "Take a seat, if you please, sir."

"Good morning, Mr. Raye," Roland said. The office was on the second story in the front part of the warehouse, and commanded a fine view of the Savannah riverfront. From the wide, cushioned armchair he accepted, Roland could see down to the harbor, see bronzed sailors scurrying up the riggings and across the decks of ships and boats, see innumerable canoes and dinghies crossing the river, dark against the flat reaches of Hutchinson Island across the way. Heat haze rose like smoke off the silvery water. It promised to be a sweltering day. He loosened his collar with a finger. How strange it is to see Raye at Ira's desk, he thought, but he did not say so.

"You have come into a big job," he said slowly.

"God willing, I shall prove equal to it," Raye said with a humility he did not feel. He had despised and ridiculed Ira's business until this opportunity had arisen. He had not known Ira well. Raye was confident that he could manage the ginning and shipping business, and yet he knew he needed the custom of men like Roland Barstow, who had been, after all, connected with Ira Barstow's family in some way—not by blood, of course. What the connection was, he had never been sure, nor did he care. Ira Barstow had been a freed slave—for that alone, Georgia was well rid of him. Free Negroes were a bad influence on the others, everyone said so, and half of Savannah's residents were slaves. Raye had been Ira Barstow's figurehead partner; Barstow's death had given his own life a renewal, and he was eager to see what he could make of it.

"You shall have my support," Roland said. "This year, as usual, you will receive my full harvest, and sell it at your discretion. Your fee will be two percent?"

"As usual," Raye said. In fact, he had not known until this morning that Roland Barstow's fee was one percent less than any other client's, or that Ira Barstow had loaned Roland one thousand dollars, without interest, earlier this year. Raye was new to the many interconnections among the privileged, but he was inspired by them and expected to be making some private deals on his own.

"The relationship between a planter and his factor is one of honor between two gentlemen," Roland said. "For years I have trusted Ira to handle all my accounts, buy and sell for me, keep me in touch with the world . . . and much more. We have never known each other well, Mr. Raye, but from now on . . . until Ira's sons are of age . . . we must necessarily be partners."

"Yes, of course," Raye said. He preferred not to think of the end of his tenure. It seemed so far off, and in the meantime he recognized his back-door ascendancy to the leadership of this thriving business as the opportunity of a lifetime, one denied nine out of ten men in any lifetime. He flashed his yellow teeth at Roland Barstow, delighted with the notion of being his partner. The Barstows were known to be high and mighty—now he was suddenly elevated to their status. He rose and extended his skinny hand.

"I shall make every effort to fulfill your trust in me," Raye said.

Roland returned the handshake and then hesitated. There was no more to say. "We will communicate through the mails, then, as usual," he said, and left, unaware that he was shaking his head as he descended the stairs. It felt wrong; he felt oddly disappointed and discouraged; he could not warm up to Raye; he did not fully trust him. And yet, how could he expect to feel for a new man what he felt for Ira?

Roland went on along the Bay, walking slowly in the increasing heat. Before the morning was out, he planned to place an order with his wine merchant, endure a fitting at his tailor's, and choose a length of fine silk as a birthday present for Jenny. Cities exist for such things, he thought as he marveled at the amount of commerce on Savannah's streets, even in summer, even on a desperately hot day.

Already depressed, he was further disheartened by the sight of a red-nosed drunk with a belly like a sack of flour who lay collapsed against a half-staved-in hogshead. I have noticed before, he thought, how in a city one always meets everyone one doesn't care to meet. The drunk he recalled from his military days. He saw a pockmarked fishwife who had lost her first husband to a firing squad; now she lived with a black man who was half Creek. Roland hated to see so many of the world's unfortunates at once, and to do him credit, he would have chosen to see them all redeemed; nonetheless, the stench and dirt of the waterfront repelled him and he walked briskly, anxious to do all his errands and sail south.

As Roland proceeded on his business, another man climbed the steps to confer with Carlton Raye. Roland would have been very surprised to see that it was James O. Dunlie; Raye was surprised himself, but Dunlie lost no time in introducing himself and stating the purpose of his visit.

"I have not lived in Savannah since before the war," he told Raye, "and I have, naturally, lost the title to my business at that time."

"Yes, sir," Raye said, his eyes wide. He recognized Dunlie as an ex-Tory and appreciated his good breeding and importance. Besides, he was dazzled. Dunlie was splendidly arrayed, like no one else in town. Raye wondered if a red coat would look well on his own lanky frame. At the very least, he must have a waistcoat with a touch of silver lace. . . . "I believe I understand. If there is anything at all I can do to help you . . ."

"There is," Dunlie said. He refused the armchair and strutted in front of the windows like a gorgeous red bird. "Before the war I was an importer of African laborers. I intend to resume the business, but I find that I will be spending the summer, at least, out of the city. Thus, I need an agent to receive goods already en route from Africa. Perhaps you will agree to be that agent. It appears obvious to me that cotton production is inexorably connected with the importation of laborers."

"So it is," Raye agreed. "Every cotton planter is always

in need of more land and more slaves. . . . But are you aware, sir, that the most recent state constitution prohibits importation of slaves directly from Africa? No matter, we shall declare them as coming in from Carolina; 'tis no doubt only a temporary injunction, sir, at the worst, and totally unenforceable."

"Ah!" Dunlie smiled, "I see you know what you're about. What price do they bring, Mr. Raye?"

"Fresh from Africa, they fetch three to five hundred dollars, sir. Those from the Gold Coast are preferred, then the ones from the Congo, then the Ibos. Ibos make the best rice workers, sir, but they tend to do away with themselves."

"So I have heard. I contracted for three ships, before leaving London—all to pick up cargo on the Gold Coast. Many of them will be children; they occupy less space, of course. As you understand this business, Raye, we shall do very well together. Five percent of my profits will be yours," Dunlie promised.

"Yes, sir!" Raye said, his head spinning. Now this was the sort of private deal he'd had in mind!

"Very well," Dunlie said. "Here are the documents you must present to the captain of the slaver *Westwind*. She's due some time this month; I'm afraid I can't be more specific. But you will keep an eye out for her, eh, my good man? And practice all the necessary discretion?"

"I shall be totally discreet," Raye promised. "After all, this is a private matter, a matter of honor between two gentlemen, sir."

"Splendid," Dunlie said. He was pleased with the arrangement and delighted that the business would be carried out right under the Barstows' noses, practically across Ira Barstow's dead body, in a manner of thinking. Raye was the perfect partner in this enterprise: weak, calculating, and greedy. It was a dirty business, but cotton growers must have slaves, and the profits would be enormous. Dunlie's spirits were high. Everything was going well. The Barstows had no idea what sort of an enemy they were taking to their bosom, no idea at all.

"Have you any beaux?" Livia Dunlie asked Juliette Barstow. The two cousins were seated together in the longboat that would carry them to Skidaway Island. It was past noon and so hot and humid that blinking an eye was an effort that released a salty stream of perspiration. The young ladies, entirely wrapped in innumerable layers of cotton and lace—including chemises, corsets, camisoles over the corsets, four or five petticoats, vests, stockings, garters, and whalebone crinolines—were damp to the skin and flushed rosy red. Of course they could not complain, at least Juliette could not, for she had been raised according to a strict code of modesty and self-controlled courtesy by her mother, who sat in the seat just ahead of her.

Juliette hoped most fervently that her mother was out of earshot. It was possible; the rising and dipping of the oars made a considerable and rhythmic splashing. One of the boatmen was singing. And, in the heat, nearly all of the ladies were napping. It was not that Juliette had any intention of deceiving her mother, or wanted to hide anything from her, but she felt self-conscious about her conversations with Livia. Livia in the daytime was proving to be even more unconventional and outspoken than she had been last night.

"Beaux?" Juliette answered hesitantly. "Not really, Livia. I am only sixteen."

"When I was sixteen," Livia said, assuming worldly-wise perspective on the age she had left behind five years ago, "I had more beaux than I could count."

"Did you?" Juliette whispered, praying her mother was not listening. She had promised her mother to put Livia at her ease, to make her feel at home, and she was afraid that she was unequal to the assignment.

"Of course I did. I had too many beaux, if it's possible to have too many. I guess it is."

"I'm afraid you will find our life at Sea Groves very quiet," Juliette whispered.

"Oh, I'm sure I shall. What do you do all day long out there?"

"I find many things to do. Of course, I try to help Mother. I like to read, Livia, and I love to ride my horse, Bermuda. He was a present to me on my birthday, from my parents. He's so beautiful, Livia, dark chestnut . . ."

Livia frowned and sighed. They were seated so close that Juliette felt their knees and thighs pressing together.

She took a deep breath of the hot, salty air. At this range Livia provided Juliette with a good opportunity to appreciate every detail of her gown and admire her pale, creamy skin and dark, tousled curls. It was all perfectly lovely and reduced Juliette's already flagging confidence.

". . . about the same color as your hair," Juliette finished, and then felt embarrassed. Was it gauche of her to compare a horse's coloring to her cousin's? Oh, dear, of course it was!

Livia snorted. "I doubt it! Anyway, Juliette, I don't care for riding. What else is there to do?"

"Mother has a handsome flower garden," Juliette suggested.

"Really?" Livia snapped with her brisk London accent. "I believe that gardening endangers the complexion. I should prefer to have a gardener. Why do you suppose it is, Juliette dear, that you aren't yet interested in having beaux?"

"I don't reckon . . . I'll ever be a belle," Juliette whispered miserably, stiff with embarrassment. She closed her eyes to hide tears, but she could not shut out the sunlight reflecting off the water, so strong that she saw red and felt quite faint.

"Goodness, it's hot," Livia complained. Cousin Juliette was no fun at all, she decided. The silly goose wouldn't even fight back; she seemed to have no self-respect. Livia yawned. She had done her best to rile Juliette, but it would seem that she was too unimaginative to rile, no matter how she was teased.

Silence settled between the two cousins, then, and the chant of the boatmen was the only human voice to rise above the splashing of the oars and the soft slipping of the big wooden boat through the water. The boatmen seemed oblivious to the heat; they passed a cask of rum between them, and one of them led the others in a song:

> We are goin' down to Georgia, boys,
>   To see the pretty girls, boys,
> We'll give 'em a pint of rum, boys,
>   And a hearty kiss besides, boys . . .

All of them joined in the chorus, their deep voices harmonizing in "Aye, aye, so we will; Yoe, yoe, so we go."

Presently, Livia's regular breathing assured Juliette that she had dozed off, but Juliette was too upset to fall asleep. Livia, with her unerring cruelty—a characteristic Juliette would have a lifetime to observe—had touched on one of her deepest fears.

What is wrong with me? Juliette worried. Livia can tell right away that something is. It must be perfectly obvious that I am not like other girls. I am so moody, and shy as a rabbit. I guess I'll never be popular, even in my own small circle of acquaintances, most of whom, I reckon, are kind to me only because they know my family. Oh, dear!

Writhing with self-conscious misery, poor Juliette felt hotter than ever. She was dissatisfied with everything about herself—her thin body, so slim and undeveloped compared to Livia's, her freckled face, her slow drawl, her want of conversation. Whatever will become of me? Juliette fretted. The best I can hope for is that some day some doltish neighbor will ask me to marry him, and I'll be so afraid that it's my only chance that I shall accept him. I shall snatch at him! The thought amused her, oddly, and with a lightening of her spirits she lifted her bonneted head and looked up, toward the bow of the longboat, where her brother and Angus Dunlie were seated.

Morgan caught her eye, and winked, and Juliette felt better. At least there was her own dear brother, the one man in the world who genuinely preferred her to all others. She smiled, and Morgan made a few abbreviated leaps and waves toward the water which she easily read to mean "Let's go swimming!" Juliette giggled under her breath. It was their secret—that he had taught her to swim off the beach on Saint Simons Island, something no lady ever did—and that she was good at it and enjoyed it, especially on days as hot as this one.

Shaking her head warningly, Juliette waved back at Morgan. Her gesture woke Livia, who shook out her fan and began to wave it slowly.

"Your brother . . . is quite handsome," Livia said.

Juliette's heart sank. It meant nothing, of course, and it was perfectly true, and yet she dreaded Livia's expression of interest. Jealousy seared her brain, and without thinking of the consequences, she said, "He is the handsomest and finest man in the world, Livia! But he is too young for you!"

Livia laughed, and then, seeing the expression of shock and consternation on Juliette's face, she laughed even harder. "Is that so?" she teased. "Is that so, dear Juliette?"

After a calm and tranquil moonlit sail south from Tybee, the party of travelers, with all their baggage and companions, arrived at the Barstows' private landing on Saint Simons Island at about seven o'clock the next morning. The journey, in the cool of night and favored by calm seas, had been an easy one. The ship was roomy enough so that each of the ladies could recline, if she chose; a light picnic supper had been served, and the gentlemen of the group had drunk rum and ale far past midnight.

Juliette had been awake most of the night, feeling that it was too beautiful to sleep, savoring the cool silver light of the moon and the soft refreshing breeze from the northeast. It was a voyage that all the Barstows had taken many times; at this time of the year, it was truly a pleasure cruise, and they all took delight in it.

And even more delight in approaching their beloved home.

Sea Groves had never looked prettier than on that June morning. The Barstows' seaside plantation had grown into its name. There had been no groves there at all when Roland's grandfather had come to the island and built the first modest two-story house within sight of the sea. In 1744, on the first eight hundred acres—five hundred of them granted by the king of England as a reward for heroism at the battle of Bloody Marsh, which drove the Spanish, forever, out of the colony—he had set out the first one hundred orange trees. In the next few years he had planted lemons, peaches, and dates, and next to them mulberry trees.

Careful husbandry through the intervening years had preserved these trees through bad storms and frosty winters. The trees had grown strong, putting deep roots into the sandy soil and rewarding the concern and care of their owners. In his lifetime Roland had replaced dozens of trees and set out many others, so that the orchards at Sea Groves were now the most extensive and magnificent on the island.

As he was able, Roland had added more land to his holdings. They now amounted to a full two thousand acres, a good part of which was planted in sea-island cotton, a part still in rice. He had also enlarged and improved the plantation house.

It stood in sight of the landing but at the end of a hedged avenue, approximately a mile in length, which led through a spacious lawn of twenty or thirty acres. The lawn was set out with live oak, magnolias, cedars, and pines, arranged in clusters and lines and interspersed with rosebeds, an herb garden, patches of perennials sent from England, an arbor of grape vines, and a small pond.

The house itself was ample but not pretentious. It was a double-sectioned, two-story structure. Porches on the south side extended from the dining room, the drawing room, and the parlor. The north side was more secluded, and the gallery running between the dining room and the kitchen house, at a remove of some fifty feet, was covered by a wooden roof and paved with brick. All of the rooms, including the bedrooms on the second floor, which were quite small, were airy with tall floor-to-ceiling windows that admitted light and air in good weather and could be closed by cedar shutters when storms blew.

"How happy I am to see Sea Groves," Jenny Barstow murmured to her husband as their boat was secured to the landing. Some score or so of the Barstows' servants lined the beach, and according to the custom of the household, those who worked in the house would be waiting outside the front door to greet them.

"How far are your neighbors?" Livia inquired.

"Not far," Jenny told her. "We are on a point of land. Beyond the house are the groves and the servants' quarters, then it's about three miles to the nearest public crossing."

I certainly hope there'll be a carriage for me to use, Livia thought. She had told Juliette she wasn't fond of horses; in fact, she was deathly afraid of them, and could not think of riding by herself.

Letting the young people go ahead, Jenny and Roland strolled up the walk arm in arm. James Dunlie had accepted a ride in the carriage that transported all their baggage, and Kate Barstow had gone with him.

"I have always been as fond of Sea Groves as you have, my dear," Roland told Jenny. "How many happy years have we passed here together!"

Why does he speak as if our happiness is past? Jenny asked herself. A frown tightened her forehead, but she said nothing. The Dunlies had come, and there was no changing that, although she was instinctively afraid that their visit would alter their lives, perhaps mar them.

"Darling, see how the roses have blossomed!" she said brightly, pointing to an arbor heavy with massive and outrageously pink blooms.

But even the sight of her well-trained housemaids, Posy and Judina, Flora and Reba, neatly dressed in homespun blue cotton dresses with starched white aprons stretched across their chests, could not dispel the feelings of apprehension that gripped Jenny. Nor could the smell of fresh-baked bread or that of home-cured ham frying for their breakfast, for this breakfast and many others to follow must be shared with the Dunlies and eaten in their company.

It will be a trying summer, Jenny thought as she greeted the maids, and reached down to gather Reba's baby into her arms.

"Thank you, thank you," she and Roland replied to their servants' cries of "Welcome home, Miss Jenny! Welcome home, Master Roland!" Out of the corner of her eye Jenny could see James Dunlie striding through the downstairs rooms, examining everything, like a soldier home from the wars.

CHAPTER FOUR

Women Talk; Girls Dream and Scheme; Men Take Action

It was the end of August, nearly the end of the summer, and the bright red noonday sun hung overhead like a burning blood orange. Everything at Sea Groves was in readiness for the party, a splendid barbecue and dancing party to which the Barstows had invited all their neighbors, in honor of their guests from New York, Abby Warrington and her daughter Aimee.

The guests would arrive within the hour. Inside, the house was just settling down from a morning of tumultuous confusion and excitement. House slaves in starched white aprons scurried across the polished wood floors, carrying dishes of food and baskets of snowy linens. Everything that could be polished shone—all the crystal and glass—all the windows, mirrors, furniture, lamps. Flowers stood in baskets and vases on every table and in every empty corner and lent their fragrance to the fresh salty breezes that swept across the lawn and the mouth-watering smell of molasses-basted beef turning on a huge iron spit outside the detached kitchen.

All the field workers had been given the day off, except for those who had been drafted to aid the house servants. Since dawn, a mood of celebration had gripped the entire plantation, and a quartet of self-taught fiddlers—who would play for dancing later—sang and played in the quarters, drank homemade ale, and ate roasted ears of corn.

"Jenny? Jenny, dear, can you spare a minute or two to walk out with me?" Abby Warrington asked, putting her head into the little pantry just off the dining room, where Jenny was in consultation with Virginia, a tall, broomstick-thin black woman who was in charge of all the cooking. Behind Virginia the shelves of the pantry were lined with cakes: seedcake and buttercake, coconut cake and brown-sugar cake, and besides the cakes, amazing puddings colored to match every stripe of the rainbow.

"Of course, Abby. There's not another thing to do here, is there, Virginia?"

"No, ma'am, everything's nigh ready," Virginia said, helping her mistress out of the big white apron that had covered her pale green silk gown made with a low neckline and puffed sleeves.

"I just hope it's not too hot for dancin'," Jenny said to Abby as they walked past the herb garden, away from the outside kitchen, scattering a pack of small boys who had gathered around the turning side of beef.

"Not at all," Abby reassured her. "There's always a lovely breeze here at Sea Groves; the weather has been delightful all summer. I declare, it's more comfortable here than in New York."

"How I have enjoyed your visit," Jenny said. Abby had come to them by sea, almost directly after receiving Jenny's letter, and had stayed with them for six weeks. Jenny had found her old friend changed—plumper, more sedate, sophisticated—but their friendship unaltered and unblemished by the passage of years.

"No more than I," Abby vowed. "Seeing you again has made me realize how much I have always missed you."

Together, the two women walked away from the house, across the huge, rolling lawn toward the sea, enjoying the sensation of freedom as the wind blew through their light, sheer gowns and tossed their long, loosely curled hair. The wind was variable, almost whimsical, bringing them at one moment the smell of the orange groves and at the next the roar of the sea.

"Look! Look at that splendid bald eagle!" Jenny exclaimed and they stood silently, faces uplifted, watching the huge white bird wheel and circle in the sky. "What a wingspan! What a handsome bird!"

"Oh, Jenny, I am so sorry to leave . . ." Abby said.

"Stay, then. Stay another month."

"I cannot. I fear to leave you, in a way . . . but my

little boys need their mother. And my husband, of course, requires me at home."

"At least you have agreed to leave Aimee here with us a while longer."

"Yes, this visit has been good for her. She has never spent enough time in the country, and I don't believe I have ever heard her laugh so freely. She has always been such a serious child, so devoted to study and music. And I am happy to see her get on so well with your Juliette."

"Juliette adores her. We all do, and find her accomplishments an inspiration."

"Thank you, Jenny." Abby Warrington had entertained some concerns about presenting Aimee to her Georgian friends, but she need not have. Roland and Jenny understood immediately whose daughter she was, and knew that Abby had explained to her husband, when first they met, that she was the widow of a Georgia patriot. William Warrington had taken in Aimee as his own, and the Barstows had accepted her on the same terms. It was a situation sufficiently irregular to escape any discussion whatsoever, especially among old friends, who had loved and suffered together in the days when Ira Barstow and Abby had been lovers.

Among the Barstows, as among many of their peers, there had developed a powerful sense of family connections, an idea of the importance of consanguinity as the main measure of status. Acutely aware of the precise relations of their ancestors—many of them mutual, as they were first cousins, children of sisters—Roland and Jenny had forged a concept of family trust and responsibilities—a powerful, far-extending system that bestowed benediction, banns, license, forgiveness as needed, to any of its members. Any family member was loved, to an extent that permitted him or her any transgression, as long as it was not against the family or its interests, and forgave any family member transgressions against the rules of outside society.

Abby was included in Jenny and Roland's concept of family. "She is as dear to me as a sister," Jenny often said, and, "I love Aimee as if she were my own." Love was the thread that bound the family together, and held them in, too, as it provided support.

It was this sort of family structure that Roland Barstow

felt obliged to offer James Dunlie, and he had honestly tried to do so. All summer he had provided James Dunlie with all the conveniences of his house and his land, overlooked his frequent unexplained absences and losses of temper with the servants. Dunlie had kept up appearances, barely, with an air of biding his time, and his children had gotten on well enough with their hospitable cousins.

But beneath the surface of daily life, Abby and Jenny had observed James Dunlie closely and ceaselessly, and their dislike of him had not mellowed.

"Aimee will always do well," her mother said. "It's not of her that I must speak, now that we have a moment alone. I must speak of a much sorrier subject."

"I daresay I know who you mean," Jenny sighed. Her face clouded.

"Yes, of course you do. I wish I could say that my visit had quelled the outrage aroused in me by your letter. I wish I could say I have found your suspicions unfounded."

"But you have not?"

"Most assuredly not. Evil, dear Jenny, surrounds that man like a choking fog. It threatens to smother all the sunshine of your lives. His greediness, his ruthlessness, his ambition are pervasive. He is a wicked man, I'm sure of it, and I have received a letter from my uncle's lawyer in Savannah, saying that there has been no suspect yet found in Ira's murder. Without a scrap of proof, I suspect that Dunlie was connected with it. He hated Ira, you know he did, and he hates all the rest of us who crossed him in those days."

Jenny gave a soft moan. "What can we do?"

"Nothing. I'm afraid that we are perfectly helpless against him."

"Oh, Abby, why do you say so?"

"There is nothing specific we can accuse him of. Our best hope is that he will leave us alone. I feel sure he dislikes the country and will return to Savannah at his first opportunity. I have never seen such hospitality as Roland has offered to him, Jenny. I could not do it, nor would I, even to his children. She, his daughter, is as charming and deceitful as Cleopatra's asp, and he! Dear Lord! I see that the young ladies admire him, but I find such vanity in a young man quite repulsive."

Jenny sighed. "I'm afraid that I agree with you. It gives

me strength to hear you speak so frankly. But I do not feel as helpless as you say I am. I confess, my resentment and anger and suspicions give me strength as they seethe below the surface, and may the Lord pardon me, I shall remain vigilant in my surveillance of him. I am strong, that you must grant me, especially when it concerns my own."

Abby nodded and smiled wryly, and walking as they talked, the two women passed under the drooping feathery branches of a huge willow. "You are as passionate and indignant as you were at sixteen, Jenny."

"Perhaps I am. I'm forty-four years old, but I don't feel any different inside. Do you, Abby?"

"Today I do. Today I feel quite weary and consumed. Coming here has opened doors to my past, Jenny, that I believed forever closed. My early life, in Savannah, with you and Roland and Ira, seems so long ago. One day I decided to put it behind me and go on with whatever was next . . ."

"Darling, you have been so brave," Jenny said, and she embraced her friend. "I appreciate your coming here to see us—opening old wounds and exciting old passions. Sometimes I am ashamed, Abby, to be such a grown woman and still subject to such wild feelings and strong desires . . ."

"Never feel ashamed of feelings, Jenny," Abby insisted, holding her old friend in a tight embrace. "It would be feeling shame for being alive! Life, so wondrous in its mysterious origin, is as wild and awesome and troubling as the sea. We must cling to it—and welcome its passions!"

Both women shed tears as Abby spoke, her voice rising as high as the wind, and then they turned to see a line of carriages rumbling up the avenue to the house, and to see Roland coming across the lawn, waving at them.

"Your husband," Abby said, and Jenny's heart quickened, for she was still in love.

"You resemble a pair of wood nymphs," Roland called out. "Can a mere man capture you and lure you inside to greet our guests?"

"We are coming," Jenny promised, giving her husband her cheek to kiss.

"My sweet, you look radiant," Roland whispered.

"I think it's from temper," Jenny confessed, and arm in

arm, the three of them strolled past the rose arbor and called out "Welcome!" to their neighbors.

It was dark. Fireflies twinkled in the trees and hedges, shining on–off, off–on, as real and unsubstantial, as brave and brief and brilliant as first love, and Juliette, examining her heart for signs of the same, sat alone on the lowest branch of a peach tree planted by her great-grandfather.

Juliette's head was spinning. The party, it seemed, had been going on forever. She could still hear music, voices, laughter coming from the house and the porches and the lawn just beyond the porches, on which guests strolled arm in arm, resting from the dancing and taking air. It had been a lovely party, everyone said so, it was still a lovely party, for few of the guests had departed or showed any inclination to end the evening.

I tried to have fun, Juliette thought, I should have had fun, but I am hopeless—everything makes me miserable—everything! Dear Lord, why am I so jealous and ungrateful? Why must I envy even those I love? Oh, I suppose it's the usual thing—it will poison my life! I want nothing more than to fall in love, with almost anyone, but I am not desirable to young men, not at all, I am too serious and too thin and unwomanly . . . they all know it and despise me . . . and women, too. How can Livia possibly respect me? Or Aimee either?

Writhing with self-conscious self-hatred, even moaning aloud, Juliette swung backward off the tree branch and neatly, if childishly, for she was still mostly child in her makeup, although with full-blown adult emotions stirring and troubling her, hung upside down from her knees, her dress mostly tucked under her legs. From this angle, with her slim, bare arms dangling and her hair streaming backwards, she could study the house, the dark lawn, and the fireflies from a new angle.

"*Mon dieu!* Darling Juliette! Don't fall! Oh, help!" Aimee trilled, running up to Juliette through the dewy grass.

Blood rushing to her head, her cheeks pink, her eyes sparkling, her good humor amazingly restored, Juliette hauled herself back up and faced her friend.

"Don't worry, Aimee, I am really all right."

Breathlessly, in the way that had already become dear

to all the Barstows, Aimee laughed. "You are so silly, dear Juliette. But I love you for it."

Juliette swung off the branch and landed at Aimee's feet. Aimee, who had been raised in New York City and had even been to school in France before her father deemed the political situation there too dangerous, was so polished and sophisticated that she would have intimidated Juliette except that she was so unaffected and affectionate that it was impossible to fear her. Aimee was seventeen and deliciously pretty: dark-eyed and dark-skinned with a tangled mop of lustrous curly hair.

"Why have you left the party?" Juliette asked, gasping.

"Oh! They are all too exasperating. I cannot bear it any more. Your cousin Angus will give me no peace, always teasing me and holding me too close when we dance . . . while I would rather dance just once with your dear brother—but Juliette, there is no hope of parting him from Miss Livia tonight. What is her magic, do you think, Juliette? I know Morgan likes me, and I am sure he does not wish to hurt my feelings, but why is it, do you suppose, that Miss Livia is so irresistible?"

Aimee's ingenuousness touched Juliette—it was so unlike her own secret melancholy—but furthered her feeling that she was unique among all the young people, the only one excluded from the network of romantic intrigue which possessed other young ladies of her age—and might have possessed her, also, except that no one offered her even a chance, let alone a kiss, welcome or unwelcome.

"I would be the last one to know," Juliette said. "Oh, Aimee, I suppose we must go back in. I know my mother wants me to have a good time. Come, take my arm . . ."

"Livia is pretty, but so am I," Aimee complained, following Juliette back toward the house.

There, seated together on the side porch, on a backless bench under a trellis of honeysuckle vines, Livia held Morgan enthralled; had the two younger girls heard her, they would have gasped in surprise.

"Goodness! You are not the first man to fall in love with me," Livia informed Morgan. "Two men have already killed themselves over me—one drowned and one in a hunting accident that was no accident at all."

"You poor thing, how awful," Morgan exclaimed, his eyes wide.

"Of course it was awful. I did nothing to deserve it," Livia vowed. She sighed, and her breasts rose and fell under the soft, shiny, sheer stuff of her teal blue dress, cut so low and tight across the bosom that her mother would have worried for her health, had she been living.

Morgan was mesmerized by her. She was enchantingly sensuous. Her proud, pale throat invited his kisses, her blue eyes teased and provoked, her supple, slim body wordlessly promised satisfaction. Other girls were moonlight; Livia was the sun. She shone, she gave off heat, she drew men to her.

"Your sister has treated me cruelly," Livia told Morgan. "She and that Aimee. Oh, Morgan, I am so glad that we have become close friends! I so needed a confidant. You know I am so far from home!"

"I would do anything for you," Morgan promised. He was not stone, nor was he clay; he was flesh, and his flesh moved in response to Livia's power. As he stood and held out his arms to her, his groin ached and his blood pounded. I have never felt so before, he thought. I suppose I am in love.

Angus, watching Morgan and his sister through the window from the drawing room—as ever the observer, as ever with one eye on Livia—was beyond confusing love with lust. Lust was what he had exorcised before coming down to the party, in the usual way, meeting with the slow-witted but voluptuous girl he had selected from the girls he saw in the fields—all of whom he assumed to be his if he cared to take them. Her name was Ella; he found her enormous breasts—and utter willingness—to be satisfactory. At the beginning of the summer she had been a virgin; she had screamed and bled the first time he had taken her to bed. Now she was changed. She was slower, wise-eyed, and her belly had begun to harden with Angus's child.

Angus remained at the window, watching Juliette and Aimee come toward the house. He had drunk a good deal, but he was not drunk. Morgan, he noted, had no head for liquor. Nor did the young ladies, of course, although everyone had drunk punch all day—it was too hot not to.

As he waited, he studied Aimee. How dark she was; he wondered what her father must look like. Juliette was just a child, with a child's innocence and illusions. Both of them, Angus thought, with a confidence that bordered on arrogance, are in love with me. Juliette is the more intelligent and more sensitive; Aimee is riper, but Father has asked me to be discreet. He has higher hopes for me, no doubt; I know he has plans for my marriage.

Father has never misled me, Angus admitted. Since childhood, he had been privy to his father's ambitions and plans, had taken pride in his confidence, and respected it. Lifelong habits of discretion had become ingrained habits of deceit. Deceit was a pleasure in itself. Habitually, Angus kept his own counsel; he took in information but rarely released any. He observed and remembered, but he never explained. No one knew his whole life, no one at all, not even Livia, and he relished that, smiling as he thought of the time he had passed with Ella before the party, and the outrage that his uncle Roland would feel when he saw Ella's "bright" child.

Angus had enjoyed the summer. He relished the physical freedom of life at Sea Groves, its miles of seafront trails to ride, marshes full of birds to hunt, enough good fellows nearby to do for companionship. He liked Georgia; it seemed to him a veritable land of opportunities peopled by polite, slow-speaking men and easy, vulnerable women. He enjoyed his rivalry with his staid, serious cousin Morgan and he was delighted to see his father so happy. It seemed to Angus that the world revolved around him; he had only to stand still and enjoy it.

"Where have you two young ladies been?" he asked, surprising them at the door. Inside, lines were forming for "Eastern Star," one of the best-loved dances. Which one shall I choose? Angus asked himself.

"To London, to visit the king," Aimee answered, smiling, but her eyes slid past Angus to see where Morgan had gone.

"Picking fireflies," Juliette said, her eyes seeking Angus's, hers dazed with confused adoration.

"Come and dance with me, Miss Warrington," Angus said, and watched Juliette turn away to hide her disappointment.

A few weeks later, after Abby Warrington had departed and the first signs of fall were beginning to be seen on the island, James Dunlie rode swiftly through the orange groves on a fine black stallion from Roland's stable, past the fields of workers bent over the rows of cotton. He saw Morgan standing among the workers—the full force, including women and children, for the cotton was ripe and haste must be made. The sight of Morgan filled him with amused contempt. Fool, he thought, he is no better than a farmer!

For his own children, Dunlie had much higher hopes, much grander plans, and some of them were coming to fruition in good order. Dunlie had ridden in from the village of Brunswick, where he sent and received mail at the inn. Today he had received two letters and was anxious to discuss their contents with his son.

The stallion was hot and breathing hard as Dunlie rode up the avenue to the plantation house, reined him to a stop, and dismounted. A groom appeared at once and led the stallion off toward the stable.

"Good even', Master James," the groom mumbled, but Dunlie paid no attention and did not reply. He was tired and hurried. It was late afternoon—to think that Morgan and his work force had been in the fields for twelve or fourteen hours already!—and the red sun hung low over the horizon. His own muscles ached, just from riding, and he would relish a tub, but only when he had spoken to Angus.

Accordingly, he turned away from the main house and mounted the outside stairs to the west wing, where "the young gentlemen"—Angus and Morgan—occupied rooms at some distance from the rest of the family.

"Angus! Angus, where are you?" he called. Angus was usually alone in his room at this hour of the day, unless he was out riding or otherwise enjoying himself. He had taken no interest in planting or any other work done on the plantation, nor did his father expect him to. What his host might have expected was of no interest to either of them.

"Here, Father. I'm just dressing," Angus called. Stomping awkwardly with one boot on and one off, he cursed at the young black valet who held out his long, tight trousers. "God damn it, hurry!"

"Be off, you!" James Dunlie snapped at the unfortunate servant. "I want a word with you, Angus, without filling a pair of sticky ears." The boy vanished, trembling. James

Dunlie's temper and ready crop had made him famous—and hated—in the quarters, not that Angus was well loved, either.

Angus was looking a bit nonplussed. His blond hair was tousled, his face flushed, his stock missing, his shirttails hanging crumpled and loose. His girl, Ella, had just left him; she had slipped in from the fields on the pretext of a terrible toothache, and he had dusted her off in good order. He felt good—relaxed and at the same time raring to go. Smiling to himself, he tucked his shirt carefully into his long black trousers and turned to face his father.

James Dunlie was seated on a low, rush-seated chair from which he had a view out the window toward the lawns and gardens. He stretched his dusty boots out before him as he spoke.

"I received two letters today which will be of interest to you," he said. "The first was forwarded from Savannah by Mr. Raye. It is from west Georgia, from Wilkes County—from our relatives out there, a family by the name of Stone. You've heard me speak of my efforts to reach them."

"Yes, Father."

"The letter is from Pittman Stone—he's Jenny Barstow's brother, although I gather they have been out of touch for some years. He inquires after them . . . but no mind, it sounds very promising."

"How so, Father?"

"Your uncle is remotely situated, but he has an immense tract of land, I gather, and some business enterprises as well. He's well established, I expect. I have it in mind that you should go out there, Angus, and see if it suits you. You are not appreciated here."

"Certainly not."

"And Stone has a daughter of the right age: about twenty-one or two, I gather. I speak frankly, as ever, son. You know I want you to marry into the family, and Livia as well. She will take Morgan, and I think this Nancy Stone will do very well for you."

Angus, who had been raised with European ideas of arranged marriages, was neither surprised nor distressed. After all, what did it matter? Marriages were business alliances like any other. Whoever he was married to, he would always have Livia, and plenty of women like Ella.

He was glad enough to be going west to Wilkes County—it was there that he had been born, although he had only a confused recollection of the days before the war.

"What do you think of my prospects out there, Father?" he asked.

"I think them excellent!" James Dunlie exclaimed. "I believe the future of Georgia to be there—since the war there has been heavy migration into the upper and central parts of the state, almost out to Indian territory. Wherever there is flux there is great opportunity. You know that I had a fine plantation out there before the rebellion—I want you to reclaim it—and the capital has been moved out there to Louisville already."

"I see," Angus said. He was not displeased with the idea of getting away from his father, who had kept him on a short rein for his entire life.

"You are a good son," James Dunlie said. "I have never been disappointed in you, and I trust you realize that all my efforts are in your behalf. I want nothing more than your success and prosperity—and the corresponding downfall of our enemies."

"I want it as much as you do, Father."

"I hope you do. I hope you realize, Angus, how they have swindled us and used us, cheated us and betrayed us. I am the rightful head of the family, Angus, and you are my direct heir! To think that when we arrived in Georgia there was a black monkey named Barstow rich enough to build the Cotton Exchange! How fast he fell! To think . . ."

"Did you . . . Father, did you kill Ira Barstow, then?"

"Of course I did. As swiftly and surely as I shall kill the others. They must all die, Angus, they must lose everything, they must wander in exile for twenty years before I am satisfied. And should I not live to see it, you and Livia must see it, and mark it, and remember that I wanted it so. Do you hear me, Angus, do you heed?"

"Yes, Father," Angus answered, somewhat subdued. His father's passions had been watered down in his veins, but he had been raised to hate the family's enemies, and hate them he always would.

"Never forget, Angus, never!" James Dunlie shouted, and Angus winced to see the rage and resentment burning in his eyes as he strode back and forth in the low bedroom, switching at his boots with the tip of his riding crop. For a few moments he was too aroused to go on, and his breathing was loud. Then he began again.

"Now, as to the other letter I mentioned, Angus. It's from Raye directly. Apparently, because of an attempted insurrection in the state of Virginia, led by a servile blacksmith named Gabriel, the port of Savannah is temporarily closed to incoming slave ships."

"I trust the insurrection did not succeed!"

"No, of course not. This is no Santo Domingo. The wretched slave was betrayed, and he and thirty-five others apprehended, but the people of Savannah are, as ever, too cautious. Raye has been in contact with the captain of the slaver, a Dutchman. Unfortunately, some of the cargo are sick, and he deems it wise to get rid of them as soon as possible, so he has sent them on, down the coast, to us."

"Good Lord, Father! What are we to do with a shipload of sick Africans?"

"Whatever we must. This is business, Angus. Your father has capital invested in the miserable savages. The earliest they can arrive, I judge, is tomorrow. On the morrow, I want you to go out early, ride to the point at the northernmost tip of the island, and wait for a sight of the sail. Then, when the ship is safely anchored, we shall see what to do next. I believe the best plan is to feed them here temporarily. The port of Savannah will reopen soon."

"Yes, Father."

"Excellent. Now I want nothing more than a drink and a bath, in that order. And then we will meet, for the usual delightful dinner with our charming cousins, shall we not, my son?"

"Why not? They set a fair table. 'Tis better than dining at an inn."

And father and son laughed together as the bell calling the hands in from the field began to toll and the red sun slipped out of sight.

CHAPTER FIVE

A Most Peculiar Day; A Long, Wild Ride; A Sort of Adam and Eve

Juliette's mood, when she had finished breakfasting the next morning, was as unsettled as the weather. There was something very peculiar about the weather, that was certain. The sky was pale, not precisely gray but a pale silvery blue scattered with immense dark, fast-moving clouds that were swept from horizon to horizon in a matter of minutes, it seemed, by a strong wind from the southeast. The air was electric, although there did not—as yet—seem to be any thunder or lightning. Instead there was a tension, a sense of suspended animation, that communicated itself to sensitive Juliette and made her anxious.

"Where is everyone?" she demanded of Judina, the placid black housemaid who was tranquilly dusting an oak and marble sideboard as Juliette drank her tea.

"Nobody 'cept you slep' late today," Judina said. "You mama and Miss Aimee drove off to visit Missus Reynolds who's been sick. You papa and Master Morgan be in the fields a'ready four hours, Miss Juliette. Who else you care 'bout? You care 'bout those others?"

"Not really, Judina," Juliette admitted. "I fell back to sleep."

"I know, and you mama said let her sleep, she's a growin' girl."

I didn't want to go with Mother, anyway, Juliette thought. Livia almost always took her breakfast in her own room, and though she loved to see Angus, he was generally in a bad temper at breakfast. Far, far better to see him later in the day, especially just before dinner, when he was often friendly and made her feel like a grown-up lady, even an attractive one.

"I'm goin' for a walk, Judina," Juliette announced. She took her needlework and her journal, a sixteenth-birthday present from her mother, and went alone out to the garden to sit on the low branch of her favorite peach tree.

"It's a family tradition," Jenny Barstow had told her daughter when she presented her with the unlined, calf-bound book. "When I was about your age, I found the book which my mother, your grandmother Fayette, had kept, and I began to keep one of my own. It is your own private forum, dear, your own secret friend, who will hear your confessions and keep all your confidences. No one can tell you what to write; you must decide yourself what and when, or even if. Perhaps you are not interested at all," Jenny had said, for she was a wise mother and knew more than a little about her daughter's troubled state of mind, and how to coax her to do something.

"Oh, I am! I am interested. I'm purely delighted with the present, dear Mother!" Juliette had vowed.

But since that day she had scarcely written a thing. All my thoughts are so tiresome, she thought as she settled herself on the branch, and I should be mortified if anyone read them. She sat very still for a bit, staring up at the sky. It was pewter gray, and the wind rustled the leaves of the peach tree in an odd way, not playfully, but warningly, relentlessly. A rabbit hurried across the lawn about twenty feet away. Strangely, there were almost no birds about, although usually the flowering bushes and fruit trees were full of them and the air was loud with their songs.

The strangeness of this observation motivated Juliette to open her journal. "Cursed be he who reads this without the permission of Miss Juliette Catherine Barstow," she wrote clearly inside the front cover, and then she flipped ahead a few pages and made an entry.

> *September 15, 1800, Sea Groves. A Most Peculiar Day.* Or is every day of my life to be peculiar, simply because I am in it? Shall I relate my mental state? I am, I confess, unworthy of much attention. I am generally disturbed and resentful these days, jealous of Livia and Aimee, jealous of my brother Mor-

gan's affection for them—although who can blame him, for they are both far prettier than I—and still hopelessly in love with Angus. Oh, can I admit it? The writing of the word gives me unaccountable joy, but I must admit that I have never been in love, so am not sure if this is what others mean by this term, and believe unrequited love to be such an utter bore!! Anyway, it is he whom I think about night and day. I could just die, though, with the despairing thought that he might never love me back. He is so handsome, so brilliant, more so than any other man I know. But how can I make him notice me? Sometimes, I just despair—everyone else knows the rules of the Game and I just don't. It's certain that I'm totally inexperienced, but I should rather die than have an experience with anyone other than Angus. . . .

Here a gust of wind caught the pages of the journal and flipped it out of Juliette's hand. Reaching to secure the inkwell which she had set in the fork of a branch, she knocked it over, too, and the blue-black ink immediately striped her pink and white morning dress.

"Oh, no!" Juliette gasped, and forgetting her workbasket, she dove for the journal and ran for the house, calling "Judina! Judina! Help! Oh, dear!"

"Everything is ruined," Juliette announced to Judina. She stood, arms across her chest, in a froth of petticoats streaked with ink as Judina dipped them, one by one, into the washtub.

"Now, why do you take on so?" Judina said with a calm Juliette could not fathom. "I'll fix ever'thin'. It's a day for droppin' things. Ever'thin's bin droppin' all day. They's somethin' evil in the air, I do b'lieve."

"I feel terrible," Juliette said. "My head is just full of worries, all spinnin' round and round. Do you know what I mean, Judina?"

"I b'lieve I do. Now, why don't you go for a walk, Miss Juliette, like you said you was goin' to in the fust place. They's a wind out there'll blow worries out of your head."

Perhaps I'll take Bermuda and go for a long ride, Juliette thought. "Yes, Judina," she said, and rushed to the chest where she kept her brown linen riding dress. Once the idea had entered her head, it seemed altogether the right one. She dragged the long, full dress over her head and fidgeted impatiently as Judina helped her fasten it.

"Lorry! Lorry!" she shouted out the window. "Please! Could you saddle up Bermuda for me? At once!"

"You sure are a hurrycane, honey," Judina called down as Juliette ran out of the room and off toward the stable.

I can't help it, Juliette thought, I just can't help it. Perhaps I'm possessed.

Lorry, the groom, had never moved more slowly, it seemed to her, but at last his stiff old fingers had settled every strap and buckle into place, set the bridle and girth at the correct point, and helped Juliette to mount.

"Careful, Miss Juliette, not to go too far. I'd say a storm's blowin' up 'fore too long."

"Lorry, you know I'm a good rider," Juliette said, and patting Bermuda's neck, she walked him carefully out of the yard and along the avenue, waving at Morgan in the field before she urged her chestnut into a trot, then into the loose, limber gallop they both enjoyed, and which, for more than an hour, absorbed Juliette completely, giving her relief from all her worries, romantic and otherwise.

She was nearly halfway down the length of the island before she realized that the sky, instead of clearing, had darkened, and that the wind, rather than decreasing, had gathered strength. Instead of frightening Juliette, the developing storm exhilarated her.

"Let's run, Bermuda, let's really run," she whispered, bending low over the chestnut stallion's neck, and he snickered in agreement.

And run they did, with the roar of the sea in their ears and the sky as dark as night, the big horse moving at a smooth and steady gallop, Juliette urging him onward, clinging with all her strength, and letting her dark hair blow straight out behind her. I am never happier, she thought, than when riding; I believe I was born to ride with the wind.

The air was soft, that afternoon, and as warm as it was wet. For hours the sky threatened rain but did not give in to it, holding it instead in a gradually thickening mist, absorbed into the wind until it seemed impossible that air could absorb any more moisture. Juliette lost track of the time. Time moves very quickly, she thought at one point, when I am very happy, so perhaps it is late. On the other hand, she was not at all tired, nor did Bermuda seem to be, so it could not be very late.

Still, the sky had darkened ominously, and Juliette, pricked by the consciousness that her mother would be looking for her by teatime, kept to the coastal road, and gave Bermuda his head. He moved faster and faster. The rice paddies on the Butlers' plantation were a dim gray swamp in the fading light; she passed them at breakneck speed. She passed the deep, still waters of the inland channels on the island's rim, passed the junction of the east-west road that led to the Brunswick ferry.

"Just a little longer, dear Bermuda," Juliette called out, "we shall take the shortcut, shall we? Through the swampy place, then along the sandy ridge home, and you shall have apples as well as oats tonight!"

Accordingly, when she reached the familiar swamp, Juliette turned Bermuda's head and urged him through it, splashing, and up the short, steep incline to the hard ridge of sand that formed a barrier against the Atlantic and stretched along the easternmost side of the island, all the way south to Sea Groves.

But the minute Juliette and Bermuda gained the heights she could see that the storm had shifted its course and its character. The sea, as she looked down into it, was as wild as a bubbling cauldron and as dark as wine. Its roar was deep and desperate, and the waves that lashed the beach below the bluffs were ever higher and higher, foamy as new milk, and they slapped onto the white sands with a cargo of weeds and branches and dark, indescribable sea things that seemed ripped from the bowels of some mid-ocean caves.

"Shall we go back, Bermuda?" Juliette whispered, but Bermuda was no judge. He snorted, and Juliette, swayed by his strength and power, decided to stay on the bluff and make a run for home.

Before she was more than a mile along, she realized that she had made a mistake.

The entire end of the sandy ridge had been sucked away, engulfed by the encroaching sea. There was no end to the sandy road, no connection with the high ground where Sea Groves stood. There was no way off the ridge—she would have to go back, through the swamp again, and along the mid-island road.

"Oh, no!" Juliette cried out. She was soaked to the skin now, with the rain that had begun falling—no, beating down in long, slanting sheets of water, driven by the wind off the sea. And she was tired, suddenly and utterly exhausted by the long hours of riding. "Poor Bermuda," she said, but her voice was lost in the wind—an odd experience, so odd that she tried it again, unbelieving, but it was so—she could not make herself audible, nor could she hear Bermuda, although she gathered from his stamping feet and rolling eyes that he was snorting and whinnying in fear.

"Poor Bermuda!" she screamed, and bent forward to cling to his rain-drenched neck. We shall have to go back, she decided, that's all. There is no other way off this ridge.

And she turned Bermuda's head, pointing him upwind, and he was somewhat assuaged, and with the wind behind them they fairly flew back along the high ridge, heading north, away from home. It was cold now, and Juliette felt it—both the chill of the wind and the dampness of her wet riding dress, the heavy linen saturated with salt and water, stiff and heavy as armor and nearly as cumbersome, her long skirts and petticoats pasting her to her saddle and making her legs feel as if they were encased in sand.

Bermuda ran as if the hounds of hell were chasing him, sure-footed, massively powerful, and Juliette clung to his back with all her strength. Her hair was drenched and clung to her neck like seaweed, and her arms ached with fatigue at holding the reins for so long, but she was encouraged by the comparative ease of riding out of the wind, and she kept a sharp eye out for the stretch of marsh to the west that they had crossed before. It seemed forever in coming.

There? Is it just ahead there? Juliette wondered. She peered through the rain. It was hard to see more than twenty feet ahead, but the tangled, green-brown marsh would stand out, the reeds and grasses and the main island rising beyond the narrow marsh—surely they would be visible.

But everywhere she could see was gray, the gray of rain, of sodden white sand, of sea unrelieved by any blue of sky and frosted with a churning white foam. It was gray in every direction. Fog as thick as snow seemed to rise off the land and roil in massive clouds, steamy clouds, themselves beaten down by the torrents of rain that blew in from the east, off the sea.

Panic rose in Juliette, and as she began to fear that she was lost, had passed the marsh, she realized that she was just abreast of it—abreast of where it had been. For instead of marsh, there was sea all around her, a wild, rolling sea reaching west as well as east, not a spear of marsh to be seen. It was under water, completely under water, and water how deep? She reined Bermuda in. He reared to a halt, wheeled, tossed his head and then stood trembling under her, a feeling that did as much to terrify Juliette as the sight of the vanished marsh.

Something told Juliette not to enter the water. The current, always considerable, swirled in every direction—rushed past the edge of the ridge with the strength of a riptide, and there was no way to judge direction. If she and Bermuda went in over his depth, which seemed unavoidable, she would not know which way to direct him. Bermuda could not swim far, not with her on his back, and they would be swept along with the current, sucked under before they could know which way to swim.

"It's too hard to see," Juliette shouted to Bermuda, as if in explanation, and as if she could be heard. Without thinking, she acted. She slid off Bermuda, hugged him fiercely, and with one arm around his big, strong neck and the reins twisted tightly around her wrist, began to walk and lead him on, still heading northward toward the very end of the sandy ridge formation where maybe, just maybe there would be something left of the tabby fortress that had stood there when the island was the last outpost against the Spanish colony in Florida.

Walking was much harder—and slower and more frustrating—than riding, and Juliette's admiration for Bermuda increased as she realized how expertly he had picked his way along the crumbling ridge. Every second step set her on loose, saturated sand and pitched her forward, or back, or twisted her ankle, so that she stumbled and staggered at a minute pace with Bermuda nuzzling between her shoulders.

It can't be far, she told herself, and if some of that old fort is standing, it will give us shelter for a few hours. I know Papa and Morgan will come for me as soon as they can; I'm sure they are out looking for me already, but oh, how foolish I was not to turn home at once, when the wind began to blow so . . .

With no one to see, after all, Juliette gave in to tears, as much of exhaustion as of misery. She blamed herself for this terrible situation, and regretted the concern that she was undoubtedly giving her parents. Minute by minute, the storm worsened, the visibility declined, and the force of the wind—incredibly—seemed to strengthen. Her face tilted up, dashed by tears as salty as the sea and as cold as the rain, she fought to see a dozen feet ahead, then ten, then only six, and then a kingfisher that flew suddenly at her head startled her so that she screamed.

Poor bird, he blew from west to east, into the wind, beating at its enormous strength with desperate cunning, heading straight into it, daring not to turn or tack, dipping, then soaring up again, then dropping, dropping as densely as a stone to the sand, where he clung—but for how long?—to the edge of the bluff, a crumbling anchor at best.

The tide was high, higher than Juliette had ever seen it, in a lifetime of living by the sea. Every wave was more immense than the last, encroached farther, approached and threatened the top of the bluff. Waves sucked greedily at the highest point of the ridge, then retreated, pulling down a slide of sand and beach grass, making the whole east side of the ridge shift and shudder, all motion, no foundation, not a foot of solid ground.

Hurry, hurry, hurry, Juliette coached herself. The tabby fort must be just ahead, if it were there at all, and she dared to remember a tree or two there, also, blessed trees which would lend the strength of their taproots to the ridge and help it hold against the rain and the sea.

Juliette had never felt more alone. She *was* alone, completely marooned without any hope of immediate rescue. The storm was everywhere; in every direction it was gray and wet and cold and wind-driven. She had not heard a human voice for hours, nor seen a sign of life, save the desperate kingfisher; in fact, she could barely see, at all.

And then, from nowhere, a riderless horse galloped up to her, his ears flat, whinnying, and thundered past. Bermuda snickered, and Juliette stared in shock, unsure whether to hope or fear. Perhaps she had died and was seeing into the next world. Perhaps she was seeing spirits. No one could be here—it was not possible, who on earth could be here, as far from home as she, as helpless, as wet and cold and frightened.

She screamed. Out of the mist came another dark, shrouded form.

She screamed again, but it drew closer. It was a human form. It was a man, a tall and broad-shouldered man, wrapped in a dark cape. . . .

It was, although it could not be, it was!

"Angus!" Juliette shouted, disbelieving. "Angus! Angus!"

"What are you doing here?" he shouted, "Why did you follow me? Why?"

Juliette stopped, stock still. Could it be real? It was real—Angus Dunlie stood there, two feet in front of her, dripping wet and scowling—and yet she could not believe he was not a creation of her imagination. Thunder crashed beside them, all around them, with the force, twice the force of exploding gunpowder, and the sky behind him went gilt with lightning.

Juliette gasped. She could not speak.

Roughly, Angus grabbed her. "Why did you follow me, you little fool? Now we are both in danger!"

His grip was too hard. It hurt, but she could not pull free. Her clear, innocent green eyes opened wider and wider.

He was angry, and her silence angered him further. Lifting her off her feet, he shook her like a small child, and her head jerked back and then forward as helplessly as a doll's.

"Oh, Angus!" she gasped at last, "what fate has brought us both here?"

"Fate!" He dropped her then, and she felt that her knees were water, that she could not stand. She buckled, and swayed, then fell forward into his arms.

"Jesus Holy Christ, how can you speak of fate!" he exploded, and Juliette, clinging to his broad chest like a bird seeking sanctuary in the hollow of a tree, murmured, completely undone by this, the most unexpected of shocks, after all the others that had brought her to this point, "I love you, Angus, I do love you so . . ."

He did not hear her. "Bloody God damn!" he cursed, "I have never seen such a storm, never seen a storm come up so fast. What is this? What is happening?"

"It's a hurricane," Juliette shouted, without letting go of his chest, around which she had wrapped her arms as tightly as she could. "Did you come out looking for me?"

"Of course not," Angus said shortly, beginning to comprehend the enormity of their meeting here, or at all, but resisting any suggestion casting fate as a stage manager.

"There's a tabby fort, I think, just up ahead," Juliette said, and tugged at both Bermuda's reins and Angus's hand, leading them on. Everything seemed possible, now that Angus had appeared, as a savior—it was impossible to think otherwise—as a heavenly answer to all her dreams and desires. She was instantly cheerful and confident; her mood had gone from black to rose-red; with all the resilience of extreme youth, she was suffused with unreasoning delight.

Angus was not. "Of course," he said, following Juliette. He knew the old fort was there. He had spent the day in it, awaiting a glimpse of the sail that would show that the slaver had found its way. He had spent the day watching the skies, seeing the storm blowing in, and felt like a fool for not recognizing its seriousness, for hanging on when he should have given up.

"There it is!" Juliette exclaimed. Much of the fort, built of tabby—in the old style, of mortared sand and crushed oyster shells—had crumbled over the years, but a semicircular bit still stood, nearly six feet high, the remains of an old lookout tower, and across this Angus had stretched a stout piece of sailor's canvas, and inside it had placed a small chest of biscuits and dried meat, intended for the relief of the ship's crew and their wretched cargo.

Juliette, seeing this, had no notion of its intended purpose but tranquilly accepted it as she had accepted the sight of Angus, as a concrete expression of benevolent goodness. Bermuda could not go into the shelter, but she tied him near, then crawled around him and collapsed, gratefully, at the back of the shelter, and turned to face her beloved.

"Goodness, I have never been so wet in my life, and

dear Angus, I confess I had nearly given up hope! God works in strange ways his wonders to perform!"

Inside the shelter, the wind's roar seemed even louder. It was not completely wet inside, but it was far from dry, for rain had lashed in at the opening, which fortunately faced northward, away from the wind, if the whirling wind could still be said to come from any one direction, and the underside of the canvas roof was slick with rain, which beaded on its taut surface and ran down at the sides in steady rivulets.

"Oh, Angus!" Juliette sighed, "it's as if we are the only two people left on earth! It's as if we are Adam and Eve!"

He scowled, and in the dim light Juliette fancied that he had smiled.

"Do you think me silly?" she asked.

I think you daft, he thought, but asked, "What on earth, Juliette, were you doing out riding in this weather?"

"Nothing special. Like you, I was surprised by how quickly the storm came up, although there were signs of it this morning. I was just riding to clear my head; it was splendid, until Bermuda and I found ourselves way back here with no way off . . ."

Her answer did nothing to change Angus's opinion. She chattered on.

"I was becoming quite discouraged, until I saw you, Angus, really it is a bad storm, of course it's the season for them, but all the same, poor Papa and Morgan were making great haste to get the cotton picked this morning, I fear whatever is not saved today will be lost, completely, but Angus, I feel I really must ask you—what are you doing up here?"

"You are shivering," he said in reply. "Here, drink some of this." And he passed her a flask of rum, the second he had uncorked to keep himself warm. "There's nothing quite dry, but I think that quilt will be better than your dress, Juliette. Why don't you take it off?"

Juliette drank gratefully, gulping the strong, honey-smooth rum and feeling its amazing fiery warmth fill her chest. "Oh, no, I couldn't!"

"Don't be a little fool! Whoever will care if you are bare naked? Suit yourself. Would you rather be ill?"

Juliette, who had not been naked in front of another human being since she was old enough to sit up, found herself taking off her sodden linen riding dress, and most of her petticoats. Angus hung them over the edge of a tabby outcropping and they began to drip. Juliette shivered, then ripped off her long-sleeved chemise and, clad only in very wet pantaloons, wrapped herself in the quilt and stared at Angus with wide-open eyes.

"Drink some more," he offered.

She did. "Listen to the wind," she whispered, when a minute had passed. "Did you ever hear such a howling?"

"So this is a hurricane," Angus said drunkenly. Although he did not admit it to Juliette, he had been badly frightened by the swiftness and ferocity of the storm. He had never seen anything like it, and seeing it rip up the old, gnarled cedars outside the tabby fort, seeing most of the beach wash away, seeing the size of the branches and leaves and boughs the sea coughed up, he had been convinced that it was surely his last day on earth. And then Miss Juliette had arrived, coming out of the mist as if this cataclysmic disaster were all part of an ordinary September outing. . . . The sight of her had made his fears seem ridiculous, although they were not. His mind was addled by alcohol. He was vastly glad to see her—to see anyone—and at the same time both annoyed by her and ashamed to be found in such ridiculous straits.

"This is a hurricane," Juliette agreed.

"Do you think we shall die?"

She considered. "We may. There's no telling what Providence has planned for any of us, Cousin Angus. But if we are to die, I pray that we both shall go to heaven."

"Heaven?" Angus took a deep swig of rum and passed the flask to Juliette, who took another long draught, then another. He snorted. His spirits were on the rise, and with his rising spirits a desire to tease and provoke childlike Juliette had reasserted itself.

"Suppose there is no heaven, little cousin?" he suggested. "Suppose this is all there is—earth and wind and water—and this is to be our last night of life?"

The rum had suffused Juliette with a warmth and freedom from self-consciousness unlike any she had ever felt. She was drunk, drunker than she had ever been with her occasional ladylike sippings of punch and wine, and the condition was one of blissful relief. She stretched her legs, conscious of every inch of her body in a new and wonderful way. She thought, seriously, for a moment and then said to Angus, "Then there would be something I would want to tell you, from the bottom of my heart."

"Oh, yes? There would be? And what would it be?"

"Come, put your arm around me and I will tell you," she suggested, with a boldness she had not thought herself capable of.

Angus laughed. "No, Cousin, you come here. Here, bring your little quilt and I will take you under my warm cloak."

Juliette did not hesitate, and as she crawled to him, he glimpsed for the first time her breasts, tiny but softly swelling and tipped with dark-red aureoles and impudent rosy nipples, and an idea for amusing himself entered his head, an idea he would have been far too frightened and tired to conceive without the aid of the rum.

Why, she is quite well formed, Angus thought. He was amazed, fancying himself a connoisseur. Urgent desire tightened his loins and he sighed, to ease it, as she slid next to him.

"Ooh! You are all wet!" she whispered.

"Undo my shirt, then."

She hesitated.

"Come on! No one will see you!"

That was quite true, Juliette acknowledged. It was only sensible that they should keep each other warm. She deftly pulled off his shirt and cast it aside. When their torsos touched, she was amazed at the warmth they created by touching; it made her dizzy and filled her with a helpless and irresistible sense of ecstasy. His skin was so soft, she thought, it's like a sweet baby's. Innocently, like a baby herself, she rubbed herself against him, arousing waves of desire in both of them; she bent her head back, her eyes slits, her dark tangled hair wantonly hiding her face.

"Juliette! You are more grown up than I knew," he said in a low voice. Instinctively, he unbuttoned his trousers and shifted his back so that his aroused manhood was between them, then held her tightly against him, pressing her to him so that she could not move.

"I am not," she whispered into his ear, "very grown up at all, Angus, but I am old enough to know that I love you. Deeply. With all my heart."

She's drunk, Angus thought, and then, Father will be

angry if this becomes known, and then he did not think anymore for a while. "If you love me, Juliette," he said, "then let me show you how to love a man."

Her answer came in kisses, insistent nibblings at his neck and ear, which Angus endured while he slid off her pantaloons and played with her sex until she gasped and moaned. Then he lifted her into his lap, and set her down, inch by inch, on his throbbing penis. She was slick with moisture, he noticed, and trembling all over, but did not seem to feel pain, so he entered her completely and then leaned back to see her.

"You are beautiful, Juliette, really beautiful," he said.

Juliette, tears streaming down her face, was speechless with shock. She had never seen or imagined such physical congress—her fantasies about loving Angus had never carried her farther than a kiss. At this point her mind and body took two separate paths. Her mind shut off. And her body was overtaken by waves of pleasure set off by his entering her. She did not hear Angus's voice, and until many weeks later she could not really remember what had happened, but she carried the feeling with her, for it was insanely powerful and continued, rocking her, longer than seemed at all possible. She, who had been tossed and tormented by her awakening sexuality all the days of summer and all the nights of fall, was entirely ready for this feeling, and it invaded her entirely; she was racked with ecstasy unlike any she had imagined or might ever feel again.

She is inhuman, Angus thought, holding the hot, moaning child-creature in his strong hands; she is beautiful. Juliette shone with light; she felt weightless to him and yet she gripped him snugly, but he could not give to her.

Perversely, he jerked her away from him as he felt his own orgasm rise in him and he spilled himself on her sleek, naked thigh as she collapsed onto him, still crying "I love you! I love you! I love you!" as the wind screamed and the waves pounded terrifyingly on the beach outside.

CHAPTER SIX

A Terrible Aftermath; Juliette Abandoned; Angus Takes His Head

The next day dawned clear with a sliver of moon just visible in the blank, cloudless sky. From the start the day had an air of exhaustion—everything was drenched, broken, beaten down into a tangle of crushed vegetation and saturated destruction. The storm had ended very suddenly somewhere in the darkest hours between midnight and first light; Angus believed he had noticed the exact moment when the wind ceased to blow. Angus had not slept. Juliette had slept heavily, stirring and crying out from time to time, but without waking.

Angus had a headache almost beyond bearing, and in the morning, before Juliette woke, even before the wind had quite stopped its ghastly, relentless howling, he had staggered out of the tabby shelter and vomited, achingly, into the sand. When he could spit up no more, he clutched his aching stomach and cursed everything: rum, the hurricane, the night, the storm, Juliette—presumptuous hussy—and the day to come, for he suspected that it would be a wearing day, perhaps nearly as tumultuous as the storm.

Whatever happened, he intended to deny it—everything. Hawking, retching, he rid himself of guilt and responsibility as he cleared his stomach of sour, undigested rum. Whatever had happened, she had asked for it, and anyway, nothing of the slightest consequence had happened.

Juliette, when she woke, was dazed and stiff and very tired. To his astonishment, she did not seem to recall much of what had passed between them. At least she did not refer to it, but dressed herself and called to Bermuda. Weakly, as trusting as a kitten, she asked Angus, "Is there anything for him to eat, anything at all? And then we must try to get home. Oh, when I think of the anxiety I have caused my poor parents. And your father, too, of course, Angus. We must make our way home as quickly as we can."

His eyes narrowed with headache, Angus barely replied. The carton of biscuits was water-soaked, the rum all gone. His horse had disappeared. There was still no sail in sight, but he did not expect one, not now.

"I shall have to ride behind you," he told Juliette.

Juliette stared at him with wide, blank eyes. She was ill at ease and, for once, had little to say. When they were mounted together on Bermuda's broad back, he fit his arms around her to catch the reins, and the warmth of his body comforted her, so that she felt a bit better, without knowing why.

Slowly, with increasing amazement and dismay, they rode together along the ridge, through the waterlogged marsh, and back onto the main island. The sea was bright, clear and shining, its present calm betrayed only by the cargo of rubbish—broken branches, twigs, leaves—that edged the sand. The larger shrubs in the marsh had been sucked completely away, as had the wooden bridge at its western edge.

On the mainland there were more awful signs of destruction. An entire row of trees all along the coast road had been felled. The huge spreading live oak, said to be the oldest tree on the island, lay massively across the way. Branches were broken everywhere, and the earth was strewn with boughs and leaves and beaten birds.

"How terrible, how terrible," Juliette murmured, seeing three familiar locust trees uprooted. Tears gathered in her eyes, but she struggled to hold them back. Only when she saw Old Billy, the venerable cooper, who never left his shop, standing knee-deep in twigs and branches by the side of the road, did she give in to the sobs that had been pent up inside her.

"Billy! Billy, hello! Is everyone all right?"

"Miss Juliette! You is safe!"

Sliding off Bermuda, Juliette ran to the old man and hugged him, laughing and crying and talking all at once.

"How glad I am to see you! Did you see—all the trees—is everyone safe at home?"

"Ever'one well and worrit about you, Miss Juliette!"

"What are you doin' way out here, Billy?"

"Ever'body sent out to look for you, miss, ever'body who can walk, we's sent all over the island since first light, that's right, you mama and papa is torn up with worry, Miss Juliette, that's right!"

"Oh, dear! Oh, dear!" Juliette gasped. "Come, Angus, we've got to hurry up. Oh, I am so glad to see your dear face, Uncle Billy!"

"You mama gone be glad to see you'se, that's right!" the old man said, beaming, and Juliette placed her small foot in his hand to remount Bermuda and, riding sidesaddle, begged Bermuda to "go fast, now, big beauty, just as fast as you can! Hurry!"

Every fifty yards or so, for the length of the mid-island road, and then even more frequently as they rode along the long avenue from the crossing, was the scene with Uncle Billy repeated. The hands from Sea Groves were everywhere—there was Lorry, there Andrew, there Selina, there Jordan, the fisherman, there Cato and Caesar, the gardeners, all out searching for Juliette and each of them delighted to see her, waving and calling out as they sighted her and Angus atop Bermuda.

With every encounter Juliette's spirits and anxiety rose and her sense of apprehension about the trouble she had caused deepened. She had known, of course she had known, that her parents would worry about her, but she had been so lost in accomplishing her own survival that she had not indulged in speculation about anything else. It was all so terrible—the storm's aftermath, the scene of ruin and destruction, that her own part in it seemed to her small, and yet she was on edge about facing her family—she could not *bear* another delay, and the tension tightened her lungs and chest like bands of iron as she clung to Bermuda and Angus for the last leg of the ride home.

And then, with the first sight of Sea Groves, there were further shocks. All the fences were flat. Half the orange trees bordering the avenue were twisted and torn apart, most of the houses in the quarters were roofless, and the cotton field, from what she could see, was a mangled swamp of muddy roots and branches—there was not a plant left standing.

"Oh, dear!" Juliette sobbed, and then, outside the plantation house—which seemed to be miraculously whole although was that a window blown out on her parents' bedroom, and there, another one?—she saw a line of people, standing, waiting, every member of the family in a row: her mother, her father, Morgan, next to him Livia, then Aimee, and just behind the rest of them—Uncle James.

Bermuda whinnied. "Here! Here I am!" Juliette shouted, and jumping off Bermuda, she ran up to her parents, a ragged, muddied, wet-headed version of herself.

"Mama! Mama!" Juliette cried, and launched herself at her mother.

Something was wrong. Something was off, something strange, she knew it at once and completely, although she did not understand. Even as she ran into her mother's arms, she was minutely aware of the sadness on her mother's face, of the awful, odd stiff way her father was standing, of the shocked misery in Morgan's eyes, of Aimee's face, quite turned away, and—in Livia's eyes—an expression of ill-concealed amusement.

"Darling daughter, I thought I would never hold you again," Jenny said in a flat, exhausted voice.

"Well, I am fine! But what is wrong? Has someone died? Papa, why do you look that way?" Juliette asked.

"Where have you been?" Roland asked. His hands were trembling; he clenched them into fists and then stiffly moved the fists behind him. "Where, daughter? Tell me at once."

Something she had never before heard in her father's voice frightened Juliette, and her own voice was fearful as she answered, "I was riding, on the outer ridge, and the marsh got flooded over, and the storm worsened, and then I came upon Angus, and we slept all night in the tabby fort."

She stopped. There was a cold silence, and gradually she realized that everyone was looking past her, looking at Angus. Casually, haggard, but as haughty and self-possessed as ever, Angus slid off Bermuda and looked around for someone to take the reins.

"Where are all the stableboys?" he asked.

Juliette watched him. For a moment she seemed to be forgotten. Her father was staring at Angus with—what was it?—it appeared to be, almost, anger. . . .

"God damn you!" Morgan muttered, and Juliette turned to him in astonishment. She had never heard her brother swear. He, too, was glaring at Angus.

"Did he touch you? Did he?" Roland shouted, and Juliette knew that his expression had been anger, for his voice was gruff with bald rage.

"Whaaat?" Juliette wailed, huddling against her mother, shocked and terribly afraid of whatever was building up, brewing as sure as the hurricane had, and seemingly about to strike as suddenly, with similar force.

"Did he touch you, Juliette?" Roland demanded.

Her voice shook. "We . . . touched each other."

There was another moment of stunned silence, and then hell erupted.

"You are a reprehensible cad!" Morgan shouted.

"Oh, no!" Aimee wailed.

"Oh, my baby," Jenny moaned.

"God damn you! God damn you!" Roland shouted, and Livia called out, "Watch out, Angus!" for Roland had stepped forward and ripped Juliette's riding crop out of Angus's hand.

Angus ducked, but Roland could not stop. Wild with anger, he raised the leather whip and brought it down on Angus's left shoulder with a violent crack. Angus screamed and covered his shoulder with both hands. He staggered backward.

Roland stepped forward and lashed at Angus's face with the whip. He left a vicious red stripe that split Angus's cheek and shut one eye. Angus ducked and spit blood.

"Papa! No! Please, Papa!" Juliette cried.

"Stop!" Livia and James Dunlie shouted, but Roland was beyond recall.

Swinging the crop like a scythe, Roland beat at Angus's face and head, his arms and shoulders, his neck, his chest, whipping the young man with violent, pent-up fury. Angus spun and twisted, he screamed and choked, he stumbled, but he could not see where to run. He moved his hands to stop the blows, but every move left another opening, and Roland Barstow struck at each opening as surely and deftly as a surgeon.

And then, as suddenly as he had begun, Roland paused. He was panting. Ignoring Angus's groans and the chorus of sobbing women behind him, he dropped the riding crop and stared at Angus with undiminished wrath, gasping for breath, each breath a tortured rasping effort.

Juliette covered her eyes with her hands. What could happen now? How could her life continue now?

"How dare you?" Livia ran to her brother. She took his arm onto her shoulder and led him away and toward the back of the house.

Silently, unbidden, unnoticed, about twenty or thirty of the Barstows' slaves had gathered on the lawn to stare at the scene, their dark faces blank with horror, their mouths open in shocked surprise. None of them had ever seen Roland Barstow lose his temper; it was well known that he never beat any of his slaves or his children, but by nightfall a report on what had happened would have reached every plantation on the island.

James Dunlie, who had stood behind the other family members, out of everyone's sight, stepped up now and joined his children. He was pale with outrage, but grim with purpose.

"You are not badly hurt," he said to Angus. "I want you to leave immediately. You know where I want you to go. Go there swiftly, and God speed. None of this matters to me."

Angus lifted his head and shook it. He was like a winded Thoroughbred, beaten but not vanquished. His deep-set eyes blazed with anger and his mouth was twisted in an evil grin.

Livia clung to her brother. "No, oh, no, don't go, Angus! You can't leave me here!"

"I will contact you," James Dunlie said in a low voice. "Go at once, my son."

Angus caught his breath and then, seeing that Roland Barstow had turned to him and stepped forward, he turned and ran toward the stables.

"Stop!" Roland shouted.

Father is mad, Juliette thought. She could make no other sense of it. She had watched Angus being beaten in speechless horror. Papa never beat anyone; it was not real, it could not be true. Everyone was mad; everything had gone awry; was it the end of their happy, normal life?

Angus did not stop, but kept running, his gait odd and sloping but swift.

"You must marry," Roland shouted after Angus's departing figure. "God damn it, you must marry my daughter!"

Juliette gasped.

Livia laughed.

Aimee burst into tears.

"Father is right," Morgan said.

"James," Roland said coldly, "I ask you to retrieve your son. He has ruined my daughter and now he must marry her."

There was silence, an awful horror-shot silence in which the loudest sound was the weeping of the women and Roland's ragged breathing.

Finally, James answered. "Angus is gone," he said simply, and then the sound of hooves and the sight of Angus, crossing the lawn at full gallop on a fine black stallion, made a fact of it.

"Stop him!" Roland yelled, raising his fist.

But Angus was moving too fast.

"Stop that rider!" Roland bellowed. One of the men standing at the edge of the avenue made a leap for the horse's bridle, but Angus kicked him aside and rode off without looking back.

In nature it often happens that a catastrophe is followed by a period of healing calm. So it was at Sea Groves, for so it had to be. The weeks following the hurricane were unusually sunny and mild, and everyone living at Sea Groves—from the clumsiest field hand to James Dunlie himself—made every possible effort to effect reconciliation, to assuage the physical damage wreaked by the hurricane, and to behave as the rational civilized beings they considered themselves to be.

Roland Barstow was—when his fury had subsided—deeply mortified by his cruel and uncontrollable display of temper. He had diverted his real feelings of concern for Juliette's welfare into the path of other feelings—admittedly also strong ones—that she had been wronged and corrupted, but those feelings were not his finest, he believed. Society might judge Juliette to be ruined, but his love for her was exempt from society's strictures, was it not? If Roland was uncomfortable with the fierceness of that love, so strong that its expression in violence had caused him to lose all control, he was far less comfortable with the idea of himself as a man of violent action.

Roland suffered in the weeks that followed, and he found his main solace in work. There was much to be done to repair the damage done by the high winds and battering rain. Windows had to be replaced, fences rebuilt, new houses built for three families in the quarters. What had been saved of the cotton crop had to be baled and shipped to Carlton Raye in Savannah. Trees had to be righted, wherever possible, and new ones planted to fill the gaps in the rows along the avenue. All this was in addition to the usual fall chores, but Roland did it gladly, with Morgan by his side, for it was work that healed.

In the first week after he had ridden away from Sea Groves, the Barstows had expected Angus Dunlie to return—expected it, it is true, with varying feelings—but he did not. Although roads had been washed out all over the island and others had been blocked by fallen trees, although the Brunswick ferry was not restored to service for several days, there had been no report of him, and he did not reappear.

How much his father and sister missed him, how much they suffered from their abrupt and traumatic parting, is not known, as a polite silence developed between the remaining Dunlies and the Barstows during the first few days, a necessary and guarded silence, broken chiefly by conversations between Morgan and Livia, who seemed to be confidants, much to the amazement of Morgan's parents.

"It is quite right that peace should be made among the younger generation," Roland said to his wife, concerning the odd friendship that had developed between Livia and Morgan. "Morgan is in every respect a good son; I pray that he and his generation can keep the peace with the Dunlie family. I confess I have failed, and I look to my son for guidance."

"Roland, the situation is intolerable," Jenny said. "How long, how long must I bear that man's presence?"

"James has spoken about going to Savannah soon," Roland said.

"It cannot be too soon for me," Jenny said bitterly;

nonetheless, she made every effort to maintain polite and friendly relations with her houseguests, as she believed she ought and as her husband expected. "Perhaps Juliette will improve when they go."

For Juliette had taken it all badly. Juliette had not recovered her spirits since that day in mid-September, and her condition was of great concern to both her parents. When Angus had ridden down the avenue, she had collapsed into a state of confused shock and could neither speak nor eat for the remainder of the day. After that, she had lapsed into a listless melancholy, so isolated and withdrawn that nothing could rouse her. Aimee had taken on the role of nursemaid and with much pleading and pampering had finally, on the eve of the second day, coaxed her to take some milk, but Juliette could not be persuaded to join the others at table, nor did she smile, or read, or sleep soundly.

"It is so terrible, so terrible," Aimee confessed to Jenny, when the two women were alone in the drawing room one afternoon. "Her spirit is simply broken, Aunt Jenny. Her pulse is low, she does not speak except to answer yes or no, and I cannot dream what she is thinking of, as she sits so calm and immovable all the day, looking out the window, uttering now and again a sigh . . ."

"I know your company does her good," Jenny said. "I am so grateful to you."

In fact, poor Juliette was more depressed and downhearted than anyone could understand. She existed in a protective state of semicoma for some weeks, pained beyond toleration, her memory a blank, numbed by the impact of shock upon shock, not only that of her night alone with Angus, but of her family's unexpected reaction to it, of seeing him beaten by her father, and of having him gone—completely and to some unknown destination, perhaps forever.

As memory returned, it brought, not relief, but further pain. She could not escape nor anticipate the flashes of recollection that came upon her at random moments with crippling force. One night she woke, screaming, with a vision of Angus's bare body and her own in soul-shattering proximity, and knew that in the eyes of God, who knew all, she had been wanton, she had been deliberately carnal, that she had sinned. On the next day she could not rise from her bed, but lay there in a shocked silence which terrified Aimee.

And under it all, under the shame and its mortification, was the sense of loss, for she had truly loved him, and did still with all the strength of her fervent young spirit, and now he was gone. Although her mourning could not be public, it must be borne, and the process, hidden and secret as it must be, did not diminish her love, no more than had its sexual realization.

Gradually, then, the life of the plantation absorbed the Barstows again, Juliette wounded and withdrawn, Livia bored but making every effort to amuse herself with serious, idealistic Morgan, Aimee content to attend Juliette and follow Aunt Jenny through her long and complicated days as chief administrator of the considerable tasks of housekeeping and slave management.

And so the days of autumn passed, with a sense of quietude and necessary healing which served only to mask and not obliterate the deepening tension between the two families.

For Angus Dunlie, on the contrary, the days of autumn were days of sudden awakening, of plentiful opportunity, of travel, constant danger, and new experiences. Angus, who had been confined and restricted by his role as house guest at Sea Groves, and even more by years of being the dutiful son, years of biding his time in anticipation of his glorious inheritance in Georgia—a notion he had been raised with and sustained by during all the years of exile in London—was like a spirited Thoroughbred suddenly freed, given his head, and encouraged to run.

And run he did, driven by rage at Roland Barstow and well pleased to escape his father, his clinging sister, his dull, provincial cousins, and the stultifying atmosphere of Sea Groves. Angus was nearly thirty years old—an age which for most men of his generation would have been full maturity, but his life had been different from most. He had been born, after all, a Georgian, raised for the first few years of his life to think that he would grow up to be a landed, moneyed planter. He was the son of James Dunlie, and not only that, he was the son of Rosalind Drayton, a wellborn Englishwoman who had given her oldest son her values and a sense that this rough period in life was to be only temporary.

Rosalind's uncle, as she often reminded her husband and son, was Sir James Wright, who had been the last colonial governor of Georgia. Just before the unfortunate war, Sir James had possessed eleven plantations along the Savannah, the Ogeechee, and the Canoochee rivers. Sir James had owned more than five hundred slaves; James Dunlie himself had owned a good-sized plantation near Augusta called Green Acres and worked by upwards of thirty Africans.

From the Wrights' and Dunlies' point of view, the Revolution had been an unjust and insane episode. The shock of losing so much, so violently and abruptly, of being shunted back to England in disgrace, had been too much for Angus's mother, and she had died—soon after bearing Livia—embittered, resentful, and miserable, at home neither in England nor in Georgia.

After that Angus had been forced to endure great loneliness and a sense of being an outcast and an exile. His father was fully occupied in business; his mother—whom he had revered and respected—was dead. Angus's accent and odd, American ways subjected him to ridicule among young Englishmen his own age. His father alternately ignored him and confided in him—always of his rage, his betrayal by his family, his resentment, and his plans to return to Georgia and reclaim all that was rightly his.

And so Angus had passed his London years, acquiring a smattering of education, a few bad habits, a taste for fine clothes, and an unusual passion for his little sister. The years passed, of course, at the usual rate, day by day, but to Angus they seemed both tedious and temporary. Perhaps it was the state of suspended time which had kept him young, for he had always been aware that he must wait, wait for the right moment to receive his expectations and exercise his ambitions. He had learned his lesson well: London was not for living—not for real living—everything must wait for Georgia. Everything was dependent upon their return to Georgia, their return to their rightful place, their coming home to wealth and glory.

When, on arrival, Angus had been forced to endure another postponement—another few months of exile from the mainstream of life on the Dunlies' seaside plantation—he bore it well enough, with a familiar sense of biding his time, but he was ready for this escape, ready to resume responsibility for his own life, ready to take on his father's crusade, ready, ready and eager—to live.

He spent his first night in Brunswick, a poor town, half-buried in sand and mud after the ravages of the hurricane, but sufficient for a night's rest, which he badly needed. There, at the inn where his father received his letters, he convinced the innkeeper to advance him a small sum of money, enough to get him to Savannah, where he felt sure he could secure a large amount from his father's agent.

There was no looking glass in the spare, drafty closet Angus hired for himself in the Brunswick inn, but he did not need one to know that the raw cuts on his face and neck were deep and would take some weeks to heal. Carefully, not without whimpering, Angus bathed his wounds.

He beat me like a dog, like a filthy nigger, he fumed. It fed his inbred desire for revenge against the Barstows. Nothing he could ever do to Roland Barstow would be punishment enough. Angus was furious, he was humiliated, and he was physically ill, but the beating he had suffered at Roland Barstow's hands had also elated him. It had awakened him, as abruptly as a fall shower, to an exhilarated sense of himself as master of his own destiny.

Instead of taking one of the coastwise vessels, Angus decided to ride north to Savannah along the inland road. The journey required two days; as he rode, Angus's outrage hardened into purpose and his sense of relief inspired a plan. On either side of the road, little more than a bridle path in parts, lay low reedy swamps, many of them flattened by the hurricane, others yellow and withered from the summer's heat. This is a dying land, Angus decided; father is no doubt right—my fortune lies inland.

In Savannah, Angus Dunlie sought out Carlton Raye, learned that the expected shipment of African slaves had been received, after all, in Savannah, and accepted the entire sum that Raye owed his father. Thus enriched, he outfitted himself with a new black broadcloth suit, a pair of pistols, and a dozen pairs of kid gloves. He laboriously penned a letter to his father and gave it to Raye to send by stage to Brunswick. For two days he lingered in Savannah, drinking Madeira in the taverns along the waterfront, but all the conversation was of politics—Thomas Jefferson would be elected, that he came to believe, for he heard it repeated time and again; the entire Georgia delegation seemed to be pledged to him—and Angus found his drinking companions to be a dull lot. He was not sorry to leave, and on the third day he set off for the West on a stagecoach drawn by six black horses.

The coach, which was of the newest and finest variety, had been built in Concord, New Hampshire. It was painted bright red and was as trim as a ship, with three benches inside, the middle one backed by a broad leather strap, the front and back facing inward, an arrangement that was cozy if not comfortable. When Angus arrived, the best seats were already occupied by an immensely fat woman, her thin husband, three children, and an aged parent, who appeared to be near death, if one could judge from his incessant coughing and spitting.

Stowing his small leather bag inside, Angus took the outside seat next to the driver, an elevated perch on the front of the coach.

"How far ye goin'?" asked the driver, a rough-looking man with massive arms and shoulders who brandished a twelve-foot whip over the heads of the horses.

"Augusta," Angus said shortly, and then added, "and from there north and west to Washington."

"How do you do—you're not settlin' there?" the driver asked, looking up and down at Angus's fine black suit and thin gloves.

"I intend to, my good man," Angus said, quite aware that he must learn the ways of these people, trying to conquer his natural reserve and habitual passion for privacy.

"You an Englishman?" the driver asked.

"Born a Georgian, born up in Wilkes County, and goin' home after many years," he answered, striving to be democratic.

"Wall, that's all right, then," the driver conceded, and Angus felt a relief that was both positive and warming. "Glad to have an able man aboard. Jake Bealor, sir, that's my name. Now should the need arise, sir, reach for the rifle under my seat. You'll enjoy the journey, sir; you'll see changes. You'll see that the country's fillin' up fast."

The coach road followed the Savannah River, north and west, through a deeply wooded valley. Angus did not find it crowded; on the contrary, it looked as wild as it had when he was a boy. They passed scattered farms and landings, an occasional church or grist mill, but for the most part the road meandered endlessly through the woods.

The days were sunny and mild. Birds called as the coach rattled over the rough, narrow road—a well-worn, well-traveled road but still pitted with chuckholes and treacherous stumps, which by law had to be less than eight inches high. "Lean left," Jake Bealor called out when he was forced to take the coach up onto its two right wheels to avoid some huge ditch or stone, and all the passengers were obliged to throw their weight to the left.

Sometimes Angus had the feeling that eyes were watching the coach pass, but whether it was an Indian peering out of the dense forest, a child hidden in a tree, or some shy settler, he had no idea.

As they drove west, the road grew narrower and narrower. The sun glinted off the river and the trappings of the coach. High on the ridges to either side of the road were deep forests of pine with some cedar, and then, as the road climbed away from the river, Angus was treated to a new and splendid sight—more beautiful than he had remembered or ever seen in England. For miles and miles they passed among hardwoods bright with colored leaves: the clear yellow of hickory and chestnut, beech and poplar, the red and gold of maples and sweet gum, the blood red of black gum and dogwood, and behind them all, the oaks—massive towering oaks fading from red to bronze to brown.

Each night the coach stopped at a small wayside inn, one of the sort also known as "ordinaries," primitive hostels run by a man and his wife who took in travelers, stabled their horses, and fed both men and beasts. Angus followed the other passengers into the low-ceilinged, smoky room, ate fresh-killed game, shared the towel and the bed with everyone else, and slept very soundly. The drink was corn whiskey and it was a sturdy potion, effective in preventing dreams and a consciousness of aching muscles.

Augusta, when Angus reached it after a long week's ride, was changed completely from the town he had last seen during the Revolution. Since its early founding, in 1735, just two years after Savannah, Augusta had been both a fort and a marketplace. Here, in the early days, Indians had brought bales of deerskins and beaver pelts to barter with the traders who came upriver from Savannah and Charleston on packhorses loaded with blankets and trinkets. During the Revolution, Augusta had been a bloody battleground which changed hands a half-dozen times, and at the end of the war the town had been so destitute that supplies had to be poled upriver to keep the people from starving.

Since those days everything had changed again. Now the boom crop was tobacco, and Augusta was once more a busy crossroads town. Immigrants streamed through it in wagons piled high with family treasures, heading for the new, fertile land which had just been ceded by the Indians. Many of them were Virginians who brought with them the know-how to raise tobacco, and by the year 1800 Augusta's streets were crowded with huge rolling hogsheads—high as a man's head—pulled by mules and oxen into town to be inspected, graded, packed, stamped "Georgia," and shipped down the river to Savannah on flatboats.

Angus lingered in Augusta only a few days, amazed by the vigor and crudeness of the frontier marketplace. He brought a copy of the *Augusta Chronicle*. Everywhere he walked he saw houses being built; the ring of the hammer and the whine of the saw filled the air. House frames lay in piles, ready to rise. Stagecoaches, wagons, carts, gigs, and sledges filled the streets. There was an organized volunteer fire company. Grocery stores and bakeries were numerous, and over several doorways he saw signs reading Attorney at Law. It was easy to see that his father was right: In the clash of wills between the conservative, stable, coastal counties and the free-swinging, fast-growing, up-country ones, it would be the western counties who would control the future.

Angus saw it, and believed what he saw. And yet, he hesitated, too aware of his Londonish fancies and his unmade reputation. He was conscious of himself as neither here nor there: he was not an Englishman, and never had been accepted as one—yet, how could he be called a Georgian? What were Georgians? Who were they—these rough frontiersmen who ate without forks, who walked in moccasins like Creeks and dressed like Cherokees in coonskin and buffalo hides?

Heads turned as Angus walked the muddy streets of

Augusta—a tall gaunt figure in cityish black—marked as an outlander by his boots, his gloves, the cut of his suit, even before he opened his mouth. "Damn it! What are you bug-eyed about?" he swore at one pack of leather-clad boys who followed him down Broad Street, and at his oath the boys took screaming flight.

Neither fish nor fowl, Angus thought. For so many years neither boy nor man . . . neither British nor American. . . . He scowled, and turning into a tavern, he resolved to make an end of it. Whatever happened, he was determined to stay here in remote, half-wild Wilkes County. Whatever the Stones were like, he would ingratiate himself with them—make them help him establish a life here. Whatever Nancy Stone looked like, he would marry her.

"A toast—to Georgia!" Angus yelled when he was seated in the dark, smoky tavern. "Whiskey's my treat, gentlemen," he shouted, struggling to conceal the London accent that betrayed him.

"Welcome, stranger," a portly man in brass buttons said, accepting the toast and the whiskey, as did his fellows, who were already drenched with rum—one of them fast asleep among the dogs lying under the rough wooden table. "We're the Augusta Volunteer Light Horse Guard!"

"A fine outfit! A famous troop!" Angus declared, although he had never heard of them. Good Lord, he thought, where am I? How far have I come? But no matter, he would stick to it, he would take this life, as it appeared to be his for the taking, he would make it work, and in time he would have it all—the comforts of his old life as well as the substance of his new.

CHAPTER SEVEN

Angus Arrives in Eden; Livia Casts Her Net; A Knight's Mission

Several hundred miles to the west of Augusta the Stone family was at home, unaware that Angus Dunlie was about to enter their life. The Stones were in some ways typical of the many back-country planters who were scrambling to settle Washington County. They had acquired their land in the usual way—immediately after the Revolution, Pittman and his family had been granted four hundred acres, according to the policy of land grants offered to veterans, and they had moved out to this remote part of the county with no more than a horse and wagon could haul. There were no roads yet, no town of Washington, no markets, no churches or schools, no law, no mail, no rules. Their neighbors were other continental soldiers who had won land grants, and the unsuccessful and restless from the older colonies: homespun freedom-loving Scotch-Irish from Pennsylvania and Maryland; stolid, God-fearing Moravians and Lutherans with barely a word of English; fierce, hard-drinking Highlanders who had fought the British with kilts and bagpipes; disgruntled Yankee farmers attracted by stories of good land; all jostling each other for room, for water rights, for the chance to succeed which was promised by the vast wilderness, despite the Indian still skulking behind the next ridge.

During the last ten years, however, unlike his neighbors, Pittman Stone had diversified his enterprises. Taking advantage of the swift, deep streams that ran through his property, he had opened a lumber mill. The mill brought traffic to him, so he opened a store, right on the road, where he sold hardware: nails and a few iron tools, seeds, tea and coffee, salt, medicines, a few kinds of cheap woven goods and almost anything else he could buy in Augusta and bring into the county. For a time, Pittman Stone had an Indian partner in the store, in compliance with a territorial regulation that prohibited white men from being traders. The regulation, like the limits of Indian land, was soon lifted and moved west, but Stone's association with the young Indian he called Tom Stillwater did not harm his business; indeed it drew to him trade from the Indians who still lived nearby and trusted him for his former partner's sake.

Stone soon fell into the usual way of doing business on the frontier. Typically, he gave credit to his neighbors, the planters, until their crops were ready for market, and then he took their surplus produce in payment. That, chiefly tobacco at first, and corn, and later cotton, he shipped himself down to Augusta, or further, to Savannah, where he had an agent sell it for him. The agents in Augusta or Savannah then extended credit to him, and with the credit he stocked his store. He was known to have the best trade in his part of the country.

Pittman Stone had a special perspective on the process of settling the Georgia up-country. Twice before in his lifetime he had seen civilization take hold and grow—first as the oldest child of Micah Stone, a very poor farmer in Wilkes County who had come to Georgia as an indentured servant, and then again as a young man, when he and his bride, Sally Martin, had left their families' well-established plantations on Saint Simons Island and moved out to new land to found their own.

The war had interrupted that second trek west. Pittman and Sally had fought bravely for freedom, followed Colonel Elijah Clark in pursuit of Tories, endured privation and hunger, and then suffered the complete destruction of their home, which had been less than fifty miles from Augusta.

Those had been terrible days, Sally said, and were better off forgotten. She had given her youth and much of her strength to the struggle; she had been a hunted woman, had fled with her children from Georgia to the hills of North Carolina to escape Tory vengeance, and had come home after the war to face wilderness, once again to face the task of carving a life out of the frontier.

"It don't do to look back," Sally said, and she had cause to say it often in the years that followed. No trouble or failure could stop her or her husband, it seemed. And they did not look back, but always forward. It was a fact that more than a desire for land had drawn the Stones and their neighbors to leave the civilized seaboard settlements, where their ancestors or their parents had been able to create a reasonable facsimile of European life. They were thoroughly American in their dreams and desires, those pioneer families, and at the same time they were characters in the eighteenth-century style—a grand, heroic, full-blown style. In moving west—and it was always farther west, and farther again, that they moved—they sought a mythical region where they would find ever more beautiful, unspoiled woods and streams jumping with fish, more wild game, a purer, healthier climate, and even more—a freer land, a land totally unlimited, unrestrained by convention; romantically, they sought an Eden where they would find, as one man put it, "something we crave and have not."

In their first year in what would be called Washington County, Sally and Pittman worked side by side with the two slaves they had owned since before the Revolution to clear ten acres, plant it in corn, and make plans for the riverside mill. That same year a strange "swamp fever" came out of nowhere. Their faithful cook and mammy, Chloe, succumbed to it, as did their two young sons. The fever and the sadness turned Sally's flame-red hair completely white. Pittman and their daughter Nancy escaped the fever entirely, although Nancy, a fragile child, too sensitive and too pretty, gave her parents other cause for worry.

The death of his sons hardened Pittman and made him more determined than ever to survive—and prosper. He sold some land and bought more slaves. With them he was able to clear ten acres of land a year, raise enough corn to pay his taxes and feed his family, and still operate his mill and his store.

Every year was a struggle after that, but every year showed a slight advance. Pittman housed his slaves in a cabin of rough, unhewn logs much like his own but without a single window. A shuttered square hole two feet wide left in the middle of the ceiling provided light when it was open; during the day the square of light moved slowly across the floor, although none of the slaves could witness it—except on the Sabbath—for during the day they were at work, following an unending, seasonal routine which Pittman set for them and to which he put his own back and shoulders in equal measure.

Sally Stone did not work in the fields after the first year, but her work was no less routine and exhausting. She ground the corn they raised for meal, washed, sewed, spun, baked bread, and cooked all their meals—for the slaves as well as her own family. For years she did it alone, then with the help of a slave woman named Darcas, who with her husband and children joined the Stones. The death of her sons had weakened Sally as it hardened Pittman; for years she did not smile and took no pleasure in life; only recently had she attained some measure of resignation, and, as a natural result, begun to raise a second family—two tiny towheaded girls now ran freely in and out of the plantation house, and her belly had begun to swell with another child, her "December child," she told Pittman.

Both Sally and Pittman were glad to have this second family, which promised to make up, to some extent at least, for the heartaches they had suffered with their first three children. For Nancy Stone was not well; she was not normal, although she was pretty enough, "too handsome," her father said, "and not half handy."

"I believe it may be my fault," Sally said to her husband. "I didn't pay her any mind when she was small, and the boys had just been taken from us."

"Nonsense," Pittman declared. "She was lacking from the start, my dear. She has always been weak-minded; there is no help for it. She can't work—nothing can make her remember what she's about to be doing—but it's none of your fault, Sally."

Pittman thought of his father, though he could never bear to speak of him. His own father, Micah Stone, had gone mad, or so it seemed, thinking back to it. Pittman could never be sure of the circumstances, for no one had told him, and now there was no one left to tell, but he remembered the empty blueness of his father's eyes. Oddly enough, Nancy resembled her grandfather physically—she was as blond and beautiful as an angel, and as empty as . . . he thought, and decided . . . as a half-staved barrel.

"Some of these things are inherited. There may be bad blood in my family," he admitted to his wife.

"It breaks my heart," Sally said, "for she's not bad, Pittman, she's not clever enough to know how, and though she'll never seem grown-up, she's near twenty, and too helpless to let loose."

"She ought to be decently married," Pittman said.

"But who would marry her? She'd be no good as a wife, dear."

"I'm afraid she'll get into some trouble."

"That she will, unless she's watched every minute. She'll go wild. Already she runs into the woods when I set her a task. She's gone for hours and I haven't the heart to whip her. She lacks proper modesty, husband, and that troubles me, I confess. 'Tis not safe to leave her in the store, and yesterday I saw her coming along the path from the men's house—if something happened there it would not be the fault of the slaves."

Pittman frowned deeply at that, for these circumstances, too, set off chords of remembering. When he was a very little boy, his mother had taken into their isolated cabin a runaway slave, against his father's wishes. He had never forgotten the man, nor that his mother had been murdered, years later, by another runaway slave, or so everyone believed. At any rate, Pittman had a deep, ingrained horror of white women associating with Negroes . . . no good could come of it, and much harm.

"We cannot confine her here," Pittman said; " 'twould be too difficult and too hard on us all. . . . But I have heard, Sally, that there is a doctor in Milledgeville, a man with the latest European methods, who takes in lunatics . . . and keeps them . . ."

"Oh, no! She would miss her home terribly!"

"And we her, but we are civilized people, my dear. Unlike some others in this county, we know that cures are sometimes made, that society has provisions for the weak-minded. Perhaps it would be the best thing to do."

"I can't bear to think of it."

But Pittman did think of it, and of his father. He

watched his vacant, nubile daughter with close attention, and worried over her, and when, a few weeks after his conversation with Sally, he came home on a damp October evening and saw Nancy standing at the well house with Big Bill, a massive black man who was his best worker—a docile, childlike man in many ways temperamentally similar to Nancy—he decided that Nancy must be sent away. Sorrowfully, he went up to Big Bill and Nancy and took her by the hand and led her into the house.

"My child, you must watch and pray that you may not enter into temptation," he said, recalling his mother's teachings.

"Yes, Father."

Pittman looked at his daughter. Her soft, straight blond hair was cut off at shoulder length like a child's, for she had never learned to comb it for herself, much less to put it up as other young ladies did, and she looked far younger than her years. Her guileless eyes were pale blue and fringed with gold, her cheeks rosy and unlined, and the contours of her full-breasted, slim body were seductively apparent in the faded calico dress she wore, baring slim ankles and bare feet.

"Papa, what have I done?" Nancy asked again, and he saw tears form in the corners of her beautiful blue eyes, a sight that wrenched his heart. There was no way to explain it to her.

"Nothing, my child," Pittman said, "but the flesh is weak."

That night Pittman told Sally what he had decided, and the next day, dressed in her finest white gown, Nancy rode away with her father to the place in Milledgeville, and he left her there.

According to his resolve, Angus made the best of his ride from Augusta to Washington-Wilkes, as it was called to distinguish it from the new capital of the republic. The road he followed north and west of Augusta made the coach road from Savannah look like a London thoroughfare. It was narrow and deeply rutted, suitable only for horses or ox carts. Rain began to fall, and on the first day he was forced to ford twenty or thirty streams. He spent a night in Wrightsborough, wondering if the town—if it could be called a town—had been named after his great-uncle, but he found no one who knew or cared.

On the second day out he was forced to sleep in the woods, finding shelter of a sort under his saddle blanket, kept awake most of the night by the hooting of owls and the monotonous, haunting call of the whip-poor-will. When he awoke, the weather had changed. It was cold. His breath showed in the crisp morning air, and frost crunched on the fallen leaves under his feet.

I shall look like a pauper, Angus fretted, brushing pine needles off his black suit after the night in the woods. The silence of the forest sobered him, almost frightened him. He yelled aloud, just for the sound of his own voice, and when he spotted smoke from a small farm in the distance, his spirits rose and he very respectfully inquired if he might buy a meal. Angus was truly appreciative when he was invited to spend the night, and savored the farmer's wife's dry cornbread and fresh-killed venison more than he ever had a dinner in the finest London chophouse.

From his hosts he learned how far he had yet to go. They knew of the Stones—everyone he asked knew of the Stones, for their mill and their store were said to be landmarks, and the next day he set out again, following a Creek trading path through the greenest, densest woods he had ever seen, along the top of a narrow ridge that gave him a view of the rolling hills and across Kettle Creek.

It was twilight when he asked directions again, and found that he was nearly there. Everything seemed very still. Angus rode briskly along the well-worn path. It was Saturday night.

And then he came to a clearing in what seemed to be the right spot. But instead of a store as he had fancied it, instead of a busy, English-looking mill, he faced a clearing edged with scrub pine, a humble split-log house of four rooms or so, and a prospect of fields beyond. From the look of it, the store and the house were the same building. Beyond it, he saw a big barn and several smaller ones, a mill house by the stream that was no more than a shed, and a sprinkling of cabins, outside of which sat a few idle Negroes.

Angus reined his horse to a stop and stared. Was this it? Was this the "opportunity" for which he had come so far? His heart sank; he was truly dismayed. A full five minutes passed as Angus looked over the premises; finally he raised his voice and called out "Hello!"

At the sound of his voice a pack of hounds exploded out of the barnyard, yelping and baying, followed by an equally unruly pack of tiny children, both black and white, all barefoot and tousled and clad in short rough-cloth shirts that cleared their dirty knees.

Angus looked down at the swarm and made no effort to dismount. A large black woman appeared in the door of the kitchen house, a column of black smoke billowing out around her. Open-mouthed and wide-eyed, she stared at Angus as she screamed at the children.

But before the ruckus could begin to subside, a white-haired woman, also barefoot, came to the door of the big house and called to Angus, "How d'y stranger . . . kin I help you?"

"Stone? Are ye Mistress Stone?" Angus asked, hoping still he had the wrong place.

"Pittman, I think it's a preacher," Sally Stone said to her husband, who was seated by the fire, cleaning his rifle. "It's an elegant man, all dressed in black."

"Well, ask him in," Pittman said, and Sally ran out to speak to Angus as Pittman put down his rifle deliberately and followed her out, reaching the front clearing at the same time as did the black woman, her hands dusty with cornmeal, and a dozen hands from the cabins in the rear.

To Angus, stiffly dismounting, it seemed as if he faced a mob, and a more shabbily dressed, mismatched, ragamuffin mob he could not have imagined. Two black toddlers tried to climb his legs, one of the slaves led his horse away, the hounds retreated, and the man he took to be his relative spoke.

"Welcome, Reverend. We're pleased to have your visit, sir."

Angus was astonished. Being mistaken for a preacher was the last thing he expected! A preacher? Pittman went on.

" 'Tis our good fortune, on the Sabbath Eve, Reverend, and we bid you come in, we're glad to have ye. I expect you're hungry, sir."

"A preacher, a preacher! He's stayin', he's stayin'," the children chorused, and danced around Angus, wild, gleeful, bobbing like corks in a whirlpool.

"I am grateful for your offer of hospitality," Angus said, "but I am not a reverend. Are you Pittman Stone?"

"I am."

"I am your cousin, sir, Angus Dunlie by name. Come from Savannah, sir, and before that from London."

A stunned silence met this announcement. Angus wondered if he had been understood, but finally Pittmàn laughed.

"Is that who you are? Well, well. If you're the son of your father, you're far from being o'er holy! I remember him well, yes, I do! Well, well!"

"I b'lieve, sir, that my father wrote you a letter . . ."

"That he did. First piece of mail to reach us in years. And here you are, now. Well, well. Sally, what do you make of it?"

"Whoever he is, I think you'd all best come in out of the dark and warm up in front of the fire. Darcas, do you think we'll be eatin' that cornbread any time soon?"

"Yes, ma'am, directly," the black woman said.

"Our life here is not up to city standards," Pittman told Angus, "but we're glad to see ye, all the same. It's been many years since we had any word from the family back east. Now what can you tell us?"

"Do you ever think of leaving Sea Groves?" Livia asked Morgan. The two of them were seated on a low wooden bench, near the rose arbor, on the lawn at the plantation. It was early evening, and the island was enjoying exceptionally mild weather for fall. The setting sun streaked the sky in orange and gold, fat red and white roses nodded on their stems, and an atmosphere of peace and beauty surrounded everything. Increasingly often, Livia and Morgan met and sat together in the evenings, a development that was not altogether pleasing to Morgan's parents, but as long as it went on in full view of the house neither Jenny nor Roland could think of any reason to reprimand Morgan. After all, they were cousins, and no one else had much use for Livia.

"Leaving? Wherever would I go?" Morgan asked, surprised by the question. For his part, he enjoyed talking with Livia. She seemed to him the most ladylike and charming of all the girls he knew. Of course she was pretty, but both Juliette and Aimee were prettier in the sweet way he was accustomed to admiring; Livia was provokingly pretty, so that sometimes he forgot the topic they were discussing and fell under the spell of watching her breasts rise and fall, or marveling at the clear brightness of her turquoise blue eyes.

"You might go to Charleston or New York or Washington," Livia suggested.

"I might, someday, I suppose. Especially if I had business to transact. But I am never bored here, Livia. The work of the plantation is so absorbing, and new agricultural discoveries are being made every year, so that it is unlikely to stop changing. . . ."

Good heavens, Livia thought. Imagine never being bored. She herself was agonizingly bored with Sea Groves, and with Angus so long gone, and no one knew where, she was agonizingly restless . . . sexually restless. It had been so long that she had considered taking on one of the slaves for a "romance of the field," as she'd heard them called in some naughty book Angus had read in London, but her father had intercepted her before she could even consider it, had forbidden it specifically, and had told her to devote herself to charming Morgan.

"Really? And you do find inspiration in the changing seasons?" Livia asked Morgan, looking him full in the eyes with her most entranced expression. Her mission, to enchant Morgan, was made bearable by the havoc and unhappiness she could see it caused Aimee and Juliette. Both of them adored Morgan. At first she had thought him dull, but she was increasingly intrigued by his calm, good-humored strength. And he was handsome: healthy and vital and masculine. Oh, he would do, she had decided, especially as her father insisted that he must do. And especially as someone must, and soon.

"I love this land," Morgan vowed; ". . . inspiration, yes, but also responsibility, both to my family and to the people over whose lives we have stewardship."

"Over the slaves, do you mean?"

"Yes, of course, dear Livia, as you have seen during your stay here. It is far from being a situation of exploitation, as some would say. Would you not agree that our slaves are far better off—better housed and fed, better clothed and cared for—than the poor in England?"

Livia had never given it a thought; to her all servants

were a lower order of beings, necessary but repulsive. As far as she was concerned, they had best do their work and then disappear into their own lives, in which she could take no interest, but surely Morgan was right—he seemed so fervent about it. She agreed, wondering how she could turn the conversation to a more interesting subject, for instance, herself. "Yes, of course, it's obvious that you are right," she said, leaning closer to Morgan and looking up at him from under her eyelashes in her most flirtatious way.

"In fact," Morgan went on, warming to his subject, already warmed by Livia's flattering attention, "I have thought of writing something about this. It is my thesis that nowhere else in the civilized world does a situation exist in which the interests of the laborer and the employer are absolutely identical. It is a situation of mutual need and dependence. For the slaveholder, both interest and inclination, both the desire for profit and the sense of his duty compel him to be kind . . . benevolent . . . protective . . . in fact, fatherly, to call into play the highest sentiments Christians embrace, when dealing with a people who come to him from the darkest corners of the globe, untaught and untrained."

"Yes? Yes?" Livia breathed, admiring the note of power and aggressiveness in Morgan's voice. Perhaps she thought, he would be masterful in bed. It was all she hoped for. . . .

"Do you realize, Livia, under what new and auspicious aspects we live? Here we are, in the first truly democratic republic the world has ever known. Ours is the chance to make a heavenly empire of it—a world of kind masters and happy slaves, united in cultivating the earthly garden and building an empire of freedom. We are poised on the edge of a new century, we have as our president a great and brilliant man, we have the best and most fertile earth, the most marvelous climate . . . ah!"

"It's quite true, Morgan," Livia nodded, beginning to feel restless. Would he never suggest a stroll? Would he never even try to kiss her?

"It's a great opportunity . . . and a great responsibility," Morgan concluded. "But . . . I hope I haven't bored you . . ."

"Bored? Morgan, of course not!" Livia jumped to her

feet. "I am quite stimulated by your ideas, Morgan, truly I am!" Her cheeks were bright pink and her eyes sparkled remarkably, he noticed.

Falteringly, unused to feeling such desire, unused to speaking so, Morgan framed a compliment. "You are an ideal Eve, for the garden, Livia. Why, your eyes are as blue as the clear Georgia sky . . . and your skin as beautiful as Mother's roses."

"Morgan!" Livia was delighted. If this was the result of talk about gardens, she would endure hours of it. "Dear Cousin, let us walk together. I long to breathe the sea air."

Morgan agreed, and when they were out of sight of the plantation house, he followed his instincts and kissed her. After that, he thought often of the kiss, and longed to kiss her again.

Determined as he was to succeed as he had never succeeded before, to find his place, to gain power and riches, Angus had a hard time of it during his first few weeks with the Stones. He had everything to learn about this new life, and nothing he had ever previously learned seemed to be of any use here at all.

At first it seemed to him that the Stones lived a life of miserable poverty. He struggled to conceal his shock at seeing that Sally Stone and the children habitually ran barefoot, that Pittman worked in the fields with his slaves, that the first meal he shared with them, a meal of pork and cornbread and bacon and greens, was repeated at breakfast and dinner and supper, day in and day out. He was equally surprised to see Sally smoking a clay pipe and playing, quite sweetly and competently, on a harp. Pittman, who wore his hair long and tangled and dressed in the coarsest of homespun, was eager to talk with Angus about the conflicts of the Federalists and Republicans in Washington, of the latest literary fashions in London, of the changes and developments that had taken place in Savannah in the years since he had left there.

It was not poverty, it was simplicity, Angus began to understand. Everything in the Stones' life was simple and dignified, from the solid, comfortable furnishings in their small house to their countrylike hospitality.

The Stones, for their part, were utterly amazed by Angus. It was clear to them that he had never worked. His hands were as soft as a baby's; his arms and legs weak and stiff. His accent fascinated them, particularly Pittman, for it reminded him of his mother's. The children were afraid of him and ran when he strolled out of the cabin, a tall gaunt scarecrow in black.

'Twould be better if I were a preacher, Angus thought desperately, as he sat up alone by the fire one night. He felt cornered; he could not go back—where could he go back to? He was unused to this life, but he had never embraced any other, never really made London his life, and certainly had no prospects at his cousin's plantation on Saint Simons Island. He questioned his father, darkly—why had he sent him here, why banished him to this confused, unnamed, unknown, untamed wilderness? What was he to do? What could he make of it?

Cut loose, adrift, Angus wrestled with his pride and his sanity. He could not hate Pittman Stone, could not even dislike him, for the man was decent, pious, hospitable. Everything he had he had clearly made for himself or wrested from the land. Instead, he came close to hating himself, for he felt his weaknesses and his lack of direction keenly, and he felt a sense of haste.

Awkwardly, for he was so unused to making decisions for himself, Angus struggled to make a plan. He had never considered himself a businessman, but he was not physically suited to clearing land or planting. He had some money—his saddlebags still held the gold Carlton Raye had paid him for the shipment of slaves. He longed to be established, but knew that he would never succeed without Pittman's aid. Perhaps, he dreamed, he could buy some land and slaves to work it, perhaps he could somehow help Pittman expand the store and the mill. . . .

Furthermore, Angus, who had lived his whole life under the influence of a powerful, diabolically determined father, was experiencing a complex and odd, if predictable, reaction to Pittman Stone. Initially he had been shocked by Stone's backwoods appearance and had felt superior, but he had quickly come to respect Stone for his versatility, his strength, vigor, confidence, and his obviously superior adaptation to the frontier environment. Respect for an older man triggered all manner of behavior in Angus, foremost among it an ingrained, passionate desire to please.

It was in response to this desire, as well as his own desperate need to find some way of life, that Angus approached the other part of his two-fold plan to become accepted by the Stones. Ever since the night of his arrival he had been confused and mystified by the absence of Nancy Stone, the daughter of the family. His father had anticipated her; Pittman had referred to her in the letter he had sent to his father, but now there was no sign of her. Her likeness, in a handsome silhouette that Sally Stone told him had been done last spring by a traveling Frenchman, hung on the wall, but the girl herself was missing, and neither of her parents was at all easy about it.

"She has gone . . . to board . . . in Milledgeville," Pittman told Angus and then said no more.

Angus could not understand it, but there were many aspects of the Stones' life that he could not understand. He could see that Nancy was sorely missed; he saw tears in her mother's eyes when she told him that Nancy had been gone only a few weeks. He became attuned to references to her and savored them, but his attention shed little light on the mystery.

One day he drew the oldest child aside, a tiny girl named Emmaline, and asked her, kneeling to get her ear, "Is she fair? Is your sister fair?"

"Sister Nancy is the prettiest girl in the world," the child vowed. "Patty 'n' me miss her. Don't you wish Papa would go off and fetch her home?"

It was Angus's first intimation of what became, by leaps and bounds of his imagination, a noble and romantic mission. Nancy Stone was a ghost in her parents' home; she became to Angus a vision of an exiled fair lady. It became his chivalrous mission to find her, rescue her, and carry her off. The idea appealed to the finest side of Angus's character and began to seem a logical step toward winning his rightful place in the Stone family.

Partly, then, to please Pittman Stone, partly in obedience to his own father's instructions, partly to fulfill his romantic dream, Angus told the Stones he had to ride to Milledgeville, on business, and set out very early one day, after he had been staying with his relatives at their bustling, busy establishment for about a week.

Angus had little idea of where Milledgeville was, or

how long it would take to get there, but he rode hard, and enjoyed the ride. It was crisp. The fall air had a tang of pine, seasoned with woodsmoke and sunshine. He followed a river trail and stopped two nights at small roadside inns; it was a hard trip but he felt confident, increasingly confident—both of his mission and of his ability to deal with this wild forested country.

"I've come to buy land," he told one innkeeper with a ring of bravado in his voice that well supplanted his characteristic tones of anxiety and studied displeasure. "And I'm going to fetch my wife," he added.

A light rain was falling when Angus rode into Milledgeville. Under the gray skies it did not look like much of a town, although there was already talk of moving the state capital there. Broad thoroughfares had been planned and laid out but they were still unpaved and muddy. Only a few houses had been built, and as Angus tied his horse to a railing in front of the town's only inn, a herd of wild pigs ran through the main street, grunting and squealing, well in the lead of a barefooted black boy who ran after them, shouting and waving a switch.

"I'm looking for Miss Nancy Stone," Angus told the barkeeper, when he had ordered a rum.

"Who? Miss Who?"

"I must find Miss Nancy Stone; she's staying here somewhere," Angus insisted, setting down a silver coin, adding "you fat fool" under his breath.

The barkeeper picked up the coin quickly. "I expect my wife would know."

But his wife, when she emerged from the kitchen, did not know. "Miss Stone?" she asked, "would that be a young lady or a woman of years?"

"Young! A young woman! Very fair!" Angus insisted. He was depressed by Milledgeville and this situation. It seemed hopeless. Why had he assumed he could find Nancy just by asking?

"Ah!" the woman exclaimed. "Would she be stayin' at the doctor's place, perhaps?"

"Perhaps," Angus said, "who is the doctor? Where is he?"

The barkeeper and his wife exchanged a look which riled Angus as much as their hesitation. Were they slow-witted? Pounding on the bar, he demanded directions, and received them, but when he left the tavern he felt oddly disturbed. Why would Nancy Stone be boarding at a doctor's . . . and why had the innkeepers spoken so reluctantly?

Strongly suspecting that something was amiss, Angus stopped outside the inn and looked up and down the street. It was quiet. A riderless horse stood tied to a tree; a few schoolboys chased past, laughing and hitting each other with switches; an old woman staggered under the weight of a wicker basket full of carrots, her head bent and covered by a black scarf. It's the far end of nowhere, Angus thought. He was baffled, and for a moment quite forgot his sense of mission. What on earth was he doing here?

CHAPTER EIGHT

Nancy Stone Saved from Torment; Juliette in Torment; An Unusual Duel

A nation of idiots, a world of fools, Angus thought as he rode out of Milledgeville in search of Doctor Poker, who the innkeeper had told him lived about five miles west, on the mountain road. "At the end of the mountain road, just keep going till you can't go no further," the man had said, and Angus had to accept it. He was tired and frustrated. His idea of riding after Nancy Stone seemed less and less practical, and his hope waned that claiming her as his bride would change his life.

The truth was that Angus was outlandish—he looked it and most of the time he felt it. Coming to Milledgeville was a defiant act—defying the reality of his being as out of place in the Georgia backwoods as a fish in snow—but it was making him feel no better.

"Damn, God damn!" he howled to the silent trees and fields that he passed. "Where will this end?"

"Ennnd . . ." an echo came back to him, and he kicked his horse onward.

Rain had begun to fall steadily as Angus left town, and a cold wind blew through the red oaks and gum trees along the mountain road. He passed a few dreary farms and splashed his way across a rocky stream before the road began to climb.

It was no mountain, but it was a hill, and his horse was winded when he reached the top and saw a farm that fit the description of being at the very end of the road. The sight of Doctor Poker's place was so grim and desolate that Angus nearly turned back. A black dog was chained to a maple tree in the front of the house and leaped and howled through bared teeth. Smoke rose from the chimney of the big square log house, but there was evidently more going on in the outbuildings behind the main house—he could see several of them and heard odd noises from that direction—more howling, a shriek. Perhaps Poker had a kennel full of hounds, Angus thought. Or could there be slaves housed back there?

Leaving his horse, Angus gave the dog leeway and knocked, a bit apprehensively, at the front door of the main house.

There was no answer. He knocked again. God damn it, he thought, what if she's not here? Why have I come all this way? He shivered, wet to the skin. It was getting dark, and it was a damp and dreary night, that much he knew for sure.

"Yes, suh?" a man's voice asked, and Angus turned to see that a huge black man had come up behind him, carrying a pail, dressed in boots and a thick blue jacket.

"Is this Doctor Poker's home?" Angus asked shortly.

"Yes, suh. Now, the doctor's just inside, suh. He's a bit hard of hearing, suh, so jest walk in . . ."

Frowning, Angus entered the house. The room he entered was large and well heated by a huge fire leaping in a stone fireplace. In a chair in front of the fire a gray-haired man, well padded and looking very much the English gentleman in a red vest and stout boots, sat in a sturdy armchair, fast asleep.

"Doctor Poker?" Angus asked, and then, shaking the man's arm, "Are you Doctor Poker?"

"Goodness!" The man sneezed twice, then wiped his nose on his sleeve and looked up at Angus. His face was as red as his vest, which was as splotched and spotted as his pantaloons. "Give a man arrest, you will, sneaking up on him that way!"

"I'm sorry, sir," Angus said. He shook his sleeve toward the fire. The flames jumped and there was a steamy, sizzling sound.

"Damn it, watch that!" the doctor snapped. "Now . . . what was it you wanted?"

"I've heard," Angus said cautiously, "that there's a young woman presently staying with you . . ."

The doctor smiled.

"Now where did you hear that?" he chuckled. "How their dirty tongues do wag! Did Colonel Pierce tell you? No? Was it Mr. Thomas? Eh? Eh? It was?"

"It was the innkeeper," Angus said, a bit awkwardly, not at all sure what was going on.

"The innkeep! Well, damn him, he can't afford her! Neither can the rest of 'em! I've set a fancy price on her, young man, for she's a fancy-lookin' lass. I don't know . . . you look to be a gentleman. Where you from? Maybe you'll take the prize . . . but if you squawk at the price I've set, damn it, I've decided to keep her for myself!"

Angus stepped back. He'd been in enough whorehouses in London to recognize the language of a whoremaster. He couldn't believe his ears. The Stones had been duped by this repulsive man. Surely, Nancy Stone, if she was here, was being kept without the knowledge of her family. His gorge rose like mercury in a glass, his heart pounded, and he swallowed hard, struggling to keep his temper and his composure before this vulgar, immoral man.

"How do I know she's worth it?" he asked, half-shutting his eyes.

"If ye don't think she's worth it, why are you here?" Poker countered. He laughed heartily at his own wit, then pulled a pipe out of his pocket and lit it from a candle burning on top of the mantelpiece. "She's worth it. She's as pretty as a yellow-headed princess, and it's all new to her. Brand-new. Why, I've examined her myself, and furthermore, young doubter, her parent gave her to me for safekeeping. *She's* not a pauper, like some of 'em. Her parent's paying her board, that I promise ye."

"I'll . . . take her, then," Angus stammered. He was so angry, so outraged, and so excited that he could hardly speak.

"Without asking the price? Well, well, you are a good fellow, I must say."

"What is the price?"

"Twenty dollars."

Angus reached into his pocket.

"Gold," Poker added. He had just doubled the figure he'd had in mind. A good businessman knows when he's got a live one, he thought.

"Where is she?" Angus asked.

"That's for just tonight, of course," Poker said, "paid in advance." He held out his hand.

It was dirty, Angus noticed, as he put a twenty-dollar gold piece into it. Fah! The man was repulsive. It was obvious that he had deceived the Stones. Angus was more determined than ever to find Nancy and get her away from this man.

"Where is she?" he demanded.

"She's out back. I'll send my man after her." Poker tried to rise, found it too much of an effort, and sat back to yell "Wash! Wash!"

"He'll never hear you over this wind," Angus said impatiently.

"Well, go out and look for him, then. Out back. He's a big nigger, big and mean-lookin' and very smart. Oh, very clever, you'll see. He's my lieutenant. I couldn't manage without him." Poker laughed, horribly. Angus pulled his collar up and went out the front door, calling for Wash. The wind had risen and the rain was a fine but steady spray. There was no sign of the black man, so he walked around behind the main house and looked into the first of the out-buildings.

At first he couldn't believe his eyes. Inside the structure, which was a low-ceilinged, slat-sided box that looked as if it had been built for a corn crib, were six filthy half-dressed old men, all in leg irons, chained to an iron bar that had been fixed in the middle of the floor. The men lay on their backs in soiled bedding and loose straw, all of it reeking with filth. The smell alone would have driven Angus away, but the howling that arose when he put his head inside the door was even more terrifying.

Retching and gasping, Angus backed out and turned to flee, but before he could, he ran into Wash, massive and implacable, still carrying a pail.

"It's their dinner time," Wash said, by way of explanation. "They're no better'n pigs, suh. Just a minute, suh. Master says to get you the young lady."

"What's wrong with them?" Angus gasped.

"They're pauper lunatics, that's all." Wash reached into the little shed and set the bucket, which looked to be full of burned meal, in the center of the room. All the men scrambled for it, howling, and Angus turned his eyes away.

"Who sent them here?" he asked Wash.

"They're paid for by the state. Oh, in fine weather they come out—they don't stay in dere all the time, suh, but they're no good as workers, too mad. One of 'em, suh, all he does is roll around, barkin' like a dog. It's funny to see, suh. I think they might as well be killed as live here. Why, they might get away."

"Does that often happen?"

"Nope, that's why we've got the dog. At night he's unchained. He roams the grounds, keeps 'em safe."

"Where is the young lady?" Angus asked.

"Over there's the house for women. Ladies upstairs. We keep the ladies quite apart, suh."

"Of course," Angus mumbled, too stunned and disgusted to do more than stumble after the Negro caretaker, past another small cabin, in which, from the smell and sound of it, more madmen were confined.

"I expect you want to take her back into the house," Wash said. "There's no fire out here."

No fire, in this weather, Angus thought. "What does the doctor do . . . to help these people?" he asked.

"Oh, he has his instruments, suh. I don't know what all. Very scientific. You'll see 'em inside, but mostly it's keepin' 'em locked up. That's the main part. You see, these are people who can't be kept at home—too dangerous. That's why they can't have fires. Some of 'em, suh, would do anythin' to get away. Wait here."

Angus waited, his stomach churning, his head spinning. It was all more ghastly than he could ever have imagined. Clearly Poker was a fraud and a charlatan who had fooled Pittman Stone as he had fooled others. And what did that make him? He had no more hope that Nancy Stone would be worth having, but at any rate he must try to get her away from here. If he couldn't manage it himself, he would send her father, of course, but if there was a shred of life and decency left in the poor girl, he would try to take her away with him this very night, before it was too late.

Waiting, Angus tried not to hear but was very aware of the women's voices coming from the rough log building. He heard sobs, a thin, pitiful voice calling "Please! Please!" and one long scream that was ended by the sound of an iron gate clanging shut. There were no windows on the ground floor of the house, but when he looked upstairs he saw one, and in it a young woman looking out, her pale face a reverse silhouette against the darkness. It was unmistakably Nancy Stone.

His heart leaped. He recognized her—without a doubt. With revived hope and interest, he ran to the door and looked into the downstairs room.

"Wash! Where are you?" he called.

"Come on in, sir!" a woman's hoarse, scratchy voice called, and then another, unnaturally high and wheedling, "Ooh, ain't he pretty!" In the dim recesses of the room Angus could see four cells, more like horses' stalls than rooms, and in each of them, behind an iron gate, a woman, a simple bench, and a pewter chamber pot. For beds, the confined women obviously used the loose straw piled against the back walls. Angus stared, touched and horrified, and one woman, white-haired and thin, opened her arms to him and sang out, "Son! Son, take me home!"

"Don't pay her no mind," Wash told Angus, coming down the ladder from the loft with a fragile-looking young woman in a white dress in his arms. "She thinks everyone's her son, even the doctor."

Angus backed away, transfixed by the sight of Nancy Stone. She was all that he had dreamed; even in this horrible place she looked completely lovely. Her blond hair was badly cut, shaggy and uncombed, her dress was stained and rumpled, but her face was angelic and her eyes met his with an expression of peace and serenity that inspired and compelled him.

"Can't she walk?" Angus asked in a pained voice.

"Oh, she can walk all right," Wash laughed, lifting Nancy's skirt to show Angus that her legs were clamped together by two ankle irons and a two-foot iron bar. "She was always tryin' to run away, till the doctor put the Iron Minder on her. I'll just carry her into the house for you, then I'll take it off. Doctor Poker's gone into the inn for dinner; he says you can use the front room till he gets back, if you please."

Wash tossed Nancy over his shoulder and strode off toward the house, Angus following helplessly.

"Can't she speak?" he asked, when they were inside the main house and Wash had found the key that unlocked the cruel ankle irons.

"She used to. She screamed and cried terrible, at first, but now she's shut up. Better if all women would, eh, suh?" And Wash laughed, but Angus saw no joke.

"Well, there you go, suh," he said, "She's yourn. I'll be outside, if you need me, and the doctor'll be home in a few hours."

"Yes, yes," Angus said, considering the possibilities. He would have to carry her off immediately; there was no time to waste. His eyes rested on her. She sat, slumped in the doctor's chair in front of the fire, all will gone, too weak and abused to struggle.

"My poor darling," Angus whispered. He fell to his knees in front of Nancy. "Look at me. Can you hear me? I have come to take you home. Home—to your papa and your family."

Nancy stared at him without expression. Her pale blue eyes were clouded, but it was a cloud that seemed as if it might blow away any moment. Then she turned her head, and the purity of her profile touched him.

Angus put his hands on her ankles and rubbed them. They were cold, and the flesh had been chafed and reddened by the irons. Nancy winced, and then shuddered. She made no move, either toward or away from Angus.

"I am going to save you," he promised, his voice so sober it sounded hollow. "Trust me. I'll take you away. I'll take care of you till you get well. I know you will, once you are far away from here."

Nancy smiled weakly. Still, she did not speak. He had not heard her utter one word.

I have to get past that monster of a Negro, Angus thought, and his damn dog—then I have to get away. He paced the room. All of a sudden an idea came to him, a plan to match his rage and desperation. Picking up Nancy—her weight was nothing, less than a child's—he carried her to a bench near the room's only window.

"Wait," he said. "Wait. Do you understand?"

And then Angus went into a fury of action. Roughly, carelessly, taking pleasure in the physical release of his emotions, he swept off the table all the doctor's papers and his few books and threw them into the fire. As they caught, the flames leaped up. Into the crackling, leaping flames he threw the doctor's pillows and his shawl, his fur rug, his blankets, the clothes hanging on hooks at the side of the room, then a linen tablecloth, a box of candles, a can of tea, then one of sugar, a deerskin, a pair of stiff leather shoes, and the woolen stockings stuffed into them. The fire danced hungrily around these offerings.

Immediately the room grew hotter, and the fire began to smoke. Angus stepped back from it, and then, for good measure, hurled a bottle of rum on top of it all and poked at the blaze with a leg of the doctor's chair, which he smashed against the grate.

He turned to Nancy. She was huddled against the wall, her eyes wide and terrified.

Don't look so, Angus thought. Her fragility and passivity stirred him as he had never been stirred; all his life he was to be touched by Nancy's saintly face, and now it inspired him.

The smoke billowed out of the fireplace, black and thick. It began to fill the room, first a gray cloud, then, as the fire continued to smoke, a darker one, blacker and blacker, until it was hard to see or breathe.

Now! Angus thought. He ran to Nancy and covered her with a quilt, then flung open the door to the front of the house and stood behind it and yelled, "Help! Fire!"

Immediately, Wash ran into the room. Angus stepped around the door, stepped out, shut the door, and ran for his horse. "Fire! Fire!" he heard Wash shouting as he untied the reins. As he set Nancy on top of the horse he felt the dog jumping at his legs. Angrily, he kicked back and had the luck to catch the creature in the side of its head before he jumped onto the horse and turned its head toward the road.

"Run!" Angus begged the horse. The animal was cold and hungry, he knew; so was he, but there would be no food or rest for either of them until they had put many miles between themselves and Milledgeville.

"Hold tight," Angus told Nancy, and he arranged the quilt around both of them and put his arms around her gently and firmly. "Are you all right?" he whispered, putting his mouth to her ear.

Nancy turned her face up toward him, her eyes wide and wet with tears. He waited. Was she about to speak? He leaned forward eagerly, and she did speak, very softly and distinctly, her voice clear and sweet as a singer's, coming from who knew what remote realm, what far-off kingdom.

"Now that you have come for me," she said, "shall we be together . . . always? Shall we?"

"Of course we shall," Angus promised. "Always, and forever."

The promise cheered him. Nancy was the first person in his lifetime whom he had ever found and saved, all on his own. She was more beautiful—in an eerie, unworldly way—than any woman he had seen, and none could be so sweet and fragile. He was confident that he could please her, could possess her totally; she would never tease him or contradict his opinions, she would never order him about, or make him feel helpless or stupid.

Purely, directly, he loved her. Finding her in this wretched place had been a miracle. It had enabled him to act heroically, more nobly than he had ever acted before, and the action had elevated his spirits. With the impression that he was acting with a force of destiny, he kissed the nape of Nancy's neck. She shivered.

"My poor darling, I know you are cold." Shifting the quilt off his own back, he wrapped it double around her, and shifted her small body closer to his.

"As soon as we find a preacher, darling," he promised, "we shall be married. And when we are man and wife, we shall never be apart."

More than two months had passed since Angus Dunlie's departure from Sea Groves, and life at the Barstows' seaside plantation had, in most respects, returned to normal. Despite the damage caused by the hurricane, Roland Barstow had enjoyed a good year: The price per pound for his fine sea-island cotton had never been higher, although he had lost much of it to the hurricane, and in addition there had been a good harvest of rice, sufficient to feed the community of nearly one hundred slaves who lived in the rows of cabins close by the Barstows' house, and whose care and supervision was a major project of their masters' lives.

Sea-island cotton, so named for the Bahamas, from which islands the first seeds had been carried to Georgia in the late eighteenth century, was said to be the finest cotton raised anywhere in the world. Experiments on Sapelo and

Saint Simons islands had led to the systematization of its cultivation, and it had been found that the long-staple cotton could easily be raised on former rice plantations and that the long, silky fibers, even before the advent of the cotton gin, could be fairly easily separated from the seed.

There were a variety of disadvantages involved in the cultivation of this fine, long-staple stuff, one which Roland Barstow had suffered this year. The region was subject to sudden, violent storms. Also, the harvest was slow, and careful handling was required in certain stages of cultivation.

It was the custom on the island, and in the coastal region of the state, to perform the work of the plantation by tasks. Drivers, trusted slaves with a talent for leadership and organization, apportioned the tasks according to the strength of the workers, who were either full hands, three-quarter hands, half hands, or one-quarter hands. The cotton fields at Sea Groves were divided into square patches of 105 feet each way, about a quarter of an acre. Each was called a task and was laid out in beds five feet apart. In the spring, cotton was planted, in the summer hoed to keep down the weeds, in the fall, harvested. In each operation the amount of work expected by a full or half-hand was clearly agreed upon.

Young slaves came into the system as one-quarter hands and were gradually raised. When a Negro had finished his task for the day, he was free to tend his own garden, fish, or pursue any other occupation within the limits well known by all the slaves, and in most seasons a field worker could manage to have at least part of the afternoon free.

Roland and Morgan Barstow took pride in personally supervising the drivers and the work of the slaves at Sea Groves. They had never hired an overseer. Both of them worked long hours in the fields and were familiar with every aspect of cotton growing. The two men habitually rose very early and rode out together, seeing the slaves begin their work in the fields before they returned to the house for breakfast.

On a crisp and clear December morning, after such a ride to see a gang of men rebuilding a seawall torn down by alligators, Morgan and his father rode together down the long avenue toward the house.

"This year is nearly ended," Roland said.

"Yes, Father. A year which has brought many changes to our lives."

"Not the least of which is the arrival of our cousins."

"Not the least . . ." Morgan agreed.

"Dunlie has gone up to Savannah again," Roland said.

"He goes on business?"

"So he says, although I am not sure what the business is. He never goes without petitioning me for traveling expenses, but I begrudge him nothing. Privately, I consider him a sorry man; but I still hope for a bridge of good will between our two families. I look to your generation for that, son."

"I do my best," Morgan said. He paused for a moment. "Juliette, I fear, does not get on well with Livia."

"Your sister is in a difficult phase. She has not recovered from that incident with young Dunlie. How I regret my part in it."

"I doubt that Angus has suffered as much as Juliette," Morgan said with a bit of irritation. For his part, he was glad to be rid of Angus Dunlie; everything had improved since he had left, including his relations with Livia. Where she had seemed before to be distracted, she was now devoted to him, and he enjoyed it immensely. In fact, he wondered if he were in love with her, a circumstance not to be taken lightly. Being in love was a condition he had always expected he would some day enter into; he also expected it to result inevitably in marriage. Morgan was a very serious young man.

"I don't know what to do about Juliette," Roland said. "Her mother is also concerned."

Juliette herself, on that fine December morning, was still in her bedroom, unconcerned that she would soon be late for breakfast, seated at her small cherry writing table, addressing herself to her journal, as had become her habit in the past few months. Her behavior, her fitful sulks and silences, her glooms and occasional fits of temper convinced her family that she was still upset by the incident, as they called it, with Angus, but none of them had any real idea of the depth of her humiliation and pain.

> *December 15, 1800. Sea Groves.* Perhaps I am foolish to think so, but I feel that I love him and miss

him even more today than two months ago. I am so much older now. When I think with what greedy innocence I sought experience! How determined I was, how desperate to learn about love! How fast I learned, how disastrously. Now he has left me—forever? I feel it so keenly that sometimes I cannot bear the pain, all the more that no one knows—they think me childish and naughty—except Livia, perhaps. I think Livia knows everything—she is as wise as a sibyl, and as dangerous. And I confess it—I hate her! For that and other reasons, foremost among them that I can see that my brother Morgan cares for her. She has fooled him—I know it; she has deceived him into thinking she is honest and sweet, but I know she is not. She is utterly false. For too long I have suffered, seeing her bewitch him (and sometimes I think she may actually be possessed of evil spirits, God help us if it is so!) but now my apathy is ended. I have decided to act. I have written her a note—which I shall slip under her door today—asking her to come to the ruins of Fort Frederica tonight at twilight, alone, and when she arrives I shall challenge her to a duel, with Father's pistols. This is a desperate act, but I am desperate, and I do it to save my brother—to stop their romance. To do it, I will risk my own life.

Juliette was rosy with temper when she finished the entry in her journal and set down her pen. Her mode of expression was extreme, but her fears and feelings were utterly sincere. All her instincts told her that the romance between Morgan and Livia was deepening, and that it was wrong. Her mother, she suspected strongly, agreed with her, and she knew that her dear friend Aimee despised Livia as much as she did.

But none of them, except me, will act, Juliette thought. I do it because I love my family so—my dear brother, so moral and good he cannot conceive of Livia's wiles, and my parents, who would suffer so if it develops that Morgan and Livia do marry.

"Miss Juliette! You late again, honey," sang out Lizzy, Juliette's maid, bursting into the room, "What? You ain't even started dressin'? Oh, honey, you mama is waitin' on you at the bre'fast table. As usual!"

"Now don't you scold me, Lizzy," Juliette said calmly, "everybody else does and that's enough." Coolly, she slid the letter to Livia into the pages of her journal. She would deliver it on her way down to breakfast; Livia always breakfasted in her room.

And she knew Livia would reply to the summons, for she had signed the note, "With fond admiration, Morgan."

Toward midafternoon Juliette called for Bermuda and dressed herself in her riding habit, told her mother and Aimee that she was going out for a ride, and left Sea Groves alone. Livia, she expected, would take the little buggy, which she preferred to riding astride. It was a cool afternoon with a brisk sea breeze, and she took pleasure in the ride, taking the main road straight across the island and passing many people she knew on horseback or in carriages of one sort or another.

Parts of the road were quite deserted, and those suited Juliette's mood. She passed the clear, swift-flowing river, then a poisonous-looking swamp, thick with tall sedges. Beyond this were low rice fields, in rough stubble at this time of year, and divided into regular squares by manmade dikes. Evergreen bushes, also called saltwater bushes, along the dikes were covered with glittering green-brown ivy hanging in thick garlands, and huge cypress trees stood at a distance behind it all.

What can be more beautiful than Georgia, Juliette wondered. Even in mid-December the roadside thickets were green, in every shade of green from bronze to bright yellow-green. The magnolia bay and the grand magnolia, the wild myrtle, the spiked palmetto hung with evergreen creepers—with the mockingbirds singing in the low bushes and the hawks and buzzards wheeling high in the sky.

Perhaps, Juliette thought morbidly, perhaps I am seeing all this for the very last time. Tomorrow at this time, I may be dead. Or *she* may be. This latter thought sustained her, and she gave Bermuda his head as they neared the deserted village of Frederica, once the only English settlement on the island, long ago destroyed by the British and never rebuilt.

Juliette had explored the crumbling ruins of Frederica many times. It was a favorite spot for picnics, and young ladies who liked to sketch picturesque ruins were inevitably drawn to this end of the island. But there was little chance, she knew, that any tourists or pleasure seekers would be there now. Now, she felt sure, it would be deserted and a bit gloomy, and she was not disappointed.

Just at sunset Juliette tethered Bermuda to the base of a live oak, well out of sight, and chose a spot protected from the wind but good for a lookout, a much-weathered but still-standing powder magazine from the days when this fort had been the southernmost outpost of the British Empire in America. The tabby walls of the structure, smoothed and softened by the action of wind and rain and the passage of years, were now adorned by a cloak of creeping ivy.

It could not help but remind Juliette of the tabby ruin where she had spent that fateful night with Angus Dunlie, and remembering pained her and hardened her heart, so that she was in high temper and firm resolve when she spotted Livia's buggy coming into the fort grounds and heard her high, lilting voice calling out "Morgan! Morgan, where are you? Are you here?"

Juliette set down the small leather satchel in which she had carried her father's pistols, taken from the cabinet in his study where he had kept them for years, and clasped her hands. Dear Lord, she prayed, steady my hand and guide my aim, for I know what I am about to do is right.

"Oh, Morgan!" Livia called. She had left the buggy and rather awkwardly climbed down out of it. Wearing a bare-shouldered, low-cut blue silk gown with only a light shawl around her shoulders, she looked out of place and a bit underdressed in the settling gray-purple twilight. Juliette stared at her with narrowed eyes, then took a deep breath and stepped out from around the foundations of the old powder magazine.

"Juliette!" Livia exclaimed. "Why . . . what are you doing here?"

"I came to meet you."

"Oh!" Livia looked confused, then irritated. She pulled her shawl more tightly around her shoulders. She sniffed, and then said, in the clipped Londonish accent that Juliette had come to hate, "Why are you always bursting in where you're not wanted, Juliette? Really, it's very childish of you, and not appreciated."

"It's you who are bursting in where you're not wanted! I wish you had never come to Georgia, all of us do!"

"Really? I believe you are quite out of control, Miss Juliette. Your family has made me feel very welcome—especially your brother. I believe your nose is out of joint over that. I believe you are quite jealous of your brother's affections for me. Ah, is that it?"

Juliette's eyes blazed with temper. She stamped her foot. "I *would* like to see him pay his attentions to a more worthy woman!"

"Such as your pathetic little friend Aimee? Oh, no, Juliette, you cannot manage our lives—you had better try to manage your own! You have already disgraced yourself over my brother Angus—caused him, through your willfulness and lack of discretion, to be parted from us! *You* have driven him away!"

"Hush, Livia!" Juliette lowered her voice and stepped toward Livia in a threatening way.

"*You* made a perfect fool of yourself over Angus! My much-missed brother. Of course he did not care for you, and now he is gone—Lord knows where. Pretending to be very immature and innocent, you have done a good deal of damage, Juliette, but you have met your match in me, I am not . . ."

"Have I? Have I? By God, you go too far, Livia! It's you who are deceitful and dangerous, and now you have insulted me! It's our custom, here in Georgia, Livia, to settle disputes and avenge insults directly, and I invite you to do so. Now!"

"Whatever do you mean?" Livia laughed.

"I mean that I challenge you to defend your honor, and I mine!" As Livia laughed harder, Juliette ran for the leather satchel and returned with it, throwing it down into the grass and pulling out the two long-barrelled duelling pistols.

"I am quite serious, Livia, and I advise you to be, also."

"You are serious about everything you do, and so silly at the same time, Juliette." Livia accepted the pistol Juliette held out to her and turned it over in her small hands.

Juliette backed away, holding the other, pointing it straight at Livia.

"I don't suppose you imagine it, but I am quite a good

shot," Livia said. "My brother taught me how to use a pistol, just for fun. But this old thing—where did you get this antique?"

"Watch out, Livia, I am ready for you," Juliette said in a strained voice, close to tears, high with fear and misery. In fact, she thought less about hurting Livia, although she wanted to, than the imminence of death. Death felt so close—she had never felt it so keenly as here, in this gloomy old ruined fort with the gray mists of twilight blowing in on a cold wind, with the eerie call of the whip-poor-will loud in her ears. Her hand trembled as she held out the heavy old pistol; she did not want to die, but she could not keep her mind from wandering into images of herself bloody and gasping, of a cruel piece of shot lodged in her brain or her breast, poisoning her, of her own body lying limp and breathless on the grass . . .

"Really, this is too silly," Livia said, and her aggravating tone of voice brought Juliette crashing back into the moment at hand. Juliette held out the pistol, her arm trembling uncontrollably; Livia examined the other pistol knowledgeably, lifting the hammer, turning it, and finally aiming it into the air and pulling the trigger.

Juliette stopped breathing, watching her. She waited.

There was no report.

"This old thing doesn't even work," Livia said with an air of irritation. She fiddled with the pistol again, then tried it a second time, aiming into a cypress tree. There was a harmless clicking.

"Some duelling weapon!" Livia said sharply. "You see how silly you are?"

Clenching her teeth, Juliette threw down the other pistol, and completely frustrated, lunged at Livia with a pent-up rage and violence that amazed them both.

"Damn you! Damn you! I can't *bear* you—I can't bear another minute, another second of your nasty superiority, I can't stand . . ."

Slapping and pinching, Juliette attacked Livia—a wildcat in pale green petticoats, her eyes blazing, her cheeks bright pink, her chestnut curls flying—scratching and ripping at Livia's bare arms, her shoulders, pulling at Livia's dark hair.

Livia was caught off guard. She staggered, stumbling backward, lifted her arms ineffectually to stave off

Juliette's ferocious blows. She gasped for air with a rasping sound.

Juliette was screaming and pressed her advantage. "Take that! There! There!" she yelled, "I hate you! Leave my brother alone! Do you hear me? Are you ready to give in?"

Livia tried to turn away, got part way, and tripped. She fell headlong into the grass and Juliette dove on top of her, pounding her back with her fists, sobbing now, in between breaths and her demand, "Are you? Are you?"

Livia struggled but Juliette sat across her back, then ripped her dress open with a violent jerk, and applied her fingernails to Livia's white back.

"Stop! You are mad! Stop! Oh, help! Help!" Livia managed to yell, crawling to her knees and scrambling to get away, with a loud ripping sound as her bodice separated from her skirt at the waist. Half-dressed, Livia could not move; she was entangled in her own clothes, her shawl had trapped her arms and her legs were caught by her skirt.

"Promise me," Juliette commanded, sitting atop Livia, "that you will leave my brother alone!"

"I will not! I won't! I won't promise anything, except . . ."

Juliette began to box Livia's ears.

"Owwww! Stop!"

"I shan't stop, until you promise!"

"Nooooo . . ." Livia moaned, stubbornly, although surely more weakly, and then her cry trailed off as both women heard the sound of a horse's hoofs, heard a rider approaching at a fast pace, and before they could get up, saw that it was Morgan Barstow.

In seconds he was there, sliding off his horse, his face aghast, shocked by the sight of his sister and Livia rolling around in the grass, Livia's dress ripped half off her, Juliette flushed with anger.

"What—what is going on here?" he demanded.

Juliette burst into tears.

"Get up, get up, Juliette! What has happened? I got your note, Livia, and I came at once. I don't understand at all. *What* has happened here?"

Sniffling, Livia rolled away from Juliette and shrieked, "Please, Morgan, help me! Your sister has gone completely mad. She has attacked me ferociously. . . . I can't believe it . . ."

"I hate her!" Juliette shouted, tears streaming down her face. "I absolutely hate her! I wish I had killed her, I tried to, and I wish I had! Oh, Morgan, help me!"

But Morgan, to Juliette's misery and astonishment, turned to help Livia.

"I am so sorry, I do apologize. I am distraught to see you so, Miss Livia. My sister has behaved shamefully, it appears. I am so sorry . . ." Scooping Livia up into his arms, Morgan set her on her feet and ran to lead her buggy horse nearer, then tied his own horse to the rear of the buggy and lifted Livia into the seat.

"I shall take you home directly, Miss Livia. Juliette, you'd better follow right along. You shall have to answer to Father for this. There is no help for it. You have behaved wickedly. I am so ashamed of you! This time you have gone too far!"

Juliette cried harder, and kicked her feet in fury, feeling totally betrayed, burying her face in the grass, shattered but unrepentant as she heard the buggy creak away and heard Morgan's dear, familiar voice apologizing endlessly to Livia and crooning words of comfort.

CHAPTER NINE

Morgan Is Caught; Angus Takes His Bride Home; A Wedding, A Party, A Funeral

"How could she have done such a thing?" Morgan asked, holding Livia close to him in the small buggy. He had wrapped her gently in her shawl and smoothed her hair, and Livia's color was returning. She had been quite pale but was not really hurt, save for some red scratch marks Juliette's fingernails had left on her back and shoulders.

"She is mad," Livia said simply. "And she is very immature, for her age, unfortunately. I'm sure it causes your parents a good deal of grief."

"And me, also," Morgan said. He wound the reins around his left hand so that he could encircle Livia with his right. She was half naked under the thin shawl and he could not help seeing that.

"I knew that something odd was happening when I got your sweet note," Morgan explained.

"She sent *me* a note, signed by you," Livia said. "Oh, Morgan, she is very jealous of . . . of my love for you."

"She is?" Morgan asked. His heart had leaped; he couldn't believe his ears. He loosened the reins and the horse slowed to a walk as he bent over to Livia, near trembling. "She . . . I mean, do you? Do you mean to say?"

"Yes, Morgan, I love you very much," Livia whispered, lowering her eyelids shyly, and batting them a bit, just a bit.

"You do?"

"Yes, I do, and not as a cousin loves her cousin. As a woman loves a man. I admire you, Morgan. I think you very handsome, and I shall love you until the end of my days."

"Oh, Livia!" Morgan exhaled. He dropped the reins and turned to her, taking her in his arms. "I think . . . no, I do love you, too, although I am so shy. I had been afraid to admit it to you. You are beautiful, Livia; any man would love you. But no one could love you more purely or faithfully than I!"

Livia cuddled into his embrace. It felt wonderful, strong, firm, utterly comforting. There was something fatherly about Morgan, she thought; he was so staid and sober and serious. Well, she would do her best to corrupt him.

"I am delighted to hear you say so," she whispered, and turned her face up for his kiss. It had grown dark, but the moon was full and shone on the scene with a pale, silvery light that caught her face. He noticed it and was struck by it; he hesitated.

She opened her eyes to see what was keeping him and saw him staring at her—like a big-eyed calf, she thought, rudely and cruelly. "Oh, Morgan," she sighed, "kiss me, please, darling."

And then he did, and his kiss was neither staid nor fatherly but eager and passionate. Livia opened her mouth to it, and responded to it gratefully, then with mounting passion. It was so long since she'd been kissed—far too long, she thought. I need this, she told herself; I must have it. I must have him.

Playfully, teasingly, she sucked at Morgan's lips and tongue, she ran her tongue along his teeth. He shuddered in excited pleasure; he had never been kissed like this; he had never made love to a woman. Although it was common for planters' sons to "sow wild oats" in the slave quarters, it would have been unthinkable for Morgan, at Sea Groves; it would have been totally contrary to his father's protective, paternalistic attitude toward his "people." Morgan had concealed and denied his sexual instincts, but he had never quite conquered them, and under Livia's experienced touch they surged to the fore.

"My darling, my darling," she whispered. "You are so passionate, so strong. You thrill me."

This confession stirred Morgan even more. Moaning, he

covered Livia's bare shoulders with soft kisses and experimentally touched her breasts.

"I can feel how excited you are," she went on. "Please, Morgan, lift me down. I want to feel all of your strong, handsome body against mine."

"Is it not . . . too cold?" Morgan asked breathlessly. He would never have suggested such a thing, but the idea delighted him.

"Your arms will keep me warm," Livia suggested, sliding out of the buggy, pulling Morgan behind her. "There." She stood on tiptoes and fit her body tightly against Morgan's. "Oh! Darling, I have never been so happy."

Morgan, who was hard with arousal, was embarrassed by the feeling of his penis against Livia's stomach, but instead of moving away from it, she pressed herself against him and wriggled.

"Oh, Livia, I love you so," he gasped.

"I can feel your desire for me," she said bluntly, and he blushed. He had never heard a woman speak so, never imagined that any woman would, but then she began kissing him even more passionately, and he forgot to speak.

Inevitably, instinctively, his hands moved to her breasts again. Her shawl fell back and access to them was easy. He bent his head and kissed her neck, her chest, the fullness of her breasts swelling above the white lace camisole. She trembled in pleasure and let her own hands drift downward to cup his buttocks and hold them in her hands, driving him on.

"Morgan," Livia begged, lifting her head so her throat was extended, slim and silver in the moonlight, "please make love to me . . . as a man does to the woman he loves."

"Do you want me to? Will you let me?" he gasped.

Her hands slid between them and felt for his penis. It was hard, and as she touched it and fondled it, he broke out into a sweat, and for a moment he saw everything bright red.

Dizzy, he clutched her and whispered into her ear, "Do you really want me to?"

"I do . . . if you truly love me."

"Oh, I do! Shall we be married, Livia?"

"Yes, I want to marry you," she said softly.

"I will do anything . . . anything . . . to please you,"

he promised. "But should we? Is it right? Shouldn't we wait?"

"Not if you truly love me and we plan to marry," Livia said.

He sighed, with all the wonder and pure bliss of extreme youth and desire, as she deftly unbuttoned his trousers and held his penis in her hand.

"Yes," she whispered, hoping only that Juliette would not choose this moment to come along the road. Why hadn't she suggested they pull the buggy farther into the bushes? "Hurry, darling," she said.

And hurry he did, stunned by the speed with which all this had happened, stunned by everything about it. Livia pulled up her own petticoats, thrust them aside, held Morgan's erect penis against herself and took it in easily, smoothly, delighted by the pleasure and relief she immediately felt.

"Oh, Livia, oh, my love!" Morgan shouted as he felt himself surrounded by exquisite warm wetness, swallowed up by it, by hot darkness, by a living vise, all more wonderful, more natural, more immediate than he had ever dreamed it could be.

"Oh, oh, yes!" Livia murmured, rocking herself into climax, such a welcome feeling, so missed, so needed, so overdue. And when it came, she clung to him, kissing his shoulder, wetting it with her kisses, whimpering a little, biting his soft skin in appreciation and relief.

"Darling, you are a wonderful lover," Livia said, finally, when he too had finished and held her for a long time, still unable to believe the wonderful turn his life had taken.

Anyone but Morgan would have sensed the comparative in her compliment, but Morgan did not.

"I am yours," he promised, "forever."

After spending the night in an inn, a drafty, flea-ridden establishment hardly suited for any sort of a romantic event, Angus Dunlie and Nancy Stone rode on past Lake Sinclair into the town of Eatonton, where they were married by a circuit-riding Methodist preacher.

Angus celebrated by buying Nancy a warm cape from an Indian woman, a doeskin cape with a hood and intricate red and green embroidery all around its hem, and a tame, sure-footed Indian pony to ride.

"You are my wife now," he explained to Nancy, and she smiled. He was not sure if she understood; it was hard to tell if she understood anything. She rarely spoke, but smiled increasingly often, and as they rode together along the narrow, wooded road back toward her father's home, she sang aloud, odd, lilting tunes he had never heard anywhere before. Her voice was delightful—clear and high and sweet—and Angus was content and sure that he had done the right thing.

He was less sure when they reached the Stones' establishment and he saw the look of thunderous astonishment on Pittman Stone's face as he met them at the gate.

"I have rescued Nancy from Doctor Poker—the man is cruel and a charlatan—and married her," Angus said proudly.

"Nancy is not well; she is not normal," Pittman said darkly.

"She is well enough for me; I have taken her as my wife and I intend to take care of her," Angus insisted.

"She will need constant watching," Pittman warned.

"I will buy her a slave woman who will stay at her side."

"Very well," Pittman said, "it's your own doing. But where do you intend to live? What do you intend to do?"

"I would like to put some money into your store and mill and live here, near you," Angus said. "Nancy will be happiest near her family. Her young sisters want to see her. And I would be proud to work with you."

"That we can discuss," Pittman said, but he was not opposed to the idea. Angus's determination to be part of the family was obvious and flattering. His own sons were gone; Angus was distant kin, after all, and he had accomplished what Pittman had thought impossible: Nancy was well married and would be looked after all her life.

And in the weeks that followed, Angus did all he had promised. He went into Augusta, and at the slave market there he bought a bright, handsome young mulatto named Rebecca to look after Nancy; he gave Pittman a considerable sum of money for an interest in his mill and store, and he bought one hundred acres of land adjacent to the Stones' and hired an overseer to look after its clearing. The land, which had belonged to a man who wanted to move farther west, had a small cabin on it, and Angus and Nancy and Rebecca moved into it.

In that small, one-room cabin, Angus and Nancy became man and wife in the full sense of the word, and he was pleased with that, too. Nancy was smooth-skinned and perfectly formed. She would do anything Angus asked her to, after he had showed her how. She was without fear or inhibitions. She would lie naked on the hearthrug all the evening while he read or made calculations by candlelight, and when he called her, she would come to him and please him exactly as he asked.

Sexually, it was both relaxing and calming. With her eyes wide open Nancy would take Angus into her mouth and hold him, gently, teasingly, for what seemed like hours, as he grew more and more excited and pretended to be interested in his book. When he could bear it no longer, he would enter her and enjoy her, never tiring of her saintly face and air of utter innocence.

It was a game to Nancy. She did not mind. If she relished it, no one knew. It was not something she spoke of; she spoke of few things, and usually they were games she had played with her baby sisters, or something she had seen in the store that she wanted.

Rebecca was never more than ten feet from Nancy, day or night, and Angus soon came to see the necessity of this. If she was left alone at all, Nancy would wander off. She would follow the Negroes into the field and—for all he knew and strongly suspected—would have done to them sexually all the things she did to him.

In time, when Nancy became pregnant and grew too big to interest Angus in the same way, he waited until she fell asleep and then took possession of Rebecca. The young mulatto woman was strong and very quick; she was witty and fast-moving; she was all the things Nancy was not, and Angus was delighted by the contrast and the combination.

For the first time in his life, Angus felt as if he were gaining control of his own life. He had acted boldly; he felt independent. He was pleased that he was about to become a father and satisfied with Pittman Stone's approval. The business of milling and selling was highly profitable and he looked forward to the day when he would be a rich, landed gentleman like the ones he had seen from afar in England. His ideal was something much grander and more gracious than the planters he had seen on the Georgia coast; his ambition was to build a manor house that would make Sea Groves look shabby and homespun. He affected a large, wide-brimmed hat for wearing in the sunshine, and quickly became a well-known figure in Washington County.

It was only then that he took paper and pen and carefully composed a letter to his father, reporting on all that he had accomplished.

As it happened, Angus's letter to his father arrived on the same day that Morgan and Livia were to be married. The news from Angus added to his father's happiness, which seemed nearly complete and was in direct proportion to the concealed distress of Roland and Jenny and Juliette, none of whom were at all pleased with the prospect of Livia becoming Morgan's wife and the prospective mistress of Sea Groves.

But Morgan had insisted. He was a man possessed, possessed by love—and lust. Since the first time he had made love to Livia, they had made love every day, with increasing ardor and confidence. He was mad for her and quite changed by his sudden plunge into sexual activity. He woke thinking of Livia's soft white body, aching to lie with her. He arrived late for everything, flushed red and dreamy-eyed. Every possible waking moment he spent at her side, neglecting his work, his friends, forgetting appointments, unable to focus on conversations or remember names.

Morgan was obsessed with Livia. He was deeply, helplessly in love for the first time in his life; everyone could see it, and bowing to the inevitable, Roland had given his permission for the wedding.

"There is no help for it," Roland told Jenny, in the privacy of their bedroom. There was a fire in the small fireplace, kindled by the slave girl Kitty while they still lay abed; now Kitty had left, and Jenny had risen to comb out her long hair. Roland stood at the window looking out toward the sea. It was a fine morning; the sky was a clear and cloudless blue; a hundred birds were singing; altogether it was a day that promised much and augured well for a wedding.

"I cannot adjust to the idea. Until it is firmly accomplished, I shall pray that it will not be," Jenny said bitterly. Stubborn as always, with the firm forthrightness that was as much a part of her nature as her sensitivity and charm, she had opposed Morgan's decision to marry—publicly at first, and now privately, confiding her apprehension and alarm to Roland.

"Dear wife, you must do nothing to stop it," Roland said.

"There is nothing that I can do, as you point out," Jenny said. "I do want my son to be happy, of course, but I can scarcely tolerate James Dunlie's pleasure in this. No, Roland, I have given up. As you say, there's no help for it. I shall smile and accept everyone's congratulations at the ceremony, you may be sure, but it is with an aching heart and a keen sense of wrong."

"*You* are as beautiful as the day we were wed," Roland said, leaning over Jenny as she sat at her dressing table.

"Oh, darling, of course I am not!" Jenny protested, but she was pleased.

The hour appointed for the ceremony was two in the afternoon, and carriages began to roll up the long avenue at noon. According to local custom, the wedding would take place at home, not at Christ Church, where the Barstows and all their neighbors met to worship—a rustic chapel under great broad-spreading oaks, a half mile east of old Frederica. The banns had been read there, however, and the minister from there would come to Sea Groves to perform the wedding rites. As befitted their position as one of the leading families on the island, the Barstows had issued a general invitation to all their fellow planters and parishioners to attend the wedding.

And come they did, the Butlers and the Coupers, the Baillies and the Pages. Captain Alexander Wylly, Lieutenant Colonel Wardrobe, and retired Captain John Fraser arrived in close sequence, greeted each other as ceremoniously as if they had not ridden to hounds together only the day before, and gratefully set to drinking Madeira in the parlor.

Jenny Barstow, who had dried her tears and mustered her strength and best spirits for the occasion, appeared in blue velvet, cut in the latest fashion from New York. The gown had been a gift from her friend Abby Warrington and suited her remarkably.

Everything is in order, everything looks well, Jenny told herself as she moved among the guests in the parlor and sitting rooms, smiling and greeting friends and neighbors with a brave show of happiness. The tables were spread with fruit cakes, pies, and puddings; a great Yule log blazed in the fireplace, and the downstairs rooms were all adorned with red-berried cassina and blue-berried cedar, glossy dark green magnolia leaves and delicate palmetto fans. Garlands of smilax festooned the doorways and mantels and encircled the huge silver punch bowl, full to brimming with a sweet and spicy rum punch.

Upstairs, Livia was dressing in her bedroom, and just down the hall, Juliette was dressing in hers. Against her wishes, over her most tearful and fervent protests, Juliette was to serve as Livia's bridesmaid.

"Please, Juliette, I ask you to do it as a special favor," Morgan had pleaded.

"She has no friends, that's why I must," Juliette had said spitefully.

"Please, Juliette. It will show Livia and everyone else that you two have resolved your differences . . ."

"Have we?"

"I hope you have. I pray that you have. Oh, dear sister, I so want you to share my happiness!"

"There is little chance of that!"

"Don't sound so . . . so bitter and miserable, Juliette. You know I don't love you any less, now that I have Livia to love, also."

"Oh, Morgan, you are impossible!"

"Nonetheless, you will do it? Juliette, she will never come between us, I promise. I will love and protect you all my life. Nothing has changed between us, I assure you."

"Oh, very well," Juliette had agreed, giving in. Poor Morgan, she pitied him; in the weeks since her tempestuous encounter with Livia in the ruins, she had struggled with her conscience and managed to come to terms with her negative feelings for Livia, or at least managed to bury them. Juliette was young; her moods were as violent and changeable as the weather; she bent like a willow and straightened up at once, and so had she recovered from her furious battle with Livia—who had been oddly reluctant to make an issue of it—and her father's stern scolding. Morgan was so hopelessly in love; the sight of it fascinated Juliette and she had made many notes in her journal, comparing what she could see of her brother's state of mind with her own, in the happier days when she had considered her love for Angus an interesting state.

Juliette, then, would attend Livia at her wedding, wearing a handsome gown of white velvet and a wreath of holly in her hair. Lizzy had buttoned her into the gown, and she stood now at the window, watching the guests arrive and waiting to be called downstairs.

The bride-to-be, at the same moment, was far from being prepared to descend the stairs. On her wedding day, Livia had awakened feeling dreadfully ill.

In fact, Livia had awakened feeling dreadfully ill every morning for more than a month, and she knew very well why it was: She was pregnant. She had known she was pregnant when she had seduced Morgan Barstow, she knew that the father of her child-to-come was her own brother, she had dealt with these realities alone. A lesser woman would have mourned and despaired; Livia raged and acted. There was no cure for her condition except matrimony, in the sense that it was a cure, and Livia had deliberately arranged it. It had worked out well enough, better than she thought she deserved, even, but she was not one to disparage herself—she was far too keenly aware of her own needs and she focused, instead, on how to satisfy them.

After waking, then, Livia had drunk some hot tea, tossed it into a chamber pot, drunk some more, and gone back to bed to lie flat in bed, her eyes shut, passively waiting for the dreadful dizzy, nauseous feelings to pass. They would pass, she knew; they did pass, finally, toward noon, every day, and at noon she rose, weakly, quite pale, and allowed her maid to arrange her hair and lace her into a corset.

"Ouch, damn you, you clumsy thing!" Livia complained as the corset cut into her swelling belly and thickened waist.

"Ah'm sorry, miss. Seems like it don't fit as good as las' week," the maid said mischievously, and Livia boxed her ears for her impertinence.

"It fits well enough," she said, and put up her arms for

the white satin gown that she had long since had sent from England, anticipating her wedding even before she had known the identity of her bridegroom.

I look lovely, she told herself, and pinched her cheeks in front of the looking glass as the maid piled her hair up on her head. And at least Papa is pleased; well, of course, Morgan is pleased, too.

"My pearl necklace," she told the maid. The pearls had been her mother's; the earrings, which matched beautifully, a wedding present from Roland and Jenny. Livia was well aware of her prospective family's feelings about her, but she could not help it, nor did she care. I am not used to a mother's love, she had reflected, and I have my own father's. Still, she missed Angus. Morgan's passionate lovemaking had only made her miss him more acutely, and resent Juliette all the more for having, as she thought of it, "driven him off."

No sooner was she dressed than Livia heard the grandfather clock in the downstairs hallway striking two. Fighting a last surge of nausea, she rose and stepped into white satin slippers. There was a knock on her door.

"Come in, Father," she called out, and James Dunlie entered, dressed in his finest and beaming with delight.

"Be off," he said to the maid, and then, taking Livia's hands into his, "what you are doing today pleases me immensely. You know that."

"Yes, Father."

"You will be mistress of Sea Groves one day; your children—my grandchildren—will be born here! It is *just* what I wanted when I came back to Georgia, and I have accomplished it in far less time than I thought I would need. I acknowledge that it has been possible because of the obedience and cooperation both you and Angus have shown me. You are a good daughter, Livia. I am well pleased with you. And . . ." James reached dramatically into the pocket of his tangerine brocade waistcoat and pulled out a letter, "I have received a letter from Angus."

Livia flushed with excitement. "Oh! Tell me what he says!"

"He has found a home with our relatives in Washington County. He has established himself well there. He has married the daughter of the family, and he expects her to bear his child soon!"

"No!" Livia's eyes widened with shock and then narrowed with jealousy. "Does he ask for me?"

"Of course he does, my dear."

"Give me the letter! Let me see it!"

"Certainly, my dear," James Dunlie said smoothly. He knew the attachment between his children was strong, and he did not regret it. It made both of them more vigorous in their family feeling.

"I read slowly, Father. Let me carry it with me and savor it later," Livia suggested, and her father watched her slip the letter into the pocket of her wedding gown.

"Miss Livia! Mister James! It's time!" Judina called at the door.

"Take my arm, dear daughter," James said, smiling like a cream-sated cat, and together they descended the stairs to the parlor, where everyone was waiting.

Two hours later, the ceremony had been conducted, the vows exchanged, toasts made "to the newly married couple," "to their parents," "to President Jefferson," "to the memory of General Washington," "to the governor," "to the memory of General Oglethorpe," "to the land we live in," "to the wine we drink," and finally "to the day itself," the roast turkey and duck and suckling pig carried in from the kitchens, the big punch bowl emptied and refilled several times; the children had been released to roll hoops and chase puppies on the lawn, the candles had been lighted, and the dancing had begun.

"Darling wife—how sweet the name is to me—I am so happy!" Morgan whispered to Livia, leading her to the first quadrille. "Are you as happy as I am?"

"Very likely," Livia said, smiling her secret smile. She touched the letter from Angus deep in her pocket. The expression of discontent on Aunt Jenny's face was alone enough to amuse her.

"Tonight we shall sleep in the same bed," Morgan said contentedly.

Tonight and forevermore, Livia thought. With luck, Morgan would not notice her thickened waist until she was ready to tell him. How delighted he would be! She had drunk a good deal of French champagne and the thought made her giggle, for after all she was very young and had succeeded in solving a serious problem without either strain or difficulty.

"I adore your laugh," Morgan said. "I declare, it's infectious!" He laughed, too, and the sound made poor Aimee wince. Aimee was heartbroken to see Morgan, whom she loved wholeheartedly and without hope, married to Livia. She had borne the weeks of their engagement poorly; she had languished, and tomorrow she would set sail for New York. Is he laughing at me, Aimee wondered. I suppose they all are. Well, I shall never forget him, never, and never love any other man half so well.

Aimee looked around the room for Juliette and saw her dancing with a young rice planter from across the island, a handsome dark-haired man in a scarlet coat. As ever, Juliette's spirits were as changeable as the skies, and the proximity of friends, music, and her favorite brown-sugar cake were enough to put her in a good mood, despite Livia.

"I expect you'll be the next to marry," the young planter said to Juliette teasingly.

"I have decided never to marry," Juliette said.

"You will when the right man asks you."

"Not at all. I intend to live an independent life, to read and study . . . and perhaps to write. Life is full enough without marriage. Marriage is slavery, I believe. It drives one to moral crimes and constricts the mind."

The young man laughed. "Juliette, you say the most extraordinary things, really you do! I know no other girl like you."

"That is very likely," Juliette said, whirling so that her white velvet skirt swayed gracefully and giving a little leap, just for fun.

Jenny Barstow stood at the side of the parlor, watching her two children dancing—Juliette with their neighbor, and her son, Morgan, with his new wife. More than ever, the sight of Livia and Morgan pained her, and unlike Juliette, she was not diverted by the party and the congregation of their friends and neighbors.

Jenny's mood, which had been low at the start of the day, had sunk further during its course, and the rum punch, which she had drunk with atypical liberality, had depressed rather than cheered her.

I cannot bear the sight of them, cannot bear it, she

thought, and with tears of disappointment and frustration in her eyes she fled from the parlor, the wedding guests, and the sound of the violin playing for dancing. What I told Abby is still true, she thought. I feel as passionate and unruly as a girl of sixteen. I am still ruled by my emotions. . . . I have none of the calm and serenity I always expected I'd have at this age.

So thinking, Jenny gave in to tears and ran to hide herself—just for a moment—in her *cabinet*, a small room, little more than an alcove, set off from the dining room. It had been used as a morning room when the house was first built, and Jenny now used it as her office for keeping household records and receipts. It was her private sanctuary, and she was amazed, when she burst into it, to see that it had been invaded.

At her desk, on which he had set a half-empty decanter of brandy, sat James Dunlie.

"Oh!" Jenny gasped. "What are you doing here? This is *my* office!"

Dunlie jumped. In truth, he had been looking over Jenny's private papers and journals as he drank brandy. He had drunk an enormous amount of brandy during the afternoon, and he was very drunk. He looked up at Jenny, whose green eyes were glowing in outrage.

"Excuse me, Mrs. Barstow. I thought I was alone. You must pardon me."

"Why? Why must I?"

James Dunlie laughed. He was drunk enough to be very relaxed; he had lost all inhibitions and taken on a few delusions, one of which was that he was very powerful, another that no woman could resist him. Although caught trespassing in her office, he felt no guilt toward Jenny or sense that he had overstepped the bounds of courtesy, and seeing her, so rosy and stimulated, the years fell away, and in his mind they were back in Savannah, in the old days, the days of the Revolution, when they had both lived in his mother's house and he had lusted after her.

"You must because I ask you to, Mrs. Barstow . . . although I confess you are always Jenny to me, and have always been . . ."

"What are you doing here, Mr. Dunlie?"

"The same thing you are, I expect—getting a few minutes' relief from the collection of bores and lumpkins you call neighbors. Ah, Jenny, we are still so much alike, we two! I rejoice to see our children married, although I suspect it displeases your husband. It's right, this wedding—the symbolic coming together of the two branches of our family, severed so many years ago . . ."

Listening, Jenny seethed and reddened with anger and resentment. Was there no limit to his presumptions? He misunderstood everything, interpreted everything according to his own views, his own desires. And he had the gall to assume that she would side with him, against her beloved husband, Roland.

"We are not alike! We have never been alike!" she said, almost speechless with rage.

"Perhaps you are right. Perhaps that is why we have always been so special to each other," Dunlie said, draining his brandy glass and filling it again. "But where are my manners? Would you take a seat? Would you like some cognac? Your husband has imported a very fine brandy. I find it delicious."

"No, I will not sit with you," Jenny said. Thinking so fast she amazed herself, she was concocting a plan, an outrageous plan but a powerful one, a plan that would hush James Dunlie for once and for all. She was dizzy with anger and still aware of it, but slipping ever closer and closer to the edge. She was about to act recklessly, without forethought, out of passion.

"Not here," she amended. "It is too public here."

Dunlie's head lifted. "What? Where?"

"You are right," Jenny lied. "I too am weary of this crowd. Let's go together . . . for a drive along the beach. Yes, never mind the rest of them! We shall be together . . . and talk. I don't believe we've had a private conversation, James, all the time you've been here."

"No, no, we haven't," Dunlie said. He was too drunk to remember how assiduously Jenny Barstow had avoided being left alone with him, how unlikely it was that she should arrange a private rendezvous. Her suggestion flattered him, it fed his self-esteem and stiffened his masculine pride.

"Meet me in the orange grove," Jenny said as coquettishly as she could manage, nearly choking on the suggestion of infidelity. When she turned away, her stomach ached, and she clenched her teeth, but her resolve was ever firmer.

"How soon?" Dunlie asked eagerly.

"I will get my carriage and be there in ten minutes," Jenny promised. "I will tell the groom I have to leave suddenly to visit a sick neighbor. Will you be there, in ten minutes, ready to drive with me?"

"Yes, yes."

"Very well, then," Jenny said and fled as James Dunlie up-ended the brandy decanter into his glass. She did not see him, but she did hear his laugh, and the sound of it rankled and drove her on.

Dunlie was staggering when he left the cabinet a few minutes later, and burped as he passed through the dining room, sending the maids into giggles. "Stand aside, stand aside," he muttered, navigating the passage with difficulty, knocking over a ladder-backed chair. Through the doorway he caught sight of Roland talking with Captain Wylly in the parlor and felt a secret satisfaction that Jenny was willing to leave the wedding party to be with him, satisfaction, but no surprise, for he had always fancied Jenny, since she was a girl of sixteen, and she was still a handsome woman, damned handsome.

The raw cool air outside sobered him up, just a bit, but enough so that he called to a servant to bring him a bottle of brandy, and waited on the verandah to take it before he walked toward the orange grove.

Jenny had moved very quickly after she left James Dunlie inside, and with fierce determination. Within the ten minutes she was perched high in a neat black two-seater, her brand-new buggy, a stylish creation with a silk-lined hood, two big-spoked wheels, and high sides.

"It's gettin' on toward dark," she told Lorry. "Please light the torches."

"Yes, Miss Jenny. You mean you leavin' the party?" the groom asked.

"Just for a little drive," Jenny explained, "and I want to be able to find my way back, Lorry."

"Yes, ma'am." He smiled, and Jenny matched his smile with one of her own. She fastened the side door, locked it, and with both torches smoking and blazing, drove the carriage out the back drive to the orange grove.

It was nearly dark, and a soft purple twilight hung over

the plantation. Stars were beginning to come out in the sky, and the sea air was bracing. How I love this place, she thought, and how many happy years I have spent here. When this is over, I will spend more, and they will be happier for what I am about to do. It will look like an accident; no one will guess that it is not.

When she was out of sight of the stables and the quarters, she opened a silk satchel she had at her feet and doused the roof, the side, and the seat of the carriage with the entire contents of a large bottle of paraffin she had taken from the supply closet. It was enough to fill three lamps; it was highly flammable and nearly odorless; when it had penetrated the side pillows, she smiled.

James Dunlie was waiting at the edge of the orange grove, already a silvery bower of shining star-shaped flowers sparkling against the dark green leaves, all of it strongly perfumed with the sweet, heavenly fragrance that, to Jenny, was and always had been one of the most delightful aspects of living at Sea Groves.

"It's so lovely, isn't it? Such a beautiful fragrance!" she called out as the carriage neared James Dunlie.

Dunlie was too drunk to smell anything but brandy, but he looked at Jenny's shining face with the admiration and wonder it deserved.

"Yes, yes," he mumbled.

Jenny's carriage was drawn by two spirited black horses—both restless from standing all day in the stable. The sleek creatures shied nervously at Dunlie, so that she had to turn the carriage in a circle before they would stop to let Dunlie climb up.

"Here, let me take the reins," he said.

"Oh, no, I am used to it," she said, sliding over so that he could sit next to her.

Dunlie missed the step up on his first try, and caught at the carriage door clumsily.

"Jump up!" Jenny called.

"Dammit, I cannot!" Dunlie shouted. "Can't you hold those horses down?"

"Just a minute," Jenny promised, pulling in on the reins to force the horses in a tight circle, turning the carriage again so that the big wheel on the left side was near James Dunlie, standing rather helplessly with a bottle in one hand.

"Now!" she shouted. "Jump up now!"

And jump he did, but not without catching his long, full cambric sleeve in the leaping sooty flame of the torch on the outside of the carriage, not without losing his footing and pitching into the carriage almost on top of Jenny.

In one minute it was too late. The carriage door swung open, then slammed shut. The little fire from Dunlie's shirt sleeve touched the paraffin-soaked side cushion and touched off a fierce, crackling blaze. That blaze leapt to the roof of the buggy and raced to the opposite side; in less than a minute, the entire carriage was ablaze.

"Help! Help!" Jenny screamed. This was not what she had planned; she had planned to jump well clear of the carriage and then toss a torch in. She panicked. Flames caught at the hem of her dress and raced up it. The door on her side was a panel of fire. The roof was a canopy of fire. The horses shrieked and bolted. She lost the reins and fell forward onto her knees.

"Fire! Jesus help us!" Dunlie wailed. He scrambled to secure his footing, to stand so that he could jump free. In doing so he up-ended the brandy bottle onto Jenny's dress and she was enveloped in a sheet of flames. Dunlie lay across her lap, kicking and struggling to rise, his sleeves burning, his face alight with horror.

Jenny knew, too, and in the seconds that passed before the smoke and fire carried her into a shocked oblivion, she screamed, crying out for Roland.

Roland heard her cry, clearly and horribly, and was the first to run out of the big house as the burning carriage, a golden chariot of fire, plunged out of the dim, sweet-smelling orange grove and hurtled through the twilight.

"Jenny! Jenny!" Roland shouted.

Stampeding, stumbling, nearly falling in their desperate struggle to escape the burning carriage, the horses dragged the fiery wreck close to the stables, then, spooked, turned and ran on toward the beach. There were a few seconds of silence, then an explosion of screams from the wedding guests, from the slaves running out of their houses and the kitchen as well as from the big house.

"Stop! Stop!" Roland yelled, pursuing the carriage on foot with half a hundred blacks behind him.

"It's my father! Father's there, see! See!" Livia shrieked,

breaking away from Morgan's grasp and running behind Roland.

"Catch it!" Roland bellowed, and a dozen young men on horseback took off after the carriage, chasing it toward the sea, leaving behind a circle of guests turned mourners, shocked and weeping.

But by the time they reached the horses and carriage, it was too late. The carriage traces burned enough to break, and the horses bolted, and the carriage stood deep in sand with the waters of the Atlantic washing up its burning wheels.

Jenny Barstow was dead, her body horribly charred, and James Dunlie was unconscious. Roland took Jenny's poor body into his arms and carried it back to the house, where he refused to be parted from it, but held it, weeping unconsolably, far into the night, surrounded by his family and some of his neighbors.

James Dunlie lingered, only a few hours, but long enough so that Livia first had hope he would recover, then slowly lost it, long enough so that she could see how little any of the Barstows cared about her father, in the face of their shocked mourning for Jenny, and long enough so that the experience hardened her heart against Morgan's family, and made her vow bitter revenge against them.

So she phrased it in the letter she wrote to her brother Angus the next day, telling him in one letter of her own marriage and their father's death.

"I am a Barstow now," she wrote, in her square, childish hand, and wrote with much difficulty, for she was not scholarly, "but in name only, dear Angus. And now that I am so close to the family, I see that our father was right—they are our mortal enemies. Indeed, Angus," and here Livia set down her pen and thought about what she suspected until she believed it was true, believed it was fact, "they are responsible for our father's death. It will be hard for you to bear it, but 'tis true. She lured him into her carriage, she set the fire . . ."

I swear, 'twas so, Livia thought, with uncanny accuracy, with one of those intuitive flashes of which she was always capable, so natural and instinctive was her understanding of evil. I know it, I know it's so, if they all call her a saint! She hated father; she never liked me. I *know* it was so!

"I tell you, Angus," Livia concluded her letter, "they have killed our father, and 'tis now due to us, as his children, the last of the Dunlies, to avenge his death, to seize without hesitation what is rightfully ours, as he would have wished it, to the utmost of our strength. I long to see you, brother, and live for the day when we shall be together again. Ever, your beloved sister, Livia."

And thus, with hardened hearts, with hatred and bitterness within, the Barstow family buried both Jenny and James Dunlie on the first day of the new year, on a day as cold and gray as the reality of their loss, a day when swift-moving clouds scudded over Saint Simons Island at midday, when the Barstow family and their friends and neighbors met in the small gloomy graveyard behind Christ Church to see the two coffins borne into the churchyard on the shoulders of sixteen strapping field hands from Sea Groves.

Everyone was there, even Aimee, who had stayed on to keep Juliette company in her misery and mourning, and there was not a one of them who did not weep, not even Livia, sick as she was that morning and bad-tempered as she had been ever since her wedding, to the confusion and pain of her young husband.

" 'Tis a sad day for the beginning of a new year," Morgan whispered to Livia, as they settled themselves back into their carriage for the lonely ride back home.

"One for one," Livia muttered, but Morgan could not make out her meaning.

"What is it, dear?" he asked gently.

"Our time will come," Livia said, and Morgan, thinking she meant theirs, sympathetically patted her hand.

CHAPTER TEN

Georgia Grows Like Cotton; Brother and Sister Meet Again: A Misunderstanding

It is often said that time seems to pass very quickly when we are happy and slowly when we are not, but it is not always so, for the slow, golden days of childhood pass, for most of us, like smooth round beads on a long string, each day much like the last, and each without much presentiment of change or awareness of it.

And so passed the next twenty years for the Barstows at Sea Groves—although each of them might not have claimed to be happy. Roland never recovered from his Jenny's death, but seemed to age and crumble as slowly and surely and irrevocably as a sea cliff, becoming almost immediately deferent to Morgan's decisions and direction, relinquishing responsibility, becoming forgetful and distracted, waiting only, if he admitted it, to die and be united again with the woman he had so long and totally loved. Juliette would not have called herself happy, although hers was perhaps a restless, creative discontent that set her to constant reflection and self-examination, as well as a vigilant watch on her sister-in-law, whom she not inaccurately suspected of malice and sabotage in every part of their lives.

Juliette, in fact, did not seem unhappy; she was the light and comfort of her father's life, and served as the hostess and mistress of Sea Groves, as it was not a position precisely to Livia's liking. To her father's deep regret and everyone's surprise, Juliette had kept the promise not to marry that she had made so gaily and casually to her dancing partner at Morgan's wedding. Despite many suitors and several sincere proposals, she passed the years in maidenhood, the belle of many a ball, growing prettier as she gained in confidence and more charming as she became more mature, although with an edge to her wit that gained her a certain reputation, all the way to Savannah, for being "sharp."

Sharp she was, and more than that—Juliette as a young woman was deep as a well and still sparkled like a running brook. She did not cry so frequently anymore, but still changed her mood as others changed their hats, was still quick to understand and sympathize, quick to anger, quick to forgiveness. She still kept her journal, and lately, on the sly, for she was as secretive as ever (as secretive as her sister-in-law, in fact), she had tried to write some little stories with the idea of publishing them in the Savannah *Gazette* or the Brunswick *Advocate,* although as yet she had not summoned the courage to send them in.

How much Juliette's aversion to matrimony had to do with Angus Dunlie, her childish passion for him and the wrenching circumstances of their night together and their parting, no one ever knew, but it is true that she thought of him often, and never without pain and confusion.

Livia Barstow thought of Angus, too, corresponded with him privately, and spoke of him from time to time. It was not Livia's way to withhold her opinions, as the rest of the family learned, nor was it her way to accept gracefully any tasks she did not fancy. So it was that Juliette had taken over the duties of plantation mistress and hostess. Livia was content to be Morgan's wife and, in an ever-increasing capacity, the mother of his children. Their first son, christened Caleb James, came into the world a scant six months after their wedding, a chronology that went largely unobserved and unmarked, due to the atmosphere of mourning and sadness which persisted far longer. Caleb, a sickly baby, was fretful and troublesome from the start, and Livia was slow to recover from the ordeal of childbearing. Although Caleb was tended night and day by an experienced slave woman, Livia made much of the responsibilities of motherhood and used it as her excuse for permanently relinquishing the other plantation duties to Juliette.

And so it was that Morgan took over the responsibilities of his father: planning for the setting out of cotton and rice, supervising the work of a large and ever-increasing labor force of slaves, handling accounts and arranging for new equipment, for supplies, for marketing, and overseeing the shipment of the crop to Savannah each fall. Juliette, likewise, filled her mother's role: instructing and managing and educating a horde of domestic slaves—housemaids, seamstresses, cooks—and training their children to do the smaller chores and to run errands. To all of them she was Miss Juliette, the last resort in times of sickness, childbirth, or trouble, on call at any moment of the day, a constant responsibility which Juliette accepted as her natural one.

And so the years passed, not without their pleasures and celebrations, both on Saint Simons Island and inland, where the Stones and Angus Dunlie and his family lived and prospered, seeing much more radical and rapid changes than his coastal cousins. Inland, it was a time of the first steamboats on the rivers, of cotton factories springing up wherever there was water power, of the first railroads, of new cities and towns, and a constant push westward. The era of the traveler on horseback or ox-cart ended; everything changed swiftly and more swiftly as Georgians spilled over the Broad River, then the Oconee, Ocmulgee, Flint, and finally the Chattahoochee, taking up the rich land formerly held by the Indians, and planting it, first the small farmer and then the land-greedy cotton planter.

It was cotton that changed the face of Georgia—everyone said so, and everyone was right. Nothing so characterized the early decades of the nineteenth century as the sight and sound and smell of cotton growing in the rich, black earth and being ginned and baled and moving away from the plantations toward the markets—moving down the rivers on steamboats and through the woods on the backs of mules.

Georgia's land had been created by God for growing cotton. The institution of slavery made it possible to plant and cultivate vast acres. The cotton gin made removing the tough black seeds easier and faster, and the Industrial Revolution in Old and New England created a market for it—a market that consumed all Georgia and her sister states could produce.

Everywhere was cotton, cotton, cotton. Cotton inspired

the pioneers swinging axes in the new land up-country, cutting down pines to clear fields. Slaves poling rafts and longboats down the rivers from Augusta sang of it; teamsters driving heavy wagons into the market towns sang of it. Planters dreamed of it—of boom crops that came year after year, each better than the last, despite the temporary recession after the War of 1812 which left Savannah with a tremendous revival of trade and made Augusta the new center of the cotton kingdom.

Cotton brought cash to the upper river country, and cash stimulated commerce, creating a market for every other sort of goods. Angus Dunlie had anticipated this, and he exploited it. In the twenty years that saw Morgan Barstow pledge himself completely to the cotton economy, Angus diversified, opening a slave market in Milledgeville, a large general store in Athens, and enlarging the lumber mill in Washington. When Pittman Stone died, he left all his goods to his son-in-law, the father of his grandchildren—for Nancy's first pregnancy had been followed by another, and another, and three little boys, all sturdy and quick, occupied the days of their mother and her maid Rebecca, whose own three children were clearly also Angus's. Like so many ducklings, the Dunlie children fought and played and ran and tumbled and swam together, white and black, all of them protective of Nancy and in awe and fear of their father.

Angus Dunlie bought land, too, with the profits from his mercantile enterprises, for large tracts of land were still changing hands in those days as men pushed westward. Westward . . . the progress of the state was always westward—west by north for the first part of the new century, later to be west by south—and as the onward-moving population deserted the old frontier towns, new ones grew up. Macon on the Ocmulgee was laid out in 1823 and five years later became a great cotton market. Columbus on the Chattahoochee began as a cluster of rough log cabins and grew into a manufacturing center.

The state capital was moved to Milledgeville, nearer the center of the state. Augusta, now a well-established cotton market, grew and took on some of the grace notes of civilization: building an academy, forming a Thespian Society and a Library Society as the wagons loaded high with cotton still rumbled onto Broad Street, bound for the wharves where steamboats and a fleet of flatboats waited to take on cotton for the trip downriver to Savannah.

And Savannah, proud Savannah, was still the Queen City of Georgia. Savannah had much to inspire pride—with her broad streets, laid out so long ago by the far-seeing General Oglethorpe, now lined with flourishing pride-of-India trees, her riverfront warehouses and counting houses and taverns busy all day and all night. She was still the cultural center of the state with her theaters, her portrait painters, her dancing masters newly arrived from Paris and London, her new Public Library, her Golf Club, her Jockey Club, her Chatham Academy, and her flourishing, much-lamented tradition of duels to the death, fought blatantly in full view of the city at the Jewish cemetery or at Fort Wayne on the waterfront. Almost anything could provoke a duel: a toast to a New England politician, an anti-Irish jingle, a suggestion of a gentleman's dishonesty, a suspicion of cheating at cards, an argument over politics or the quality of a bottle of Madeira, or a slur on a local lady's honor.

But cities like these, and even towns, were the exception in Georgia. Georgia was an agricultural state in a society already changing from the purely agricultural. Cotton was king, and despite her varied climate, topography, and soils, Georgia resisted efforts to develop a diversified agriculture or to turn wholeheartedly toward commerce, manufacturing, or shipping. Land was cheap and plentiful, and slave labor—except for the initial investment, which in many families had been made generations back, and small expenses of upkeep—was free. Inevitably, large plantations grew up in the up-country, and though plantations were economic organizations and businesses, they were more than that as well—they were the symbol of southern living. Everyone aspired to be a planter; even in the most remote backwoods counties, men nourished the ideal of the English country gentleman and a stern code of conduct that upheld personal honor; hand in hand with the mania for cotton went the growth of an odd (and largely un-American) uncommercial spirit.

Thus, the cotton factor was the power behind the throne of King Cotton, but his wealth bought him no prestige. Nor did that of Georgia's few merchant princes, those who, like Angus Dunlie, bought and sold goods, acting as middlemen to the planters and the importers. Dunlie, though, with his eye to the old ideal, kept his plantation on the side, and built, in the flush years after the war with England in 1812, a grand English-style manor house outside Milledgeville. To his satisfaction Dunlie enjoyed a reputation in his county for being a gentleman with foreign connections and an immense fortune.

For after all, Angus Dunlie did have a good head for business. He had extended Pittman Stone's pioneering enterprises into a considerable network of going concerns. Angus was changed. Somewhere at his core he had mellowed; his marriage had changed him, that odd arrangement with pale, absent Nancy and capable dark-skinned Rebecca. In ways that he had never anticipated, the years brought him peace, and his way of life satisfied him. Many years passed before he traveled east to Savannah, although Livia in her infrequent letters begged him to do so.

Finally, in the fall of 1820, he decided to go, and left his wives and family to make the long journey back to the coast, where he planned to see his business agent, visit Savannah, and have a reunion with his sister Livia, who had arranged to be staying at the Barstow house in town.

Livia Dunlie Barstow, who expected her brother soon, although she could not know exactly when, awoke on an early September morning in 1820 in the largest bedroom of the house on Abercorn Street, the room where her grandparents had slept, where her father had been suckled as an infant. She did not wake alone, as she did not choose to sleep alone.

Livia, in name the mistress of Sea Groves, the wife of the distinguished, widely-loved, respected planter Morgan Barstow, was in many respects little changed from the willful, petulant girl of twenty who had come to Savannah for the first time twenty years earlier. She was still willful, demanding, and outspoken. She was often dissatisfied, although she made it a habit to demand and secure, as much as was humanly possible, exactly what she wanted.

"Chester!" Livia called, opening her eyes part way and seeing that the room was flooded with golden sunshine.

There was no reply from the man lying next to her, naked, still sleeping, completely covered by a sheet.

"Chester!" Livia called again, poking his shoulder. An

elbow, mahogany-brown, large, smooth-skinned, poked out of the tangle of bedclothes. Good Lord, Livia thought, I feel perfectly dreadful. My neck is stiff, my head feels as if it may split, my vital arteries are constricted.

"Get up!" she whined. "Open the window! I am sick! I must have air!"

Chester woke with a start. He was barely nineteen, recently chosen by Livia to be her carriage driver, and quite unused to being where he was, unused to drinking wine as they had last night, unused to being singled out by the mistress for her attentions—although he knew there had been others before him, many others, and he knew that some of them had left the plantation after a term as Livia's carriage driver, never to return.

Chester was grateful for Miss Livia's selecting him—how could he not be grateful? Here he was in Savannah, where he had never even dreamed of being, to say nothing of being in Miss Livia's own bed! Yet he was frightened and unsure of what to do. The best thing to do, reason told him, was exactly what Miss Livia asked; it was his only duty, and his only hope for surviving this unexpected interlude in another world.

"Yes, Miss Livia," he said, scrambling out of bed, stumbling to the window. "But Miss Livia, they say the fever come in with the mornin' air."

"Never mind what they say, Chester. Mind what I say."

"Yes, Miss Livia."

"Ohhhhh! I feel ill! How much wine did we drink last night, Chester?"

"All of it, ma'am."

"All of it? Four bottles? Impossible. Don't lie to me, you bad boy. Further, open it wide. Ah . . ."

Chester stood in front of the window, naked, confused. He was broad-shouldered, slim-hipped, and well muscled. Last night Livia had looked at him with approval and lust; today she glared at him through narrowed eyes and cursed him.

"Damn you, Chester! Don't just stand there. Go down to the kitchen and order me some tea. Don't go like that! Dress! And wash yourself. And then come back here . . . to me."

"Yes, Miss Livia." Chester pulled on his tight purple trousers and a loose, long-sleeved shirt dyed brown. He would do all he could to please his mistress; he had pleased her last night—he knew enough about women to know that—and it appeared that white women were just like black women, after all. Who would have guessed it?

Livia lifted her head from the feather pillows. "Don't stand there grinnin', you monkey! Run! Ohhhh, my poor head."

I must get him some decent clothes, Livia thought. Perhaps livery. She had seen it on some of the carriage drivers along the road up from Darien. It would be worth it, no matter how long she kept Chester on, and he seemed promising. He was young enough, wonderfully vital, tractable, and yet so massive that he offered her that edge of fear that she liked to have along with the pleasure of it. He could hurt me, Livia thought, titillating herself with the thought; he could break me in two, but of course he doesn't dare. He's not stupid, not at all. I suppose he has white blood in him somewhere; although he's dark as Lucifer, his face . . . and nose is narrow, and his lips are thin for a darky's.

"Good Lord, my head," Livia moaned. How had she drunk so much? In truth, she did not recall the latter part of the evening at all. She had dined with some friends of Roland's—terrible bores, really, with their endless talk of Missouri entering the union as a slave state. For some reason this did not please them, although she'd be damned if she could see why not. All her life she had heard Americans talk politics—they seemed to thrive on it—and never had it made, to her, the slightest sense.

After dinner she had driven with Chester along the riverfront, seeking a cool breeze. It was very hot for September, and drippingly humid, of course; when was it not in Georgia? Savannah was horribly damaged—there had been a fire at the beginning of the year, a dreadful, devastating fire that had burned for two days and destroyed more than four hundred and fifty houses. They said that the destruction totaled four million dollars, but already a great deal of rebuilding was taking place, and she had been curious to see it. The ride had soothed her and excited her at the same time, for the spicy night air stimulated her nerves, and she had decided that it was as good a time as any to take Chester into her bedroom and try him.

So she had, and there had been four bottles of wine in a leather case—that she remembered. But then . . .

"Yes, Miss Livia," he said, his head wet from the dunking he had given it in a bucket of water.

"Kneel down here, near me," Livia instructed, "and rub . . . there. Yes, and there. Ummm. Your hands are so big, Chester. I know I shall feel better when you . . . massage me. Yes, just so. Now harder. Harder. Ummm."

Chester complied, nearly dizzy with the nearness of his mistress, a woman who had been a far-off deity to him all his life; not that there wasn't talk about the mistress in the quarters, but he had never expected to see for himself how true it was. Slowly, firmly, he rubbed Livia's soft, white skin, kneading her shoulders and back. His thick penis rose against his stomach, blood-gorged and erect, and he tried to hide it, but Livia was watching out of the corner of her eye.

"Why, Chester! Look at you. I don't believe you learned a thing from the lessons I tried to teach you last night. Did you?"

"I . . . uh . . . I don' know, miss . . ."

"You are so big, Chester. I declare, you are a . . . brute!" And she laughed delightedly.

What shall I do? What shall I do? Chester agonized. His own head ached; it was terribly stuffy in the upstairs bedroom; he was as afraid as he was stimulated; he was as unsure as he was confused. Then, remembering how she had reacted last night, he leaned forward and began to bite the skin on Livia's back, taking small but distinct nibbles of it, and let his hands slide around to knead her big, soft breasts, as roughly as he dared.

"Ohhhhh . . ." Livia sighed. She writhed in pleasure and began to whimper like a puppy. Instantly excited, she felt sweat bead in the small of her back, felt her nipples harden under his huge, rough hands, felt her legs slide apart. "You beast, you animal," she said in a strange, low voice, and began to wrestle with him, to fight against his grip, all the while whispering "yes, yes, don't stop, don't stop, you nasty brute, yes!"

A few hours later, just after noon, when Angus Dunlie rode into the yard of the Barstow house on Abercorn Street, he was informed that Miss Livia was still abed.

Angus grinned. So much had changed in Savannah—he could not recognize the town; it seemed most of it had burned down in January—but at least that had not changed. His sister was still fond of lying abed late.

"Tell her I am here," he instructed a neatly dressed slave girl, "and bring me some cool water—at once!"

"Yes, master," the girl replied, and backed out of the parlor, headed for the kitchen where she could report to her friend the cook that a strange-looking gentleman was here looking for Miss Livia.

Unaware that Livia was not coming, Angus waited in the parlor. The old house looked shabby to him—and small. His new home, Dunlie Hall as he liked to call it, was both spacious and grand; this house, built so many years ago, although enlarged far beyond the original structure, had the small close rooms characteristic of the eighteenth century. Still, it was a miracle that it had been spared by the fire in January, and he supposed it served well enough for a town house; from what he understood, Morgan rarely left the island and the house was kept mainly for Livia's convenience—and also Juliette's—on their occasional trips to the city.

Where is that girl, Angus asked himself, when a few minutes had passed. He was thirsty; it was a hot day, and he had risen early to ride in from the inn five hours outside of town where he had stopped for the night. He rose from his chair and looked out to the back yard, where he saw the recalcitrant slave girl sitting on a three-legged stool, chatting with the cook, her hands and mouth full of johnnycake.

The sight enraged Angus. Over the years he had trained his own servants very well; they jumped to do his bidding. Actually, it was Rebecca who trained the household servants, but she and all the rest of them knew that he was master and would readily enforce his discipline with blows from his silver-handled riding crop. His hand settled on the cool silver grip as he saw the young maid out the window, eating and talking and laughing. Isn't it just like these damn Barstows, he thought, and Livia has become as lax as the rest of them!

"Cool water!" he bellowed out the window and had the satisfaction of seeing a look of consternation and fear cross the maid's face—but then he saw her taking off down the garden path, clearly a long way from bringing him the water he wanted.

"Damn them all, black savages!" Angus muttered, and searched the parlor for a flask. He found a glass decanter of rum and took a healthy swig, although it had been years since he had drunk rum; his taste had turned to whiskey, far more common up-country.

Doubtless Livia still has no idea I'm here, thought Angus after a few more minutes. Well, he would find her. Far from silently, his big roughly made boots clumping on the old, worn stairs, he climbed to the second floor and heard his sister's laugh coming from behind the closed door of the master bedroom.

She's not alone, Angus realized. He paused. He heard another laugh, a grunt, muffled gasps, and then the sound of creaking bed cords. He smiled. What a minx she was—had always been. In a flash he remembered all his sister had once been to him; he became aroused, although he had thought he had put all that behind him.

Without thinking any more of it, he knocked loudly on the bedroom door and called, "Livia! It's Angus!"

"Angus!" Livia screamed. She stopped short, in the midst of what she was doing, which was mainly teasing Chester with a long-handled feather duster as he lay, exhausted and nearly asleep, on the thin rug at the side of her bed.

"Get out!" she said to him in a low, tense voice, immediately wide awake. He woke instantly and scrambled to his feet, heading for the door.

"Yes, Miss Livia," he said, too loudly.

"No!" she shrieked, "not that way! Go! Jump out the window! Now!"

"Wha . . . t? What you say?" Chester's voice was high with fear.

"Faugh! You stink!" Livia said, wrinkling her nose at the raw smells of sweaty skin and soiled bedsheets and stale air that indeed permeated the room. "Just a minute, Angus," she called clearly and then, to the young black man, "Out the window! You must! Jump!"

Angus, his ear to the thin door, listened with increasing excitement, laced with no small measure of incredulity. Could Livia be forcing her lover to jump out a second-story window? Why should she bother? He laughed heartily. "May I come in?" he called again.

"No! Just a minute, Angus," she shouted, but he disobeyed. Lifting the latch, he stepped into the bedroom just in time to see Chester's bare back outside the open window and hear him scream as he leaped the twelve feet to the ground below.

"Oh, Livia!" Angus said, his voice gruff. "After all these years. How naughty you are."

There was a moment's silence as Angus looked out the window, watching Chester crawl to his feet and walk slowly away from the house, limping as if he were in great pain. Livia collapsed into the mess of tangled bedclothes and pulled her sheer, rumpled nightgown closed. She felt guilty . . . and foolish. It was not at all the way she had imagined her reunion with her brother, and he . . . he seemed a stranger. She blushed and looked glancingly at him. He looked a positive cracker, as they called backwoodsmen: His gray-streaked hair was long and shaggy; his coat dusty and of a rough, oldfashioned cut, and yet he had told her in his letters that he was prospering. He had aged; there was no doubt that he had aged—not only the gray in his hair, but the wrinkles around his eyes and—yes, unmistakably, a thickened waistline and the hint of a belly. Disappointed, Livia lowered her eyes. Of course she was wrong to consort with Negroes, it *was* disgusting, but what else was she to do? It was a violation of the system they all lived by—the worst possible violation—but she had made an effort not to flaunt her affairs, and she had never before been caught.

But now she was. Caught and cornered and confused. She had no idea what to expect from Angus. Perhaps he would tell Morgan. Well, if he did, Morgan would never believe it. She decided to take the offensive. She had found that, for her, it was always the best way.

"What else was I to do?" she asked petulantly.

Angus stood across the room, his voice, hardened and older, was stern. "Precisely, my dear sister, my own! What else? Did I expect you to become pious? You are a woman in her prime, eh? What else could you do? I see that the young buck is well formed, eh? No doubt you did not choose him for his poetic nature. Oh, Livvy! You have not changed. You are, as you were as a girl, very naughty

. . . perhaps I shall have to punish you." His head swimming with rum, Angus felt, and was, out of control.

Livia looked up uncertainly. It was just what he had used to say to her, so long ago . . . but in what sense did he mean it now?

"Perhaps I shall," he said, "just as I should punish that presumptuous nigger, as I would any unruly servant or naughty child."

Livia's heart soared. "What will you do to punish me?" she asked.

"I shall beat you, of course," he said, drawing out his silver-handled whip.

"Oh, Angus!" she sighed. "Oh!"

Later that day, when both Angus and Livia had rested and bathed and rested again, they sat down to a cold supper and a bottle of the fine Bordeaux from the cases Morgan Barstow had imported for Sea Groves.

It had been a hot day, and the late afternoon sun glared in the dining room window. Clouds of flies buzzed overhead and the smell of burned cornbread from the back kitchen was pervasive. Livia was tired; her poor head still ached so badly from the excesses of the night before that she thought she might as well drink the wine liberally—it could not feel worse.

Angus, too, was tired, and he felt uncommonly reflective. How quickly he and Livia had slipped back into the old roles. He did not feel entirely good about it. He did not feel good at all, he decided. It was wrong—years of plain living and domestic accord had convinced him of that. It was wrong for animals and it was wrong for men. Children born of such congress were too often warped; he had seen it among the lowest poor whites, and it had caused him to wonder.

He squinted at his sister. She was painted up like a London poppy. How different she seemed to him from the little girl he had raised. It was he who had cultivated her sexual tastes; he had spoiled her, no doubt. Now she was bedding with Negroes. He hated to think of it. No decent woman would do such a thing; he believed it deeply, although he had teased his sister. The truth was that she was not a decent woman. Even half sober, the realization disturbed him. Livia was all that was left of his old life—and just look at what she had become!

He had a strong urge to get away, away from the crassness, the licentiousness of the city, back to his own world.

"I shall be in town less than a week," Angus said. "There are many pressing matters of business awaiting my return to Washington."

"Business?" Livia asked. How cold and cruel he sounded. She sniffed. How heartless he was to speak of leaving her again, when he had just come back. For her part, there was nothing pressing her to come or go; there never was; it seemed she had fewer responsibilities and fewer friends than anyone else she knew.

"I have many responsibilities, dear sister," Angus said. "You do not understand, I suppose. Things are quite different in the interior. I prefer it there."

"Doubtless I should, also," Livia said. "It is terribly tiresome on the island. All the same people, year after year. So provincial and proud. I have never liked them or they me. We belong together, Angus. Father would have wished it."

"Father's plans for us seem . . . long ago," Angus said.

"To you, perhaps," Livia said, miffed. "I think of him daily. I think of you daily, Angus. I am sorry you think so little of me."

"Livvy! I think of you often, have thought of you. But you have your own life, your children . . ."

"They are all *his* children," Livia said fretfully. "All of them care more for him and his sister Juliette than they do for me. Except Caleb. Poor Caleb. Oh! There is something I want to tell you, Angus, about Caleb."

"Perhaps you should come out . . . for a visit," Angus suggested, not quite sincerely. He was not sure how Livia would view his domestic arrangements, if she would be able to accept Nancy, to say nothing of Rebecca. But how could she not tolerate them—she of all people. "I am very pleased with my children," he said, absently, thinking of all of them. Of the lot, his favorites were the two youngest boys, one by Nancy and one by Rebecca, both just five years old. The boys were named Peter and Leon; they were inseparable and played together like puppies.

"Caleb is expected here . . . in Savannah, very soon,"

Livia said. Perhaps she would not tell him just now that Caleb was his son; perhaps she would wait until they had met. "Morgan wants him to work with Jacob Barstow, our factor, for a few years, to learn that business, to understand it. Caleb is no ordinary boy. I should say young man. No ordinary young man . . . why, he is nearly twenty. He . . . well, he will just have to do his best."

Twenty, Angus wondered? No ordinary boy? What was Livia suggesting and why did she not come right out and say it? Livia's subtleties had always annoyed him. Was she suggesting that this Caleb was his son? He stared at her. Her hand rose to pat her hair. The suggestion of vanity revolted him; he had grown strict as well as proper. What business did a woman of her age have playing the courtesan—and with blacks! Half-submerged jealousy fueled Angus's anger at Livia, had fueled his lapse into sexual patterns he had not meant to indulge.

She can be nothing to me; my life is complete, Angus thought. Her weakness and willingness made him cruel. His own weakness made him crueler still.

"I am sure he will do well enough," he drawled. He would take a look at the boy; one look would tell him whether or not he was responsible for him.

"Oh, Angus, I have missed you so!" Livia exclaimed, a note of emotion plain in her voice.

"It has been many years," he said baldly. Would she cry now? He should never have indulged himself; what obligations did it put him under? He forked a slab of cold pork and lifted it, glistening and dripping with juices, to his mouth.

Perhaps I could get away . . . to visit, Livia thought. Of course Angus would rather be with me than with his wife. 'Twas only a marriage of convenience, like my own. I have never loved Morgan; he has never loved Nancy. That is the way it is. That is how it had always been with us. Thinking of her life, her marriage, Livia felt her eyes swim with tears. She thought of the dullness of life on the plantation. She thought of her sphere of influence at Sea Groves; it was limited, and since his high fever a few years ago, Morgan had been impotent—thus reducing her ability to control him through sex. Although she was his wife and the mother of his children, he no longer listened to her in the same way. It disturbed her; and it more than disturbed her, it infuriated her, that Juliette was Morgan's true helpmeet—it was Juliette he consulted about important decisions. Together they planned for the future of the family and the people. Morgan would never easily let her go to Angus; only a catastrophic, devastating event could move him in that direction. Livia sensed it, and her mind began to toy with the possibilities. . . . It could be done; she could set events into motion that would sway him. What were they?

Angus interrupted her reverie. Gagging, he spit out a mouthful of Morgan's imported Bordeaux. "Dammit! What is this swill? Isn't there any whiskey in the house? This rotgut tastes like medicine . . . or poison. A man likes his whiskey, Livia, don't you know that?"

Livia stared, thoroughly lost in a world of her own imaginings—a world that existed nowhere in reality—forgetting for a moment that this vulgar backwoodsman was her own beloved brother. She recoiled a bit at the loud coarseness of his voice, breaking into her dreaming of a way to shake Morgan Barstow to the roots of his soul, and then the lifelong habit of wanting to please Angus gripped her again and she jumped to her feet to run for the green bottle of whiskey hidden in the fireplace cupboard. Angus's disapproval excited her; that was still true above all. His strength and superiority challenged her. For the first time in many years she felt truly alive. How pale and weak Morgan seemed, in comparison; her husband never demanded or commanded. He was conciliatory, tender, and loving, and it had never suited her, never!

"As you wish," Livia said, presenting the bottle, and when she sat again, she was trembling, tossed by awakened feelings, again desperate to please, knowing in her heart that she would do anything, risk anything to be with Angus . . . forever.

CHAPTER ELEVEN

Caleb Barstow Meets His Partner; Trouble Spreads; Juliette Meets Her Editor; Trouble Ignites

As his natural parents drank and schemed in Savannah, Caleb Barstow approached the city in the mail stage. It was a journey of some twenty hours from Brunswick, and he passed the night as uncomfortably as could be expected in the rattly old stage, a drafty wooden coach drawn by two strong horses. The route passed through dark, dense swamps, enveloped in thick, unhealthy mists. Alligators slid off the narrow road as the stage approached, writhing into the green, stagnant water, choked with reeds that bordered it. The night was damp and cool for September, and the day dawned hot and hazy.

Typically, in Georgia's coastal counties, September days were as intensely hot and humid as the nights were cool and humid; the unpaved roads were muddy in all seasons. Caleb woke to the sight of vast cotton plantations and of slaves already at work under a driver's lash and a broiling sun.

He saw it all coolly, as a matter of course. Caleb, described by his mother as "no ordinary young man," was in fact an extraordinary one. Nature herself had seen to it that he would never be ordinary by inflicting him, since birth, with an ill-proportioned body and a twisted spine that forced him to walk with a slight limp and cock his head just slightly to the left. His posture was a curse and not his own fault, although it had occurred to his mother that it was surely hers—and also, of course, his father's.

As if to compensate, Caleb was naturally handsome, as handsome as a man can be when his eyes are bright, commanding blue, his dark hair thick and shiny, his features regular, his teeth strong and white, and his height just in excess of six feet. In many ways the product of his secret and complicated heritage, Caleb was like no one part of it, like no one parent. He was as clever and secretive as Angus Dunlie, as willful and spoiled as Livia, and as intelligent and aristocratic as Morgan Barstow, who had raised him in the full tradition and expectations of a rich, well-connected planter's son.

Yet there is, in all human lives, a point at which heredity is surpassed or circumvented by personal will. We are what we make of our lives. Caleb was clever, but he was not kind. He was willful but thorough and deliberate—he could and would wait years to work out a grudge or set even a score. He was ambitious and reckless, and yet he was vulnerable—to love, to flattery, to a certain sort of unquestioning attention which he had been denied in infancy and childhood because of his sickliness and the accompanying family troubles.

And now Caleb Barstow was on his way to a new life. In many ways it promised to be a life well suited to his abilities and tastes. Because of his infirmity, he had never been able to participate fully in the man's world—the outdoor life of the plantation—neither in its work or its play. From the start, his younger brother Cole had beaten him at games, been a better hunter, fisherman, rider, and had displayed a natural talent for agriculture and managing workers. Caleb had, perhaps in reaction, cultivated a slight talent for scholarship. He had made friends with the tutor, a slight, nervous boy from Connecticut hired to teach all the Barstow children. He had loved the tutor better than a brother, and had progressed in his studies even after the frail young man had succumbed to yellow fever. He had read every book in the small library at Sea Groves, and he fancied that he knew mathematics. There had been talk of sending him to university, but Caleb did not want to go—he hated meeting strangers. Instead he had agreed to be placed in the office of Jacob Barstow, the free-born son of Ira Barstow, now successfully managing his family's cotton brokerage business in Savannah.

It was not an unusual arrangement—planters with large families sometimes spared a son to business. What made it unusual was the special relationship that existed between the two branches of the Barstow family, the main branch being Roland's family—now represented by Morgan and his children—and the free black Barstows, Ira's sons, and their families. Even though large slaveholders, Morgan and Roland had always respected the free black Barstows and their right to live a free life.

"Jacob Barstow's father saved grandfather's life," Morgan had explained, not for the first time, to Caleb as they had stood waiting for the mail stage that would take him to Savannah.

"Yes, Father," Caleb had answered with half his attention. The rest of it, the greater half, was trained on a very pretty yellow-haired young woman also waiting for the mail stage. She was laughing to her companion. Is she laughing at me? Caleb wondered, and he grew red with anger. Women were so false, so deceitful—all of them! He did not care for women. If he could avoid it, he would never marry.

"You must respect him and learn all you can," Morgan told Caleb. "His place in the world is not an easy one, but he has done very well and he can show you the system. You will live comfortably enough at the old house on Abercorn Street. We look forward to seeing you home for Christmas."

"Yes, Father," Caleb said. His eyes were on the young woman; hers, he now noticed, studying, not him, but his younger brother Cole, who had come along to Brunswick and was now walking his roan stallion up and down the roadside, a creature as handsome and good-tempered, loose-limbed and graceful as Cole himself. Caleb's self-consciousness burned off and was replaced with jealousy. Jealousy was the coin of exchange between the two brothers at any time; theirs was a rivalry so keen as to trouble even optimistic Morgan, and it was a large part of the reason their father had decided to sent Caleb to Savannah.

And then, in the next moment, the mail stage had rattled into Brunswick, and Caleb had the satisfaction of seeing the yellow-haired woman greet an ugly, whey-faced soldier and fall into his arms. Slattern, he thought, hussy!

"Good-bye, my son," Morgan said, awkwardly reaching to embrace Caleb, who stepped sideways to avoid the embrace and climbed partway up into the stage.

"Take care of your health, dear boy," Morgan called. "Remember me to our friends, respect the Sabbath!"

"Yes, yes," Caleb called back, embarrassed.

"A safe journey, brother," Cole called out, and Caleb repressed a shudder at the gay, triumphant ring of his voice. How glad he is to be rid of me, Caleb thought. Well, I shall be well rid of him, too, and I shall more than better him, someday . . . be richer, more successful, more famous, happier. . . .

"Farewell!" Roland called, and Caleb waved, too choked with emotion to speak. Hours passed before he could get the memory of Cole's smile out of his head, and when he did, somewhere during the raw, chilly night, he dreamed of running behind Cole in a footrace, a doomed, breathtaking scramble in which he could never catch up.

Waking, then, with vague feelings that he had already lost the race, Caleb stared sullenly out of the stage's small windows. Northward past the cotton plantations, the route took him westward along the river's edge from the sea, offering a fine view of the broad, shining Savannah River and the network of swamp islands that intersected it. The islands dividing the river into different channels had been converted into rice fields, lying very low and easily flooded at the proper seasons. Negroes working the fields were out in them as the stage passed, and he saw behind them the small wooden huts in which they lived.

Such continual moisture and dampness would kill a white man in a month, they said, and Caleb thought of it as he passed by; all the slaveholders said that Negroes were naturally particularly fitted for field work under a hot sun. God had intended them for such toil, just as he had intended white men to be masters. How, then, could the existence of free Negroes like Jacob Barstow be justified? Caleb had no idea; he resolved to think on it later.

Although it was early, the city of Savannah had long since stirred to life as Caleb rode into town that September morning. All along the Bay, the principal street, moved carts and carriages and men afoot, endeavoring, as was the city's sensible custom, to do their business in the relative cool of the forenoon. Seeing the traffic, Caleb decided to go directly to the Exchange, where he might be expected to encounter Jacob Barstow, rather than going to the house on Abercorn Street, where he should most certainly find his mother—another demanding, deceitful woman—still abed.

The Cotton Exchange, spared by the fire that had destroyed so many of Savannah's wooden buildings, which were in the majority, stood just on the verge of the river bluff and nearly in the center of town. It was a large brick building containing some public offices, and an assembly room where fortnightly concerts and balls were held during the winter. Atop the Exchange was a steeple which commanded a panoramic view of the city.

Seeing all this, which he had seen before, Caleb Barstow walked straight into the assembly hall and asked the first man he met for directions to Jacob Barstow's offices. He was told to seek a warehouse, marked with the Barstow name, just along the Bay, and found it without difficulty. The front door of the warehouse was open, but there was no activity within, and Caleb's curiosity mounted as he climbed the narrow dark stairs to the second floor.

"Who's there?" a man's voice called, slow and deep, neither young nor old.

"Caleb Barstow, sir, at your service." He hesitated.

"God bless you. Come on in," the voice answered, and Caleb climbed the rest of the way up to meet the man with whom he would be in daily association for the next forty years.

Jacob Barstow rose to meet his cousin, and stood calmly, aware that he would be inspected and that much would depend, as it always did, on what a white man made of his appearance. Caleb noticed that Jacob Barstow was small and light; he liked that. He was handsome, in an inoffensive way, and looked neither positively white nor black—his blue eyes were Caucasian, but his black hair was obviously Negroid; his skin was no tanner than that of any outdoor man. In fact, as Caleb was to learn, he never went into the sunshine, not deliberately to avoid the sun's rays, but because his life—and his passion—was his work.

"With all my heart, I welcome you," Jacob said seriously. "You know we are somehow related . . . distantly, I suppose . . . it matters not how. May I call you Mister Caleb?"

Caleb nodded.

"I will open my heart to you, Mister Caleb," Jacob said, thinking that he had no choice. How young he was, how pale, how ill-formed. "If you had not arrived today, I would have been forced to close my business. There is great antagonism toward free men of colored blood in this town. Do you know of it?"

Caleb shook his head. Though he had not, he found it unremarkable. He had never considered the black man's point of view; it would have seemed to him that any black man should be grateful for any white man's indulgence, and yet clearly, this black man was different. Jacob Barstow was obviously intelligent and clever. He found his fervor and attention flattering.

"It matters not that we are distant cousins, if indeed we are; what matters, indeed what I cling to as a drowning man to a life rope, is the support and toleration which has always been extended to my family by your good father and his father before him. Bless them! Bless them! And now, when I need it most, Morgan Barstow has sent me you—his first born son—his chosen son!"

Caleb, who had generally felt himself to be the rejected son, could not help but be pleased to see himself cast in such a light. "What . . . now? What has happened just now?" he asked.

"It is always something," Jacob complained, feeling more sure he had a sympathetic ear. "Whatever happens we are blamed for it. Now it is as a result of the charity of the people of New York. They have sent our city three thousand dollars—just think of it!—three thousand! 'Twas to aid the people who suffered as a result of the great fire, but 'tis given with the stipulation that it be used to aid black and white sufferers alike. The mayor has returned it! All the city councilmen are aroused. . . . They resent the reflection on their impartiality, of course, but that is not my concern."

"May I sit here?" Caleb asked. His back ached after the night in the mail stage.

"A thousand pardons, Mister Caleb. Sit here! Take this chair. 'Tis the best! It commands a view of the river."

"Thank you," Caleb said, looking out over the bustling wharves and the rows of anchored sailing craft.

"My concern, and yours, too, now that you are here . . . my partner! . . . is that they have further restricted the commercial license of free Negroes, as a result. We cannot bear or use firearms, Mister Caleb, for fear we should incite insurrections. We cannot dispense medicine for fear of . . . well, 'tis of no matter. But now the Council has levied a new tax on our profits and forbidden us from selling goods outside of the county. I am ruined! How can I sell cotton to the markets in Liverpool? I cannot! I am out of business! Except . . . with your aid. You will aid me, will you not, Mister Caleb?"

Caleb was beginning to get the drift, and was not averse to his role as savior and figurehead. "Why, of course I will. That is why I am here," he said and was rewarded by the expression of gratitude and relief which settled on Jacob Barstow's worried face.

"Hallelujah! You will become my partner, this very afternoon. I must register it with the city. You will be the titular head of our concern: Barstow and Barstow. Why not? I will register it and we shall move that cotton off the wharves by noon tomorrow! I have been offered a good price, Mister Caleb, a very good price. What do you think of twenty-five cents a pound? I tell you, Mister Caleb, the British cotton merchants do not care for the color of a man's skin, only the quality of his cotton!"

Caleb nodded. It made sense. If some men of color were more intelligent than the others, if they rose above the others, in this case obviously because of a measure of white blood, then why should they not be allowed to do business? Like Jews, he thought. He had never met a Jew, but he had heard of them; there was a community of them here in Savannah. Doubtless there was a place for Jews in society, also—some lowly place.

The place for white Americans would, of course, remain the dominant one. White men should be the patriarchs—black men the children. Flush with the notion of himself in this new, patronizing position, he who was sick to death of being the weakest, the least masculine, the unfit pariah, Caleb rose and expressed an instinct he had not even known he possessed.

"Let us shake hands on it, then," he said to Jacob Barstow, putting out both hands for Jacob's aid in rising from his chair. Jacob accepted them readily, and pulled Caleb up. Caleb rose slowly, feeling a twinge of pain, and Jacob, seeing it, grasped him firmly by the shoulders, grinning broadly.

It was just then that Angus Dunlie looked into the door

of the office, seeking a glimpse of the young man Livia had described as "no ordinary" one. Neither Jacob nor Caleb knew that they were being watched. Angus stopped cold. He looked searchingly; he saw many things and his mind leaped to conclusions. The young man, he saw, very much resembled himself—in fact, he resembled his own father, except that he was crippled—"hideously" it seemed to him. Worse yet, he was engaged in an unnatural embrace—a full embrace with another man—and even worse, the man was a Negro.

Retching, gagging in disgust and guilt, Angus backed away from the sight. He turned and ran down the warehouse steps and across the Bay. With scarcely a word to the servants and a brief note to Livia, who was out shopping, he left Savannah that day.

Livia, when she returned home in a new blue silk bonnet, was incredulous.

"I don't believe you, you little liar!" she screamed at her maid, when the insolent girl had given her the news.

At first she suspected foul play. The note was no explanation, none at all, just a few lines telling her that he had gone, which she could see perfectly well for herself. She was hurt, confused, outraged. She felt rejected, robbed, frustrated, and out of this confusion of feelings came a strange resolve. It was nothing another woman would have resolved; a lady would have languished in disappointment, but Livia was no lady—she was a woman in a troubled stage of life who had been offered a renaissance of youth and passion and then had it immediately ripped away from her.

First she turned to Chester, seeking some outlet for her awakened lusts. She found him, after screaming at the housemaid and the cook, seated in the spacious airy side parlor that served as an office for the men of the family. Chester, surprisingly, was seated at the handsome old mahogany desk, holding a book.

From the first moment, Livia, whose intuitions always far outstripped her reason, sensed something changed in him, but she had no clear notion of what it was. She laughed, a bit uneasily.

"What are you doin' here, you bad boy! You can't read, Chester!"

Chester, who was holding the book upside down, could not, but he wished he could. Deep changes, deep longings were stirring in Chester, had been stirring for a number of months, but had been fanned to life, as a fire from a spark, during his last few days in Savannah. He glared at his mistress, emboldened by the whiskey he had drunk and the exhortations of his new friends—for it was these new friends who had inflamed him.

Chester had been deeply humiliated by his encounters with Livia, especially their last encounter, when he had been forced to leap naked from the window at the risk of his life. He had been used by white people all his life, used as a draft horse is used or a domesticated milk cow, but he had never before been used sexually, and it cut into his very soul. It embarrassed him; it frightened him; and it had touched his spirit in a new, profound way. What had a man left if he had not his own sex to call his own? All his life he had been told to love God and respect his white masters—but he did not respect Livia.

The downcast look Chester offered Livia hid not only fear—for he knew himself to be at her mercy—but smoldering anger and resentment.

"You are a worthless fool, Chester," Livia snapped, but she could not have it both ways. If he was her vassal, he could not be her master, and that was what she craved.

"We shall leave for the island in the morning," Livia said, wretched and unsure, settling on that course—it seemed as good as any. She stared at Chester. What was he thinking, he with that flat, blank stare? What did he think—he or any of them? They were as inscrutable as the stones on the beach—no white folk knew them, not really.

"Yes, Miss Livia," Chester said, but his tone revealed nothing, and a thrill of terror ran through Livia at his mystery and power—his and that of all black men, and she wavered, feeling him a poor second for her brother, but still . . .

Chester gave her no chance. Rising, he dropped the book so that it bounced on its spine and fell, open, to the floor. "I'll be gettin' the horses and carriage ready, then, ma'am," he said, and stalked out of the room.

Livia would have felt more than a thrill of terror had she known what was to occupy Chester that night.

For Chester had met and fallen in with a coterie of

Savannah Negroes—some of them slaves, a few of them free—who gathered together at night to discuss inflammatory and dangerous ideas. Freedom was primary among them; some of their number had moved from thought to action and had run away to the North in search of it, and some of them had survived—against impossible odds. Even more astonishing to Chester had been the talk he had heard of insurrection. Not that he had never heard, before, of armed resistance—always in some far-off place, the Carib, or long ago, in Virginia—but here, here and now, these city Negroes were talking of getting together, or getting guns and ammunition, of taking over a town, a neighborhood, an island, and holding it for themselves to live in and run, all alone, as free men.

The talk was heady; it was preposterous, and Chester had listened without speaking, but when he left the midnight meetings he could think of nothing else. His head was completely filled with it; it had come to him at an age when he was most vulnerable, when he was full grown and not yet broken by hard work and the habit of submission. The sexual experience with Livia had aggravated his restlessness and uneasiness—in its way it was as spiritually unsettling as the hope of insurrection, arousing a sense of his own power as well as a fatalistic awareness that it was not his own to use.

It had been the housemaid, Su-Anna, who had taken Chester to the meeting, and when he left the parlor, after his conversation with Livia, she was waiting for him outside the kitchen.

"Mistress says we leavin' already in the mornin'," he said to her.

"She screamin' mad that her brother gone west without seein' her again," Su-Anna said sagely. She was a "bright" mulatto, far too clever and energetic for her role in life; had Livia devoted half an eye to overseeing her servants, she would have noticed that Su-Anna was excessively independent and freethinking.

"I want to go with you again tonight," Chester said. He was half frightened by the bold, impulsive feelings rising in him, but exhilarated, too. They said, the men at the meetings, that plantation slaves could take hold of chances God gave them and turn them to violence. Fires, floods, big storms . . . those were the times to seize control . . .

and kill. Every white man, woman, and child in the near region would have to die; there was no other way.

Chester shook his head, thinking of it. He knew Master Roland and Master Morgan were kind men, as white men went. And Miss Juliette . . . He felt his head spin at the idea of hurting Miss Juliette. It went against all his teaching, all his life so far. But that was how it had to be, if the slaves were to take hold and take over. So they said, the men at the meetings, and one of them was a minister of Christ and one of them had read aloud out of the Bible, and they all said that it was the only way for black folk to get some of what was owed them in this world.

"Yes, I want to go to that meetin'," Chester said stubbornly. "I got to find out more and carry it home."

By a fitting coincidence, the same month that Angus Dunlie had journeyed from Washington-Wilkes to Savannah and Livia and Caleb Barstow from the plantation to the family's town house, Juliette Barstow had, for the first time in her life, also undertaken a journey, one of considerable length.

Juliette's old friend and lifelong correspondent, Aimee Warrington, had become engaged to marry and had written to Juliette, begging her to come to New York for the event. That Aimee should marry was not in itself surprising, for she had always been pretty and well connected, but in truth both she and Juliette had long since passed the age when most young women marry.

"I know most people would call me quite an 'old maid,' Aimee had written Juliette with her customary good humor,

> and they probably have, but what can be done, dear friend, for I have fallen in love! And so it is with all my memories of you and your dear mother and all she meant to my own much-missed female parent, that I implore you to come to New York—and it's not, you will find, such a dull town as all that—to see me in my "fallen state" and to meet Rawley and complete my happiness. . . .

Juliette had laughed, reading Aimee's letter, and then, most uncharacteristically, she had decided to go. For years she had not left the plantation for longer than a few days' trip to Savannah; for years she had devoted herself to affairs of home and family, partly out of an inborn and well-developed sense of duty, partly by preference, and partly out of an obsession with self-renunciation that had been part of her personality since the days when Angus Dunlie had stayed at Sea Groves. But this . . . this seemed an invitation it would not be kind to refuse.

Juliette's spirits soared and she felt years younger as she packed for the journey—by sea. Her own personal maid was awaiting confinement; she chose one of Lizzy's grown daughters, Patience, to accompany her, and passed many busy weeks in cutting and sewing dresses and accessories that would not shame the family, the state, or the South itself, in far-off New York.

Finally, all was ready. All the laces, silks, and ruffles were hemmed and stitched and styled to perfection and packed into trunks; Patience was properly outfitted; and then, unaccountably, Livia took it into her head to make a trip to Savannah.

"I shan't go, after all," Juliette said, but Morgan was adamant.

"You must, for all of us," he insisted, and she did. She left the island on a bright moonlit night, just three days before Livia and Chester had set out for Savannah, to sail straight north along the Atlantic coast in a trim two-masted schooner with a crew of thirty. It was a strenuous sea voyage, but everything was new and wonderful to Juliette, and she wondered why she had never traveled before.

New York itself seemed a carnival of wonders staged for her amusement. Aimee's family—her younger half-brothers and her aged but cheerful father—were more than amiable, and far wealthier than Juliette had expected, or perhaps it was just that Yankees did things differently. Instead of slaves, the Warringtons employed a corps of Irish servants; instead of a plantation's affairs to turn to, Mr. Warrington went every day to his bank, as did Rawley Clinton, Aimee's fiance.

Juliette was taken wholeheartedly into the bosom of the family and swept into a network of social events that kept her rushing up and down town from morning to midnight. The day began with a heavy breakfast—once even at a hotel, where oysters and ice rose in dazzling mountains at each place. Mornings were occupied with shopping and visiting; lunches were formal and sociable; afternoons were sociable and musical, ending with visiting friends for tea, then more friends for strolling along Fifth Avenue (it was sleighing, in winter, Aimee said) before dinner parties.

And at all of them, all the lunches and parties and dinners and balls, there were the fashionable and pleasant people of Aimee's acquaintance, all strangers to Juliette, at first, although when she began to sort them out, she found that she liked some of them very much. In particular, she came to realize as the days of social events continued, she liked one man—an old friend of Aimee's family, a Mr. Taylor Bruce, who was not completely a Yankee, for he had been born and raised in Virginia, a man who seemed to her the embodiment of the finest sort of gentleman, and who worked as an editor at Harper and Brothers.

To Aimee's obvious satisfaction, to Juliette's astonishment, the acquaintance of Juliette and Mr. Bruce progressed daily toward friendship, a sort of lively, argumentative friendship that challenged Juliette's intellect to its limits and delighted her soul.

" 'Tis nothing like a romance," she confided to her journal, one rainy afternoon when she had a rare moment for reading and reflection:

> There can be no question of romance, for he has been married, and indeed is the father of a son by that unfortunate union which ended in divorce. But, oh, my soul! It does me good, I am sure, to associate with a man of his fine intellectual calibre; he fascinates me! I have confided in him that I am interested in writing stories and he has encouraged me. He is a very handsome and clever man, that is obvious; his company stimulates me, and I look forward, at the end of each day, to seeing him the next. . . .

But that evening, at the Metropolitan Opera House, Juliette did not encounter Mr. Bruce, either in the lobby or in their box, and for the first time in New York, although the performances and production were splendid, despite the company of Aimee and Rawley Clinton, she felt disappointed and dissatisfied.

How foolish I am, she chided herself. I blush to think how ridiculous such feelings are in a woman of my age and expectations. She forced herself to concentrate on the opera, which was an Italian tragedy, and to put thoughts of seeing Mr. Bruce out of her mind.

But directly after the concluding aria, when the audience rose to its feet and cheered and shouted "Bravo!", Juliette heard a man's voice behind her speak her name, and she felt her heart leap.

"Why, Mr. Bruce!" she said, her natural delight irrepressible. "Are you just arriving now?"

"I was detained," he apologized, "at my club." He bowed to Juliette, then to Aimee and Rawley Clinton, and added, aside, "I could not relinquish the opportunity of seeing you, even for a few minutes, for I have something of particular interest to discuss with you."

Particular interest, Juliette wondered. Lost in her own thoughts, she was silent in the carriage that carried the four of them from the opera house to the Warringtons' elegant brick house on Washington Square. Whatever could he mean?

She had not long to wait. Taylor Bruce, who had joined the crowd of theatergoers who were now gathering in the Warringtons' high-ceilinged parlor—a splendid room lined with tall gilt-edged mirrors—cornered Juliette at once, a glass of cold and delicious French champagne in one hand.

"I have a wonderful surprise, Miss Barstow," he said. "I have spoken with my publisher on your behalf."

"My goodness, Mr. Bruce, you have what?" Juliette exclaimed. She had a sinking feeling.

"Spoken on your behalf. Pardon me if I have been premature, but as we were dining together at my club, I recognized the precisely appropriate moment."

"Oh?" Juliette said, immensely flattered and disappointed at the same time.

"Of course it is far from done, but he agrees with me that pieces by an intelligent Southern woman might catch the public's fancy. We had spoken of stories, Miss Barstow, but would you not think of trying a longer work?"

"I had never thought of it at all," Juliette protested.

"Well, you must," Mr. Bruce said persuasively, leading her away from the others, to a spot where she was able to see the shape of their two heads coming together in reflection in one of the tall mirrors. "I believe you owe it to the rest of the nation, Miss Barstow, to write a tale, and if it be romantic, so much the better, of how Southern life really is!"

"I cannot deny that I am of a romantic turn of mind," Juliette sighed, "but your expectations, I fear, far outstrip my abilities." She took a gulp of the champagne to steady herself. Why should I not try it, she thought, why not? I shall never marry, and the gaieties of social life can never satisfy me. Other women are totally occupied with the bearing and raising of children, but that is not the sum of women's God-given talents, I know it is not.

"I believe you are a writer," Taylor Bruce said. "I believe you should succeed, if you dare to try."

"Dare?" Juliette said, and she lifted her head to give him a brilliant smile. "Why of course I dare. If I fail, it shall not be for want of courage, Mr. Bruce. I am a Barstow, and a Georgian!"

Livia, returning to Sea Groves with her driver, Chester, and, by a last-minute impulse, the housemaid Su-Anna, who usually remained in the Savannah house, had no inkling that she was taking a lighted fuse into the tinder box. But even a lighted fuse could not have been more dangerous, more inflammatory, or more inevitably explosive.

Chester, who had begun to stammer uncontrollably, could not look into Livia's eyes, or into Morgan's when his master addressed him, on the morning after his return to the plantation.

"Chester," Morgan began hesitantly, obviously upset about what had happened, what might have happened, and what he felt he had to do, "I am very sorry to hear that you have been insolent to Miss Livia. You were born here at Sea Groves and raised here; I have always trusted you and regarded you as one of our finest young men. But what I hear from Miss Livia is very serious. She says you have talked back to her, have disobeyed her orders, and worse—exposed her to danger on the ride by drinking while you were driving the carriage." He paused. Chester's downcast look did not please him; he had noticed that the most unruly slaves could not meet his eyes. It was a sure sign of a runaway, too. It made him sad to see that Chester had gone bad.

"What have you to say for yourself?" Morgan asked.

Chester was seething with anger. He felt cornered. What *could* he say? Nothing he could say would be accepted as true, if it was contrary to what the mistress said. Besides, he was so angry he could not speak. He felt his palms go cold and his head swim. Never in his life had he hated anyone as he now hated Livia, and by association, Morgan, whose questions trapped and humiliated him, who was likely to punish him no matter what he did now.

"Why won't you speak, Chester?" Morgan said. His regret and disappointment were changing to a desire to have the inevitable over with. Chester was acting guilty if he had ever seen a guilty Negro.

"So it's true, then," Morgan said. In frustration, he touched the handle of his riding crop and Chester jumped at him, his big hands reaching for Morgan's throat.

Quick as Chester was, Morgan was quicker. "God damn it!" he swore, and lashed out at Chester with the riding whip.

"You ain't gone beat me, you ain't!" Chester choked out. He spun awkwardly, too passionately enraged to have much control over his muscles, stumbling over his feet, falling onto his knees.

"Stop immediately, damn you!" Morgan shouted. It was too late now; no slave could be allowed to get away with attacking his master; it would lead to a complete breakdown in the system; it would corrupt the other slaves; it would lead to an epidemic of rebellion and resistance. "If I wasn't gonna beat you, I have to now, you black fool!" he said in a terrible, low voice, switching at Chester's unprotected head and shoulders as the black man raised his hands over his head and howled in pain.

Their encounter, which was taking place just outside the stables, had drawn a crowd of grooms and hostlers. Now Chester's wife, Patty, ran up to them, as did Morgan's youngest son, Hugh.

"Stop! Stop!" Patty yelled. "Have mercy, Mister Morgan, you gonna kill him! Stop! He good man!"

"Daddy! What happened? Why are you beatin' Chester?" Hugh screamed.

Silently a crowd of about twenty slaves from the stables and gardens formed a crowd at a distance of about twenty feet, and seeing them out of the corner of his eye, Morgan was afraid of his own slaves for the first time in his life. White people were outrageously outnumbered at Sea Groves; of course they were all over the island, all over the state. It was the way things were. Everything depended on the system; discipline had to be maintained, but Morgan knew that he had already violated one of his own long-established principles of slave management—never to strike a slave in anger.

He lowered the whip. "Chester," he said, "I'm sorry to see you like this. Tom, Bucko, come here!"

Answering Morgan's call, two of the most trusted and respected men on the plantation, both gardeners, came over.

"Chester has gone bad," Morgan told them sorrowfully. "I want you two to hold him. He's goin' to the jail."

Chester's wife Patty screamed. "You ain't gone sell him, Master, is you? Please, Mister Morgan, please!"

"No more cryin' and screamin', Patty, and the rest of you get back to work," Morgan said, and his voice was once again level and controlled. "Chester has been very bad. He must be punished. It's a capital offense for a slave to hurt a white man. Chester tried to hurt me, but I believe he did it out of weakness. He will have time to repent his crime. Now the rest of you go along. Don't you have work to do?"

The crowd dissolved, and Morgan put his arm around Hugh as the two of them walked away from the stables. Hugh was crying.

"Son, it can't be helped," Morgan said, but there was no anger at all left in his voice, just sadness and understanding.

CHAPTER TWELVE

A Night of Horror; A World Overturned; Some Moments of Truth

And so it happened that on the night Angus Dunlie returned home to his family at Dunlie Hall, on the night that Aimee Warrington married her handsome banker and Juliette cried tears of happiness for her, the slave Su-Anna left the quarters at Sea Groves and crept through the dark, starless night to visit Chester in the slave jail.

The jail, a wretched structure converted from a woodshed, was not located on the Barstow plantation but was shared by several of the plantations on the island, and stood in an isolated patch of scrub oak, about two miles along the main island road from Sea Groves.

Chester had been there three nights already, and when she found him he was in a debilitated, dispirited condition. The slave jailer, an old man with a streak of cruelty who had been a foot soldier in the same Revolutionary company as Roland Barstow, had drunk heavily and was asleep.

"Chester?" Su-Anna called in a low voice as she crept closer to the jail. She carried a lantern, partly covered by a cloth. "Chester, you hear me?"

There was a low groan. She followed it, looking into the jail easily through the half-sided walls. Four wide-open eyes stared at her from one room; there were two field hands from the Barclay plantation, both in stocks, confined for willful destruction of the cotton gin. Su-Anna winced to see them. The stocks that held them were built according to an ingenious and terrible design that allowed them neither to stand, nor sit, nor lie, but to hold themselves on their arms, half raised, in a position scarcely endurable.

"Help," one of the confined men groaned. "Help me, sister!"

"Dear Lord, save me," the other moaned.

"The Lord ain't gone save us, we gotta save ourselves," Su-Anna muttered, "but hang on, there; the day of salvation comin' quick!"

Stumbling a little in the blackness, Su-Anna made her way around the stocks to the back of the jail, where Chester was handcuffed and shackled to a heavy rust-coated ox chain. He had been beaten, and his legs and back were deeply crossed with lash marks, dried now and barely crusted over with new-formed scabs.

"Chester?" she whispered, holding the lantern up to his face for a long moment before he blinked his eyes. "Can you walk?" she asked.

Chester, who had finally fallen into a sleep that was his only relief from the terrible pain of his back, did not at first recognize Su-Anna. The lantern light was too strong; her coming too total a surprise.

Su-Anna produced a flask of whiskey from her pocket, still half full although she had gulped a good deal of it on the way over from Sea Groves. With shaking hands she held it to Chester's lips and he drank as she talked to him. "You gone be saved, Chester. A lot happened since you went away. A lot happening tonight, you see. You gone be part of it, sure you are. Here, drink some more. I come to get you, Chester, but I ain't alone. The others comin' along quick—all of 'em. We an awful force, Chester, a real army, yes, we an army of God and we gone beat them down. There! You hear?"

"I hear," Chester said, his head swimming already with the combined effects of raw whiskey and the hope of deliverance. "Who comin'? Comin' here?"

"They was a meetin'—just like in Savannah—at the old slave cemetery. Our people come from all over the island—old and young—and they comin' here first to git you. . . . They comin' armed, yes, sir!"

"What they gone do?"

"We . . . we, Chester, you too—we gone set fire to this nasty jail, first off, then we gone march on the plantation and kill 'em all."

Dizzy, Chester shut his eyes. A sweat broke out on his forehead.

"No good closin' your eyes to it," Su-Anna said, prodding Chester in the side so that he shuddered. "Can you walk? If you cain't walk, someone gone have to carry you off. Git yourself pulled up as best you can, Chester, here they come!"

Behind them in the darkness there was a stirring, as subtle as wind in the trees at first. Su-Anna ran to tell the others that the jailer was asleep and where he lay, then returned with two men who carried a saw and a hatchet.

"Here! Cut him loose and they's two others," Su-Anna said. Chester cried as the heavy chain was cut away from the iron staple that held it to the floor of the jail. He stumbled as he tried to walk with shackles on both feet, but he made haste, for Su-Anna had already set fire to the piles of filthy straw on the wooden floor, and the crackling of the fire grew louder as the flames rose.

Mumbling and sobbing, the two men who had been locked into the stocks lay stiff and cramped on the ground, too crippled to walk unaided, but Chester found that he had the strength, despite the agony of his back, despite the stinging pain of the open sores on the backs of his legs.

"That's it!" Su-Anna yelled, "you can do it!" Her voice—high and ringing with confidence—cheered on all the men.

"Let's go!" one of them yelled, "we got to catch up with the others now! They marchin' down the island road. C'mon, brothers!"

Torches high, stepping faster and faster, the crowd left the burning jail. They were armed with scythes and axes, with wooden spears, with hand knives, with homemade bayonets. One man carried a shovel, which was all he had; another carried a peck of stolen bullets and ten pounds of powder, ready for the moment when he would relieve some white man of his gun.

With Su-Anna near the front and Chester struggling to keep up, the little army marched to the mid-island road, where they saw the lights of the others just ahead, and heard, through the stillness, the tolling of a bell in Frederica, a warning bell, the one used to signal fire somewhere on the island.

Hearing it, the marching slaves broke into a run. Surprise was their strongest weapon, that and their numbers; if they were only a small part of the slaves on the island, they would still outnumber the whites by a large margin. Even yet, they faced nearly hopeless odds; they had no habit or tradition of organization, no experienced leaders, no far-reaching plan. The tolling of the bell reminded them of the white man's world, a wider world than their own, a finite, legitimate world in which theirs was only a poor, wretched part. Would the bell wake the white people at Sea Groves? It was late, past midnight, and they were all asleep. Perhaps they would not hear it.

"Liberty!" Su-Anna screamed, feeling the fear stirring among the men. "Damn the bell! They sleep like the dead—like the dead they gone be tonight! Liberty or death!"

And the others took courage from her, and a chant rose up: "Free-dom! Free-dom! All white men die! Die! Die! Free-dom! Free-dom!"

As the slaves bent on murder and destruction approached Sea Groves that night, all except one member of the Barstow family was asleep. Livia slept soundly, her rest undisturbed by dreams of any sort. Beside her in the master bedroom, Morgan slept fitfully, his conscience still troubled by the incident with Chester three days earlier, his mind reviewing and recalling the ghastly moment when Chester had sprung at him, his hands at his throat, his dark eyes blank with hopeless rage.

Both Cole and Hugh, the youngest son, now fifteen, slept as deeply as young men will who have spent the day outdoors and eaten heartily. The brothers were good friends and much alike. Since his childhood, Hugh had imitated Cole in all things, following his older brother everywhere he went, learning from him how to ride, how to load and shoot a gun, how to handle slaves and women. Neither Cole nor Caleb had wanted to go away to college, but Morgan was determined that Hugh would go—in less than a month he would journey off to Georgia's own university, already a flourishing institution at Athens. Until then, and it was a prospect Hugh dreaded, he would spend every daylight moment working outside with Cole; it was the season for cotton picking and both of them rode out daily with their father, overseeing the slave men and women who moved slowly through the fields, filling huge homespun sacks with cotton bolls and dragging them to the gin house, which stood between the stables and the boat landing.

Roland Barstow, now a white-haired man in his seventies, slept and dreamed; although he did not always sleep well, that night he had doubled the size of his customary nightcap of rum, sugar, and water. Perhaps more than any of the others, Roland missed his daughter Juliette; she was the only one who did not make him feel old—to him the house seemed empty without her light step and cheerful voice—and cotton-picking time was hard for Roland, for he was too weak to ride out with the other men and the lint and dust in the gin house made him wheeze and gasp. Roland's dreams, as they so often did, took him to a far-off realm—the past, a time he missed more sorely than his waking self could ever admit, a time when he had been strong and hearty and with his beloved Jenny at his side had been master of Sea Groves in more than name.

While all these older Barstows slept, the youngest member of the family did not. Polly Barstow, the baby of the family, everyone's favorite, was engaged in an act of rebellion no less dangerous and radical for its being conceived and perpetrated by a cherished and cosseted girl of ten. Perhaps it was because she had been so spoiled and adored since her birth that Polly was so self-assured, so active, confident, and independent—none of them qualities that society, her family, or in particular her mother would have rewarded in a female child.

Polly had been allowed to grow up in a gentle atmosphere of indulgence, created and protected by her father, who favored her above all his sons, even as her mother ignored her. From the moment of her birth, Polly, as was the custom, had been under the care of a black nursemaid and in the company of her own personal handmaid, the child, in this case, of the same black woman who suckled and looked after her.

Together, the little girls—blue-eyed, curly-haired Polly and smiling, round-faced, brown-skinned Berlinda—had made the entire house and all its grounds, its gardens and fields and orchards and huge, rolling, well-kept lawns, their playground. They had, in Livia's view, "run wild."

It was Morgan who had spoiled them, more than anyone else. As soon as they were old enough, he took them everywhere with him, riding all over the plantation in front of him on the saddle of his mare, to visit neighboring plantations, to market in Brunswick. When the girls were six, he bought them both tiny well-trained ponies, for Polly's birthday, and when they were seven, they learned to embroider, and made twin samplers, which Morgan had hung on either side of his desk.

Thus busy and happy, Polly and Berlinda learned not to "bother" Mama, who was always short-tempered and often absent, to go to Papa or one of the boys for any indulgence, and to take willful advantage of their freedom, which became a habit for both of them.

Inevitably, it was a habit which led to trouble, for Polly as well as her friend, for if Berlinda was, after all, a slave, Polly was a woman—another restricted condition, and a single incident served to illustrate the restrictions on both of them. There had not been a tutor at Sea Groves for some years, before that spring, when Morgan had managed to secure one, in a last-ditch effort to prepare Hugh for the university. Thus it happened that young Hiram Van Peele, a university graduate himself, came to the plantation, the first formal teacher there since Caleb's tutor had died six or more years earlier.

Van Peele's main responsibility was to teach Hugh, a considerable task, for Hugh's interests ran to horse racing and duck shooting rather than to history and calculus, but at the same time he set about teaching Polly to read. Polly was to learn reading; she was not introduced to the mysteries of arithmetic. History was safe enough for girls, but there was no thought of Polly's being prepared for the university. That was for boys. Polly—used to her way in everything—protested a bit. She wanted to learn whatever Hugh learned, but that was not as disturbing as the tutor's other injunction.

To Polly's astonishment and chagrin, Berlinda was not allowed to go into the classroom with her. She was not allowed to hear Mr. Van Peele's stories about George Washington and Alexander the Great, and she was not, in point and particular, allowed to learn to read, which became the great pursuit and passion of Polly's days.

"Why, Papa? Why can't Berlinda learn, too?" Polly demanded of her father.

Her usually permissive parent was firm. "Negroes have no use for reading, Polly. Their minds are not suited to it; in general they could not learn to read, and if some of them did, it would ruin them—make them unfit for the work they have to do."

"I don't believe it!" Polly insisted. "Berlinda can do anything I can do!"

"No, she cannot," Morgan said. "Reading makes Negro people restless and rebellious, and that is why it is against the law."

"Against the law?" Polly asked, still disbelieving.

"Yes, it is against the law in Georgia," Morgan insisted, and even his pretty daughter's tears could not move him.

But Polly, not to be stopped either by law or custom, took it into her head to teach Berlinda all on her own. She realized well enough that it would have to take place on the sly, and their lessons began, with the keyhole blocked in Polly's bedroom, at night, when Berlinda was supposed to be brushing out Polly's long, curly hair.

Berlinda was an apt, intelligent pupil, and the secret lessons progressed well. "A—t—at, b—at—bat, c—at—cat," the girls sounded out together, and surrounded by Polly's copy books, her little wood-framed slate, her Bible, and enough apples and cookies to sustain them for hours, they worked together every night.

And so they were on the night the army of angry slaves approached Sea Groves. The oil lamp had been put out, both girls were clothed in frilled and tucked white batiste nightdresses, and lying belly-down on the floor by the light of a single candle, they studied together, Polly taking an almost malicious satisfaction in how fast Berlinda could learn.

"Why, I think you will be a better reader than I am!" Polly said.

"I want to be just as good," Berlinda said.

"You are . . . just as good," Polly promised, and their eyes met, and they clasped hands, just as they heard the tolling of the bell that meant fire.

"Listen!" Polly said.

"I know! It's the big bell, isn't it?"

"Do you think we should wake Papa?"

Berlinda hesitated, but as the bell continued to toll, she had a sudden, sure feeling that something was very wrong.

Pulling Polly up with her, she ran to the window—it was open—and there, framed in dotted swiss ruffles, the two little girls saw that the front yard of Sea Groves was filling up with men carrying torches, filling with a menacing crowd—it seemed huge—of dark-skinned men, a few women among them.

"Who is it?" Polly gasped.

"What are they here for?" Berlinda asked.

They stared down at the incredible scene. The crowd seemed huge; they were milling around at random, trampling over the rose bushes and the beds of flowers. They were oddly silent.

Each of the girls knew that the mob was bent on trouble, and each felt, at the same time, a shock of terrible fear such as they had never before known.

"Oh, Berlinda!" Polly whispered, "I'm scared."

And then she screamed. Her voice was weak and high-pitched, but it cut through the darkness like a thin, sharp knife. Several of the men looked up at the window, at the weak, pale light of the candle the girls had been reading with, and the crowd surged forward, toward the front door.

Polly screamed again, screamed with all her strength, and Berlinda began to sob.

In New York City, a week later, Juliette received her brother Morgan's letter bringing her the awful, unexpected news of what had happened on Saint Simons Island. Before she had finished reading the letter, Juliette felt her vision dim and her head go blank. She dropped the letter and fell to the floor, in a dead faint for the first time in her life.

Patience, her maid, was nearby and ran to Juliette's aid; Juliette was unconscious for only a moment, but when she came to, and felt her face being cradled in Patience's black hands, she shuddered, and, as she never had before, she winced at a slave's touch.

Bit by bit, Juliette absorbed the sum of the news. It was not all bad. Although Roland was dead—"my poor father," Juliette wept—no other family member had been killed, or even injured. Roland had died in Morgan's arms as the family had fled the big house. They had "found refuge," as Morgan's letter put it, "in the quarters, in the very homes of those who were attacking us, for you see, Juliette, and you will realize the importance of this distinction, it was by no means the majority of our people who were involved."

Juliette shook her head. It was not surprising to her that most of the Barstow slaves had not been involved; it was surprising that any of them—any of their faithful, contented, well-cared-for people, most of whom had been born at Sea Groves, all of whom had *always* been—well . . . *seemed*—happy to live there, could have participated in this terrible insurrection. She could not understand it; she could not adjust to the idea—it contradicted all her beliefs and feelings, it went against the entire experience of her life.

Shocked and profoundly disturbed, she tried to digest the rest of the news from Morgan. The plantation "big" house, almost eighty years old, built by their grandfather, had been totally destroyed, burned to the ground.

Juliette sobbed when she thought of it. It was wrong, she supposed, to set such store by material things. The Bible said not to expect salvation through worldly goods; it was spiritual treasures that were of real value, and yet . . . she felt desolate when she thought of such an end for her fine old home, her family's home. It had been more than a dwelling place; it had been a symbol and solace to all of them for all their lives.

"The offenders," Morgan had written, "have been apprehended to a man, have been taken into custody and are being severely punished. I regret to say that there are some among them whose names you will recognize." Juliette's fingers trembled as she read the names of those from Sea Groves who had been part of the insurrectionary force: Chester, the driver; Jim, field hand; Randall, groom; Levi, field hand; and Su-Anna, the housemaid who usually stayed in Savannah.

"They have all been put to death," Morgan wrote. Juliette cried anew. The perfidy, the treachery, the ghastly disloyalty of it! She could not believe it. Juliette stayed alone in her room for an entire day after she received Morgan's letter; she could neither eat nor sleep. The Warringtons assumed her to be wrestling with her grief; in fact, she was questioning the entire foundation of her society.

Slavery was wrong, Juliette willingly admitted. As an abstract concept, it was wrong for one human being to own and manage another. Slavery led to cruelty; some slaves were unhappy; some masters unjust. And yet—the reality of it was something not easily dealt with, nor easily understood by nonslaveholders. Negroes were an inferior race, she believed. A violent insurrection like the one that had grown up on Saint Simons Island seemed to prove it, not deny it. Negroes were altogether different from white men; they were next to savages; they were uncivilized, uncontrolled, prone to violence; they had come from heathen Africa, denied any form of education, any knowledge of civilization as it had developed in the rest of the world.

What could be done, Juliette asked herself, and she pondered the question very seriously. What could be done? The wisest southern thinkers regarded the peaceful coexistence of the two races on a basis of equality to be impossible. Perhaps it was. Should they, then, all be sent back to Africa? She had heard of movements organized to promote this. She had heard, of course, of abolitionists, who advocated an immediate end to the buying and selling and holding of slaves. But everyone she knew, including her brother and father, considered this position wild, naive, irresponsible, impossible. If the abolitionists had their way, what would happen to southern agriculture? What would happen to Georgia if she took on the added burden—for burden it would be—of a free majority of uneducated, unguided, illiterate, violence-prone Negro people in her midst?

It was hard to understand, hard to reconcile, but Juliette was forced to confront it, and so, she knew, must Morgan and the others at Sea Groves. The cataclysmic end to the "trouble," the actual burning of the plantation big house, made it impossible to go on as they had been. Juliette was not surprised to read that Morgan was considering a radical change. One seemed due. The slave revolt and the destruction of their home had effectively ended their family's happy tenure on Saint Simons Island.

Morgan wrote his sister that he was thinking of moving west, moving everything that was left, all their animals, all their people, all the possessions that had escaped the fire, to new land somewhere . . . far from Sea Groves. Juliette felt sad to think of it, but she was not completely surprised or opposed. For years the coastal region of Georgia had been emptying out to the West. Many people she knew and others she had heard of had left their old land and headed toward unsettled areas. All America was shifting to the West—there was rich, fertile farmland out there, and reports came back of wonderful cotton crops, of towns and cities that were fast acquiring all the advantages of eastern communities.

"Come home, dear Juliette," Morgan had written, "for of course, I would not think of making this decision without you, nor in opposition to your will. I am distraught, sister, and know not which way to turn, except this. Just now I am occupied with my grief, but there are the children to consider. The family survives, and it is our duty to make provisions for its future. I know you will come home to us as soon as you are able."

Sadly and shamefacedly, a troubled Juliette made preparations to leave New York. She was truly sorry to leave; her visit had been in some ways the greatest adventure of her life, but it did not leave her unchanged. She met with Taylor Bruce on the eve of her sailing.

It was difficult to talk to Mr. Bruce about what had happened at Sea Groves—indeed, it was difficult to speak to any of her New York friends about it, for discussion aroused painful and dangerous differences of opinion and outlook.

"I cannot understand why you must go back," Taylor Bruce said.

I cannot understand how you cannot understand, Juliette thought, but she hid her trembling hands and said merely, "Mr. Bruce, I have a duty to my family . . . to our people . . . to carry on . . ."

"Could not your whole family come here? How can you remain? The region is a tinderbox. This can only happen again!" Mr. Bruce said fervently. "Miss Barstow, you are too fine, too sensitive, too talented a woman to disappear again into that troubled wilderness. . . . I have to contemplate it! Is there no way I can persuade you?"

"None, sir," Juliette said.

Taylor Bruce tossed his large, handsome head. "Miss Barstow, I admire you immensely. I shall look for your manuscripts in the mail. I beg you to respect your talents, to use them. I beg you to take all possible care of yourself. And not to forget . . ."

Juliette felt the weight of what might have been. Her soul felt robbed, wrenched. "Sir, I must go," she said. "I am exhausted by my arrangements for traveling. Believe me, sir, I have considered all this. I have considered everything. Mr. Bruce, I look forward to going home! Does that surprise you?"

"It does," he said, and they managed to exchange a smile before he took his leave.

The next day, Juliette and Patience sailed for Georgia.

Two weeks later, Juliette rode out alone to visit her father's grave for one last time. Roland Barstow had been buried next to Jenny in the little graveyard next to the church in Frederica, as he had wished to be, and Morgan had seen to it that a carved marble monument was erected with both their names, and inscribed "Dear Father, Dear Mother, God rest you both, from this your fond children, who pledge you our troth."

Since returning from New York, Juliette had ridden to visit the little graveyard every day. Somehow, seeing its unchanged mossy stillness gave her a measure of peace and relief from the sadness, confusion, and bustle of Sea Groves, where the Barstow family had made a temporary home for themselves in the plain, primitive suite of rooms in the eaves of the stables, while preparations were being made for the trip west.

For Juliette had encouraged Morgan to follow his plan to leave Saint Simons Island, and they had decided to go. En masse, the family and their slaves would make the trek west in a vast caravan of forty-five big, wooden-wheeled wagons, already gathered at the mainland side of the Brunswick ferry.

This is the last time, Juliette thought as she rode slowly down the avenue that led from the ruins of the big house to the mid-island road. For the last time she passed the acres of banked-up cotton fields, bare now, and the low-lying rice fields which had been laid out in squares by her grandfather. All along the avenue slaves were busy raking and cleaning and tidying the fields, busy getting together their own possessions and putting into good repair and order the tools and equipment they would move with them.

Morgan had presented the matter of moving west to his slaves, asking them if they wanted to come along or to stay. Those who elected to stay, he had said, would be sold to other masters on the island. He did not intend to take along one unwilling slave, for the route was hard and long, and the future uncertain. There would be no quarters waiting for them in western Georgia, no fields cleared, no trees felled. Everything would have to be done before they could plant a cotton crop and plan and build a house for the family. Morgan had explained all this to the slaves, and yet all but two of them had chosen to go. There was a new spirit among them now, a changed spirit from the first days after the insurrection when they had been quiet and sullen or quiet and ashamed, according to the extent of their involvement.

Most of them, as Morgan had written Juliette, had nothing to do with the uprising, had stood by helplessly, and some of them had acted bravely to protect the Barstow family—hiding them in their own homes in the awful, crazy hours while the big house burned and the small army of vigilantes from all over the island and as far away as Brunswick had ridden to Sea Groves. Those Barstow slaves who had been involved had been put to death violently by the posse of vigilantes.

Juliette shuddered as she rode to the end of the avenue through the familiar acres, thinking of it. All five of the rebels had been well known to her. When she reached the plantation gates, she looked away from the sight of their five heads impaled on tall oak saplings. There they were: Levi and Jim, Randall and Chester and Su-Anna, their dark faces set in grimaces, their eyes forever blank, their black hair soaked with blood.

Sobbing, Juliette whipped up her horse and cantered toward the graveyard. Once she was alone she made no effort to act cheerful and confident; in truth she was not. A part of her had died, too; her innocence was gone forever; the worst had already occurred, and when the worst was past, the future, however new, must inevitably be shadowed. For Morgan's sake, for the sake of Polly and the boys, she would muster her spirits tomorrow, she would do her best to encourage the others, but as for herself, she did not want to leave Saint Simons Island, and indeed, did not want to go on holding slaves and raising cotton.

How must it be for the children, she asked herself as she stood at her parents' graves. She thought of little Polly, her goddaughter, her favorite. Polly seemed—quite rightly—terribly shocked by the realities of the revolt and the fire, and unable to conceive of the idea of moving west. How different it was for me, Juliette thought. My own mother was a rock, an immovable stable force. Why, I grew up thinking nothing could change, or ever would, that I would live here on Saint Simons Island all my life, that the slaves and the plantings and the parties and the community affairs would go on season after season, year after year, just as they always had.

Of course, I was wrong, Juliette conceded, strolling in the shaded mossy churchyard. Nothing had been the same in any of our lives since the day Ira Barstow died, since the day James Dunlie came home from England, perhaps. But I never really knew it until now. And Polly? Praise God she has the courage and faith to maintain her sisterly friendship with her little maid Berlinda. Had the clash of the races shattered even the love of little children, it would have been impossible to go on, Juliette decided. Her own innocence might be totally gone, but without a good measure of innocence and trust, she could not fathom how Polly . . . and the others of her generation . . . would go on living in their society.

Perhaps, even so, Juliette thought, they will change it. Who can say what great and good changes, what new mornings Polly will live to see? Many, I hope, many, many, and of such a considerable magnitude that my poor imagination cannot encompass them.

Wiping away tears, Juliette returned to the graves where her parents lay and bid them farewell forever. Nevermore, nevermore, she thought, and then she smiled. The past had been happy; now it was past. They had been a loving family, a family united by caring and mutual concern; despite her mother's tragic death, she had been the happiest of wives, the most loving of mothers. Her father had missed his wife sorely and long; now he was united with her in heaven. I do not envy you, Juliette told her parents, but I know that you are both well content to be together again.

And as for myself, Juliette thought as she remounted for the ride back to the bare, defaced plantation, I must bear these losses and go on. Nothing is left but to endure.

CHAPTER THIRTEEN

A Wilderness Exodus; An Overseer's Obsession; Passion Quashed

For all the Barstows, the trek across the width of the state of Georgia was, as might well be supposed, an unforgettable experience, although for each of them it was to be remembered for different reasons and in different ways.

Generally speaking, it was for Morgan a sort of Pilgrim's Progress, a voyage of atonement, for he believed in his heart that he must have sinned, must have transgressed in some moral way, to have brought down upon his home and his family the wrath of judgment. Only some great wrong could have earned for all of them such a terrible punishment of destruction and death. Morgan began the journey in a very sober, remorseful frame of mind, but as it progressed, his spirits lifted, gradually, and he began to hope for redemption, for a new start, a second chance at Jordan, when they should all arrive in the promised land.

For his two sons (Caleb having been left in Savannah) it was a relief and a reprieve. Hugh was glad enough to postpone his entrance into the university until they had settled in the West; Cole accepted the change and adventure gladly and willingly, as he accepted everything else in his life. The two young men, in the first full flower of their strength and courage, easily turned their backs on Saint Simons Island and faced the future where it lay—across the Altamaha River, across the dense boundless swamps, through the pine barrens, and farther west in Jasper County, where their father had contracted to buy two thousand acres of land reputed to be good for growing cotton. Cole and Hugh rode at the head of the Barstow caravan, each mounted on a spirited, sure-footed mare, each armed with pistols and a sword, for dealing with the foe ahead, be it Indian or rattlesnake, and as they rode, they sang, and shouted to each other and the family and slaves who came behind.

For their mother, for Livia, the trek was an epoch of misery, discomfort, and privation. Livia rode in a small, open-sided carriage near the end of the caravan; but she was not accustomed to pioneering and became ill from drinking some bad water, or some turned milk, and suffered terrible cramps and agonies from the start, even before they had left Brunswick fairly behind. It fell upon Juliette to care for Livia, an arrangement which pleased neither woman, and as often as her conscience allowed, Juliette left Livia to groan alone under her coverlets and rode ahead on her steel-gray stallion, to talk with Morgan or one of the boys.

Despite her illness, the hope of reaching the new land sustained Livia, for as far as she could tell, the land, described as partway between the towns of Macon and Milledgeville, could not be far from her brother Angus's home. Livia had written Angus before they left Saint Simons, informed him that she was coming—with the rest of the family—and expressed her happiness that she would see him again very soon. The prospect of seeing Angus Dunlie was not one that would have drawn any other member of the Barstow family to the region, but Livia had talked with Morgan and had gotten Morgan to agree that a reconciliation between them would be advisable, if possible, and that he was not averse to it, if it should indeed come to be.

Each day en route, then, seemed to Livia to be one day closer to her destination, and she began to live in the future, ignoring as much as she could the current miseries of aching bones and muscles, the damp chill of the nights in the woods, the constant breakdowns that slowed their progress along the roads, rough at best and in some cases barely half-stumped paths.

But if Livia lived in the future, and the other adult Barstows daily struggled to forget the past, young Polly Barstow and her dear friend Berlinda lived completely in the present, thoroughly enjoying every day of the journey, waking every morning to birdsongs and the smell of the campfires, riding back and forth all day on their tiny ponies, sleeping snugly each night in the back of a covered wagon. For the little girls it was a wonderful time, a time of constantly changing scenery and freedom from restraint and supervision, a time to see new wonders—logs that turned into alligators, handsome Indian women offering beaded capes and moccasins for sale, bright-feathered birds swinging in the branches of wonderfully tall trees—and all this going on while their parents hardly remembered to wash them or comb their hair, often forgot when it was bedtime, and could never punish them by sending them to their rooms.

"I love travelin'," Polly whispered one night, deep in the thickly wooded swamp which stretched for hundreds of miles along the Altamaha. She and Berlinda were not asleep, as everyone supposed them to be, but peered, wide-eyed, out of the back of a long, low-roofed tilt wagon laden with goods and bedding. All around them in the wilderness stretched the small tents where the slaves slept by night. Joshua, the fiddler, was playing a rollicking song; some twenty of the younger people were dancing as their elders sat on logs around the campfire, smoking pipes and looking into the flames and the unfathomable darkness of the surrounding swamp.

"Me, too," Berlinda agreed. "Let's never go back."

"Never," Polly promised. "And let's always stay together, you and me."

"Always," Berlinda vowed, and finally, unwillingly, the two girls fell asleep.

But as delightful as the journey could be in good weather, it became far less so with the advent of the rains of December. For days, for more than a week, the rains were heavy and unceasing. They swelled the river and streams with ominously black water, turned the rough roads to beds of mud, and soaked into every wagon and carriage. As the rains continued, as the family and the slaves woke day after day to gray, sodden skies, as every garment they owned became dank and mildewed, the dancing stopped and spirits fell.

On such a rainy morning, Morgan and his sons met a party of travelers heading east. It was a melancholy-looking party, every one of them soaked and shivering, from the master, riding at the head with heavy holsters swinging across the pommel of his saddle and a black bearskin over his shoulder, to the women, mother and grandmother, piled into a large black carry-all wagon with four small and tearful children.

"Good day, stranger. Could you use some help? What's ahead?" Morgan asked the man at the lead.

"Bridge is out and it's a bad ford. The creek's high and risin' up ahead," the man said tensely, and rode on without saying more.

Where were they going? Cole wondered. They were turning back, but back to where? It was days to the nearest town; how bad could the ford be, and why had they not waited it out?

When the Barstow party reached the ford up ahead, Cole's questions were answered, at least in part. The stream was broad and higher than its banks on either side; the footbridge, or what had been a bridge, was completely collapsed—thick logs cracked in two—and caught in the debris were the carcasses of two good-sized horses, the loss of which must have so discouraged the party of travelers that they had turned back.

Morgan and his sons faced the sight with dismay. It was morning, and rain had fallen all night and was still falling; the level of the water could only continue to rise. Silently, Morgan and Cole and Hugh studied the turbulent black flood as the others—the wagons, the rolling hogsheads, the slaves on foot and the women and children on horseback—came up behind.

"We can't cross," Livia complained. "We shall all be drowned!"

"We can't wait much longer," Morgan said. "It's rising fast."

There was no way of knowing how deep the water was—that it was rough and dirty was obvious. Part of the footbridge still clung to its traces, but it was in parts only a single log wide.

"Let me try to drive the biggest wagon across," Cole suggested.

It was a desperate suggestion, but sensible. If Cole could get a wagon and a rope across, then the rest of them could cross in turns, floating goods when necessary, sending most of them across the log bridge from hand to hand.

Emptying the wagon, they piled its cargo beside the

stream, and Cole took his seat on the high bench, behind the two best horses in harness.

"Go! Go, Red! Go, Big Boy!" he urged them. Both sturdy draft horses snorted and whinnied and rolled their eyes, but they plunged ahead resolutely under Cole's cracking whip.

"Take it straight!" Morgan called out, thinking that perhaps the logs of which the road had originally been made might somehow be in position under the floor.

And such appeared to be the case, for the wooden wheels groaned and creaked and sank to their tops in the water, but the horses never lost their footing, and when they scrambled up the embankment across the stream, a cheer rose from all the watchers and Cole raised his arms in triumph.

For the rest of the day, then, bit by bit, the Barstows and all their goods passed perilously over the sunken bridge or were floated across on the wagon beds. By nightfall they had gained only about a hundred feet, but with their backs to the stream they built a huge campfire and roasted a score of the chickens they had carried from Sea Groves in slat-sided coops.

"Will it ever stop raining?" Livia demanded fretfully as the family sat together huddled under a makeshift tent and a broad-branched white pine in the midst of a huge, encircling mass of dark-skinned servants.

"It must, I promise you," Morgan said with a wry smile. His eyes met Juliette's across the shadows, and he gave her a wink that was both encouraging and commiserating.

"Did you ever hear the story about the rains that lasted for forty days and nights?" Polly asked innocently, and wondered why everyone laughed.

If Angus Dunlie had seemed a backwoodsman in sophisticated Savannah, had seemed a "cracker" to his sister Livia, and had shrunk in horror from the effete abnormality suggested by the sight of his son Caleb embracing Jacob Barstow, in his own land he seemed neither shrinking, nor rude, nor out of style. In his own country, his own town, at his businesses, and at his own Dunlie Hall—already a Washington County landmark—he was lord and master, he was the *grand seigneur*, the father of all and the ultimate authority.

It was with relief that Angus Dunlie returned to Dunlie Hall from his visit to Savannah and with pleasure that he took up again his life there. Perhaps it was not the life he had contemplated living when he had been a young man in London, or even one to fit his expectations when he had come west in 1800 wearing kid gloves, but it was a life that suited him, a life that—like his own character—was built on compromises and contradictions, that had a strength and a style of its own, and a strong streak of violence as well.

Dunlie Hall was not the mansion its name and reputation suggested—not yet, for it was to undergo many additions and remodelings in the years to come. It would not have been so remarkable in Savannah, or Charleston, and certainly not in Boston or Philadelphia, but for northwest Georgia it was impressive indeed.

To design Dunlie Hall, Angus had hired a foreign architect—an itinerant from England who had come to the county by chance and left immediately afterward. There were no other houses like it, and there never would be. It was well proportioned, being twice as wide as it was deep and two and a half stories high. Eight brick fireplaces stood at either end of the house, opening into two tall brick chimneys, and there were eight rooms on each floor, all paneled with pecan wood. Verandahs opened front and back, a sensible concession to the climate, and over the front porch rose an impressive balcony, supported by a dozen sturdy white-painted columns of the Corinthian order, as the house's mistress liked to explain to visitors, although she had no idea who or what Corinth had been, and supposed it, had truth been told, to be some village in England.

A tall glass-paneled door opened onto the balcony from the master's bedroom, which was central and large. The whole house shone with glass; there were countless windows, all of them neatly framed in pecan and finished outside with deep sills and blinds, and inside with painted shutters, showing imaginative views of the English countryside rendered in a somewhat primitive, if nostalgic, hand. Free to amuse himself, the architect, a Mr. Colin Whitbread, had given license to his fancies and had peopled the pastoral scenes with nymphs and satyrs, elves and fantastic fruits and ferns and foliage that had never before come together in a single climate or frame.

Without quite understanding it, Angus Dunlie was very proud of it all. He had furnished the house to the best of his ability and imagination, had imported tables and chairs and sideboards and bedsteads from Savannah shops and workshops, had ranged them in all the rooms and hung up curtains of pale brocades until the effect was both soothing and startling.

Outside the house there stood two kitchen houses, made of rough-hewn logs, a smokehouse, a well house, and then, far behind them, hidden from view by a row of poplars, a little village for the slaves, whose number had increased steadily since the days when Pittman Stone had brought in the first four or five to till his corn. There were now no fewer than he needed for his own enterprises, even taking into account his mill, his stores, and his late, almost reluctant venture into growing cotton.

To direct and coordinate it all, Angus Dunlie employed an overseer, or rather a series of overseers, for none of them had stayed long. It was not a post, poorly paid and difficult as it was, to attract the most intelligent and capable sort of man, and Dunlie was not an easy master. His current overseer, a redheaded Scotsman from Pennsylvania, Jack MacPherson, had hung on already the better part of a year, which was nearly a record.

MacPherson's job was by no means an easy one. He was expected to rise at first light and ring the bell that roused the slaves from their beds. He assigned the tasks and saw that they were done; he supervised the storage and distribution of food and firewood; at night he was responsible for feeding and housing the livestock and for seeing that all the tools and equipment were put away and the storerooms locked. It was his duty to see that no strange Negroes were about the place; at nine o'clock he rang the curfew bell, inspected the quarters, and reported to the big house that all was well before he himself was free to retire.

And retire he was expected to do—alone—to his own little house, a simple two-roomed cottage set under some pines near the stables. MacPherson was a bachelor, and—of course, as he was a Yankee—likely to remain one in this county where pretty girls of good family were at a premium. MacPherson's rank and origins set him well apart from the other white folk; he was included in none of the social events and activities which increased yearly in the county.

Angus, insofar as he thought of him at all, except as a necessary part of the plantation work force, thought MacPherson a bit odd. The man was a reader of newspapers; he was solitary, and seemed—as one expected of a Scotsman—practical, thrifty, and dour. Nonetheless, he got on well enough with the Negroes—there had been no runaways since his tenure began—and he did not trouble Angus with endless questions and problems, as most overseers did. It was partly due to MacPherson's interest that Angus had increased the number of acres he planted with cotton; there seemed no reason not to, the land was there, new and fertile, the hands were available, and the price of cotton was rising every year.

MacPherson had his own reasons for advocating the increased cotton plantings; although Angus did not yet know it, he was the sort who had his own reasons for everything he did. Jack MacPherson was the sixth son of a Pennsylvania farmer; he had never expected to inherit land; he was independent and hard working and ambitious. He did everything for a reason, everything toward a goal, and his goal was to learn all he could about the best ways of planting cotton and then to move west with his salary from four or five years of overseeing, to buy his own land and set up his own cotton plantation.

It was this dream that sustained him in what he regarded as an exile in the desert, this and another secret dream, this one more of a passion. Shortly after his arrival at Dunlie Hall ten months ago, Jack MacPherson had first laid eyes on the mulatto woman Rebecca, and had fallen directly in love with her.

However inappropriate this passion, it was genuine. At first, MacPherson had no idea of Rebecca's role in the household, of her relationship with the family, or her character. At first, it was purely a physical attraction, complete with the emotional and sentimental longings and fascinations that make up the sickness we call love. MacPherson was young; he was in his early twenties. Rebecca was a good ten years older than he, but she was a remarkably healthy, fine-featured woman with a graceful, robust figure that her years of childbearing had done nothing to harm. She had beauty, strength, and intelligence to match any other woman, white or black, that MacPherson had ever met. It was these qualities that had led Angus Dunlie to select her for his wife's keeper, so many years ago when she was a very young woman; it was these qualities that had led to his taking her into his own bed and keeping her there over the years.

In every way, Rebecca was a wonderful woman. She was cheerful, beautiful, clever, hardworking, and submissive. In almost every way, she was the mistress of Dunlie Hall, except that Nancy Dunlie held title to that position. Nancy Dunlie sat at the head of the table; Rebecca stood behind it. Nancy Dunlie walked, pale and disconnected as a zombie, through the quarters and through the house; Rebecca walked beside her, carrying the basket of keys, deciding to whom would go favors and medicines, to whom needed articles of clothing would be assigned, which child set to work weeding the flower beds or shooing flies off the children in the nursery.

Rebecca did it all gracefully, and she seemed to do it willingly. Her own dreams were small ones, and before she met Jack MacPherson they had been all her own. She was a woman of strong feelings, and the corner posts of her life balanced each other with a solid regularity that both supported and enclosed her. She loved, in turn, her children (who were all by Angus Dunlie, although she did not love, had never loved him, and could not love him), her God (she had been converted to Christianity and believed in it with all her heart), her dream of freedom for herself and her children, and with an admixture of duty and pity, Nancy Dunlie. These four callings, then, were the poles of her life, the life of a woman who would have been admired as an honest and devoted wife and mother and community leader in any other time and place, but whose existence, because of the conditions of her servitude and exploitation, was sharply limited and without expectation or hope.

In this life, at least. It was Rebecca's habit, as she went about her daily chores and rounds, with Nancy at her side, to sing to herself about the life to come; Rebecca's voice was strong and true, and her favorite song was one which included the words "Oh, one of these days, my time will come. . . . Ah'll heah that bugle, Ah'll heah that drum." Nancy's voice was light and clear, and she, too, loved singing. "Ah'll be there, when they open up Heaven's gate," the two women sang, and their voices melded into one of heart-stirring richness.

Rebecca, a mature and intuitive woman, could tell quickly enough that Jack MacPherson was attracted to her although she was surprised by his attraction. She avoided him, but his eyes followed her everywhere. Whenever he had cause to speak to her, her replies were as short and businesslike as she could manage, but he took every opportunity to see her and speak to her, he sought her out by day and by night, and always, unfailingly, he treated her as no other white man had ever treated her, as an equal, as a desirable woman. Neither presumptuously or demandingly, he courted her, bringing her gifts such as yards of cloth, a store-made shawl, and a parcel of tulip bulbs to plant in front of her cabin.

One day he wrote her a note, and Rebecca cried, for of course she could not read, although she longed to read the Scriptures. He offered to teach her, but she shook her head. "If you want to read to us some time, Mr. MacPherson, we'd be honored," she said, and he did, sitting on the back verandah with Nancy Dunlie and Rebecca all one Sunday afternoon, reading aloud from the testament. It was the first time she had ever looked at him, and Jack MacPherson took some hope from it, for he was both awed and infatuated. His own mother had been a Quaker, and he was well acquainted with the Scriptures and in his heart a believer—even more so since Rebecca had awakened in him such pure adoration and longings.

MacPherson's intentions toward Rebecca were honorable. He loved her; he wanted her; he aspired to buying her freedom and carrying her off with him to live with him in a free state, as his wife. He told her so, and though Rebecca was too astonished to refuse him outright, and though she was far from believing that such a thing could ever be, it unleashed her fantasies and troubled her mind, so that she went about her duties for the next months troubled with dreams of freedom and what might have been.

As he grew more accustomed to the workings of the plantation and the peculiar setup of Dunlie Hall,

MacPherson realized that Rebecca's four children, all of them quite light-skinned, were those of the master. True to his nature, strict-minded MacPherson was angry and disturbed when he realized this. To him, Angus Dunlie was an old man, a hard and stingy master, and now an immoral and deceitful man, for it was hard to imagine how his relations with Rebecca could have been carried out without the knowledge of his wife. Rebecca and Nancy were seldom parted. They spent every waking moment together. Only when Nancy had been given her medicine and put to bed, only when the key to her bedroom (of which only Angus and Rebecca possessed copies) was safely in Rebecca's pocket, was she even free to go to her own little house.

But it was there that MacPherson now sought her, increasingly often and openly, somehow liberated by the knowledge of Angus Dunlie's exploitation, and it was there, in her tiny cabin, that he begged her to leave Dunlie Hall and to flee with him to the West, across the Mississippi.

With tears in her eyes, Rebecca told him she could not.

"I beg you not to speak of it again," she said sincerely. "My ties here are too strong, sir. I am bound to this place. There are my children. I could never leave them. And the mistress. She could never get on without me, sir."

"Miss . . . Rebecca," MacPherson vowed, "the children should come with us."

"He would never allow it!" Rebecca gasped. The enormity of the overseer's misunderstanding of the situation both horrified and impressed her. He was so unlike any other white man she had ever known. Of course, she had never known another Yankee. Everyone said Yankees were strange, still . . . He must be unique; how could there be others like him? Perhaps he was mad. She stared into his face, lined with sincerity, red with passion and excitement. She had seen him work; she knew him to be a good man, but she had no real hopes for herself. She was not old . . . not yet . . . but her life was over. She was fixed here; too many doors had closed for her ever to pass on—in this life, at least. On the day Angus Dunlie had bought her, a girl of fifteen, on the auction block at Milledgeville, the die had been cast.

"We should try him," MacPherson suggested. "He is a

man who will do anything for a dollar, I believe. I can get money from my family, borrow it against the day when our Kansas farm shall prosper."

"You ask too much. You do not understand how it is . . . with him," Rebecca said sadly, shaking her head.

"We could defy him!" MacPherson suggested. "I would dare anything . . . with you."

"Say no more. You misunderstand us. He, too, is attached to the children." She knew it was true. He would never give them freedom, but he enjoyed seeing them grow, so curiously like his children by Nancy, so strong and healthy. The oldest boys had already been put to work in the lumber mills; he trusted them above the other slaves. He took pleasure in owning them all, and in owning her. She shuddered.

"Only tell me that you want me to do it," MacPherson said.

Rebecca shook her head again. "There might be lots of things I want, sir. I might want the moon. I might want life over again, some dif'rent from the fust time around, but there's no way I'm gone leave my children, sir—this life's too hard for us people without we hang together onto our fam'lies. I mean to trust in God, sir, that I do, but I b'lieve the children, sir, dey got to look to us."

"And I look to you, as a man to a woman," MacPherson insisted. "I tell you I love you, Rebecca. I can't go on without you, don't want to . . ."

"I'll tell you an old secret," Rebecca said in a low voice. She leaned toward MacPherson. The two of them were seated together on the narrow front porch of Rebecca's cabin. Although it was September, it was a hot, muggy night and the smell of the oleander bushes blossoming in front of the cabin was strong and sweet.

"Tell me," MacPherson begged.

"When I was young, when I was a very young woman and only bin with Master Dunlie a few years, I tried to run off. Yes, I tried, and I tried again. Twice I took my little baby and went into the woods with him tied up in a basket. But every time, you know what happened? Miss Nancy, she come right along behind me. She run off, too! Miss Nancy, she's stronger and stranger than anyone else knows. It's the truth. Somehow, whenever I go to run, she got away, too, and she come after me."

Rebecca laughed when she told the story, but then her eyes filled with tears, and she hid her face in her hands.

"So did you come back on your own?" the overseer asked.

"Yes, sir. I come back, what else could I do? Miss Nancy taggin' along with me, I come back, back with my little baby in the basket. And Master Dunlie, he beat me bad for it. Both times he beat me, sir, and he told me that next time he gone beat me till I die. And I 'spect he mean it, sir. He own me, don't you see that? He'll never give me up. That's how I know I'll always be his. That's how I know he'll never ever let me go, not for all the money there is."

"Oh, Rebecca," MacPherson sighed, moved to pity and acutely aroused by the thought of Rebecca's sufferings, her lifelong desire to escape Dunlie, the terrible limits of human nature. "I would never do anything to risk hurting you so."

"You are a good man," she said softly, and without speaking, she put out her arms to hold him. MacPherson came into them gratefully, resting his head on her soft breast and stroking her strong, firm arms—so smooth-skinned, so warm and capable.

"How long I have wanted to touch you," he said. His hands trembled and Rebecca did not move away. His touch was so gentle it reminded her of the embraces of her own children. What's the harm in it, she asked herself, what's the harm? He's so young, he's not long for this place; he's goin' away, soon, I'm sure of that.

"May I kiss you? May I?" he begged.

Rebecca's eyes were closed and her cheeks were tear-streaked, but she did not refuse. How different he was from the master, and yet both were white men. All her life this had been her lot, and her mother's before. It was so strange, so unlikely. All her life she had been the sexual possession of one white man, and now another one held her and kissed her; why was it so? Where were the strong, gentle men of her own race? How had they gotten to a position where they were so helpless? How had she? Why was it so?

"I jest can't understand," Rebecca whispered, and MacPherson, himself misunderstanding, promised her, "I wouldn't ever hurt you. I . . . love you, Rebecca. You're the finest woman I know."

Rebecca did not answer, but she could not relax; she felt the eyes of the night on them. There were many at Dunlie Hall who resented her privileges as chief housekeeper, who were jealous of her proximity to the white family and all their goods. And there was always the master, although he was still away, not expected back until tomorrow at the earliest.

Starved as she was for kindness, she who had for so many years sacrificed herself and her own needs for everyone else's, Rebecca lost herself, bit by bit, to MacPherson's wooing. His touch was gentle, adoring, hesitant; it was almost reverential. Her heart beat faster as he caressed her, but a rustle in the bushes made her jump.

"Let's get inside," she suggested, and from there MacPherson took the lead. Sighing with longing, he scooped up Rebecca's solid frame and lifted her inside her little house.

"We shouldn't, we mustn't," Rebecca said at first, but his lovemaking was unlike any she had ever known; it was more like massage, it was soothing and seductive, it caught her unaware. Her eyes closed, she allowed herself to be kissed, kissed as she had never been kissed, stroked and petted and rubbed. Gradually he undressed her, rolling down her petticoats, controlling his own passion, hiding all signs of haste.

"Pretty, pretty, darling," he whispered to her, covering her ears and neck with soft, brushing kisses, kneading the tired muscles of her shoulders and arms, "so soft, so warm, so lovely."

Her skin was smooth and unlined; it was soft brown in color, and in the moonlight it looked honeyed gold. Her hair, hidden under a wrapped cotton kerchief, was cut short and pressed tight to her head, and as he loosened the scarf and ran his finger through it, rubbing her scalp, she sighed in ecstasy.

He can't bring no harm, she thought. It's late, we're all alone, and no one will ever know.

"Do you believe I love you?" he whispered, but she could not answer, nor was love what she cared for, at this moment. At this moment, the physical pleasure was enough, it was overwhelming, intoxicating, and arousing; it carried her into a realm of sensation and relief that she had never known.

She lay, collapsed, in his arms and he began to kiss her mouth. At first she stiffened, but she did not pull away; then she relaxed, softening, melting into his embrace, parting her lips, drinking of his love and caring.

"Tomorrow," he promised, "tomorrow we will go away. Both of us . . . all of us, all your children . . ."

Never, she thought; it can never be. But she only said, "Tonight, tonight, sir, let's take tonight. . . ."

Gently he set her down on her hard, narrow bed and kneeled beside her, stroking and petting her as he did. To him she was a goddess of golden flesh, the woman of his dreams and months of fantasy; she was a creature from another age. With her, so exotic and so long desired, he felt totally free, and he explored her body as he had never explored any woman's body, touching and kissing every part of it, stroking her smooth, bared thighs, until the tremors that shook them stopped, kissing her knees, her calves, her belly, finally putting his mouth to the lips of her sex and kissing her there as she groaned with pleasure and gripped her own breasts.

"See? See?" he whispered. "See how I love you, Rebecca?"

"Oh, oh!" she gasped. Warm, wet waves of desire swept through her body, defined every muscle and washed to every nerve. Hungrily, she pulled him to her, onto her, into her, he kicking aside his clothes and sliding into place with a hard, muscular weight that aroused her, aggravated her longing, maddened her so unbearably that his entry was a need fulfilled, a completion of parts, the last piece in a puzzle that their two bodies had begun to assemble ages earlier.

As soon as he entered her, he began to move with a fluid, rocking rhythm that locked into her own. She screamed, once, in full realization that she had never felt such pleasure before; it was the moment of her sexual completion, and as her blood seethed, her brain blacked out, and for a moment longer she believed she would never come back again, would die of it, would pass on to a life where life was all a world composed entirely of this exquisite, white-hot sensation.

She screamed again, and then, with an unspeakably terrible shock, she felt him go rigid, felt his liquid weight change to painful pressure, felt a rush of coldness as chill as the grave, opened her eyes to see a lantern shining above them, to see him—him, the master—standing there by her bed, towering over them, his sword glinting, its length silver and terrible, its point thrusting into her lover's back.

"No!" she screamed. "No, no, no, no. . . ."

MacPherson yowled in pain. He struggled, but he was fixed, pinned to her body like a bug on a pin. Every motion set off waves of excruciating agony; the sword's tip was lodged in his spine.

CHAPTER FOURTEEN

A Healing Season; A Love Affair Concluded; Plans for a Sunday in May

The winter had passed, and it was spring. Spring comes gently to the rolling hills of central Georgia, touching her woods and fields with soft green fingers in late February, awakening the wild plum trees to delicate white blossoms that shine like stars in the dark branches and against the unfolding green leaves.

Spring is a healing season, a season that forgives the land the rough injustice of winter, promises everything warm and rich and fertile to come and soothes and subdues all memories of chill nights and frosty mornings.

It had been a hard winter for the Barstows, the coldest they had ever known, a winter of settling into their simple, plain new house, of learning the wants and ways of new land and new neighbors, of becoming attuned to the spirit and vigor of a raw, lusty land just quickening to life, just awakening to full promise. Twenty years ago this had all been Indian territory, had all been dense primeval forest or lush, undisturbed, river-fed plains. Now it was going into cotton, being shaped with desperate haste by the backs and bones of the new settlers and their slaves, clearing it, plowing it, planting it, reaping white gold from the red earth.

The Barstows had settled into a double log cabin with lean-tos behind and an attic above, and there they had passed the winter, but already Morgan had selected the site for a proper house, and as spring came, the slaves were set to building their own cabins as well as preparing the land for planting cotton.

In late February, Juliette, who was busier than she had ever been carrying on the many duties of plantation mistress as well as managing to find time every day to spend alone, working on her writing, made an entry in her journal.

> Despite the rigors of the journey and the difficulties and discords of settling into a new life in a house that is no more than a frontier cabin, despite the pain with which I—and I think Morgan, as well—remember our dear home, so far behind us now, despite all this, I am truly of the opinion that we have done well to make this move. It has unsettled us all so violently that it has cleared our heads of the terrible and mournful events that forced us to the move. This is, truly, a new land, a new Georgia, and I pray to God that we will soon be happy here. . . .

Juliette sighed and wiped her pen. It was a splendid, sunny afternoon; all the children were outside; all the men and hands were at work, and her sister-in-law, Livia, who had unfortunately caught a lingering flu from the journey, had been moved out into the sunshine, where she slept now, sitting up in a rocking chair under a pile of shawls.

"I have made great efforts to work on my stories," she wrote,

> "not with any prideful expectation that they will ever see print, but more as a means of fulfilling my promise to Mr. Bruce, as well as trying to please myself. Poor Livia has been very ill, and it has fallen on me to nurse her, so fretful is she that none of the servants can really manage. It seems she is better now, thank God, although still very weak. The children do well. Hugh has gone off to the university; Morgan was adamant that he should go, and Cole daily accepts more manly responsibilities for the work of the plantation. My dear brother is not free from troubles, but I believe I see his spirits lifting as the weather improves. Perhaps mine, too, will find a natural elevation in the coming season. I confess, dear journal, that I have not been as happy as I ought. What stone have I for a heart that I have never embraced life as

other women do? Ah, still I grieve for what might have been. Love touched me once; I was too young; it spoiled me. I am forever marked. Lately I have thought 'tis better to grieve for lost love than never to have loved; happiness brushed past me when I was only sixteen, leaving my heart cold and hard and forever remembering. Perhaps it is Livia's illness that has rekindled my thoughts of those days, that love, for in her delirium she had spoken of him often; she loves him, too. No matter; I embrace my work and my family. So God has willed it."

The loud cawing of a jay distracted Juliette as she put aside her journal, locking it away, as always, in the bottom of her red leather-bound casket, and she walked out into the fine, heartwarming sunshine. Its heat was at once soothing and stimulating; she raised her arms to the blue sky, still slim and healthy, still a fine-looking woman, and she smiled.

Perhaps, she thought, this is the spring that will heal all the old wounds. Why should we not put down roots here, why should we not all thrive and prosper? Why should we not sow our talents and reap peace and happiness?

The singing bird and the seductive sunshine promised that it could all be so.

A few months later, early in the afternoon of a fine day in May, Angus Dunlie rode alone from his store in Washington, toward Dunlie Hall, which lay in the rich, well-watered land between the Oconee and Ocmulgee rivers, west of Lake Sinclair. He went less often to Washington these days; the passage of years had slowed him, and his son Francis lived in the old Pittman Stone house in Washington. Francis was eighteen, old enough to show a good head for business; Angus had enlarged the operations at Washington for him and given him two of his half-brothers to run the mill. Already he talked of opening another store and mill in the town of Madison.

His ride was a day-long one and he had suffered a late start; still, in a few miles he had passed a company of Indians with their guns and blankets, a coffle of slaves en route from Augusta to New Orleans, and a group of emigrants in wagons, moving toward the Alabama territory.

The sight of the latter caused him to think of his sister. She had written more than a few months ago that she and her family were undertaking the trek west to new land, but he had never heard further. It was not like Livia to cease their correspondence; still, the mails were atrociously bad, as they always had been. Likely he would hear soon, and whenever it was, it would be too soon.

My domestic life is complicated enough, Angus thought. The afternoon sun was hot on his shoulders, and he shrugged off his jacket and loosened his collar. He had never relinquished his own style of dress; under his jacket—black broadcloth in summer, buckskin in winter—he wore the same style of shirt he had adopted when he was a young man in London. Oddly, it still suited him. His pale, big-featured face was still handsome, his expression still haughty enough to suggest both aristocracy and depth. His hair had never grayed, but was longer, in the style of the day.

Thinking, then, of the situation that lay ahead of him at Dunlie Hall, Angus frowned. Rebecca was pregnant again; she would deliver in less than a month. He supposed the child was his own, although there was always the chance that it was not. Angus thought of the overseer and a shudder of horror passed through his frame. He had been uncontrollably angry; his jealous rage had possessed him. In a sane moment, he would never have done it, not even for Rebecca. He had sent the man off in a carriage; it was the least he could do, and for some time he had feared reprisals, but none had occurred. Perhaps he had died. When he left, he had been in great pain.

All my life, Angus thought, I have been ruled by my passions. He thought of other occasions when he had lost control of his temper and appetite. It had always seemed disastrous, but always he had escaped somehow. After all, perhaps it was these significant moments of passion that determined the course of a man's life. Perhaps they were necessary to shape lives. Children are conceived in such losses of control, he thought; men die, paths are chosen, perhaps that is how it is.

On the night he had attacked MacPherson, he remembered, he had immediately replaced the man in Rebecca's bed. He had wanted her terribly, all the more for the smell of another man's body, all the more for her hysterical panic, her dazed, helpless efforts to repel him. It had to be, he thought, and he liked to think that their congress that night had planted the baby to come in her body. God willing, it would be a boy and grow to resemble him.

Rebecca had returned to normal since that night, he told himself. Oh, at first she had seemed sulky and moody, but he had not punished her, not beyond the light whipping she surely deserved. MacPherson had been hurt badly enough for two, and he needed Rebecca, they all needed her, especially Nancy. Only Rebecca knew the routine of her medicines and could control her intermittent rages.

As she grew older, Nancy's condition had not improved, but as long as he kept Rebecca to watch her and manage her, she was no trouble to him, and he liked having her. She was his wife; he still took pleasure in the sweet helpless beauty of her face, and she was the mother of their children, none of whom, thank God, seemed to have inherited her condition.

Angus rode through the town of Washington, seeing a few people that he knew and raising his hat to them. Beyond the town the road was rough and passed almost wholly through dense pine forests. It was shadowy and gloomy and so narrow and sandy that it could not be traveled by carriage. Thus it was all the more unlikely, all the more surprising, that a turn in the road brought into his view the silhouette of a well-dressed lady standing inside the gates of the town's small, stone-walled country graveyard.

Angus knew the church and graveyard well; it was here that Nancy's parents and no few of her brothers and sisters had been laid to rest. He had been here on several solemn occasions, although not for some years. The lady, for she was unmistakably one, had apparently ridden in alone, for her mount, a huge, well-outfitted gray stallion, was tethered to the wooden gate.

Reining his own horse to a slower pace, Angus stared at the unusual sight of a woman alone—and in the deserted cemetery. The woman turned, hearing the sound of his approach, and he stared again. She was quite remarkably pretty, her dark curls covered by a pale green shirred bonnet, her face clear and handsome, her arms uncovered by the cut of her lilac-plaid gown. There was something oddly familiar about her, but he was sure he had never seen her in Washington, or anywhere in the county.

"Pardon me, madam," he said, just a trifle awkwardly, for he was unused to dealing with strangers, "are you looking for someone? Could I be of some assistance to you?"

Juliette stared, for she knew him at once. It is impossible to record the sequence of emotions, all of them larger than could be easily tolerated, that coursed through her at the sight of him—alone and so abruptly, so unchanged, so totally unexpected. She put her hand to her throat and felt the pulse throbbing there, so fiercely it threatened to jump out, so erratically, yet still in tune with the sudden wild throbbing of her heart.

"Madam, do I know you?" he asked. If he did not, it was quite rude to trouble her in what looked to be a moment of private mourning.

"I believe you do," she said simply, lifting her head to face him. "Angus, I am Juliette Barstow."

Angus could not hide his surprise. His face paled, and in one fluid motion he slid off his horse and stood before Juliette, swaying a bit unsteadily.

Juliette took comfort from the sight of his discomfiture. She herself was stunned and unaccountably frightened, yet not unaccountably, for if this man had so affected her life once, could his power to do so be totally gone? She looked him over. He cleared his throat, and the sound seemed loud in the quiet burying ground, deserted save for themselves, with the wind sighing softly through the pines and a single mockingbird scolding its mate.

To do him credit, Angus, whose life had involved so many shabby moments, could not lie at this moment.

"I am very surprised to see you," he said. "I don't understand how you come to be . . . right here."

"I have come," she said and her voice strengthened as she spoke, "to visit the grave of my mother's brother, my uncle Pittman Stone. They told me at the inn that I should find it here."

"Of course," Angus said. "So you shall, and right over there. . . . I am most amazed to see you, Miss Barstow."

"I daresay you are," Juliette said, turning partway from him. She was aware that she was in a state of shock, yet being even partly attuned to her somewhat stunned feelings, she felt a battleground for their ravages. Love for him melted her—and she was astonished to feel it untrammeled by the passage of years, amazed even as she identified it. How, how could she love him still? Oh, the weakness of her heart that it could so easily be tapped, the strength of it, that it could seize and hold so securely, securely enough to bind her for twenty years!

And even as love suffused her and flowed, hot and vital to the tips of her nerves, so that she tingled with pleasure and longing, its contrary, hatred, tightened her veins and constricted her breath. Love and hate, so like and so unlike, so close and so contrary, so quickly interchangeable. She seethed with it. Her hands were ice cold; she clenched them and turned to him, and her voice was sharp and silvery-clear as she spoke.

"You ruined my life," she said.

Angus winced. The power of her voice frightened him, even as it only hinted at the ferocity of her emotions. He stepped away from her. He flushed.

"Miss Barstow, I owe you an apology."

She did not answer.

"I did you a great wrong. I took advantage of you."

It seemed to Juliette that she was imagining this moment. It was a moment that she might have arranged in her fantasies many years ago; it had no place in the present. She was a grown woman now, and he a grown man; what had happened between them had happened between children; she had no moral right to hate him so much, for so long, unless . . . unless . . .

"What is the value of one life ruined?" she asked, and as she raised her eyes to meet his, his slid away and he could not face her. I am foolish, her heart cried, it is of no use, nothing can change. What has happened is past. Nothing can alter the past, and I do not want him now.

And yet, in some awful, undying way, she did still want him, and she knew it. Her heart pounded at this staggering physical closeness to the man she had loved for twenty years. Release me, she asked her own heart. End this now!

To Angus, she had never looked so much like her mother, Jenny Stone, and he was suffused with remembering how Jenny had looked, in Savannah, in those even more long-gone days when he had been a boy, admiring her as his father held her captive in her own family house on Abercorn Street. What strength these women have, what wills, what tenacity, he thought, and he could not help but admire the firm, graceful line of her throat as she tilted her head up, up toward the blue sky, toward heaven.

"May God forgive you, Angus. I have," Juliette said, and her voice was bitter, but her hands fluttered apart and she felt a loosening around her heart, as if the bonds, the cords of tension and sadness and longing that had constricted her for years had suddenly burst. It was true, all at once it was true! She was free of him! It was ended, her strange sustaining passion was dead. And what was left? She must have time to examine herself, her heart and mind, before she would know.

"Thank you, Juliette," he said.

"Please go," she said in a steady voice. "I do not wish to see you again."

"Our families . . . are connected now," he said.

"Of course, but I do not wish to see you, ever again. Angus, you would be advised to contact your sister. She has been ill. Very ill. We are all settled now . . . in Jasper County."

"Yes, yes, I will," he agreed, as if he had been given absolution by the Church. "I will do it at once," he promised, the eagerness of youth rising in his deep voice. "And perhaps you will change your mind, and we, too, will meet again."

"No," she said. "Never."

Less than a week later, a slave on horseback brought a letter from Angus Dunlie to the Barstows at their home, the plantation they had begun to call Waverly, on Juliette's suggestion, for she was an appreciative reader of the novels of Walter Scott.

The letter, which was addressed to the Barstow family, to the particular attention of Mr. Morgan Barstow, Esq., was handed from one family member to the next as they sat together at dinner that night. In it Angus Dunlie apologized for not contacting them earlier, welcomed them to central Georgia, speaking on behalf of the community of older settlers, offered them his support and assistance in any endeavors where it might be of use, and invited them all to a family reunion at Dunlie Hall on the following Sunday.

Juliette read the letter in silence and passed it back to Morgan without comment.

"I think we should go," he said. "It is time that peace was made between the two branches of the family. He is married to our cousin Nancy . . ."

"He is my brother!" Livia interrupted. Her voice was weak. She sat with them, wrapped in a wool shawl despite the heat and humidity, but she had not been able to eat at all.

"Of course, my dear. He is your brother, as well," Morgan said evenly. He looked at Juliette, searching for a response.

Juliette, who was the only one not surprised by the letter, revealed nothing by her expression.

"I should like to see his plantation," Cole said.

"Please, let's go," Polly begged. "Will we go in the carriage?"

"It is quite a distance, I think," Morgan speculated. "I should say nearly fifty miles. We should have to go and come in two days." He looked at Livia, and a frown creased his forehead. "I don't know, dear, if you are well enough for such a journey."

"I shall die," Livia said frantically, "if you try to prevent me from going." Two feverish red spots burned on her pale face, and her hands were thin and yellowish as she gripped the edge of the table. "I must go! I want to go more than anything in the world!"

"I think you should all go," Juliette said, finally. "I won't go, myself. You may remember that I have spoken of going to a preaching appointment at the Pine Groves church on Sunday. I am looking forward to it, and I would prefer to attend that."

And so it happened that at dawn on the following Sunday, Juliette stood alone on the verandah and watched the carriage, with Morgan and Livia and Cole inside and Jerry the groom driving, roll down the dusty road away from her. Morgan had decided that Polly, whose vivacity and high spirits upset her mother, should stay behind with Juliette, much to Polly's disappointment.

Livia, who had postponed visiting or even contacting her brother out of shame at her weakness and sickly appearance, had spent hours fixing her hair and dressing herself for the visit. She had put on her finest gown, a rose and mauve sprigged silk, but the dress was sizes too large for her, she had lost so much weight during her illness. Juliette was touched, seeing her skinny arms reaching up weakly as Morgan lifted her into the carriage and Cole received her.

"Why does Mama always look so tired?" Polly asked Juliette, coming out on the verandah in her nightgown, rubbing her eyes.

"It's because she is still not well," Juliette told her. "When we go to the prayer meeting, we can ask God to help her get well, shall we?"

"Oh, yes!" Polly said. Although she was disappointed not to be allowed to go to Dunlie Hall, an outing with Aunt Juliette was almost more of a treat. "Can Berlinda come along with us?" she asked, and smiled with delight when Juliette gave her permission.

CHAPTER FIFTEEN

An Amazing Confession; A Disastrous Reunion; A Time to Die

By the time Juliette and the little girls arrived at the log cabin church at Pine Groves, there was already a good-sized crowd assembling there. It was a fine, warm day, and preaching appointments, in a community like this one where there was no regular minister, were festive occasions. It was a day of socializing as well as spiritualizing, of fun and fellowship as well as saving souls. Blacks and whites attended the services, men and women and children, and everyone brought his guns and his dogs.

The preacher had not yet arrived, and Juliette, recognizing very few of the faces in the crowd, stood shyly at one side, but it was not long before a pair of plump, plainly dressed women bore down on her, smiling welcome and extending their hands.

"Welcome, welcome, sister," one of them said. "We're the Powell sisters. Congratulations on yer comin' to our meetin'. Pass round the yard, sister, and shake the hands of the lot of 'em, that's our way!" And so Juliette, trailed by Polly and Berlinda, passed around the churchyard, shaking hands and meeting dozens of her neighbors, many of them poorly dressed and barefoot, some of them surprisingly well arrayed. Poor whites mingled with their betters and their slaves at prayer mettings on the Georgia frontier. Almost all the men and some of the women were smoking pipes; a few had come from the fields and wore dusty blue-denim overalls. One man wore a string of fresh-killed partridges and possums around his shoulders.

"Pete Gowan, Mrs. Call, Will Martin, John Kirk,

Tommy Barndegger, Sally Fox, Mrs. Abrigail Baldwin, Susie and Peggy Wheeler, Doctor Nat Brown, Sarah McMillan, General May, Deborah Sue McCutcheon, Mr. McCutcheon, Mrs. Kingsley, Rob Gowen, Jake Fox, Mrs. Avery, Herbert Burke, Jenny Ashton . . ." Never had she heard so many new names at once, it seemed to Juliette. She nodded and said softly "Miss Juliette Barstow" as she shook each outstretched hand.

"Welcome, welcome, God bless you . . ."

"Praise God!"

Suddenly a trumpet blew, and all present looked toward the road. At a full gallop, mounted on a fine high-stepping black mare, the expected preacher rode into the clearing.

A swell of excited "ahhhhhs" rose, and the people swarmed toward the church, rushing to find seats.

Juliette stared at the preacher. He wore a black cloth suit cut full with long black tails, a spike-collared white shirt, and a broad-brimmed black felt hat. It was obvious that he carried his entire household on the back of his mare. A sheepskin blanket lay across her back, and hung from the saddle were bags of books, a rolled-up blanket, and an umbrella, a gun, a Thermos, a knifecase, and a coiled rope.

As she watched, the preacher slid off his mare, took a long drink from the Thermos, and patted the horse on her rump. Then he swaggered toward the church, calling back "Come in, ma'am, enter into the house of the Lord."

As fast as they could, Juliette and the girls obeyed him, taking seats near the back where they could see everyone there, a crowd of about forty-five people.

The service began with singing. "Ah'll passel it out and you pass it back," the preacher yelled, and then shouted out the first two lines of a hymn. The congregation sang it back, in a variety of keys and with a mixture of voices that at first surprised, then pleased, Juliettte. Only a word or two changed in each line of the hymn, so she and the girls were soon singing along.

After the singing there was the first collection, a "lifting," as the preacher called it, and then the congregation settled back to enjoy the message of the day. During the preaching they were far from quiet. Loud shouts of "Hallelujah!" "Amen!" and "Glory be! Glory be!" punctuated the preacher's description of hell and promise of heaven.

The preacher—his name, Juliette gathered, was Reverend Spyker—had a rhythm to his delivery that caught up his listeners. It was a singsong, a rise and fall, broken with pauses and a deep, intoned "ahhhhh" that ended each phrase.

"Promise me, pro-o-o-omise me," Reverend Spyker proclaimed, "your hearts and your minds and your souls, ahhhhhh. Promise me your love and your true repentance, your faith and your charity, ahhhhhhhh. And ah will promise you that the love of God will come back to you one hundredfold, ahhhhhh. It will save you, it will lift you up from this troubled eaaarth, ahhhhhh. Yes, it will, yes it will, promise me and ah will promise you, ahhhhhh."

"I promise, I promise!" a woman yelled.

"Glory be! I feel it liftin' in my heart today!" a young man called out.

"Yes! Yes, ah do promise you, ahhhhhh. Ah promise you it will be so, and ah speak with the power of God, the love of God, the strength and loving kindness of the master of us all, ahhhhhh." Reverend Spyker went on. Juliette looked over at Polly and Berlinda. They were rapt, spellbound. She smiled and relaxed, letting herself enjoy the preaching. Reverend Spyker was a powerful speaker, and she had not heard a preacher since they left Saint Simons Island.

"Ah have come her today, brothers and sisters, fellow Georgians, all of us children of God, ahhhhhh. Ah have come here today with an invitation to you all, to all of you, ahhhhhh. Ah come here to ask you, to beg you, to invite you to give up sin and join up with Jesus Christ, Our Lord, ahhhhhh. The only man on earth who has ever been free of sin. Yes, we all have it, you and you and you! You have it, ma'am, and you, sir, and you, little boy, you were born with sin, riddled with it, yes, ahhhhh. Is there anyone of you here today who ain't got it? Is there? Is there? Ahhhhhh?"

"No! No! Amen, we all sinners," an elderly black man roared, and there was a murmur of "Praise God, help us" from every side of the room.

The temperature in the little log church was rising, though all the windows and the door stood open. Sweat streamed off everyone's bodies; some of the women were fanning themselves, and some of the men waved their hats and mopped their faces with handkerchiefs.

"Sinners, sinners, sinners, you are all sinnners!" Reverend Spyker shouted, jumping in the air as he waved his arms. "Ah can help you! Yes, ah can help you! Ah can promise you help, and that's through repentance, yes, ahhhhh. Ah can if you get down on your knees before the Lord, get down and promise me . . . and Him . . . that you will put Him first, put Him above men and all the cares and troubles of the world, ahhhhhh. Yes, all of them! Get down, promise me, and we will pray together, ahhhhh."

Juliette saw all the members of the little congregation slide to their kneees. Nodding at Polly and Berlinda, she did the same, with a whoosh of her best silk dress, landing squarely on the rough board floor. Some of the women around her, she saw, were crying, others embracing each other, still kneeling, their arms entwined.

One bald old man near her knelt rigidly, his face buried in his hands, his head bowed, and it seemed to Juliette that whenever he lifted it, he peeked through his fingers at her. His arm, she saw, was tattooed with a blue horse's head. Poor man, she thought, he looks to be suffering. The man's face was white and tear-streaked; his hands trembled. She looked back up at the preacher and forgot the tattooed man, but when she looked back, some moment later, he was still staring at her.

"Dear Lord," Reverend Spyker prayed aloud, "help these, your children kneelin' before you, to repent truly of all their sins, ahhhhhh. Help them to admit them freely, to you and to themselves, ahhhhhh. For he who comes openly unto you, as you have taught us, is saved and will live forever in your love, but he who hides his sins, he who denies them, for nothing can be hidden from your sight, nothing, nothing, ahh he will burn forever in hell, he will suffer torments until the end of the eternal night, he will be damned!"

"No-o-o-o-o-o-o," the congregation wailed. "Save us, dear Lord!" "Amen!" "Save us sinners!"

"Come forward!" Spyker bellowed, waving his arms like a bird lifting into flight. "Who? Who among you will be the first to come forward and confess, ahhhhhh. Who has fear enough in his heart, in her heart, ahhhhh. Who feels the spirit stirrin'? Who is ready to confess his sins and be lifted up to the Lord?"

Juliette felt her heart pound. Her spirits were high. I believe I am already saved, she thought. I am a new person now that I am free of the terrible love that tied up my heart for so many years. I believe I can feel the lifting he speaks of. She looked around her.

Several men and women were crawling forward in response to the preacher's call. Still on their knees, they moved forward clasped and shaking, amid a chorus of "Amen!" "Praise Him!" "Glory be!"

And then the old man who had been staring at Juliette rocked forward and began beating his head on the floor. "Forgive me, Lord! Ah'm ready to confess! Forgive me, Jesus, ah'm comin' home to you at last!"

Juliette stared. The man was frantic, crazed. With every motion forward his bald head crashed on the floor; he trembled and blubbered with harsh, choking sobs. Polly gave a little whimper of fear.

"It's Jake Fox; he owns the livery stable," someone whispered to Juliette.

Still shuddering, rocking, the frenzied man edged forward on his knees. Reverend Spyker took notice of him.

"Clear the way, for a brother in deep need of salvation! Come on, brother, come on right up here before the Lord, ahhhhhh. That's right, you got the spirit, come forward. Stand aside for the man who's comin' through! Make way for him!"

Slowly, painfully, Jake Fox attained the front of the room, and with Reverend Spyker's help staggered to his feet. He turned to face the crowd.

"Ah confess! Ah've sinned, bretheren, ah've sinned, Lord, in the wust way there is. . . ." Sobbing, Fox wrung his hands and then wiped his face with them, leaving dark streaks.

"Ah've killed! Ah killed a man, an innocent man, for money, Lord, and ah thought You didn't know! But You did, Lord! He did, Rev'rend! Ah know He did! He sent 'er! That one! He sent 'er to confront me with my sins, that lady there!"

And shaking and trembling, Jake Fox pointed at Juliette. She was still on her knees, but with all eyes on her she rose slowly and stood facing Reverend Spyker and Fox across the kneeling crowd.

"I don't know what he means," she said.

"Yer a Barstow, ain't ye?" Fox demanded. "From Savannah?"

"My family . . . is from Savannah."

"May the Lord forgive me, may He strike me dead if ah eveh lie agin, ah killed the old man, Ira Barstow," Fox blurted out. "Ah did it for money; he hired me to do it, that other one, the English one, Mr. Dunlie. Ah took the money, and on the blood money ah built my life!"

"Jake! Husband, what are you saying?" a woman moaned from one side of the room.

"Sally, 'tis true," Fox moaned. "We can't never escape the Lord's justice. Ah knew it was comin' when I saw that lady sent here today. . . ."

"Jesus! Save him, the Lord's will be done, ahhhhh."

Juliette was dumbfounded. There was no reason to think Fox was not telling the truth, and nothing much to do about it, not now anyway. The man was old; his crime had been committed twenty years ago; anyway, the blame might as well be fixed on the man who had hired Fox to do it—James Dunlie. Or—a new thought came to Juliette as she gathered her wits and left the church, grasping each of the girls by a hand—perhaps it had been Angus Dunlie.

"Why are we leavin'? What did that man say? What did he mean?" Polly demanded when they were outside in the sunshine again, the voice of the Reverend no less strident and compelling.

"We're goin' home," Juliette said firmly, and led the little girls to the buggy she had tied to a pine tree. She was too aroused and amazed to speak. So it had all come together at last. Had God arranged it? The coincidence of meeting her uncle's murderer, here, after all these years, was too sharp to make little of it. After all these years, and so soon after her chance meeting with Angus Dunlie, opening, perhaps closing another old wound that she had never expected to air.

Her head was spinning, and she could not speak for some time as she climbed up into the buggy and started driving back home. What did it all mean? For one thing, she saw clearly that they should never escape the past, and that an end to the trouble between the Dunlies and the

Barstows was not yet in sight. She tried to remember the sequence of events, twenty years ago. Why, the first time any of them had seen any of the Dunlies had been at her uncle Ira's funeral. They must have come to the funeral puffed up with sin and shame, poisoned with guilt. And after killing Uncle Ira, they had moved into her father's house, bringing more trouble there, starting all the events in motion that had never come to rest.

As she thought about it, horror and amazement settled into revulsion and hatred, and despair that the blood rivalry between her father's generation had not died with James and Roland, but lived on. Meeting Angus Dunlie forever shadowed my life, she thought, and as for Morgan . . . did he really love Livia? And even if he did, had she not made his life a hard one?

"What did you think of the preaching appointment?" Polly asked Berlinda, as Juliette pondered all this.

"It was wonderful," Berlinda sighed, and Juliette stared at the two little girls. It was hard to see their share of the blame, even Polly's, daughter of Livia Dunlie as she was. She thought of Cole, Hugh, Caleb. She remembered that Angus Dunlie had married her own cousin Nancy Stone. In the next generation all the goodness and badness would be mixed together, but would it end? Could it end?

With an immensely troubled and sorrowing heart, Juliette reached Waverly and began to wait for the others to return from Dunlie Hall.

When the Barstows reached Dunlie Hall at about midday, there was no white person in sight. The Barstows' driver stopped their carriage in front of the big, white-painted house, and Morgan, Cole, and Livia stepped out and waited a moment in the blazing sunshine, but no one came forward to meet them.

"It's the most beautiful house I've ever seen," Livia said, looking up at the dozen white columns, the balcony resting on them, the wide expanse of front verandah.

"Cole, fetch your mother's parasol," Morgan said. "The sun will weaken her."

Cole obeyed, climbing back into the carriage as Livia clung to Morgan's arm. "Isn't it the most beautiful house you've ever seen?" she asked. "There is nothing like it anywhere else in Georgia! Is there?"

"It is handsome," Morgan admitted, wondering where everyone was. It was strangely quiet; of course it was Sunday, and they had seen a few blacks walking along the road into the plantation, although the fields were empty. Dunlie, he assumed, gave his slaves Sunday off. It was the custom all over Georgia.

Livia sighed and swayed slightly as Cole raised her parasol. "Look at all those windows," she marveled.

"We had better go on inside," Morgan said. It was rude of Dunlie, he thought, to keep them standing out in the sun. With Livia on his arm, he crossed the lawn and proceeded up a white stone path to the front door, and as they passed under the edge of the covered verandah, he thought he saw a woman's face in the room above, but he was not sure.

Cole knocked on the big front door, but for some moments there was no answer; finally, a light-skinned housemaid opened it and stared at them with obvious surprise.

"We are the Barstows," Morgan explained. "Your master is expectin' us, I'm sure."

Still the girl stared, and in the moment's awkward pause a woman's high-pitched scream cut through the stillness. All of them started. It did not come from the house; it seemed to come from somewhere behind the house, but not far behind.

"What's that?" Cole asked.

The maid rolled her eyes. Ignoring it, Morgan helped Livia step up into the front hall, which was much cooler than the verandah.

"It sounds like a woman in childbirth," Livia said frankly, though no other well-brought-up lady would have mentioned such a thing.

"Dat's right. Miss Rebecca, she been at it for two days," the maid said. "Master jest went down to see to her."

"I see," Morgan replied. "Well, we will wait for him in the parlor. Where is the parlor?"

"Oh, 'scuse me, I done forgot my manners," the maid said, eyeing Cole saucily as she led them to the left into a cool, airy, well-furnished drawing room.

"My goodness, look at the elegant paintings!" Livia murmured as she collapsed onto a dark walnut curved sofa, displacing a pair of pink satin pillows. "Just look at that scene, Cole. Now that is the sort of thing we saw a lot of in England."

"Perhaps we could have some cool water," Morgan said to the maid, and she flounced away.

"It's very rich-looking, isn't it?" Livia asked. "My brother has elegant taste in everything. Just as my father did." Her voice was thin and anxious, but she sounded happier, Morgan observed, than she had in many months.

Just then Angus Dunlie himself appeared at the door.

"Angus! Darling brother!" Livia cooed. She struggled to rise.

Angus, who was appalled at the deterioration in her health and appearance since their last meeting in Savannah, could not for a moment speak. He could not bear to look at the skeleton of his once-beautiful sister, but he stepped over to the sofa and bowed low over her hand.

"Welcome to Dunlie Hall, dear sister. And welcome to you, Morgan. I apologize for not meeting you directly. This must be your son?"

"This is my second son. This is Cole," Livia explained, her voice weak but proud. "My oldest son Caleb is in Savannah. What a beautiful house you have, Angus. We are . . . only just beginning to settle into ours."

"Of course," Angus said, and the smoothness of his voice concealed his anxiety. Of all the days for them to come. . . . He was frantic over Rebecca. He simply could not manage without her. "But where is Miss Juliette? Did she not come with you?"

"She had a previous engagement," Morgan said. "And your wife?"

"My son Augustus has just gone to fetch her," Dunlie said. "I must explain that Mrs. Dunlie is not well. She has been in her room. She is generally not restricted to her room, but as her personal maid is presently being confined . . ."

"We heard her," Livia said.

"Ah. Yes, her time is very near. I am sorry for the somewhat disorganized state of the household today, but you will understand why. Let us drink some sherry together, and then we will all sit down to dinner." Angus moved toward the decanter of sherry that stood on a mahogany side table, but Livia stopped him.

"Please, Angus, I should like to see the house first."

"Surely you are too tired," Morgan protested. This social occasion was proving to be more wearing than he had expected. Now that he and Dunlie had met again after all these years, what were they to say to each other? He had no interest in the man; in fact, he never had. The sooner this was over, the better. Directly after eating, he would insist that they leave.

But Livia had already struggled to her feet and was leading the men out of the drawing room, shrieking with delighted admiration as she saw the windows and the painted panels in the dining room next to it.

The men had no choice but to follow her.

"Oh, Angus, how splendid! Look, Cole dear, this is an antique sideboard! French, isn't it, Angus? I think it quite lovely, truly I do! Oh, look at this wonderful mirror!"

And so it went, from dining room to parlor, from library to music room, through all eight of the rooms on the first floor, in each of them Livia marveling and exclaiming over every single piece of furniture, every painted panel, every picture, every mirror, every tall window. In the last room a tall light-haired young man, slightly stooped and strongly resembling Angus, joined them.

"This is my son, Augustus," Angus said. "Where is your mother?"

"I left her in the drawing room, sir," the young man answered, and to the amazement of the Barstows he passed Angus a large brass key.

"Let us go back there directly," Angus said, leading the way, leaving the others to trail behind, Livia still trilling in delight over all the house's furnishings.

The sight of Nancy Dunlie, who was waiting for them in the drawing room, proved to be as much of a shock to the Barstows as the sight of Livia's illness had been to Angus. She was thin to the point of emaciation, ghostly pale, and they soon determined that she was beyond ordinary social intercourse; although she sat quietly and smiled sweetly at all of them, she did not utter a word.

"What a lovely house this is," Livia said to her, but Nancy did not seem to hear. Instead she stared at Angus, and though he was looking away, all the Barstows saw an awful look of passionate hatred cross her face, replaced by bland passivity as soon as he turned back to her.

Whatever is wrong here? Morgan wondered. He could

barely repress a shudder. Nancy Dunlie was clearly very ill, and she was clearly very unhappy.

"How long has she been this way?" he asked Angus, confused and upset; why, the woman looked to be a lunatic.

"She has always been so," Dunlie said. He lifted the decanter of sherry and poured it into tall, stemmed glasses. He disliked sherry himself. He preferred whiskey, but as he recalled, the Barstows had a passel of foreign tastes, at least when he had known them on Saint Simons Island.

"Can nothing be done for her? Has she no treatment, no medicines?" Morgan asked, his natural, polite reserve overruled by the horror and pity he felt at the woman's depraved appearance.

"She has seen many doctors," Angus said in a low voice. "She has medicine, a powerful medicine that keeps her subdued and manageable. Ordinarily, she is never without her maid, Rebecca. Only today . . ."

"Ah, yes," Morgan said, accepting the glass of sherry.

"Excuse me, Father, I will join you at the table," Augustus said. "I want to show Cole the stables."

"Ten minutes, no more," Angus said.

"This is delicious, dear brother," Livia said, sipping the golden wine with enthusiasm to equal that she had displayed for the house and its furnishings.

Dunlie found it rather bitter, but he drank it and refilled his glass, hoping the alcohol would take the edge off his nerves. "No, my dear," he said to Nancy as she reached for a glass. "No, dear, you know you are never allowed to drink wine."

Nancy whimpered and sat back sullenly. Morgan avoided looking at her as Livia chattered to Angus about someone she remembered from England, but whenever his glance wandered her way, he could see that she was glaring at Angus. That woman looks dangerous, he thought. He had never before seen such a look on a woman, but once, on a mad slave . . . The slave had killed his overseer and then himself. He shuddered and drained his glass. There could be no similarity between the two cases.

Still, he was relieved when the maid reappeared to call them to the table. As soon as we have eaten, we shall escape this unhappy place, he thought. We have only come for Livia's sake.

The meal, to all present, seemed interminable. Livia was tired, Cole and Augustus bored, Angus distressed and distracted, and Morgan anxious to have it over and be gone. The menu included cold ham, boiled mutton and turnips, some rather fresh trout, peas and beans, a berry pudding, and both red and white wines. None of it was particularly tasty or well prepared, and the progress of the conversation was thrown off by the occasional screams from the back yard, each of which caused Nancy Dunlie to start from her chair and try to leave the room.

"She wants to go to Rebecca," Augustus explained to the Barstows, and they were forced to nod in understanding, though in truth none of them did understand what Rebecca was to Nancy and how deeply she resented what she dimly understood to be Angus's fault.

"Take her back upstairs," Angus said finally, weary of the continuing struggle, weary of the occasion itself, of which he had expected, somehow, much more. Perhaps if Juliette had come. . . . At any rate, nothing could go well without Rebecca's management; none of the servants was controllable without her. Without her the food was bad, the service slipshod. No one could manage Nancy but her. He was worried about her, none of her other labors had been so difficult or prolonged. As soon as the damn Barstows had left, he would go back down to her cabin and do whatever he could, not that there was much a man could do at this point.

With each of them distracted by his own thoughts, a silence fell over the table when Nancy had left, and when the port had been served, no one was surprised or sorry to hear Morgan suggest that they should be on their way. Livia was so weary she could hardly sit straight.

Poor woman, Angus thought. She looks morbid. My little sister. Well, there is none of the coquette left in her today. Their son is handsome enough, though. Side by side, Augustus and Cole walked ahead of their elders toward the front door, and as the rest waited on the verandah for the carriage, the two young men strolled out to examine the well house that stood at some distance from the front of the house.

"How do you like this part of the state?" Augustus asked Cole.

"I like it," Cole smiled, exercising on his cousin the

charm that had never failed him, " 'cept I've not seen any pretty girls around here yet."

"You ain't? Why there's plenty of 'em! Hey, I'll see that you get invited to the next party I hear of. You'll see 'em there!"

"Sure enough? How deep is your well, Augustus? Ours was just dug to thirty feet."

"Thirty? That ain't nothin'! This one is sixty," Augustus lied. Lying was a habit of his, a habit born of confused fears and a terror of his father.

As soon as the Barstows' carriage had rolled out of sight, Angus turned to his son. "Did you give your mother her medicine? Did she take it?" he asked.

"I couldn't," Augustus said. "There wasn't any in the vials. It was all gone."

"Gone?" Angus gasped. Nancy's medicine, an extract of the herb hellebore, was a very powerful pacifier, and had to be taken in minute doses, according to the doctor. It could be poisonous otherwise, could damage the nervous system. Or so her doctor had said. "You fool!" he shouted at his son and started to run toward Nancy's room, but then he heard a scream from Rebecca's cabin that was sharp and agonizing enough to freeze his blood, and he ran that way instead.

"It's come! It's come!" a barefoot peasy-headed child informed Angus as he neared the cabin. She scowled at him, but he burst into the cabin. Besides the midwife, the slave doctor was there, and the herb medicine expert, a woman they called Oola, and Rebecca's oldest daughter. All of them glared at him, but he dropped to his knees beside Rebecca's bed.

"What is it?" he demanded, and the midwife held up a tiny girl. Rebecca turned away from him to face the wall and her eyes were shut, but he could tell from her exhausted panting that she was still alive.

Only a few hours later, though, Angus himself began to feel very very ill; cramps and shooting pains in his stomach attacked him as he sat on the front verandah sipping whiskey. He was alone; Augustus had ridden off to visit one of the MacIntosh girls at Pine Bluff Plantation soon after Rebecca's baby was born.

The pains were severe, in fact they were excruciating;

they were unlike any pain he had ever felt before in his life. It was not long before he thought of Nancy, thought of her hostile, sulky rebelliousness at dinner, remembered what Augustus had told him about the empty vials of medicine. But when would she have had access to his food . . . or his wine?

He doubled up with pain; he screamed. He could not think, could not remember. What could he do now? Was he dying? Perhaps one of the slaves had poisoned him, or that old witch Oola. But in his heart he did not think so. He remembered Nancy's face at the dinner table, for he had seen more than he acknowledged; always, he had seen more than he acknowledged. She hated him; she was mad; she had access to a dangerous drug.

But when had she done it? He had contrived not to leave her alone. When could she have done it? He bent over in a gripping contraction.

"Help! Sally Ann? Cissy? Adam? Where are you all?" he called out weakly when he could speak again. Where were the servants? How could they all be missing at once? He staggered toward the door.

As he crawled through the front hall he remembered that his son Augustus had left Nancy alone, for just a few minutes, while he was in the far end of the house with the Barstows. He knew very surely that there had been enough time for her to have dumped all her hellebore into the sherry decanter. There had been time enough, and she had taken that time, with all the malicious cunning of which she was capable.

"Nancy? God damn you, Nancy!" he gasped, as he lay collapsed on the floor in front of her locked door, when he had managed to crawl up the stairs. The key was in his pocket, but he was too weak to stand and open the door. Inside, he heard Nancy moving about, singing to herself.

"Aaaugh!" he screamed, as the pains came and went. The tremors had started as he climbed the stairs. His tongue was dry and his vision blurred. He felt sure that he was going to die; all he wanted was to make it to his own bed.

In the space between gripping pains he managed to slide into his room, to cross the threshold on his belly, to save his last strength for climbing up into the bed. Sweat streamed down his cheeks; his strength was going; and still the pains paralyzed him. He was too weak to cry out, and his vision came and went in a confused blurring of frightening images, but one of his last clear sights was the lot of them standing around his bed, watching and grinning.

They were all there: Sally Ann, Cissy, Adam, and the rest of them: Levi and Lize and Randall and Tom, Margaret and Bet and Jerry and Peter and Wade, and more, all who could fit into the room. He was alone with them and then he died.

Livia died at nearly the same time, limp and wretched, in Morgan's arms, even as their carriage drew into the front gates of Waverly. She had been sick for two hours, increasingly ill. She had screamed with pain, and Morgan had been nearly out of his mind with anxiety and grief and fear.

Of course, Morgan was ill himself, but he was too distracted by Livia's suffering to heed his own, nor did he understand his own. Livia's collapse was not unexpected; she had been sick for months; she had grown progressively weaker and weaker. The events of the day had exhausted her and her illness had overcome her life. So it seemed to him, and when he had carried her frail, still-warm body into the house and laid it out on the big pine chest he had ordered built for her to store her linens, he was still too wracked with sadness to fully realize that he was sick himself.

Juliette realized it, though, seeing his pale, dry face, so unnaturally clammy, seeing his hands and arms and legs begin to tremble.

"You are ill also, brother," she said to him in a soft, motherly voice. "Please leave her now and lie down. You need to rest. You must rest, Morgan." This is no time to talk to him about Jake Fox, she thought. It must wait until he is better.

Privately, she asked Cole what had happened at Dunlie Hall.

"Nothing of importance," he told her. "It was very quiet. Mrs. Dunlie was quite strange, Aunt Juliette, and we all ate dinner. Oh, poor mother."

"You have always been a good son to her," Juliette said and left to go to Morgan.

Morgan had grown much worse since Livia's death,

since he had retired to his own bed. It was as if he had postponed dying until he had fulfilled his duties to his wife. Now he wanted his children about him, and so he told Juliette. "Please, sister. Quickly. Both of them. And you."

Juliette believed him and ran to wake Polly and to find Cole.

By the time they returned to Morgan's bedside, he was shaking all over, clenched with pain, but he sat up to speak to them.

"Children, I am dying," he said. "No, don't cry, there is no time, I am sorry to leave you, but God's will be done, on earth as it is in heaven." He paled, shuddered with pain, and then, as Juliette bathed his forehead, he went on, "Cole, you are grown and strong enough to run Waverly for the family. God bless you. I want to bless you, also. Kneel here."

Holding back tears, Cole did as Morgan asked. "You are the head of the family now, Cole. Take care of your sister and your Aunt Juliette. She will advise you and inspire you, as she has me, with her faith and spirit and beauty. She is what it means to be a Barstow, look to her. . . ."

"Yes, Father."

"And Polly?"

"Papa!"

"Be a good child, my pet. Be happy and follow your heart. Grow with our beloved land. Juliette? Juliette, are you there?"

"Morgan, I am still here," Juliette cried out, holding his hand as he passed on.

CHAPTER SIXTEEN

Polly Goes Home; Gus Dunlie Gets His $'s Worth; An Afternoon at the Turf

One warm spring day, almost exactly seventeen years later, Polly Barstow, now Mrs. David Strawbridge Todd, wife of the Reverend David Todd, drove in through the gates of Waverly, now her brother Cole's plantation, to pay her family a visit.

The intervening years had been years of enormous growth and expansion for the republic, for Georgia, and for the Barstow family. If any one thing characterized the era it was a strenuous pursuit of material gain. Not that religious, intellectual, and humanitarian experiments were not being carried out as well; it was the time of spiritualism, Mormonism, Unitarianism, transcendentalism, and utopias. It was the time for the organization of abolitionist societies and societies advocating the rights of women, and all of these movements sent feelers into Georgia, and stirred her, however slightly, but idealistic as Americans and Georgians were in the twenties and thirties, they were even more restless, demanding of quick material prosperity, and greedy for land.

Land, land, land. It had been so since the first European set foot on the Atlantic shores; there was even talk of pushing on toward the Pacific, although that was still a notion that seemed amusingly preposterous. Land greed was a fever, an obsession; enough was not enough; land wore out, towns grew up, neighbors crowded in, and everyone wanted more and moved west to get it. The attitude of a west Georgia farmer summed it up: "I ain't greedy for land; all I want is jist what jines mine."

As well as land, Georgians wanted slaves to work their land. They had slaves; they needed them; they wanted more. Ever since the closing of the African slave trade, interstate traffic in slaves had been pursued vigorously and slave smuggling carried on. The number of slaves in Georgia rose yearly, as did the percentage of slaves in the total population, and the price of a prime field hand, which had been about seven hundred dollars in 1821, was now, in 1838, about thirteen hundred dollars. The system of Negro slavery came to be part of the spirit as well as the substance of Georgia life; it had come to her early and set her on a path of changelessness that was to lead to disaster in the years to come. But in the twenties and thirties it was a changelessness that seemed to spell peace and permanence. Life had its routine; the routine was built on farming, on tobacco, rice, corn, and—especially—cotton. The pattern was set; there was little change in the basic pattern of getting land, planting cotton, ginning cotton, and selling cotton even as the system expanded to its limits.

Among the land coveted by land-hungry Georgians was that which had been set aside and ceded to the Cherokee Indians, a large tract of lightly wooded highlands in the northwestern part of the state. The Creek Indians, after a long and bloody struggle, had in 1827 ceded the last of their lands to Georgia and moved west to others, said to be of equal value, beyond the Mississippi. Getting the Creeks out of Georgia had only been accomplished by the determination of her strange, stern governor, George Troup, for Troup threatened to take Georgia out of the union and into war unless the Creeks were paid off and forced to move.

There remained the Cherokees, a much more acculturized and considerable part of the native population. The Cherokees numbered about fourteen thousand. Like their fellow Georgians, they had become an agricultural, slaveholding people. One of their young intellectuals, Sequoya, in 1825 invented an alphabet so their language could be written; at their capital city, New Echota, they published a newspaper, the *Cherokee Phoenix*. Their communities had organized public schools; they built public roads and churches and hired preachers, and considered themselves a nation within the state of Georgia.

Because the Cherokees' mountainous land was not good for raising cotton, for many years Georgians left them pretty much alone, but in 1828, the year Polly Barstow married a Presbyterian minister and moved with him to the Cherokee territory, gold was discovered at Duke's Creek, or Dahlonega, as the Indians called it, and everything changed. Georgia experienced her own gold rush. Speculators invested thousands of dollars on the prospect of instant wealth. A stampede of at least six thousand gold diggers rushed into the region from every state in the union, on horseback, in wagons, and afoot, carrying shovels, pans, and crude cradles. Within a few months the quiet Cherokee farmlands were trampled by a wild, lawless horde of miners who had failed to strike it rich. Some of these were men of the most disreputable character; they looked around the Cherokee corn and cotton fields, saw the orchards and villages, and helped themselves to food and forage. Some "squatted" and began to farm Indian land; others organized "pony clubs," bands of thieves and cutthroats who roved and robbed Cherokee farmers of their livestock. Nonetheless, the mountainous valleys yielded some gold; the mining towns of Dahlonega and Auraria sprang up, and a federal mint was opened at Dahlonega.

Polly Barstow did not think of all this, of the Cherokees' noble and tragic history, of the Georgia gold rush and those first months in Dahlonega, as she rode toward Waverly Plantation. She did not think of it, although it was all of vital importance to her; it was the stuff and fiber of her own life, past and present, and the reason that she sat alone in the carriage, alone but for her son Bridge Todd and her faithful servant Berlinda, holding her baby daughter, Delight Todd.

"Will we see Aunt Juliette, Mama?" Bridge asked Polly as the carriage proceeded slowly along the red earth driveway which led into Waverly Plantation.

"I expect so, dear," Polly said. Juliette, who had been more of a mother to her than her own mother, especially since both of her parents had died—so suddenly and on the same day, a terrible tragedy, a case, so everyone thought, of food poisoning—was equally beloved by the younger generation, and seemed like a grandmother now to young Bridge and Delight, as well as to Cole's eight children.

Juliette still lived at Waverly. She had never married, although she was still the prettiest, most charming and graceful, wisest and most understanding aunt anyone could ever have. For years Juliette had sacrificed herself to her family, and there had been some lean hard years among them, when Waverly was still a small, struggling plantation, years when Cole had worked day and night to clear land for planting cotton and Juliette had worked even longer hours to manage the difficult, demanding, and above all, never-ending duties of plantation mistress.

Three years ago, though, Juliette had surprised them all. Her family had been shocked at first, and then proud. One of Juliette's manuscripts, a long and amazingly convoluted story about a Georgia family living on a sea-island plantation, had been accepted by a New York publisher and actually printed as a book. It was a novel entitled *Who Can Know the Heart?*, which was a quotation from Jeremiah, and everyone who read it agreed that Juliette's book was both beautiful and inspiring, in every way a credit to her family, and a lively, exciting story to boot.

Now Juliette worked on her writing more openly, after years of working by lamplight behind her bedroom door when all the chores of the house were done. She admitted she was writing another book, although she was not yet halfway done with it. All the Barstows knew it would be a great success.

"I hope we see Aunt Juliette, Mama," Bridge said.

"Yes, dear, I hope so," Polly answered absentmindedly. She hoped to see both Cole and Lucy, his wife, as well as Juliette. Polly had come to see her family in most desperate need; she needed money, as much as she could borrow, and as fast as possible. Polly sighed; the events of the past years, the past months had exhausted her. She had witnessed injustice and misjustice, the violent rule of greed; she had seen the Cherokees her husband loved, and she had come to love, cheated of their land, their gold, and their heritage. And now they were all to be moved off their ancestral lands, moved west forcibly, those who would not go otherwise.

She and David Todd had been caught up in it all. Eight years ago, the Georgia legislature had denied him his residence permit in the Cherokee country, although David Todd had lived among the Indians for years, teaching and counseling them and working on his lifetime project, a translation of the Scriptures into the Cherokee language. His mission was part of one that had been active among the Cherokees since the beginning of the century, and all of the Christian teachers had been outraged by Georgia's effort to rob the Indians of their land and its mineral wealth. They had opposed the Gwinnett County edict, refused to leave, and refused to apply for special residence permits.

David Todd, as an example to the others, had been arrested and cruelly carried off. As Polly had watched, her husband had been chained with a yoke of heavy horses' trace chains around his neck to the back of a cart and forced at bayonet point to walk, stumbling and falling, twenty-one miles to the jail. Sick and exhausted, his feet bleeding and his neck sore and bruised, he had been jailed.

When he was tried, he had been sentenced to four years hard labor at the state penitentiary in Milledgeville.

But no force on earth could break David Todd's spirit, Polly and many others had learned. The tall, gangling, blue-eyed minister, a native of the north Georgia hills, had persevered in all his efforts; with the same stalwart faith and loving kindness that he had shown to Polly as a very young man, he had adopted a new stand on the Cherokee question: that the whole nation should obey the government's edicts, however unjust they might be, and move west to set up a new life there.

Accordingly, David Todd had already gone west to the designated new Cherokee homeland, a flat river-bottom country west of the Mississippi, west of Arkansas in the new Oklahoma territory. He had gone with a small part of the Cherokees, a tiny advance migration of only six hundred, who had set out with carriages and wagons, accompanied by their slaves, saddle horses, and oxen, following a route through Tennessee, Kentucky, the southernmost tip of Illinois, and Missouri into the Cherokee lands.

"The people must follow," Todd had told Polly only last month, "for if they stay, they must inevitably be cheated and oppressed, be perpetually made drunk by the whites, reduced to beggary, become miserable outcasts, and as a body be reduced to nothing." His was an unpopular position with many of the Cherokee leaders who had pledged to resist until the last possible moment, to cling to their lands and their property, but Polly did not doubt that he was right.

"Here we are," Polly murmured to Berlinda, as a smiling coal-black groom ran out from the stables to lead away the horses. She kissed, then handed down three-year-old Delight; Bridge jumped out and ran into the house, and she and Berlinda followed, still together after all, still closer than sisters, their lives and destinies entwined since their happy childhood on Saint Simons Island.

Polly smiled as she looked up at Waverly. How peaceful and beautiful it looked; although it had grown and changed over the years, it was still home to her. Since her marriage she and David had lived in many houses and all of them had been made happy by their love and the strength of their marriage, but she had not grown attached to any of them, as she was still attached to her family and girlhood home.

Waverly looked its best on that sunny spring day. Its white walls and immense two-story columns were all new; when the price of cotton topped seventeen cents a pound, three years ago, Cole had hired a builder from Clinton who had created an imposing mansion on the foundations of the log house Morgan Barstow had laid out seventeen years earlier. The new house had four central chimneys, third-floor bedrooms with dormer windows, and a wide verandah that ran all around between the columns on both the ground floor and second floor.

In the summertime life was lived on the cool shady verandah, or galleries, as Lucy Barnes Barstow, Cole's serene, dark-haired wife, called them. Miss Lucy, herself a Jasper County cotton planter's daughter, was an easy-going aristocratic woman who had accepted the Barstow family and their traditions as firmly and passionately as she loved Cole, and had borne him eight children to date.

"Dear me, if this keeps up, we'll need more bedrooms," Cole had joked to his brother Hugh, who had returned to Waverly last spring after an extended journey to Europe and Persia. Actually, Cole was delighted by the flock of dark-haired children who swarmed all over Waverly, each of them more like Miss Lucy than the last, but he worried about costs and payments. Ever since he had remodeled the house and ordered enough fancy French and English furniture to fill it over and over again, the price of cotton had fallen.

Some brokers called it a crash, some a panic, but whatever it was, the reality was that cotton had stood at thirteen cents a pound last fall, and no one knew what would happen next.

"Goodness, hello, Polly," Lucy Barstow called out from the far end of the gallery, where she was sitting in a white rocking chair holding her newest baby in a long and lace-trimmed white cotton gown. "And hello, Berlinda. Why, Bridge, what a great boy you are already!" Handing the infant girl to a nursemaid, Lucy rose to kiss Polly, who noticed with silent alarm that Lucy's waist seemed thickened again. Or could it be still? Surely, eight children to raise and feed and dress and educate was plenty, even on a big, thriving plantation like Waverly.

"Where's Cole, Lucy dear?" Polly asked.

"He's in his office, poor darlin'. D'you s'pose it's the taxes again? He says they have to be paid this month and I know we can't expect more money from the factor till autumn. Why, I think it's positively unfair! Oh, Polly, I meant to ask, what do you hear from Mr. Todd?"

"I had a letter from him yesterday." Polly's brow creased with a frown. "He has arrived safely in the new lands, but the journey was arduous. Many of the people fell sick and died, and their needs are great. David has written to me asking me to help find money, money for seeds and plows, for medicines, for a schoolhouse for the children, and for a church. And then I must have money for my own trip, mine and the family's, for we are anxious to join him as soon as we can."

"Yes, of course," Lucy agreed, "but oh, dear Polly, how we shall miss you! I can't bear to think of you goin' so far away! Aunt Juliette will just pine for you, I can tell you that!"

"I shall miss her, too . . . and all of you," Polly said in a soft voice, and her eyes filled with tears, but she determined not to begin missing her family until she was truly gone. There was no other way; even the Bible said that a wife was duty-bound to follow her husband and to cleave unto him, and she missed David so painfully that she could not sleep at night.

Nevertheless, Polly was not surprised, when she went to Cole in his office, to be told that he could not afford to give her much money. Cole was—as always—affectionate and charming; he was kind and considerate, as a master, as a brother, as a husband and father; he was idealistic, in his own way, being unswervingly devoted to his family, his friends, the state of Georgia, and the southern way of life. Cole was a gentleman and widely known to be one; he was well liked and had begun to have political aspirations. His name had been mentioned for the Senate, and it was not an idea that met with any opposition from his fellow planters. But like many other Georgia cotton planters on the edge of boom times, he was badly overextended.

"The truth is, dear Polly, and I am ashamed to admit it," he told his sister with an irresistible smile, "that Waverly is mortgaged to the last inch. And so is the cotton crop, not only this year's crop, which is just now beginning to gain strength in the fields, but next year's crop and the next one after that. Polly, I don't even understand how it happened!"

"How did it happen?" Polly asked, shaken and confused.

"Why, I believe it's the system. The factor—and you know we have always given our cotton to Barstow and Barstow, brother Caleb's firm in Savannah—well, Calcb keeps all the accounts. He is always ready to advance me money for whatever I need. Three years ago he gave me a tremendous amount of money for the house. You know, we needed a larger house, and it's beautiful. . . ."

"Yes, 'tis beautiful," Polly sighed.

"Even to pay for the house, we needs must have bumper crops and high prices for several years to come," Cole explained. "And then there's the furniture. And Hugh had to borrow several thousand dollars when he came back from his travelin'. Of course I was delighted to be able to secure it for him from Barstow and Barstow. Honey, I'm never sure where I stand, but I see that we are all livin' off future prospects. It's so hard to be prudent."

"So it is," Polly agreed, thinking of David so far away, of the urgent needs of the dislocated Cherokee people.

"The spring freeze gave us a bad start," Cole complained. "And now this draught. We have a long way to go, with cotton at thirteen cents as it was last fall. Perhaps it'll increase."

"Perhaps it will," Polly said, hoping so. "The Cherokee leader John Ross is still in Washington, but the President has sent General Winfield Scott to round up the people. He is determined to execute the treaty. David feels the Cherokees are in terrible danger unless they are persuaded to leave peacefully. He wants me to come at once, and I want to go! Oh, Cole, I don't know what to do!"

"Honey, what *can* you do?" Cole asked, putting his arms around his sister. "I will give you all the money I have here. I'm sorry I can't do more just now. It's only two hundred dollars."

"Thank you, Cole," Polly said. "I need to go back to Dahlonega with the children and pack up our household goods. I must hurry. Perhaps . . . perhaps I could ask our cousin Augustus Dunlie for a sum of money. You know, Cole, he made a brilliant investment in the gold mining region. I have heard that the latest strikes were all on his land. And he owns the drilling machinery used all through the gold hills."

"I believe Gus Dunlie is prosperin'," Cole said slowly. Relations between the Dunlies and the Barstows had been amicable if cool during the past seventeen years. Augustus Dunlie's father had died the same day their parents had, and after they had all been dining together. His mother had died a few years later, poor woman. Although Cole and Augustus were not good friends, they met often, at fox hunts and parties, in town, and sometimes they sought each other out to talk, politely enough if a bit awkwardly.

Aunt Juliette, on the other hand, despised all the Dunlies, and could never be persuaded to see them at all. She had communicated her antipathy to Miss Lucy, so that Cole had seen his cousins less and less often since his marriage. "They are trash, honey," Miss Lucy insisted, although Cole could not really agree, since they were his cousins.

"But don't tell Aunt Juliette you're goin' to ask a Dunlie for money," Cole warned Polly, and Polly decided that she would not, although she went to visit with her aunt directly after leaving Cole and found her already reading to Bridge as she held a smiling, babbling Delight on her lap. I surely admit I have no pride when it comes to gettin' this money, she thought. The Lord will forgive me. In fact, I know He'd approve. She thought of Jesus and David and ached for both of them.

On the day after Polly Todd visited Waverly, Gus Dunlie was awakened by the sound of a slave patrol riding into his front yard, a dozen men on horseback and another man driving a wagon with its roof and sides made of strong young saplings set two inches apart.

"Mist' Gus! Mist' Gus! It's the slave catchers, and they've got Daniel wit' 'em!" yelled Bug, the strong but slow-witted Negro who had been Augustus Dunlie's body servant since he was a child.

Dunlie woke slowly. His head felt thick and heavy from the whiskey he had drunk the night before. He spat into a basin beside his bed and realized that he had fallen asleep with his boots and pants on. God damn it, he thought, that lazy Bug. Now, why didn't he undress me?

"Mist' Gus! Mist' Gus, they here!" Bug yelled loudly, bursting into his master's bedroom and running to look out the front window, over the roof of the verandah, at the yard below. It was full of barking dogs and men and horses and had begun to draw a crowd from the house and the slave quarters.

"Where's Miss 'Rissa?" Dunlie asked, coming to terms with the fact that his wife was not in bed beside him and that he did not remember her being there earlier.

"Miss 'Rissa gone to town a'ready," Bug announced. "Ooooo-eee, they's nasty-lookin' nigger-dogs down there. B'lieve I'll stay inside."

"Long's you doan take it into yo' head to go off, yo'll be all right," Dunlie said. He took a long drink from the bottle next to his bed to brace himself, and stomped downstairs to meet the patrollers, leaving Bug still hanging out of the front window, moaning and shouting.

"Mornin', Mister Dunlie," Rake Quint said proudly when Dunlie walked out onto the verandah. "Wall, I got 'im for you. Jist like I said I would." Quint was a man who made his living tracking down runaway slaves for masters all over this part of the state. He kept and sold dogs to go after runaways—specially bred, big-boned black-and-white hounds with good noses, who chased a scent for miles through the woods, in swampy river bottoms, in the mountains. Quint bragged that he had never failed to bring back his prey.

"Where'd you git him?" Dunlie asked, looking into the slat-sided wagon at the young black man crouched there, his head between his knees, silent and stolid, refusing to look out at any of them. "Did you hurt 'im?"

"Barely a scratch," Quint said, "just like you tole me. Wall, maybe a few toothmarks. The dogs had to pull him out of a gum tree. They treed him twenty miles from here. He give us a good run, he did."

"Daniel's a'ways been a good runner," Dunlie said. Flies buzzed around the caged man and around the swarming, yelping, sweating dogs, a pack of about twenty. He felt the sun burning his bare neck and making his headache worse. It promised to be a warm day, a real warm day, and he was a big man, a heavyset man who minded the heat.

"Guess he'll stay home for a while," Quint said sagely.

"How much do I owe you?" Dunlie asked. The dogs' barking hurt his head too, and the smell of the whole lot of the patrollers was pungent. Why is it, he wondered, that when I wake up with a head like this, it's the smell of everything that hurts the most? He blew his nose into a handkerchief and mopped his forehead.

"Wall, I figger one hundred dollars," Quint said.

Dunlie stared in horror. He was a rich man, born rich and heir to so much of his father's property that at the age of eighteen he had controlled more money than most of the planters in the county accumulated in a lifetime. And he was a thrifty man, sharp and tight. He hated "like pison," to part with cash, hated to settle his accounts so much that his wife, Nerissa, had to do the household accounts and his overseer had to pay all the bills for the plantation. The thought of spending one hundred dollars to get back a runaway, even a valuable, skilled carpenter like Daniel, made him sick.

Dunlie retched and inelegantly spat into an oleander bush.

Quint read his feelings clearly enough. "We had to chase him twenty miles, goin' and comin'," he said. "Took all my men and all my dogs. That's the price, Mister Dunlie." You cheap bastard, a hundred dollars is nothin' to you, he thought. It was more than he had ever asked for a single slave, but he knew, instinctively, that he could get it, and if he could get it, he would.

"The money's inside," Dunlie said. It was robbery, but he lacked the spirit to bargain with runty, red-eyed Quint. It would be like wrestling with a rooster. Anyway, he'd gotten a large sum just yesterday from his mining machinery company in Cherokee country. Peters, the overseer, had taken it to the bank in Macon. And with the check had come another bag of gold nuggets, his bribe money from the men who did not really own the land they mined and who made it worth his while to keep quiet about it. The lumps of gold, at least twenty thousand dollars' worth, he would send on to Savannah to his cousin Caleb Barstow.

Caleb Barstow had been handling Gus Dunlie's more sophisticated investments for years, and when Dunlie had stumbled onto this rich source of raw gold, he had advised that they ship it to England, where it fetched a far better price than selling it to the U.S. Mint, although that was required by Georgia law. Once deposited in an English bank, Caleb Barstow had told Dunlie, the money could be drawn out and brought back into the country without arousing suspicion. Barstow had offered to take care of it all—for his usual factor's fee of two percent, of course.

"Lemme go inside and fetch it," Dunlie said to Quint. All he wanted was to get rid of Quint and his raw-smelling white trash posse and to get himself some breakfast before he had to face his wife. Miss Nerissa had good cause to be mad at him this time, and how that woman could wail and carry on.

Gus Dunlie staggered in and through the cool, airy downstairs of his big house, found the money in a locked metal box in his office, shuddered as he withdrew it, swore as he carried it back out to Quint, and vowed to take it out of Daniel's hide. Wretched smiley—the slave was half Indian—probably wasn't worth it, after all, 'cept a man couldn't let his slaves go off and get away with it. It was a bad example to the others, a real bad example, and Daniel had done it before. He had to be taught a real lesson; he'd have to be whipped, and publicly, too.

I'll do it myself, Dunlie decided. Peters was in Macon. It must be done right away, so that the slaves could connect the crime with the punishment in their thick heads.

Now was the time, with all the idlers and troublemakers hanging around the front yard anyway. Just let him get rid of Quint and he'd polish that Daniel's broad back with the thong.

But by the time Gus Dunlie got back out to the front yard, Polly Barstow had arrived, riding up to the assembled mob of men and dogs and horses in her small carriage with her children and Berlinda. As Polly and the others stared in horror, Quint's arm unloaded Daniel from the wagon and tied him to the tall, T-shaped crane in front of the well house in the middle of the yard. As they watched, Gus Dunlie paid Quint and the two men shook hands.

"Wall, Mister Dunlie," Quint said in his flat, slow voice, deep with pride in his work, "I'm glad I could help you out. Now, any time you need me agin, you jist send for me. I keep the best nigger dogs in Georgia and I keep 'em ready to run, day or night . . ."

"Good day to you, Quint," Gus Dunlie said shortly. A woman was getting out of the carriage, unfurling her black parasol, as one of his stable boys held the head of her horses. Now what was his cousin the preacher's wife doing here? He hadn't seen Polly Barstow . . . Todd in some time. She and her husband had been living in Cherokee country; he'd seen them there. Why, it must have been more than a year ago. Poor woman, her husband was a fanatic, a Christian gone soft on savages, but that didn't give her any cause to come riding in to Dunlie Hall for a visit, not that he could see.

"Good day, Cousin Augustus," Polly said calmly and clearly. "What on earth is goin' on here today? Who are all these men? What has that poor man done?"

It's none of your God damn business, Dunlie thought, grinding his teeth. His headache was worse and the heat was beginning to get to him. He felt sick to his stomach and the sweat was streaming off his corpulent body. God damn these women, he thought, always spyin' on a man and interferin' in his affairs.

"He's a runaway," Dunlie said. "What kin I do for you, Miss Polly?"

"I expect . . . you're surprised to see me here," Polly said, her son standing next to her, her faithful Berlinda just behind holding Delight.

"Yes, ma'am, I am."

"I have come to talk with you about somethin' very important," Polly said.

The way she said it communicated immediately to Gus Dunlie that she had come to borrow money. He had heard that tone before, heard it all his life, it was the tone of hesitant need, but it did not move him. He hated it and despised those who used it.

"I expect we should speak in private," Polly said, her voice quavering slightly.

"Wall, I'll be leavin', Mister Dunlie," Quint said, "les' you need any help with the whippin' I'm sure that boy's gone git."

"No, no, I'll handle it," Dunlie said. "You better take your children inside, Miss Polly. I have to tend to this before I get to you."

"Oh, please don't beat that young man," Polly exclaimed in horror. "Isn't it enough that he's tied up, humiliated? What has he done? I'm sure he's suffered enough already. Please . . ."

"Miss Polly, you better git inside," Dunlie said grimly. "Take the children clear in through the house to the back parlor. This is nothin' to do with you, but it's got to be done right away. Do as I say."

"In the name of God, Cousin Augustus . . ." Polly begged, but Gus Dunlie turned his back on her, calling out "Git in there like I tell you, Miss Polly, 'les you want you children to see."

And scooping up Bridge, Polly ran into the house with Berlinda at her heels, both women sobbing. Delight started to wail at the threshold and the high, penetrating sound made Gus Dunlie wince. Thank God his own children were past that stage; he had hated it. He hated to hear a baby cry, it was a noise that set his teeth on edge, and there was no stopping them once they got warmed up and really let loose with it.

Christ, I forgot my hat, Dunlie thought as he marched across the lawn, past the oleander hedge, to the well house. His blond, curly hair was thinning on top and his scalp was already burned bright red. Women! he thought. All he was going to do was whip Daniel. Some of his neighbors, he knew, made it a practice to brand runaways or let the dogs chew them up. Seth Reid, over in Jasper

County, punished his runaways by pulling out one of their toenails with a pair of pincers. He claimed it cured them every time. It was common practice to "salt" a slave after beating him—wash out his cuts with brine—and many masters flogged arrogant slaves until they were crippled, maimed, or dead. He, Gus Dunlie, hadn't the stomach for that. All he intended to do was to give Daniel a good whipping, just as he would have one of his sons if the boy had done something to deserve it.

And so, as Rake Quint and his men and dogs rode out of the yard, Gus Dunlie took up his whip, a bunch of thin leather thongs tied onto the end of a wooden stick, and began to beat Daniel across his bare back. The sun was hot and his back and arm were stiff, and he began slowly, but as they loosened up he put more muscle into it.

"How many? How many lashes you gone give 'im?" Bug asked, running across the lawn and coming up behind Dunlie.

"One hundred," Dunlie said, and Bug howled, "Oooooh, mas'er! One hun'red? Oooooh!"

He cost me a hundred dollars, he's gone get a hundred lashes, Dunlie thought, remembering the price Quint had set. Sweat streaming down his face and chest, his knees felt weak, but he kept at it, as Bug counted out loud.

"How many? How many lashes are gone give 'im?" Bug chanted, and Gus Dunlie kept at it, raising and lowering his arm increasingly slowly and heavily.

For Daniel, already weakened by hunger, exhaustion, and fear, the interval between each blow was an eternity. Each blow sent waves of pain through his body, he shuddered with it, and slumped into the ropes that bound him hand and foot. Blood rose to the surface of the cuts that the lash made across his back, collected there, and ran down his buttocks and legs in rivulets. Sweat ran into the cuts and made them sting as well as ache and throb. He fainted, then came to again, fainted, woke in a space between two blows, lifted his head and then screamed, once, as the next blow cut deeper into the raw, lacerated flesh of his back.

"Thirty-eight, thirty-nine," Bug chanted, and Honey, the light-skinned seamstress who had been born the night Old Master died, Old Rebecca's last child, burst into tears and ran into the house, sobbing wretchedly and despairingly as she ran. For Honey, who loved Daniel with all the strength and passion of her heart, it was a crucial moment, a turning point. She had suffered the highs and lows of despair this morning. Despite everything, she was truly happy to see that Daniel had been found. She was happy to see him again, to know that they were together again.

He had been gone five days. She knew that he had run away to Indian territory, where he had been born. Before he left, she had prayed that he would not go, but when he had gone, she had prayed that he would make it to freedom. Daniel had promised that he would return as soon as he could to get her. But if he did not escape, if he were returned to Dunlie Hall, as he now had been, he had promised her that she should plan their next attempt.

Now it was up to her. She was determined to go off, just as determined as Daniel, but she would not leave without him. Somehow, she would take him with her, and they would go north to freedom.

Honey had heard of people who did it and survived. All her life she had been attuned to such accounts; all her life she had known that someday she would run away, if she died trying. An urge to flee was inborn in her; it was as if she had drunk it in with her mother's milk, first gotten the idea in her head by listening to the songs of flight and freedom her mother had sung as she cradled her in her arms.

"My Daniel, my darlin', my love," Honey sobbed, and she ran to hide herself in the sewing room where she could not hear any of the sounds from the front yard. Later, when it was over, when Daniel was returned to his cabin, she would go to him and bathe his wounds and feed him and make love to him, and she would tell him of the plan she had invented while he was gone. It was a bold plan, and as well as courage and confidence, they would need money, but she had an idea about that, too, for she had watched Master take the money for the slave catchers out of a box in his office, and she had seen where he put the key.

Both Caleb Barstow, the cotton broker, and his partner, Jacob Barstow, the free black, had a passion for the turf. The two men, both so wealthy and fashionably dressed, both so refined and well-spoken, Mr. Caleb Barstow quite remarkably handsome despite his twisted posture, had been a familiar sight at Savannah's Jockey Club for years.

Accordingly, on a sunny Saturday afternoon that spring, the two businessmen left their offices on the Bay and rode out together to watch the races. They arrived just on time, and the ground was already crowded with a wide sampling of Savannah society: Men and women of all ages, conditions, and complexions were clustered before the betting booths as others arrived on foot, on horseback, in carriages and wagons and carts.

Well-dressed ladies were in abundance, although, according to local custom, most of them remained in their carriages, which were ranged some thirty or forty paces from the starting line. From their open carriages the ladies could lean out to call to friends, beckon for ices or cups of punch from strolling vendors, wave to acquaintances all the way across the field, and enjoy an excellent view of the goings-on without risking exposure to the rays of the sun or the mud underfoot.

"There is Mister Barstow," one young lady in cerise commented to another as the two gentlemen rode past.

"Ah, yes," sighed the other. "Mister Barstow is so handsome, don't you think, Mandy? I wonder why he never married."

"I expect he is shy," Mandy speculated, thinking that she might be the very one to charm the incredibly rich Mister Barstow out of his celibacy. To her it would not matter a whit that he was ill-formed. He was tall, and had such striking blue eyes. Yet, although she had met him on numerous occasions, he seemed able to resist her charms, and he was well beyond the age when most men married. She accepted a lemon sherbet from her most devoted suitor. He was not rich, but at least he was enthusiastic. "Thank you, Edward," she said sweetly, lowering her head to put out her tongue, just a bit, as he watched.

Moving toward the betting booths, the two Barstows passed through a crowd of peddlers selling apples, oranges, squares of honey cake, and roasted corn. The purse, contained in a red satin envelope embroidered in gold and silver threads, hung from a pole over the starting point. For the afternoon's racing it was worth five hundred dollars.

"Prepare your horses," a call came from the judges'

stand. The race, as usual, would be four miles in length and the winning horse would be the one able to outdo all the competition. Often two or three heats decided the winner. At a track in New York State, not too long ago, a field of America's best race mares had run a total of twenty miles in one afternoon before a winner was declared. Today there would be three heats at the Savannah track.

As Jacob and Caleb Barstow made their bets, Negro grooms saddled the four horses that were to run the first heat. Among them was a fine-blooded mare named Miss Rowena; Caleb owned her and both men bet a hundred dollars on her against the field.

Miss Rowena was to be ridden by a little Negro jockey of about thirteen years of age; he was dressed from head to toe in pink satin, and waited now, anxiously shifting his weight from foot to foot, as an ancient black trainer held Miss Rowena's head and her groom fastened her girth.

"I see that Judge Flint is in the stand," Caleb commented to Jacob. The judge was a devotee of the turf and had often been known to adjourn the court to officiate at a horserace.

"How does he look?" Jacob asked.

"Far from sober," Caleb commented.

Taking a place at a slight remove from the starting point, they waited for the signal to start. There was a roll of drums and a whoop from the judges' stand.

"Oh, dear," Jacob Barstow said to Caleb.

At the starting gun, all four horses were off, amid shouts, shrieks, and a continuing series of whoops from Judge Flint. Miss Rowena trailed a gray called Sully, pulling ahead of Ocean Pearl and Rafaella, then, as the horses completed the second mile, Miss Rowena took the lead, increased it to a length, held it, and finished ahead of the pack.

"Whoopee!" Judge Flint yelled, and the crowd roared satisfaction, swarming all over the track despite calls of "Clear the track!"

For the second heat, Jacob and Caleb increased their bets to five hundred apiece, still on Miss Rowena to take the field. The horses rested for about a quarter of an hour as the bettors crowded the booths and punch was bought all around.

"Little Jackie is ridin' well," Caleb commented. He took immense pride in his jockeys and had been known to pay as much for a handsome, well-formed young Negro jockey as he had paid for a Thoroughbred. He housed his young jockeys above the stables at his house on Abercorn Street, although his horses were kept at a farm just outside of town.

Jacob Barstow's blue eyes met those of his partner. He did not smile. None of Caleb's passions were amusing to him, even the ones he shared. Over the years the two men had developed a remarkable relationship, one that had been immensely profitable to both of them, but of the two, Caleb was the more trusting and Jacob the more secretive. Business was their overriding standard; if a thing was not profitable, they did not do it. Both were amoral in every sense of the word, yet Jacob had, in the past few years, begun to betray his partner and conceal some of his activities.

None of Caleb Barstow's affairs were unknown to Jacob Barstow. He knew that his white partner was smuggling gold out of the country for his cousin Augustus Dunlie. He knew that Caleb had been involved in the illegal African slave trade and still invested in cargoes of Africans when the opportunity arose. He knew how often they had sold cotton on margin and how fantastically they had profited. He knew about Caleb's strange sex life and loved and pitied him for it. He did not judge Caleb; they were too close for that.

But with increasing regularity during the past few years, Jacob had agreed to help his younger brother Isaiah, who was a minister in Savannah's African Baptist Church, when Isaiah had asked him to hide fugitive slaves in the Barstow and Barstow warehouses. And now he had gone further. He had helped Isaiah smuggle some miserable runaways onto steamers going north. He had concealed a whole family, a wretched, terrified family, in his warehouse for a week, waiting for the chance to send them on to Charleston. It was highly dangerous and insanely risky for a free black to be involved with slave smuggling.

At first Isaiah had mentioned money to his brother, but it became apparent that he could not pay Jacob any worthwhile amount. To his own amazement, Jacob had continued to help the runaways. In his heart he thought it was right; in his heart he was glad to be able to speed some of his enslaved brothers out of Georgia.

But in doing so he was risking everything. And everything was a great deal.

CHAPTER SEVENTEEN

Polly Goes Begging; Honey and Daniel Dream of Heaven; The Cherokees' Darkest Hour

Honey, who had sought private refuge in her sewing room, found, when she burst into the plain, white-walled workroom that overlooked the back verandah, that Polly Todd and Berlinda and children were already installed there. Clasping hands, the baby Delight with them, the four visitors were on their knees, with their faces lifted, praying aloud.

"Dear Lord, give us strength to do Thy will . . ." Polly began.

"Amen," Berlinda chimed in, and continued, "Thy will be done. Forgive those sinners, forgive us our weakness in fightin' evil."

"Amen," Polly said clearly. "We mourn, dear Lord, for the injustices we see in our daily lives, our hearts break for the cruelty of our fellow men . . ."

"Let the good triumph, let it gain in strength, let it grow in our hearts and souls and make us strong," Berlinda begged.

"Amen," said little Bridge.

"Release the oppressed from bondage, punish the unrighteous, dear Lord, we implore you," Polly intoned in a low, fervent voice, shaking with emotion.

"Let us flee from evil and do the thing that is good," Berlinda chanted.

Honey froze. She listened, transfixed. She had never heard such a thing. There was no church for the slaves at Dunlie Hall, and Master had forbidden them to go to the nearest one, five miles away at Snake's Creek. Since her mother had died, she had not heard women praying like this, but it touched her, stirred her, and, trusting them immediately, she flung herself down on the rug in front of them, crying so hard that she could not speak.

"The Lord is our help in time of trouble, we look to Him for salvation, He will stand by us, He will show us the way, He will lead us from bondage," Berlinda and Polly said together, and each of the women put out an arm to draw Honey up into their circle.

"Help me! Help me!" Honey sobbed.

"Who are you, dear?" Polly asked in a gentle voice, holding Honey's hand.

"I am called Honey."

"Why are you crying, Honey? For the man being whipped?"

"Yes, ma'am. He's the man I love. Since I love him, I love ever'thin', that's how I know I love him. I sure can't stand to see him bein' hurt, ma'am."

"None of us can," Polly said softly, stroking Honey's straight dark hair. She had pretty Caucasian features and was unusually light-skinned, even in a society where mulatto slaves were as common as blackberries. I wish I could take her with me, Polly thought.

"Are you goin' to marry him?" she asked.

"Master doan want us to marry, ma'am. He's mad at Daniel 'cause he's always goin' off, but . . ."

I wonder, Polly thought, but before she could say more they heard the sound of Gus Dunlie's boots tramping through the house toward them and heard his voice calling "Miss Polly? Where have you gone to? Miss Polly!"

"Stay here with Berlinda," Polly said, placing Honey's small, amber-colored hand in Berlinda's. As fast as she could, she straightened her petticoats, smoothed her hair, and found her parasol.

"I must talk to him; you talk to Honey," she said quickly, patting Bridge's shoulder as she passed by him.

"Here I am, Cousin Augustus," Polly said, wandering through a handsome, elegantly appointed sitting room. The house, she knew, had been built by her uncle Angus Dunlie, who had been Augustus's father. Although it was now about twenty years old, it was still the most elegantly furnished house in this part of Georgia. She marveled at the scenes painted on all the paneled window shutters and the profusion of fine European furniture. How out of keeping it seemed with Cousin Gus's blunt country ways.

I expect, Polly thought, Uncle Angus was a different sort of man, although Aunt Juliette had always refused to discuss him.

"Oh. You hidin' back there in the sewin' room, eh?" Gus Dunlie asked, coming onto Polly in the back hallway. "D'you see that fancy sewin' wench I got there? Ain't she somethin'?"

"She is very pretty," Polly said, trying not to betray any feelings at all. "Is she a good seamstress?"

"Good enough, but I think I'm goin' to sell her. Fellow who was here last week told me they sometimes bring five thousand dollars, if they're really pretty and light . . . in a fancy girl market in New Orleans."

Polly shuddered. "Mr. Dunlie, I don't know why you would speak to me of such matters," she said stiffly and miserably. He was just too crude and callous; how could she approach him on the matter of obtaining money for the Cherokees if the conversation started out this way?

On Gus Dunlie's part, the tone of the conversation was deliberate; he sensed quite accurately that only a need for money could have brought this particular cousin, a refined and religious lady, to Dunlie Hall after all these years, and he wanted to unsettle her so that she would not even dare to ask.

"Come into my office," he said to Polly, grinning. "My arm is tired. I b'lieve I need a drink. Can I offer you a drop, Miss Polly?"

"No, thank you," Polly said, thinking that Cousin Augustus might be more easily managed if he were drunk. She had seen many men come to the Lord that way, and only later be persuaded to face Christianity sober.

Gus Dunlie, who had felt sick and woozy before he had undertaken the ordeal of beating Daniel in the broiling sun, sank into his armchair with all the exhausted weariness of a man fifty pounds over his best weight. He sighed and drank deeply from a bottle of whiskey he found standing on the floor. He had not eaten all day; it was now past one o'clock, and the whiskey made him immediately giddy, although it masked his aches and pains.

Where is that woman? he wondered, recalling that Miss Nerissa was not yet anywhere to be seen. And even if she weren't home, why wasn't there the smell of dinner being cooked? God damn it, his world was a shambles!

"I wish I wuz a bachelor," he sputtered. "I wish I wuz an abolitionist. None of 'em is any good, and they stick together like wattle 'nmud." Dear Lord, he thought, one hundred dollars to get back a mean, ornery nigger! Twenty niggers 'round the house and none of 'em cooking dinner. Women hanging all 'round, screwing up their faces in judgment and looking for money.

"What can I do for you, Cousin Polly?" he bellowed.

Polly swallowed and plunged in. Having got this far, she would go on, though prospects looked grim indeed. The worst he can say, she told herself, is no. He can't beat me, and his scorn and ridicule mean nothing to me.

"I have come, Cousin Augustus, to ask you for money . . . for a cause of immediate and personal interest to me, to us all. Perhaps you are aware of the terrible peril Georgia's Cherokees now face?"

Gus Dunlie's eyes narrowed. In some perverse, convoluted way Polly's earnest seriousness aroused him. Her smooth, pink-skinned face topped by a riot of light brown curls was too pure, too good-womanly to endure. He wanted to hurt her, shock her, humiliate her somehow.

"Indians?" he asked. "You want money for some stinking savages?"

"The Cherokees are not savages!" Polly replied, her cheeks reddening and her eyes shining with outrage. "They are Christians, literate Christians who have built farms and schools and churches that should be the envy of their white neighbors!"

"So let 'em be," Gus Dunlie said, drinking from the bottle. The whiskey's smooth, smoky strength had mellowed his temper as it dimmed his vision. In the golden afternoon light that streamed into the room and across the cluttered table where they sat, Polly Barstow . . . no, it was Todd now . . . looked ripely pretty to him. Where is her husband, he wondered. What sort of a man was he, letting his young wife go out begging for the Indians?

"That's just it," Polly said fervently. "We have never let them be, we white Georgians. And now they are being driven from their traditional homeland, not because they are not civilized, but because we, who are too strong for them, want their possessions!"

"I hate Indians," Dunlie said flatly.

"Well, you are very wrong to do so," Polly snapped. She was shocked. How crass, how stupid he was! She drew in her breath sharply and started to rise as he stared at her breasts. Instinctively, she let a hand float down to cover the top of her plain blue cotton gown. "Don't look at me so, Cousin Augustus!" she said, tears coming to her eyes. She had never been so treated by a man, never so humiliated.

"And I never give away money," Dunlie said, "unless I get something I want in return."

Polly raised her head and faced him defiantly. "I am sure I have nothing to offer you, sir, except peace of mind at having done the right thing."

Had Polly been more sophisticated, she would have been even more insulted. Had she been one whit less of a lady, she might have been downright rude. Had Gus Dunlie been less afraid of the consequences, he might have proposed something specific, but as it happened Polly was fighting back tears and did not notice when Gus Dunlie, red-faced and aroused, hauled himself up and stood so near her that when she stood up she put the point of her parasol on his toe and spun it like a drill.

His boots were thin. He yelped in pain and swore. "God damn it! God damn it! Enough!"

"Oh, my goodness!" Polly gasped, "Oh, I am so sorry! Pardon me!" She stepped back from him abruptly and nearly upset the spittoon, brimful with a vile collection, that stood near the doorjamb. From the back of the house she could hear Baby Delight begin to wail, perhaps set off by Gus Dunlie's screams, which continued unabated.

"Get out! Be off," he yelled. He was hopping on one foot, and as she slipped away, Polly saw that he had landed in the spittoon himself.

"I do apologize. I am going, I assure you, Cousin Augustus," Polly called back with all the dignity she could manage. I do pity his wife, she thought as she ran to reclaim her children—how ever does she put up with him?

Men, she thought as she ran back through the house, in general, of course—not my dear David—seem to me to be one step up from animals! And the vast majority of them seem to believe that women were made to gratify their animal instincts!

* * *

As soon as Polly and Berlinda and the children had driven away from Dunlie Hall, Honey left the sewing room and ran down the back path to Daniel's cabin.

Daniel lay there, across his bed on his stomach, and Oola, the old woman who knew all there was to know about herbs and healing, was bent over his lacerated, bleeding back.

"Darlin'!" Honey sobbed, putting her cool hands on his forehead and stroking his hair. "My poor darlin'!"

"He's gone be all right," Oola pronounced, regal as a tribal queen in her scarlet turban, laying cobwebs and the leaves of some green plant over the broken, bloody skin. "Never saw no nigger as tough as this Injun."

Daniel opened his eyes and saw Honey. A light of recognition came into them and he tried to speak, but she could not hear until she kneeled beside his bed and put her ear to his mouth.

"Next time, Honey," he whispered. "We'll make it next time."

"We will, we will," she promised. "Brave Daniel, I know we will; rest now, and recover."

A week later—a week during which Daniel had already been set to work building a new chicken coop, Miss Nerissa had returned to initiate a quarrel between Master and Missus that had the whole plantation on edge for days, and Honey had spent long, solitary hours in the sewing room—Honey and Daniel planned to meet after curfew, at the old smokehouse down past the grove of willows, an isolated spot that had been their trysting place all throughout the course of their romance.

Daniel arrived alone and took a seat facing the open doorway to wait for Honey. He was tired; he had worked from sunup to sundown, lifting and carrying, hammering and sawing, each motion a stinging shock to his back, crusted now with scabs, still stiff and sore, but healing. Although he was barely twenty, he felt old and defeated. It was a beautiful spring, but he felt no part of it; he had lost hope, he felt beaten. Despite his brave words to Honey, he did not know how they could get away; it seemed entirely hopeless. Master and the overseer watched him more closely than any of the others, and if he were caught again, he would be killed, Master had promised him that. And yet, to stay here? Master would not let them marry.

Saddened and yet seething with frustration, Daniel picked up a wrought-iron hook that was used to hang hams and hefted it in his powerful hand. He longed to smash it against the smokehouse's stone walls, or through the master's head . . . or his own. There is no way, he thought bitterly, no way left to me to be a man.

His life had been better when he was a child. He had been born a slave on a small plantation owned by a Cherokee farmer, near Ellijay, in the green, mountainous country where gold had later been found. His mother had been a black African, herself born on the plantation. His father? One of the Indians, he supposed, for as soon as he could walk he knew that he was of mixed blood. His Cherokee master had been a good man, had fed and cared for his ten or fifteen slaves kindly. As a boy, Daniel had been set to learn from the plantation's carpenter, and though he was silent and moody, he was clever with his hands, and he had learned the rudiments of carpentry well.

Then, when Daniel was sixteen, full-grown and handsome, tall, with broad shoulders and shining white teeth, the Cherokee had died of a fever and all of his slaves had been put up for sale. Augustus Dunlie, traveling in Indian country, had seen a chance to get a skilled carpenter at a low price and had purchased him for three hundred dollars. Riding on a horse of his own behind the master, Daniel had traveled the length of Indian country to get back to Dunlie Hall, and what he had seen had crested in him a desire to rejoin his Indian people somehow, some day, and somehow, some day to be free.

I was young, Daniel thought bitterly, remembering the journey, remembering the shock of being absorbed into the slave work force at Dunlie Hall. There were no other slaves with Indian blood here; there were no others who had glimpsed another life, and the life they led was grim. The master himself was bad-tempered and changeable; when he was drunk, which was often, he was cruel and violent. He employed an overseer, and even in Daniel's day four overseers had come and gone—overseers who seemed to express the worst side of his own nature.

I was young and angry then, Daniel thought. During his first years at Dunlie Hall he had passively and sullenly resisted his condition, destroying tools, performing slipshod work, fighting with his fellows. I drove in every nail with hate, set every beam with malice, Daniel remembered, but I got no relief from it. I was just mad, mad and hopeless, but I never thought of trying to run off till I got to know Honey.

Honey, whom Daniel had first glimpsed "like a vision of heaven," he recalled, coming down the walkway to the quarters in a yellow dress, had been off the plantation with Miss Nerissa for several months, visiting her family in Madison. "I didn't b'lieve in love till I met Honey," Daniel had said some time later, "but I b'lieve now."

"You bet' watch out fo' dat one," the master's body servant Bug had told Daniel. "Mist' Gus got special plans for she."

But despite Bug's injunction, Honey and Daniel fell in love, and he found in her a willing conspirator, the only other slave at Dunlie Hall who had ever been off the plantation. Together they dreamed of freedom. In their love, hope was born, and Daniel turned his strength and cunning away from blind anger to calculated resistance. Twice he had run away and hidden in the woods near Dunlie Hall, once for as long as six weeks, but each time he had been caught by the slave patrollers.

This spring he had conceived another plan. Word had reached the plantation that the Cherokees were leaving Georgia and migrating west. Daniel decided that his best hope for freedom was to reach them, but to his sorrow Honey disagreed. The only slaves she had heard of who succeeded in their attempts to escape had been heading north, she had argued, and besides, the master would suspect that Daniel had gone west, as he had before. But Daniel had been determined and he had fled, promising Honey that he would return for her when he had found a horse and contacted the Indians.

But now? He had failed again. He scowled and turned the wrought-iron meat hook in his hands. He had failed Honey again, and failed his own dreams. Better to die than to live like this. He was confounded, cornered. If it weren't for Honey . . . and even Honey was not his—she might be taken from him at any time. He was completely helpless. Both of them were. . . .

Just then, in the pale moonlight, Daniel saw a slender young white man appear in the doorway of the smokehouse. He walked slowly, with a slight limp. His right arm was carried in a white cotton sling, his face was partially bandaged, and he wore a green felt hat pulled low over his ears.

Daniel jumped fearfully and stepped back into the shadows, but the young man advanced, tapping the ground lightly with a bamboo cane.

"Excuse me, young master," Daniel forced himself to say respectfully. There was nowhere to hide; whoever this man was, he would have to show himself to him, and if he was fast enough, he could warn Honey as she was coming down the path.

The young man stared at Daniel. He did not speak.

"Yes, sir, I'll be goin'," Daniel said and tried to edge around the figure. Just as he did, he caught sight of the man's eyes, and heard him say in a low, teasing voice, "Don't know me, eh?"

"Honey!" Daniel gasped.

She laughed delightedly; then, instantly sobered, she ran into Daniel's arms and held him close to her. "Daniel, it's my goin'-off costume, and I've made one for you, too. Don't you think I can pass for white?"

"Oh, Honey, Honey, but where will we run to?"

Pulling him back into the shadows, Honey began to explain, talking rapidly in a low voice that quavered with tension and fear, although she tried not to show it.

"Las' week, when that lady come to visit Mist' Gus, the day Miss 'Rissa was gone, oh, the day you was beaten . . ."

"Yes? What of that lady?"

"She lef' her servant, her free-woman servant, in my sewin' room while she was talkin' to Mist' Gus. Her name's Berlinda. She tole me, darlin', of a name to ask for in Macon, and another one in Savannah. Names of partic'lar friends we can trust. She tole me I could dress up and pass for a white man who's bin sick, and take you 'long as my slave. If'n anyone ask any questions, I'll jus' tell 'em I've got to go to Savannah to see a doctah!"

Daniel exhaled very slowly. It was an amazing plan, so

stunning by its boldness that it might succeed. How beautiful she was, and how much he loved her. He would do anything for her. . . .

"How should we get from Macon to Savannah?"

"On the railroad, Daniel. I should go with you to the station and buy tickets."

"And where would we get the money?"

"I shall steal it from Mist' Gus."

"Oh, my darlin', how brave you are!"

"My courage, Daniel, is half as strong as my love for you," she told him, and he took her into his arms, and very carefully removed her hand-stitched finery, and made love to her.

"If we are caught, we shall be killed," he said softly, as he kissed her smooth, golden skin and rested her slim body on his lap.

"But if we make it, and I believe we shall," she whispered, "we shall be free and be together. It will be heaven on earth."

Dahlonega, the gold-mining town where Polly Barstow Todd had lived most of the years of her married life, had been picturesquely situated in one of the small valleys which part the wooded mountains as they are washed through by creeks with names as charming as their clear, fresh waters: Pigeon Roost Creek, Blackbird Creek, and Cane Creek among them.

When the Todds had first come to Dahlonega, the hills and ridges, three to four hundred feet in height, had been wooded to the top and the streams had meandered through them following their natural courses, but the gold-mining operations had entirely altered the natural beauty of the hills. Now all the valleys had been dug up and the washed gravel thrown into heaps, the fine trees had been uprooted, and the streams diverted.

It pained Polly to see it, but today she had graver matters, even, than geological devastation to concern her. As soon as she entered Cherokee territory with Berlinda and her children in the carriage, they found themselves swept up into the chaos of General Winfield Scott's general evacuation of the eight thousand Cherokees who remained in Georgia.

From the first, Polly had to stop the carriage every few

hundred feet along the road, present her papers, and explain her mission. Twenty-three split-log stockades had been built throughout the Indian nation, she learned. They were manned by militia. General Scott planned that his troops would go forth every day in squads to capture and bring in all the Indians living in the immediate area and to put them in the stockades, from where they would be forwarded to one of four main emigration depots.

"How terrible! How terrible!" Polly exclaimed to the lanky Georgia militiaman who stopped her near a little hamlet where she knew a Cherokee family. "Pray treat them with all kindness, sir, for they are God-fearing souls."

"We are under orders to show all possible kindness, ma'am," he said. When the troops he had ordered from Florida had failed to show up, General Scott had mustered two regiments of Georgia militia to do the grim work in their own state. "We're enjoined to use clean language, ma'am, treat 'em easy, and to get 'em horses, those too old or sick to walk."

" 'Tis as it should be," Polly said with a troubled heart, but as she rode on toward the hamlet where the Long family lived, she had her first view of a sight that was to become commonplace, if never easy to bear, in the next few days. Ahead of her on the road was a coffle of handsome, dark-haired Cherokees, women and small children among the men, being driven along the path ahead of a mounted soldier flourishing a bayonet while five or six other soldiers rode among the Cherokees, hastening them on with blows and oaths.

"Just as if they were animals," Berlinda murmured, and Polly wished Bridge and Delight were not there to see.

A few minutes later they climbed the hilly road to the Longs' farm and found the family about to sit down to dinner. "Welcome, dear Mis' Todd," the patriarch of the family, a wise, kind farmer of almost seventy with long white hair, said to Polly. "Your husband has gone ahead, has he not? Ah, we are honored to have you break bread with us at one of our last meals in our own home."

"Thank you, thank you," Polly said, and tears stood in her eyes. She was tired after the day's traveling, and the Longs' orderly farm seemed a familiar oasis of tranquillity to her. "But what will become of your land, your buildings, your livestock?" she asked.

"Perhaps we will manage to sell them," William Long said slowly, "but it is late. There is much haste, and the house is old. My grandfather built it."

"It's old, but it's sound," Polly said, her concern revealed in her voice. If so many of the Cherokees hadn't put so much faith in their leader, John Ross, David had always said, they would have had enough time to put their affairs in order, to have sold their houses and land and livestock and their crops. But many of them had hoped, to the last, that the edict would be reversed. Some hoped it still.

"Mister Long, there is much haste," Polly said, remembering what she had seen already on the road.

"God's will be done," the old man said, and bowed his head. "Mis' Todd, in the name of your husband, who taught us all, will you lead tonight's prayers?"

"I will be proud to, sir," Polly said, and the entire Long family knelt with her in a circle, in their neat, well-swept kitchen, while the cornbread baked and the rabbit stew simmered over the fire. Beside William Long knelt his wife, still dark-haired and plump, as pretty as the bird for which she was named, Phoebe. Most of the Longs' children were grown and moved to farms of their own; only Rachel and Rebecca, the little girls who were Bridge's special friends, remained, and one other son, Thomas, who, though he was tall and muscular, was a deaf-mute and always stayed close to his home.

"We thank thee, Lord," Polly prayed, "for the many blessings of life. Make us truly thankful."

"Amen," echoed the assembled, and Polly lifted her head and looked around at the circle. When would they all be together again like this? Oh, let it be soon, she wished, and with David here beside me.

"Almighty God," she went on, and her voice strengthened and found a timbre as pure as the wind and the rushing stream outside the Longs' tidy home. "Almighty God, whose compassions fail not, we give Thee thanks for opening heathen lands to the light of Thy truth. Save and deliver us, we humbly beseech Thee, from the hands of our enemies, preserve us from all perils, guide our steps in this exodus we undertake in Thy name. Stretch forth, we pray Thee, Thine almighty arm to strengthen and protect us, Thy children; in this time of peril, keep us safe. Grant us grace fearlessly to contend against evil and to make no peace with oppression, but to reverently use our freedom. Look with pity on our sorrows, give us strength and skill, and grant that, perceiving how frail and uncertain our life is on earth, we may apply our hearts unto that heavenly wisdom which leads us to eternal life, through Jesus Christ, whom we adore."

"Amen, amen, amen . . ." everyone said, except Thomas, who smiled. I believe he feels the prayers, if he doesn't hear them, Polly thought. She settled herself in a rush-bottomed chair and took Delight onto her lap. Thank goodness this long day is nearly over, she thought. Tomorrow she would push on to Dahlonega and start to pack up their household things; although she still had very little money, she would do the best she could.

As Phoebe Long cut the cornbread and ladled the spicy-smelling rabbit stew into wide pottery bowls, darkness fell and the night birds began to sing. Polly ate with the others at the long trestle table, even the children quiet and subdued.

"When will you be ready to leave?" Polly asked William Long, finally, voicing the hated question although she would rather have not.

"Tomorrow . . . the next day . . ." he said. "It is the wrong time to go. The corn is knee-high and growing nicely. A good spring. There has been no cold weather since the first of March. . . ."

Just then, as the Longs and their guests sat without moving, there was a sudden loud clatter of horses' hooves coming up the trail to the farm, and then a series of gunshots that set the dogs barking and the chickens crowing.

William Long stood immediately, erect and calm.

"What is it?" Polly screamed.

Two soldiers with flashing guns and bayonets appeared in the doorway, more soldiers behind them. The soldiers were so big they filled the whole doorway; Delight burst into wails and dove under her mother's skirts.

"William Long and family," the first soldier said, "under the authority of the United States Army, I come to move you to the nearest stockade. Every Cherokee man, woman, and child must now be in motion to join their brethren in the West. Bring your family, old man, the time is short."

"Tonight? At once?" Polly shrieked, unbelieving. She looked toward the back door; another soldier stood there. She pulled Delight up into her arms and found that she was trembling so violently that she could not hold her.

From the barnyard they could hear the cattle lowing and the horses whinnying. There must be more soldiers out there, Polly thought. We are surrounded.

"This white lady is our guest," William Long said clearly. "She has nothing to do with this. Phoebe, take a few things for the children; take some corn; take our Bible. . . ."

"She don't look Cherokee," the soldier laughed. "Neither of them do."

Polly passed the sobbing Delight to Berlinda and put her arms around Bridge. "I know you soldiers are doing what you are ordered to do," she said, as bravely as she could, "but, really, I should think that tomorrow . . ."

"Tonight, ma'am, we got a long way to go, and more of 'em waitin' out on the main trail. You just stay out of this."

"You two men first," the second soldier ordered William Long and Thomas, nudging the proud old man with the point of his bayonet.

"Please, Mis' Todd, you must stay here . . . at least the night," Long said to Polly, and she nodded and scrambled to help Phoebe put some clothes and cracked corn in three small bags.

"Bridge, say good-bye to Rebecca and Rachel. You'll see each other again in the West," Polly said. "What else can I bring along for you?" she asked Phoebe, but the Indian woman shrugged stoically.

"Of everything, it is hard to choose," she said, looking for the last time around her neat, well-furnished cabin, seeing the pots hanging from the rafters, the bunched herbs from the window frames, the hand-woven blue-checked curtains and tablecloth. Impulsively, she seized her favorite skillet and followed the men outside, with her little girls hard on her heels.

"March!" the first soldier ordered, as William Long stood, just for a moment, his shoulders square and rawboned, his dark eyes gazing without expression out into the darkness where his cornfields still flourished.

"Left! Hey, I said left!" one of the soldiers yelled at Thomas, but uncomprehending, Thomas turned right and headed away from the soldier.

"Left!" the burly soldier yelled again, and added, "That one's a troublemaker, I can see it! Left, you dumb Injun!"

"My son is deaf," William Long said in a strong, clear voice, but it was too late.

A shot rang out, and in plain view of them all, gentle, silent Thomas Long crumpled and fell forward.

Crying out in Cherokee, Phoebe Long ran to her son and bent over him, sobbing hysterically, but Polly and Berlinda stood transfixed on the doorstep, too shocked and horrified to move.

"Git goin'! Git marchin'! Leave him be, now! Git that woman up!" the soldier in charge yelled out, without looking back at Polly and the others. I shall see that he is punished by law, if I die trying, Polly vowed, but she did not know his name.

Minutes later all the Longs had been marched out of the clearing in front of their farmhouse and the sounds of the soldiers' horses and their oaths and yells were all that echoed back to their hilltop farm.

Polly and Berlinda were left with the aftermath of agony and despair, left with the crying baby, with Bridge asking endlessly "Why, why, Mama, why did the soldiers shoot Thomas and take the others away?" and with the sad and exhausting task of digging a grave in the dark.

And when, after a sad and sleepless night, the two women left the Longs' deserted farm and continued on their way to Dahlonega, they saw even more. They saw soldiers driving their captives, shooting into the air, whooping and hollering uproariously as if the Cherokees were herds of longhorns, saw them force the Indians through rivers without giving them time to remove their shoes. They saw a man who struck a soldier goading his wife with a bayonet receive one hundred lashes on the spot. They saw lost children crying hopelessly. They saw men being seized in their cornfields or while going along the road, saw young women insulted, saw confused old people stumble along the roads with dazed, defeated eyes.

As well as the soldiers, the county was invaded by a

lawless rabble who rode behind the troops, looting and pillaging the Cherokee property. Polly and Berlinda saw homes set afire, saw outlaws driving off the Cherokees' cattle and other livestock before their rightful owners were out of sight. And then they saw white men digging up and desecrating Cherokee graves, rifling them for silver pendants and other valuable objects buried with their dead.

Dear Lord, I find it hard to forgive my fellow men, my fellow Georgians, Polly mourned, as she rode back into Dahlonega, back to her home. I despair for the nature of mankind; surely this is one of his blackest hours. Truly the innocent are made to suffer while the good are punished. Dear Lord, help Thy children the Cherokees, lead them peacefully beyond the great river, and deliver them safely to their new homeland. Consecrate me, Lord, if I am to be Thy helper in this, their crisis.

But when Polly reached her home, she found there a letter from her husband, urging her to join him, to bring all that she could, and she set about at once preparing for her journey.

CHAPTER EIGHTEEN

A Midnight Robbery; A Smooth Getaway; A Chase Across Georgia

By sundown the next day, all the slaves at Dunlie Hall knew that the slave traders had arrived at Madison and had taken the two big rooms above the tavern. How they knew was not easy to understand, but news about the slave traders, and the slave patrollers, carried like sound, the sound of doom. Planters in the area were selling slaves, everyone whispered. The traders were paying high prices, the masters always needed money, and there were so many slaves, so many in each tiny cabin, and every year more. A few could always be spared, and those few were usually the most independent, or runaways, or the good-looking ones, often with a few children thrown in to sweeten the deal.

At the supper table, Gus Dunlie told his wife that he wanted to sell a few slaves. He would go into Madison the next day, he planned, to see what sort of slaves were wanted and what prices were being paid.

"I've a good mind to git rid of Daniel," Gus Dunlie said; "sell him south," and the housemaid, Rizzy, who was clearing the table, heard him say so and ran to tell Honey as soon as she had dumped the big china plates and the silver knives and forks in front of the outdoor kitchen.

"Mist' Dunlie, I don't care what you do, or who you sell," Nerissa Dunlie said sulkily. As usual, Miss Nerissa was suffering the vapors, a malady either real or imagined but no less debilitating for the mysteriousness of its origins. It seemed the only thing that eased her miseries was visiting her own plantation home, sitting among her five sisters at their mammy's knee and tatting lace and gossiping, free from the overwhelming daily demands of being mistress of Dunlie Hall. "Per'aps, as long as you're goin' to Madison, I'll ride along and call on my family," she suggested.

"As you like, dear," Gus Dunlie acquiesced, thinking of the money he might so easily make and of the beloved collection of gold nuggets he had already stowed away in his metal box. He should have sent them off to Savannah by now; the sooner they were on their way to England the safer it would be, but he relished having them around, just to look at. Tomorrow, he thought, tomorrow is Wednesday, and there's a train that leaves Macon for Savannah. I'll send them on that train; he had already written his factor to look for them.

"Tonight, tonight," Honey told Daniel, when she found him repairing the wooden bed of a slat-sided haywain. "Darlin', we must go tonight. The slave traders are in town and . . ."

"I know, Honey," Daniel said softly, but there was a fire in his dark eyes and he straightened his sore back, for Honey's courage had sparked his own.

"There'll be no turnin' back this time," Honey said. "Once we leave here, we got to go free or die. You'll be ready tonight?"

"I'll be ready," Daniel promised. It was a warm June day and promised far warmer days to come. Where will we be, he wondered, when summer's come to an end? Far from these green hills. . . . Dreaming, he watched a barn-swallow soar out of the eaves of the haybarn and swoop low, then soar again, its pointed wings outstretched, dark against the reddening sky, tracing a graceful circle. May our flight be as easy and natural, he wished, although when he thought of the reality of it, he was so frightened that he could not bear the pounding of his heart.

Daniel had few friends among the other slaves at Dunlie Hall, but Honey was beloved, and when she returned to the Big House, she found the maid Rizzy, her half-sister, in her sewing room, collapsed in tears.

"I'm so scared for you, Honey," Rizzy wailed. "Seems Master's set on sellin' Daniel and maybe you. I know you love him so! Why does life got to be hard on us poor black folks? Why, Honey? 'Specially you, you so pretty and bright-skinned. You deserve better, I swear you do!"

"We all do, Rizzy," Honey whispered, and then she bent over her little half-sister and confessed, "ever since I was a little girl, Rizzy, I had the idea of runnin' off to freedom, you know that. Wall, I hain't lost it, ever, or put it aside, and it's gonna come true."

"It is?" Rizzy asked in a high voice that carried to all corners of the dark, shadowy sewing room. A big quilting frame stood in one corner, draped with a half-made coverlet; racks of sheets loomed, and the big woven baskets of mending were stacked half as high as the ceiling.

"Hush, Rizzy," Honey warned her, but it was too late. Gus Dunlie's body servant, Bug, who was napping in one of the mending baskets, woke and sat up to listen to the girl talk.

"What you mean, Honey?"

Putting her hand over Rizzy's mouth to keep her from crying out again, Honey whispered, "Daniel and I are fixin' to go off tonight. We're goin' by train to Savannah. Now don't tell a soul, Rizzy, till we been gone for six months or so. Then you can tell the rest of my sisters."

"You are?" Rizzy mumbled, her eyes huge with surprise. "Oh, Honey, I'm afraid for you." Tears filled her eyes. "It's so far . . . to Savannah."

"We're goin', I tell you, and you just keep you mouth shut!" Honey cautioned, and Rizzy promised, but it was too late. Bug had heard, and what kind of a man was Bug?

What kind, indeed? He was a man slow to act, that much is sure, for a few hours later, when Honey had dressed herself in the man's suit of clothes that she had designed and made, tied the white cotton sling around her arm, with part of the bandage easy to slip her right hand into, and found the green felt hat and the bamboo cane, Bug was still asleep in the mending basket.

As Honey finished dressing in her sewing room, the hallway clock struck midnight. Each stroke sent a wave of fright through her body, and when she saw her own reflection by candlelight in the big, gilded-walnut mirror hanging in the downstairs front hall, she jumped a foot off the floor.

Why, she did look white! And she looked exactly like a

young man, a young man rather wasted by disease, a bit frail, a bit uncertain. I must be sure to remember to speak softly, she thought, and with a shaky voice.

Somewhat emboldened, she crept along the dark hallway toward Mister Gus's office. The door was ajar, and the room looked to be empty. The master and mistress were always asleep at this hour, she knew, unless they had company or sickness. Honey had never been into the master's office before, but she had seen where he got the money to pay the slave catcher, from a metal box, and she moved a candle cautiously over the piles of newspapers, old pipes, tack, empty glasses, and assorted iron rings and leather straps and nails and tools that heaped both the desk and the work table.

There! There was the metal box, and it was unlocked, its latch hung open. Honey reached for it eagerly, but just then she heard footsteps, slow, heavy shuffling steps, coming down the main stairs.

She froze, shut the box. What could she do? Where could she hide? Frantically, snuffing out the candle, she whirled around the room, looking for a closet or cupboard she could crawl into, but there was no closet and the cupboard was as heaped with relics and refuse as the rest of the room.

Fear rose in her throat and she felt it choking her. The footsteps were coming closer. She did not doubt that it was Mister Gus. Should she run out the office door and take a chance on ducking into another room before he reached the office? She stood paralyzed, and then, when it was just this side of too late, she spied the coatrack beside the door, hung with Mister Gus's heavy winter cloak, a massive garment of dark blue felt.

Without thinking, Honey dove for the cloak and ducked under it. It hung nearly to the floor, and she bowed her head so that she was entirely hidden in its thick folds.

Just as she had settled the cloak's trembling, Gus Dunlie shuffled into his office, wearing his nightshirt and bedroom slippers.

"Eh? Anyone here?" he asked the darkness. "Thought I smelled a candle," he muttered. He set his own candle on his desk and lowered himself into the best chair, with his back to the coat rack. Honey waited, then she screwed up her courage and peeked out through a buttonhole.

What? What was the master doing? He seemed to be . . .

Slowly, deliberately, lovingly, Gus Dunlie was removing an immense lot of gold nuggets from a leather pouch and weighing each one in his hands before he placed it in the metal box. Honey watched, transfixed.

Breathing heavily, as if the sight and weight of the gold stirred his blood, Dunlie became completely absorbed in the process. Minutes passed, a half hour, maybe an hour. Honey had no idea how long it was, but it seemed a very long time. She dared not move or breathe naturally. She posed rigidly, but he never turned around, never heard a sound.

Finally, he was finished. He shrugged his shoulders, stretched, and sighed. "Twenty thousand dollars," he said to himself, "at least."

Honey nearly swooned. If she could get that gold, she and Daniel could go to the ends of the earth and live like royalty. But what was he going to do with the box?

Dunlie rose, then sat down again. He carefully locked the metal box, hefted it approvingly, and then set it down. He held the key up—Honey could see it—it was a very small key and shone like gold itself in the yellow candle-light. She watched, wanting it desperately, and he paused, as if he were thinking.

Then he gave a short laugh and dropped the key into the neck of a half-full whiskey bottle that stood on the floor. It splashed, then sunk to the bottom.

Honey stared. Gus Dunlie picked up the whiskey bottle and took a drink from it, then held it by its neck.

Please, Honey prayed, don't let him take it with him! Please! Oh, please!

Dunlie swallowed, gulped, burped, and took another slug of the whiskey. Just then the clock struck once, and he yawned. For another minute he hesitated, then he recorked the bottle and set it back down on the floor. Picking up his candle, he shuffled out of the office and back along the corridor toward the stairs.

Oh, thank God! Thank God! Honey thought. She felt herself flush hot all over with relief. He had left the key! The gold was theirs! Twenty thousand dollars' worth.

Shaking with excitement, she slipped out of the hot, heavy cloak and ran to the bottle with the speed of thought. Carefully, she uncorked it and poured the whiskey into one, two, three of the empty glasses that stood on the crowded desk. When she finally had her hands on the key, she kissed it, then fit it eagerly into the locked box.

It turned. Smiling in the darkness, Honey gathered up all the gold nuggets and replaced them in the leather pouch Dunlie had carelessly left next to the box. She knotted the cord at the neck of the pouch and then carefully poured the whiskey back into the bottle, spilling only a little.

It's a good omen, it's a wonderful omen, Honey told herself. We are lucky, see, we shall be lucky all the way to freedom! Stowing the pouch in the big pocket of her roomy trousers, she spotted a pair of green glass goggles that Mister Gus had worn when he had an eye infection a few years back, and added them to her costume before she flew out of the door and ran to Daniel.

By the time Gus Dunlie had realized, the next morning, that his gold was missing, the overseer had come to his office to report that the bad nigger, Daniel, was gone off again, and Miss Nerissa had flounced through the downstairs toward the same office, shrieking that she could not find Honey anywhere.

"That lazy girl! I tole her to finish those pillowcases for my sister Clarissa and the baby quilt for my sister Priscilla! She's so no-count, she's not half done with either of them! A'ways out mooning around the quarters, that one, too proud for her own good. When I find her, I'll teach her a lesson! Oooh, yes, I will! I'll show her who's honey and who's 'lasses. Oooh, I am so angry, I might faint! Gus! Gusssss!"

It was nine o'clock.

Honey and Daniel, having ridden all night on two stolen horses, sat primly side by side on a wooden bench in the Macon train station, waiting for the afternoon train which would take them to Savannah. They were both exhilarated by the smoothness of their escape so far, but extremely edgy and wary. Every slight sound frightened them; every new arrival on the station platform might be a slave catcher; every face was the face of a potential enemy, for they had no allies. Fear constricted their arteries and pinched their nerves, and still they sat, trying desperately to look at ease as the day grew hotter and hotter and traffic at the station increased.

"Calm yourself, Miss 'Rissa," Gus Dunlie begged. "I don't know where your damn seamstress has gotten off to! How the hell, pardon me, ma'am, I *beg* your pardon, now don't take on so, remember your nerves, remember how frail you are, my dear, you will excite your vapors, but Miss 'Rissa, someone has stolen something of *great* value from my office, *that* is of paramount importance to me!"

"What has been stolen?" the overseer asked.

"Some small . . . objects of great personal worth," Gus Dunlie said. He looked into the empty box again. He couldn't believe his eyes. It was too awful to be true. He remembered it all perfectly. He had locked the box and dropped the key into the bottle. Now, this morning, he had poured out the key, unlocked the box, and . . . it was empty! How could it be so?

"Bug!" he screamed. "Bug, come here!" If anyone knew anything about this robbery, it might be Bug. Bug was such a snoop and a gossip that he always knew everything.

"Well, Mist' Dunlie, what are you goin' to do about my seamstress?" Miss Nerissa asked. "Are you goin' to whip her?"

"I thought she had disappeared," Gus Dunlie said. "How can I whip her if she's disappeared? Besides, I don't want to harm her, I want to sell her for top money. Are you sure she's disappeared?"

He turned to the overseer. "Are you sure Daniel has gone off again? Didn't the damn fool ornery nigger learn anything from that last beatin'?"

"Daniel is nowhere to be found," the overseer said slowly, a bit overwhelmed by the vehemence of the Dunlie family style of exchange. Although uninvited, he reached out and closed his fingers around one of the glasses Dunlie had filled with whiskey when he emptied the bottle. On second thought, he put the glass back down. Hadn't there been a famous case of poisoning at Dunlie Hall? He had always heard that it was food, but last Friday, at the Madison tavern, he had been told a different version of the story.

"Daniel appears to be gone," he repeated, ignoring the sight of Miss Nerissa stamping her feet like a child and beating her husband's arm with a wooden spindle she had brought from the sewing room. "And two horses are missing, as well."

"Well, why didn't you say so, you fool?" Dunlie bellowed. "So someone, some god damn thief, has run off with my . . . my . . ."

"What are you goin' to do, Mr. Dunlie?" Miss Nerissa demanded. "Call the constable? Call the slave catchers, *again*? My sister Clarissa will be *very* disappointed, I can tell you that, and my sister Priscilla . . ."

"Hush! Will you hush, woman?" Gus Dunlie begged. "Do you suppose they have run off together, that seamstress and that damn half-Injun Daniel? I recall they were sweet on each other, but of course, she is too light for him. She's worth twice what he is . . ."

"Yes, suh, Mist' Gus? Yes, suh?" Bug asked, sliding to a stop in the midst of the others who filled the small, cluttered office already. "Did yo' call me, Mist' Gus? Here I is!"

"Good Lord, it's hot, I feel faint," Miss Nerissa complained, sinking into Gus Dunlie's chair so that he had to lean over her to pick up a glass of whiskey, which he did.

"Shall I send for the slave catchers, Mist' Dunlie?" the overseer asked reasonably enough.

"No-o-o-o-o-o-o! God damn it, that mean nigger cost me one hundred dollars a'ready this month, and that's enough. I'll find them myself. You'll come with me, you, what's your name?"

"Clarence Coe," the overseer said stiffly. He had been at Dunlie Hall only a month, but he had seen the master every day. He could not help thinking that it was rude to be called what's your name, after a month of faithful service. Anyway, he had never seen such an undisciplined lot of gentry in his life, if gentry they were.

"Ain't you going to send for the constable, Mist' Dunlie, to report the robbery?" Miss Nerissa asked. "That is a free service, I believe."

She is very quick to make fun of my thriftiness, Gus Dunlie thought with a sense of shame, but what has *she* contributed to this household, except children, and all of them girls, named after her damn sisters. But he did not say this, he merely said, "I don't wish to advertise to every white trash lawman in the county just what it is I have lost, do you understand, Miss 'Rissa? That is why I am determined to handle it myself . . . if I can . . . Bug! Bug, where are you?"

"Right here, Mist' Gus."

"Bug, do you have any idea where that Daniel and the light-skinned seamstress called Honey might have run off to? Do you think they've run west?"

"No, suh. I b'lieve I heard somewheres that they were goin' to Savannah, Mist' Gus, goin' to Savannah by train. Now think of that!"

"Saddle up, Mister Coe!" Gus Dunlie roared. "You see?" he said to his wife. "Bug knows ever'thin' that's goin' on and then some. Good for you, Bug!"

"Where are you goin'?" Miss Nerissa demanded. "Oh, dear, I feel so weak. This excitement has ruined my day."

"We're goin' to Macon. To catch that damn train, that's where we're goin'!" Gus called back as he stomped out of the office and down the hall.

The clock struck ten as he passed it.

As the sun reached its zenith, Honey and Daniel still sat, rigid as two clay pigeons, on the bench at the railroad station in Macon. The train to Savannah was scheduled to leave at two, but trains out of this brand-new station were often late.

Every half hour or so Daniel, who was dressed very properly as a gentleman's servant in a plain black suit with a blue shirt and a wide black hat, had crossed the station's platform to the water cooler and dipped up a cup of water to carry, very carefully, back to Honey. He had drunk some water, too, but neither of them could eat.

Neither of them had ever seen a railroad station before, and so in addition to all the other anxiety-provoking elements of the wait, they were constantly startled and amazed by the bustle of the station. Porters and conductors crossed and recrossed the platform, the tracks, and the yard. Whistles blew, steam escaped from the waiting engine, bells rang, the clock struck the quarter hour, and the loungers and loiterers of the town made their appearances, greeted each other, stayed to chat or have a smoke, then departed, to return, perhaps, in an hour or so. Every sound, every new face, every sudden motion alarmed the two fugitives, struggle as they did to appear patient and impassive.

Finally, Honey poked Daniel and told him, in a voice one degree above a whisper, "It's time to buy the tickets. See that window? Where the man is standing in line behind the other man?"

Daniel nodded.

"Go. Take a piece of gold, a small piece, from the pouch in my pocket and tell him you want two tickets, one for you and one for your sick master. To Savannah. Good luck, Daniel."

His heart pounding, Daniel took the gold nugget and approached the ticket window.

"Two fares to Savannah, if you please, sir," he said. "For me and yonder, my young master, if you please, sir."

The ticket seller stared at Daniel. He nodded. "Twelve dollars."

Daniel offered him the gold nugget.

"Oh, we can't accept this, boy. You'll have to take it to the bank and ask them to change it into dollars. I'm sorry, boy."

Daniel's eyes widened in fear.

"Please, sir, my young master. He's too sick to be left, sir, and too sick to take out in this heat. Please, sir!"

The ticket seller hesitated. He could see that the nugget was worth far more than twelve dollars. Where were these two coming from anyway? Indian country? That happened from time to time.

"Oh, all right. I'll weigh it out for you and change it right here. Mind you take gold to a bank next time, boy, you hear."

"Yes, sir!" Daniel managed a weak smile, and accepted the fifty dollars in change and the two tickets.

"What's the matter with your master?" the ticket seller asked curiously.

Daniel had his answer ready. "Vapors, sir. He's got the vapors, and he was in an accident, sir, real bad." Honey and Daniel had decided on vapors, since Miss 'Rissa had them so often and so variably; the disease seemed to express itself with different symptoms with each attack; it seemed a sufficiently vague explanation as to deflect further inquiry.

But the ticket seller had never heard of a man suffering

from vapors, and he laughed to himself and his coworkers as Daniel and Honey boarded the train, the one clinging to the other's strong arm, both of them silent and "sober enough lookin'," as a spectator later recalled, "to chill a Quaker."

All the town's loungers and loiterers recalled the pair clearly and had a chance to expound on their recollections when, two hours later, Gus Dunlie and his overseer arrived at the station on dripping, wheezing horses.

"God damn it! Those two were runaways!" Dunlie exploded, "and you nincompoop sold 'em tickets to Savannah! Holy Jesus Christ!"

"I am not at all sure, sir, that we are referring to the same pair," the ticket seller insisted. "One of the two was a very sick young white man. He was white, of that I am sure."

"He warn't white, and he warn't a man, but they are both thieves. God damn it," Dunlie raved. "What time's the next train to Savannah?"

"Eight o'clock tomorrow morning, sir."

"Why won't you hire a professional slave catcher?" Clarence Coe inquired patiently.

"Because I want to get them myself, and I know I will, you damn fool," Dunlie blustered. "I'll go on alone. Now why don't you git back there to that plantation and see if you can hang onto the rest of 'em?"

"Yes, sir," Coe agreed.

The railroad line from Macon to Savannah was the pride of central Georgia. It had been built to transport—what else?—cotton, a highly seasonal commodity. In the fall and winter the cars were heaped with cotton, stuffed with them, overstuffed with them, the huge white bales stacked high as the tree branches along the way, and threatening to topple off, which they sometimes did. Returning, the cars were often empty, and in the summer, business dwindled greatly.

On this particular June day there was only one passenger car on the run to Savannah and only a dozen or so passengers seated in the car. Slowly, cautiously, Honey and Daniel found seats together in the rear, near an open window, but no sooner were they settled than Honey realized that the portly gentleman who seated himself opposite them and opened up a newspaper was a man she had known all her life.

It was Doctor Phillip Gaywood, the respected Macon physician, the man who had come to Dunlie Hall on numerous occasions to treat Miss Nerissa, not only for her recurring attacks of the vapors but to attend her in childbed, for Miss 'Rissa subscribed to the new fangled notion that a midwife was not sufficient assistance for a delicate woman.

Honey's heart sank. What if the doctor should recognize her? How could he not? He had seen her dozens of times, and as recently as last week. She shrank back into her seat and tried not to move. Daniel could feel the increased tension in her body and her fright communicated itself to him, but he did not know the doctor. Neither of them spoke a word.

Doctor Gaywood read his newspaper, nodding a bit in the heat, lapsed into a drowsiness punctuated by a few deep snores, then shook himself awake and walked to the rear of the car to have a smoke on the outside platform.

"Daniel, it's Doctor Gaywood," Honey whispered as soon as he was gone. Her low voice was tremulous with horror. "He's seen me at the plantation a lot of times. I'm afraid he'll recognize me!"

"Keep yo' head down, pretend you're a sleepin'!" Daniel coached her, but he, too, was more nervous than ever and felt perspiration soak his shirt front and run down his neck and face.

Between Macon and Savannah, the Central of Georgia's railroad tracks ran through some of the most beautiful land in the state. The roadbed, which had been built by slave labor, mostly from the plantations it cut through, was graded of rock and sand. It meandered through fields and forests, swamps and glens, and crossed two rivers—the Oconee and the Ogeechee—and their fertile riverbed valleys. On this splendid June day Georgia's heartland was at her best: Everywhere wild magnolias blossomed, green grass waved in the soft, warm wind, and birds sang of the blue skies and safe nests for their families.

But Daniel and Honey saw none of it. Later, when they were asked to recall the train ride across the state, neither of them could remember a single detail of the landscape or the name of a single one of the small stations into which the train pulled, blew its whistle, hissed to a stop, and then started up again. Every mile, every crowded station platform was another stretch of danger, another tension-spaced wait, every new face in the train's window or in the seats around them a potential betrayer.

When Doctor Gaywood returned to his seat and spoke to Honey, she started as if she had heard a gunshot.

"Excuse me, young man," he said in his low, familiar voice. "I don't mean to disturb you, but you appear to be unwell, and I am a doctor of medicine. Is there anything I could possibly do to help you?"

"No!" Honey said, as gruffly as she could manage, staring at the doctor through her green glass goggles. "I am well looked after by my man, here, and will see a doctor in Savannah."

"Very well," Doctor Gaywood said. "However, if you require my services, they are at your disposal."

"Thank you," Honey choked out and turned her head. For the next few hours she pretended to be asleep, but a careful observer might have noticed that her left hand, the one not swathed in bandages, clenched and unclenched itself restively inside her trousers pocket.

As for Daniel, his expression was plainly one of anxiety and fear, but it was not an expression to alarm their fellow passengers. "*See* the look on that big boy's face," Miss Clara Wilkerson of Soperton said to her sister Lillian. "I declare, he looks positively wretched with worry."

And Miss Lillian nodded approvingly. She liked to see a faithful servant, a really faithful servant, one that took his master's welfare straight to heart, and so it did appear between those two young men.

Hours later, darkness fell, and still the railroad car rattled on through the heart of Georgia. After eating lunches packed and brought aboard from home, or purchased at one of the way stations, most of the other passengers settled back to sleep.

The darkness brought a measure of comfort to Honey and Daniel, and when they could tell by his regular breathing that Doctor Gaywood was sleeping, Honey whispered, "We're goin' to make it, Daniel; I b'lieve we are."

"Shhhhh. . . ." he cautioned. "Now who we lookin' for in the Savannah station?"

"She told me to look for an old black man with a push-cart," Honey explained. "You're to go up to him and ask, 'What has Isaiah promised his people?' He'll know who we are and he'll take us away. To some safe place."

"I sure hope so," Daniel sighed. "When'll we be in Savannah?"

"In the mornin', in the blessed mornin'," Honey promised. "And Daniel?"

"Yes?"

"We'll be married, just as soon as we git to freedom, won't we?"

"That we will," he promised.

Although the night was long, and seemed endless, neither Honey nor Daniel could relax enough to sleep, nor did they see the stars outside the train's windows, although the summer sky was bright with them and dark clouds scudded past the round silver moon like islands floating in a dark sea.

When the sun rose the next morning, the Macon train was not far west of Savannah. Following for quite a considerable distance the river Ogeechee, the roadbed was exceedingly flat, and the city of Savannah was visible from about ten miles away. A more welcome sight there could not have been to all the train travelers, Honey and Daniel among them, for it had been a bumpy, uncomfortable night, and they were all glad to reach their destination.

"Have you ever been to Savannah?" Doctor Gaywood asked Honey, his good spirits irrepressible at the realization that he would soon be able to avail himself of both a good bed and a bottle.

"No, sir," Daniel answered for the two of them. "Nor has my master."

"Ah, 'tis an admirable city," the doctor told them. "Philadelphia itself is not more perfect in its symmetry. It is organized around eighteen large squares, and every principal street is lined with handsome pride-of-India trees. Some call them pride-of-China trees, but surely, they are the pride of Savannah. Hah! Hah!"

Daniel managed a weak smile, but Honey could only look stunned. She was terribly hungry, but her fear was worse than hunger; the fear was like a paralysis that had gripped every bone and muscle in her body. It ached in every joint, in every tooth and nerve. She was so afraid that she was starting to shake. What would they do if there was no old man with a pushcart? What would they do if Mist' Gus was the first face they saw in the station?

"Will you stop at the Pulaski?" the doctor inquired.

Daniel, who had no idea what he was speaking about, nodded.

"Yes, 'tis the finest hotel. I shall be stopping there myself. Perhaps I can offer you a ride in my carriage?"

Daniel looked stricken, but Honey managed to speak. Her voice was quite genuinely weak and shaky. "Thank you, sir, but no. We shall be met by relatives."

"Ah, just so. Yes, the Pulaski is the finest hotel, but as the others are owned by the same rascal of a proprietor, all three have in common high prices and great indifference of service! The last time I stopped at the Pulaski, with a party of four, including my daughter and a man servant, but with no private sitting rooms, the fee was ten dollars a day! Just imagine!"

Honey shut her eyes behind the goggles, willing herself to endure whatever, but Daniel asked, "How much longer, sir, will it be . . . before we reach Savannah?"

"Longer?" The doctor chuckled, "No longer. Here we are. See, there's the Cotton Exchange, that's the tallest building in town. It's on the Bay; all the principal buildings and the shops are on the Bay. See! There is one of the new private dwelling houses built by Mr. Jay. He's the English architect who is the darling of Savannah's wealthy. I find his designs too ornate, myself. Well!"

And rising and bowing, Doctor Gaywood gathered his bags and walked down the aisle as the train slowed to a stop amidst whistles, hissing steam, clanging iron wheels, a rising tide of calls and cries from porters and vendors and the screech of brakes.

"Quickly," Honey whispered to Daniel, "lead me! Let's get off this train!"

"Savannaaaah! Savannaaaah!" the stationmaster called, and the few weary passengers staggered down the aisle toward the door as the carriage swayed unsteadily. Waving farewell, Doctor Gaywood hurried across the platform. Daniel helped Honey down the steps, and for a moment both of them stood, astonished and speechless, looking at the bustle of the station where blacks and whites, businessmen and peddlers, Quakers and Indians, urchins and draymen all moved in every direction on urgent errands of their own.

Silently, both Honey and Daniel searched the crowd for an old black man with a pushcart. At first there seemed to be none; then there looked to be several who fit that description.

They hesitated, fearful, confused.

Clinging to Daniel's arm, Honey choked back tears. "I feel . . . faint," she said in a low, miserable voice.

"Sit down over here," Daniel suggested, and started to lead her across the platform to an unoccupied wooden bench.

But before they had reached it, a tiny, wizened black man, bent as a monkey and moving at a turtle's pace, cut directly in front of them.

Gathering his courage, Daniel leaned over to the man and asked, "What . . . what has Isaiah promised his people?"

Grinning a toothless grin, the old man looked up at Daniel and said, "Freedom, brother! He done promised us freedom!"

Honey winced. Had anyone heard the old man? She looked around, but there was not a familiar face to be seen, and no one at all paid them the slightest attention.

"Follow me, now," the old man said in a lower voice, and immediately shuffled out of the station, dragging his cart behind him. It was a poor-looking low-sided wooden cart, with a pile of hay visible at the end and covered over with a blanket. As soon as they were outside, he stopped and said to them, "Now, as soon as that man in the black suit get to that willow tree, both of you hop in that cart and duck down way up at the front, and you keep quiet till I tell you to talk."

"Yes, sir!" Daniel snapped, and when the man in the black suit had passed the willow, both of them dove head-first into the wagon, dragging their one bag and the plug of hay behind them. I sure hope that old man is stronger than he looks, Daniel thought, curling himself into a spoon and fitting Honey's body into his.

It was hot, suffocatingly hot, and dusty, and the boards of the cart's bed were rough and hard, but both of them felt their hearts begin to fill with joy and hope. Every creak, every jounce and bounce gave a lift to their spirits. Honey could feel Daniel's heart beating and patted his arm.

As the old man dragged them ever so slowly and deliberately along the street, he passed a well-dressed businessman, one of the best-known men in Savannah, and stopped to lift his cap to him. " 'Morning, Mist' Barstow," he said respectfully.

"Good day," Caleb Barstow said, without really looking at the old black man. He was a few minutes late to meet the Macon train, and his client, Gus Dunlie, had written that he'd be sending the next shipment of nuggets in the strongbox on that train. Of course he wasn't too late, but he hated to be even a bit late, and there was a ship leaving for England tomorrow that he wanted to send the gold out with. Timing was crucial these days, with the customs inspectors poking their sharp noses into every single casket and barrel, always looking to increase their revenue, as if the revenues weren't already high enough to cripple an honest trader.

Despite the increasing heat of the day, Caleb Barstow hurried along the sandy walk, his odd lopsided gait a familiar sight to most of the people he passed.

As he reached the railroad station, the old black man pulled the covered cart in through the shadowy doorway of a warehouse marked Barstow and Barstow, where Jacob Barstow met it and directed Honey and Daniel to a small room hidden behind the wall of the gin room.

"Be very quiet," he warned them. "There is food and water there. When I shut the door it will be totally dark. Someone will come to you tonight and tell you where you are to go next. For the sake of your lives and mine, I tell you, be very quiet. Not a sound."

Clinging together, arms entwined, Honey and Daniel nodded. They would do as he said.

And when the door shut, the bolt slid, and they were alone in total darkness, they fell into each other's arms, and before they took time either to drink or eat, they began to caress each other and make love.

CHAPTER NINETEEN

Gold Drives Men; Blood Binds Brothers; The Sarah T. Sails

Late that same afternoon Gus Dunlie's train pulled into the Savannah station and Dunlie burst out of it, knocking through the crowd, his coattails flying, his hat askew. Stopping to look neither right nor left, he hurried straight to the offices of Barstow and Barstow and began to explain what had happened and what he proposed to do about it.

Gus Dunlie was a man outraged, a man determined to reclaim his own, however unfairly got, and a man armed. Both his coat pockets held pistols, and a belt around his waist held enough bullets to kill both Honey and Daniel twenty times over, which was what he wanted to do to them. *After* he had repossessed his gold.

Both partners, Jacob Barstow and Caleb Barstow, were present in their offices when Dunlie arrived, and after a few minutes of heated discussion each of the three men had a clear if limited understanding of the situation and what could be done about it. Both Caleb and Jacob Barstow understood completely why Dunlie had been unwilling to involve the Macon constabulary or the slave catchers in the search of the runaways—he had no legal title to the gold nuggets, and their possession of such wealth would attract official attention to his whole smuggling enterprise.

"Did you meet the mornin' train?" Dunlie asked Caleb Barstow. "Did you see an odd pair of country folk gettin' off it? The Macon stationmaster reported that a young invalid was travelin' with his body servant—I b'lieve that was them in disguise!"

"I was a few minutes late to meet the mornin' train," Caleb Barstow admitted, "but if we have reason to b'lieve we know their disguise, I have an excellent man here in Savannah, Mist' Percy Duke. He is both thorough and discreet. I would say we should send for him at once."

"Send for him! Send for anyone you trust who'll do the job!" Dunlie bellowed. "I want 'em found and caught. 'Course we don't know that they made it all the way to Savannah, do we? They might of popped off at some little station anywhere along the line."

"That is possible," Jacob Barstow said slowly. He was torn with mixed feelings. On the one hand, he knew very well where the two fugitives were: They were right downstairs in the warehouse, locked into the secret room by his own hand. Of course when he offered the fugitives refuge, he had no idea that they were carrying a vast amount of stolen gold. Now he, Jacob Barstow, was the man who held all the cards, was he not? He could betray the fugitives and turn them over to his client; he could betray the client and share the gold with his partner; or he could take it all for himself. . . .

Jacob shook his head. To think that those two young people, so frightened, so helplessly adrift, little more than children, really, with no idea where they were or where they would go next, had succeeded in robbing Gus Dunlie and getting all the way across Georgia without being apprehended. He was amazed at their courage and luck. The people's movement was growing stronger; even from his limited perspective he could see that. Now almost once every week his brother Isaiah sent someone to him; the trickle was becoming a stream of fugitives bound for freedom.

And he wanted to help them. . . . He thought it was right, but . . . the danger of it! If he were caught, if anyone even suspected he was involved with helping runaways, he would lose everything, the business his father had given his life to establish, that he had spent a lifetime strengthening, a lifetime of treading very carefully on the right side of the white man's law. Things had never been easy for free blacks in Georgia, and the strictures against them were tighter every year. He had to be above reproof, above suspicion. . . .

"What do you think, Jacob?" Caleb asked him, but he had not been listening, had not heard the question.

"Pardon me, Mist' Barstow, what did you say?" Jacob Barstow asked in his smooth, low voice.

Now that one's a fox, Gus Dunlie thought. I've never liked him. He knows more'n he says, I'll wager that!

"Get Percy Duke, conduct a thorough search of all the no-counts and free persons of color, put a watch on the train station and the waterfront. Most likely we'll get 'em, don't you think, Jacob?"

"Yes, Mist' Barstow, most likely," Jacob said without hesitation.

"Savannah's a big town these days," Caleb warned Gus Dunlie. He had the unpleasant feeling that Dunlie was trying to find some way to blame him for having lost his slaves and his gold; it was none of his fault at all, but Dunlie was in a rage that denied reason. "The population is estimated to be ten thousand, of whom about five thousand are whites."

"I shall know my property if I see it, I assure you," Dunlie said, "and I shall go out right now to have a look about. Tonight, gentlemen, you can reach me at the Pulaski Hotel. Please send this Duke to me there."

Dunlie stormed out of the offices and stomped down the stairs.

When he had gone, Caleb Barstow turned to his partner. "I'm afraid we have missed the last race, Jacob."

"Yes, Mist' Barstow, I'm afraid we have," Jacob said calmly.

"However," Caleb went on, "if you will take care of sending for Percy Duke, I b'lieve I'll ride out to the Club and see how my horse has done."

"Yes, of course, Mist' Barstow," Jacob said. He reached for his gloves and began drawing them on. He would go to Duke's usual lodgings and hire the slave hunter, but on the way he would look in on the two fugitives downstairs and see if they really had the gold.

A few hours later, in the lobby of the Pulaski Hotel, Gus Dunlie was amazed to encounter Dr. Gaywood. The two men had known each other for years; they fell into immediate conversation, and before many minutes had passed, Gus Dunlie had established that the doctor had indeed seen his runaway slaves on the train from Macon, had even engaged them in conversation, and remembered them very well.

"I'll be damned," Dr. Gaywood exclaimed. "The young invalid looked exactly like a white man, I swear he did. Of course he was wearing green goggles, so I didn't get a clear look at his . . . her eyes!"

"Those are *my* green goggles, God damn it!" Dunlie raged. "You sold them to me yourself, Doctor, two years ago when I had that miserable sty on my eye! Don't you remember?"

"Why, yes, I do recall your eye troubles," the doctor said, "but you can hardly expect me to have recognized the goggles on someone else!"

"Perhaps not," Gus Dunlie said. He was beside himself with rage and frustration and had not eaten all day, so it was not with difficulty that Dr. Gaywood persuaded him to step into the dining room of the hotel, where the two up-country gentlemen were seated, drinking and eating a roast loin of pork, when Percy Duke found them.

"Sit down, sit down!" Gus Dunlie bellowed at Duke. Duke, a lean, slant-eyed man, slim as a bean pole and dressed entirely in black with a rather dingy white shirt and a black bow tie, had a keen, cruel look that reminded Dunlie of a sophisticated version of Rafe Quint, and he was inclined to trust him. He was not pleased, however, when Percy Duke announced his terms: fifty dollars in advance, nonrefundable, and one hundred dollars, per fugitive, on delivery.

"Outrageous!" Dunlie gasped. "Robbery, sir!"

The price seemed outrageous to Dr. Gaywood, also, and he was completely amazed when Gus Dunlie sputteringly agreed to the terms.

"I have a large network of . . . connections," Duke explained to them. "They will work all night, searching all the places where runaways have been concealed in the past, questioning strangers and suspicious persons, examining passes." Duke smiled, and his yellow teeth caught the light. "Do you know, Mist' Dunlie, of any relatives or friends these fugitives might have in Savannah? Anyone they might look to for refuge?"

"No," Dunlie said. "They are uncommonly ignorant, I assure you, and uncommonly bold."

"Come to think of it," Dr. Gaywood said, "the big one told me they were planning to stop at the Pulaski!"

"Impossible!" Dunlie exclaimed, and then, in his next breath, he thought better of it and yelled, "Search every room!"

"The desk clerk will know immediately when I give him this description," Percy Duke said. "Fear not, Mist' Dunlie. Any two persons of this description who takes even one step out onto the streets of Savannah tonight will be stopped, searched, and brought in. Fear not."

"Well, I hope you are right," Dunlie said, but he could not eat another bite and followed Percy Duke to the front desk of the hotel, where the manager assured him that no invalid gentleman at all had been registered there in recent memory.

"Is there anything else, Doctor, that they told you and you only just now recall?" Gus Dunlie asked Dr. Gaywood sarcastically, when the two men stood alone again by the front desk of the Pulaski Hotel and Percy Duke had left, Dunlie's fifty dollars in his pocket. Parting with the money had been painful to Gus Dunlie, but that pain was nothing compared with the prospect of losing twenty thousand dollars worth of gold. He was genuinely sick at that prospect, and perhaps it is not surprising that he turned an edge of his anger toward good Dr. Gaywood, who had, after all, become involved in this situation by the merest chance.

Dr. Gaywood missed Dunlie's attempt at sarcasm. He thought for a moment and said, "Well, yes. They did say they were comin' to Savannah to consult a doctor! Perhaps . . ."

"Perhaps we should keep an eye on you, eh? Is that it, Gaywood?" Dunlie asked. What a fool he is, he thought; does no one realize that this is serious? Percy Duke seems to. . . . It seems my fortune is in his slimy hands. He seems to believe he can find them. Well, he damned well better, and when he does, I shall sell the two of them down South so fast they won't have time to kiss good-bye.

"I do hope you're not serious in suspectin' me," Dr. Gaywood said stiffly.

"No, no, Doctor, I am not," Dunlie sighed.

* * *

Later that night, after dining with his partner at the old family house on Abercorn Street, Jacob Barstow directed his driver to take a detour and stopped off at his brother Isaiah's home, a modest frame building that served as the parsonage for the African Baptist Church.

Isaiah Barstow was alone in his sitting room, his Bible open, reading by the light of an oil lamp.

"God bless you, Jacob," Isaiah said when his fashionably dressed brother stepped across the threshold into the tiny room. "I hoped that you might come by, and yet I was afraid that you would. Percy Duke has been here twice tonight. He suspects that I have something to do with the two packages from inland."

Jacob Barstow hesitated, uncomfortable in the cramped, poor house. There was nowhere for him to lay his walking stick; nowhere he wanted to hang his hat, either; the single coatrack was heaped with the motley capes and sweaters that belonged to Isaiah's children, of which there were ten or so; he could never remember exactly.

"How long ago was he here? Do you think we can speak safely?" Jacob asked, an edge of fear in his voice.

"Yes, I think it is safe, now," Isaiah said. "I am so glad Jacob, that they are so well hidden."

"I want them out of there as soon as possible," Jacob said, a bit sharply. "Do you know, brother, that by chance they have come from the plantation of one of our most important clients? And he has followed them to Savannah. He is here now. It is insanely dangerous to conceal them on our premises. Do you understand that?"

"Very well, brother," Isaiah said calmly.

"Why has Duke come here twice? Why twice?" Jacob demanded.

"Someone in the station recalled seeing the packages picked up by an old black man with a pushcart," Isaiah explained. "It sounded to Duke like our Uncle Joe. Of course it was our Uncle Joe, but I have sent him to safety in the country, so they will not find him here."

"Jesus! He comes too close!" Jacob exclaimed. "It gets more dangerous every month, Isaiah."

"God's work is always dangerous," Isaiah said. " 'Tis the devil who makes it so."

"Those two may have the devil's ear, themselves," Jacob said. He sighed, fidgeted, and finally sat down next to his brother. In the lamplight they looked very much alike, and both of them resembled their father, who had been Ira Barstow, the patriarch, the free black Revolutionary hero who had founded the brokerage business, he who had started it all.

"What do you mean?" Isaiah asked.

"They appear to have stolen some gold nuggets, a lot of them. Worth a lot of money, brother."

"Was it money their master had earned rightfully?"

"No, that it was not."

"So that is why he is so desperate to catch them."

"Yes, and why it will go very badly with me if they are caught in our warehouse. I want them out of there. Tomorrow."

"We had planned to send them on a steamer to Charleston."

"All the steamers will be searched from stern to 'sprit."

"And 'twould be dangerous to get them out of the warehouse, unless . . ."

"Unless what, Isaiah? Speak your mind, you dreamin' schemer. Sometimes I think 'tis you who has inherited our father's head for business, not I!"

Isaiah smiled. "My business is the Lord's. Not an easy trade. I propose you bale them up with some of your cotton and send them to Liverpool on your ship the *Sarah T.*; I have already contacted a trustworthy crewman aboard that vessel. He will release them and feed them on the crossing. Since you say they have means, it will go more easily than I thought."

"All the way to England?"

"Why not? They are young. She is a seamstress; he is a carpenter."

"The *Sarah T.* sails with the mornin' tide," Jacob said slowly, thinking of the many difficulties of the plan, of the many risks, the many possibilities for error. . . .

"And when she sails you will be completely out of danger," Isaiah said. "I'll send my son Peter home with you tonight. He is clever at packaging."

" 'Tis a preposterous plan," Jacob said, shaking his head.

"The Lord God loves boldness," Isaiah said confidently. "He loves courage, he loves a fearless man, for he has given us the example of His Son, who risked everything and brought Salvation."

Jacob stared at his brother.

"You speak of chance, Jacob," Isaiah went on. "You call it chance that the freight which concerns us comes from Dunlie's plantation. Would you call it chance also that the operator who sent them to me was none other than the freed hand maiden of your partner's sister? Yes. 'Twas Polly Barstow's woman who sent them. Not without her knowledge, I daresay."

"I am astonished," Jacob said.

"Call it not chance, but the workings of God's plan to save His own," Isaiah said. "You will do your part, will you not, Jacob?"

"Yes. Yes, I will," Jacob said softly.

The next morning dawned fair, as clear and bright as a day in deep summer. A light wind from the south whirled the sand on the city's streets into cracks and crannies, but the rows of shade trees stood square and proud, and it was more pleasant than not to be abroad, as long as one had a destination—and a plan to be out of the sun by high noon. The heat, when it came, would be as solid and relentless as a steel rod laid straight down over the town; it would beat down ambition and slow steps and put a lot of matters that might have seemed pressing into a new perspective.

Both partners were at the offices of Barstow and Barstow early that morning. The *Sarah T.* would sail for England at about ten, and much of her hold was already filled with baled cotton from their warehouse.

"A good day for a swim, eh, Peter?" Caleb Barstow called to his partner's nephew, a cheerful stocky young man who often hung around the docks and the warehouse.

"Yes, sir, Mist' Barstow," Peter grinned.

"A good day for the Club," Caleb said to Jacob, but Jacob was ill at ease and agitated. Peter had done it; he had concealed both Honey and Daniel inside two huge bales of cotton, setting up breathing tubes for them and tying the cotton around a hollow core, braced with a wicker basket of sorts.

The fugitives were far from comfortable; the question was whether they would be brave enough, composed enough, to keep from crying out in fear or panic as the bales were trundled down to the docks in hand carts and swung onto the big ship by ropes. Jacob had lost track of exactly which two bales held the fugitives, but Peter had marked them in some way and would go aboard to make the connection with the seaman his father had already contacted.

"Lord God, 'tis hot already!" Caleb exclaimed. "Let's go down to the docks and watch the sailing, eh, Jacob? For once, Jacob, take a few minutes' fresh air."

Reluctantly, Jacob agreed and followed his partner down the stairs and out to the loading area, where they could see the last bales being put aboard and see the crew of the *Sarah T*. assembling on the deck.

And where is Gus Dunlie? Jacob wondered. He expected catastrophe still. The boldness of the plan still appalled him. He sensed danger everywhere. The morning stillness frightened him; the creaking of the *Sarah T.*'s stays and moorings set his nerves on edge; the crowd of loiterers and spectators gathering on the docks alarmed him. God, he wished it were over.

"That's the last of ours," Caleb commented, and Jacob looked at the ship's gangway to see a hand cart with two huge bales going up it, his nephew Peter sitting on top, waving his red hat cheerfully at the onlookers, grinning with all the insouciant confidence of a favored child.

"Ah . . ." Jacob sighed, and just then he was aware that Gus Dunlie and Percy Duke and several of Duke's men were bearing down on him and Caleb where they stood in the shade of a striped awning.

"Halt! Stop that man! Arrest that man!" Dunlie shouted.

"Mist' Barstow! Halt!" Percy Duke said in a low, rasping voice.

"What man?" Caleb Barstow asked. "What do you mean, Duke? Have you found the fugitives?"

"I found these!" Duke said in a low, menacing voice, "and it seems to me you ought to be explainin' to Mist' Dunlie what they was doin' on the floor of your warehouse."

"What?" Caleb asked again.

Duke was holding up a pair of green goggles as if they were as dangerous as a pair of smoking pistols.

Jacob Barstow felt his heart hammer as if he were dying. He put his hand to it. Surely, his face was ashen. Surely, his guilt showed. He could not speak.

"Those belonged to that damn runaway nigger! I'm sure they did! I know they're the ones!" Gus Dunlie shouted.

A crowd of interested spectators was forming around the four men. Caleb hated it. He hated to be stared at by rabble and riffraff.

"Don't be ridiculous," he said in his coldest voice.

Howling and barking, a pack of hounds raced onto the wharf and toward them. "I've got my nigger dogs, now," Percy Duke said, "and I intend to let 'em have the run of you warehouse, Mist' Barstow."

"It may be too late for the warehouse," Gus Dunlie speculated. "What about these goggles, Barstow?"

Caleb Barstow looked at Jacob and was stunned by what he saw. His faithful partner, his respected lifelong companion, his confidant, his former teacher, looked stricken with fear. Caleb knew Jacob, knew him better than any other man on earth and knew at once that he was completely terrified, that he could not speak, that he had something to hide. In a rush of pity and love, he responded at once.

"For Christ's sake," he said. "Those are my damn goggles. I wear them riding on dusty days. Now give the damn things to me, Duke, and call off your damn dogs."

Jacob Barstow let out his breath in a long, slow sigh. Out of the corner of his eye he saw his nephew Peter come skipping down the gangway and disappear into the crowd.

"Can't stand the press of a crowd," Caleb Barstow muttered and he strode off the docks, back toward the warehouse, without looking back to see the *Sarah T.* preparing to sail, but Jacob Barstow stood as if rooted and stared at it, watching the gangplank swing aboard, hearing the first mate call out "Weigh anchors" and the crew call back "Anchors aweigh."

I suppose they are aboard, Jacob Barstow thought, sailing to freedom . . . and with all that gold. God speed you, he thought, God keep you and guide you . . . and all of us. . . .

"Hooray! Hooray!" the shout went up from the assembled crowd, seeing the *Sarah T.* execute a smart maneuver and free herself in the current of the river. Their voices startled Jacob Barstow, but he did not move. He lingered, watching the *Sarah T.*'s sails out of sight until long after the loiterers had drifted away and Gus Dunlie and Percy Duke had gone off with their dogs to inspect the steamer leaving for Charleston.

Then, with the noontime sun beating on his head with blistering force, he walked across the docks to the warehouse and an odd thought came to him. 'Tis not the end, he thought, 'tis the beginning.